THE SHARDWELL SERIES

Book 2

GUARDIAN OF TIME

A. Gerry
C. Hall

Published by Scribes of Shardwell, LLC

ISBN-13: 978-0615660547
ISBN-10: 0615660541

The Shardwell Series

Book 2

Guardian Of Time

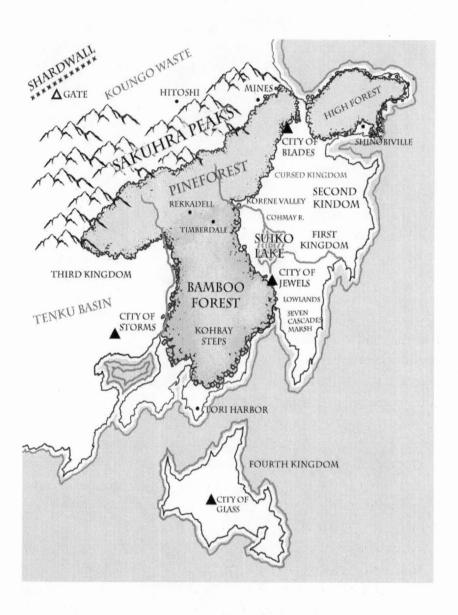

PROLOGUE

Duty has always been the focus of my life: forfeit all desire, protect the kingdom, perform with honor. My mother showed me the importance of these precepts. Though I was very young, she expected unwavering obedience to the responsibilities of my station. She taught me that serving my people and safeguarding my siblings required one thing—absolute sacrifice. And I have come to learn, through both isolation and sorrow, that sacrifice is the ultimate definition of love.

My family's reputation was marred by the greed and violence of my mother's father. Unsatisfied with the rule of a single kingdom, he instigated a war that infected the entire shard. Other royal houses were crippled, one obliterated entirely. He carried an artifact of unrivaled power, bequeathed to our lineage by Nehro, the water goddess. The conflict escalated into one final, senseless battle. Both sides suffered cataclysmic casualties. Neither could claim victory. My grandfather's remains were discovered on the outskirts of the scorched battleground, robbed of my family's heirloom.

Through kindness and even temper, my mother attempted to rectify her father's tyranny, reestablishing our claim as a great and noble family. But she grew sick from a malady our healers could not explain. Her soul passed into the netherworld before I had reached my 15th season. Moments before her death, she summoned me to her bedside.

A secret has the power to destroy a kingdom. My mother carried two.

Terrible is the burden of duty, and heavy it seems when balanced against the lives of those I love most. The obligations of my kingdom, the vow I made to my mother, and the care of my siblings forms a precarious balance that is constantly threatening to teeter into chaos. My fate was to bear this task, my duty to safeguard the kingdom.

Until Fohtian's Warden appeared and changed my destiny forever.

PART 1

1: 639 YEARS AGO

An azure bead chinked into the bowl of a glass apparatus, marking the quarter passing of another moonarc. Margariete stared into the crystal timekeeper's collection of tiny balls, silently willing its magical gears to rotate faster. Two white beads had gathered at the bottom of the jeweled assortment since her arrival in the castle library, signifying two endless arcs of her tutor's sonorous voice. Three blue beads preceded every white, a standard indication of the moon's path across the sunlit sky.

Directing her gaze away from the unhurried contraption, Margariete's glower encompassed the features of the wrinkled teacher kneeling across the room. She wondered irritably how much longer the tedious lesson would continue. Margariete usually enjoyed the quirky rantings of the family mentor: his sermons on the various factions of the Thyellan kingdoms, recitations of the universe's most intriguing legends, and most especially his dissertations on the nature of Shardwell magic. But this cycle his crooked form was everything uninspiring as he hunched over the woven bamboo floor. The absence of his customary enthusiasm left his grey eyes vacant and gave a sunken quality to his words.

5

Social propriety. What—by the Seven Cascades of Time and Space—had possessed him to lecture on this topic? For Margariete, the countless tenets layering the First Kingdom's system of aristocratic decorum were irrelevant, for she was rarely allowed to attend court. She was her family's most humiliating eyesore. Polite society required her presence only during the occasions of special significance—she was sister to the heir apparent after all— and her father assumed it prudent to remove her from all but the most essential social interactions rather than risk a witness to her exotic features.

Margariete hid an impatient breath with her teeth as her ancient teacher continued, relating the suitable way to accept an invitation to dance. Why did Malbrin believe it necessary to teach her something so superfluous? She would never actually chance upon an occasion to use this nonsense. She was more likely to dance with a temporal ghost than a flesh and blood nobleman.

Margariete shifted her aching calves as a steady throb crept into her lower back from long exposure to correct kneeling posture. Her heavy hair tugged painfully at the nape of her neck. She fiddled with the silky veil shrouding her face, a garment that left only her striking sapphire eyes visible. The smothering folds of her gown cloaked every part of her skin, its voluminous sleeves draping evenly over the ends of her fingers, trapping her body in a prison of fabric that concealed her true self from the world.

Malbrin's ramblings shifted to the topic of polite greetings. With a sigh, Margariete's wayward gaze lifted to the window. The stuffy library where they knelt squatted in the south corner of the west wing, overlooking the soldier training yards below. The music of clashing metal echoed upward through the open portal, mocking Margariete with its tantalizing freedom. The Knights of the Gem, the First

Kingdom's elite military force, had commenced their daily routine of swordplay. A sting of longing swept over Margariete, and she itched to rid her body of its confining attire.

"Your Highness, please pay attention," Malbrin's leathery voice beseeched.

Margariete wrenched her attention from the window with difficulty. Her tutor's tolerance seemed to be waning. She could sense the edges of his patience fraying into haggard threads. Malbrin shook his head, his coarse, chin-length hair scratching his face with the sideswipe motion.

"Sorry," she replied ungraciously from behind her veil, disregarding the use of a more formal apology that would have been appropriate between teacher and pupil.

Malbrin pursed his bulbous lips, his facial muscles trembling with age, but Margariete chose to ignore his disapproving response. Before his interruption, she had been mentally reviewing the most recent of her covert sword lessons, appraising the motions that led from strike to parry for a tricky maneuver. She believed the new technique harbored a fatal flaw in its intricate downstroke, although her swordmaster—who stood to lose his knighthood if their confidential training was ever discovered—would disagree with her assessment. The correction had been close to surfacing when Malbrin's untimely remark ruined her concentration. A wave of heat climbed into her throat. She couldn't even voice her displeasure—it was extremely unsuitable for a woman of her standing to participate in activities such as swordplay.

No matter, she thought to herself, brushing her annoyance aside to forestall an angry outburst. She still had the fault in the sword sequence identified, despite the interruption. Her innate talent for the blade would eventually rectify the defect. Next time, it would be the swordmaster prone at the tip of her weapon, not the other way around.

The Princess of the Jewel looked back at the bead collector. A white glass sphere was poised to drop, completing the arc. Three more blue and she would be free.

Malbrin began a tangent of discussion that outlined the responsibilities of her station. His lecture lasted nearly two full azure bead sequences. Margariete ignored him and chose to spend the remainder of her tutelage poking a loose thread dangling from her elbow-length signet glove. Its delicate pattern designated her rank amongst the elite of the First Kingdom's gentry. The elegant cloth and fine embroidery of the garment was second only to her brother's.

"Your Highness, you must consider your position. A woman of your stature must be well educated, in both learned academia and social grace," Malbrin suddenly demanded.

Margariete infrequently appreciated the veil that hid her face, but this cycle it served her well as the froth of her ire contorted her expression into an angry grimace. Who did Malbrin think he was talking to? She understood the duty of her position. She was not an infant, requiring constant supervision.

"I know my place, Malbrin," she seethed, "but the study of dancing customs, courtly speech, and suitable female behavior is useless for me," her voice dropped in pitch, "as you well know."

"You may differ from other members of the court in appearance, Your Highness," Malbrin argued with tactful empathy, reminding her that he, too, recognized the misfortune of her curse, "but you are still a princess of the realm. It is your responsibility to understand every nuance of our culture."

"Understanding of any knowledge is better learned when one practices its use," she countered hotly, "and since I will never have that chance, my time would be better served studying more relevant subjects."

Her hands tensed into fists.

"A valid point Your Highness, but your father has insisted that I instruct you in the intricacies of relationships and halt all other education," he said sadly.

"Why?" Margariete asked, suddenly cautious.

Little love existed between the king and his daughter. Margariete's unfortunate abnormality was an embarrassment to His Majesty's royal reputation. He chose to ignore her existence as much as possible. Margariete couldn't recall that His Majesty had ever meddled with her education at any point in her life.

"He did not provide me with that information, Your Highness," Malbrin answered evasively. "He simply commanded it so."

Margariete could sense the wizened teacher's worry emanating intangibly through the air. Malbrin might not know the exact motivation for the king's order, but he obviously suspected something, and whatever it was affected her future. Exhaling a whispered breath, she formed a link between herself and her mentor. She swam through his recent memories, seeking out images of her father. A quick recount of Malbrin's lesson preparation played in her mind, suddenly interrupted by the somber frown of her father, His Majesty Arahm Galenos. Her father's brisk command to alter her tutelage concerned her less than the sudden flash of supposition that alighted Malbrin's sharp instincts. The implication sent rivulets of shock through her veins.

She withdrew hastily back into her own mind, though her retreat had more to do with a need to confront her father than concern of discovery. To her knowledge, her unique talent for mind-walking lay outside any magical power that had ever surfaced in the history of Thyella. The magic users of the shard reflected the influence of Nehro, the water goddess. Only four others knew of Margariete's exclusive gift: her two brothers, her swordmaster, and her late mother.

"Are we done for this cycle, Master Sage?" she asked, inserting Malbrin's formal title.

Though officially a question, her tone indicated clearly that she was finished with his coaching. Malbrin glanced at the timecounter.

"Of course, Your Highness. We will continue these matters tomorrow."

Tersely silent, she rose from the kneeling cushion, her heavy skirts rustling against the matted floor. The paper-paned door slid open at her approach, revealing two of her ladies-in-waiting kneeling obediently on either side of the threshold, their heads bowed respectfully as the Princess of the Jewel passed. She stopped just outside the door, pausing for the soft clack as her servants replaced the panel. As the princess lifted her arms, the maids slipped an extravagant overcoat over her already suffocating gown.

Once the two servants corrected any rumples, Margariete crossed the open veranda, wondering crossly at the necessity of wearing such a massive, floor-length jacket to simply walk through the private rooms of the castle. The ornate stitching was too delicate for any outdoor pursuits. A muttered profanity escaped her tongue, causing one of her maids to gasp in distress.

When Margariete reached the tower stairs, the only path to reach the royal apartments on the sixth level, she didn't ascend. Instead, she glowered at them, unmoving. The tight-fitting structure of her underrobe limited the length of her strides. Though her outerdress was made of fine, billowing silks, the weight of her overcoat magnified the constricting pinch of the corset beneath.

Why adorn her body in expensive fabric, if she was only to be seen by her family and a handful of servants? Angry that everything in her life was so vigilantly controlled, even down to the clothing that her servants picked every morning, she threw propriety to the Cascades. Margariete turned from the turret of steps and plunged past the dignitary suites, knowing that the king was most likely in his study.

"Milady, where are you going?" the youngest of her attendants asked in a panicked squeak.

Though not a public floor, the princess required special permission to walk these halls, as an assortment of guests and nobility often requested private audiences with His Majesty.

Margariete ignored Lya's protest and continued forward, rushing past several surprised servants and courtiers. Two foyers and a stateroom later, Margariete was forced to stop, her pace having been too quick for the restrictive properties of her clothing. Leaning against one of the castle's infrequent stone walls, she gasped heavily.

"Your Highness, are you all right?" the eldest lady-in-waiting asked. "Should I bring you some water? Or do you wish to retire for your arc of meditation?"

"No, Rin," Margariete said, "I want to speak with the king."

"Your Highness, he is sure to be discussing matters with his councilors," Rin said desperately, brushing a stray blond curl behind her ear. "Perhaps you may speak with him at supper?"

"I will speak with him now. Go prepare my lavender bath, I will follow shortly."

Both maids exuded an aura of anxiety. Their station demanded obeisance to their lady, however, modesty insisted that an unmarried maiden should never be alone outside of her chambers. Rin and Lya had been disciplined on multiple occasions in the past due to their lady's reckless abandon for protocol.

"But we are not allowed—" Lya stuttered, her face pale.

Margariete interrupted with a wave of the hand. "I know. Stop boring me with your excuses, and do as I command."

"Of course, Highness," the servant answered meekly. Both attendants fled to the stairs.

Margariete continued toward the king's study. As she glided down the corridor, His Majesty suddenly emerged from a doorway, deep in conversation with one of his favorite advisers. She had hoped to overtake him alone. Approaching her father in front of an official of the court would only provoke Arahm's anger, so she ducked into the first available room and quietly slid the door three-quarters shut. Their voices carried clearly through the paper-plated walls.

"It is a good match, Your Majesty," her father's counselor flattered openly. Margariete wrinkled her nose in disgust.

"Better than expected," the king agreed. "A joining between my family and the royals of the Fourth Kingdom will unite the three houses in an unshakeable treaty."

Margariete felt a stitch rise in her throat. Her tongue seemed dry and swollen. Malbrin's terrifying hypothesis couldn't be true! Even the king couldn't force her to marry without the crown prince's sanction. Margariete knew her brother would never force her into such a distasteful union.

"And what of your daughter?" the adviser asked, his nasal voice high and whiney. "She will never agree, and may try to counsel His Highness, the prince, against the marriage."

The king snorted.

"My son has finally given his consent. Her opinion is of no consequence. The contract is already signed. Breaking the pact now would provoke war. Princess Margariete is not fool enough to plunge the kingdoms into a blood feud."

"Of course, Your Majesty."

Margariete heard the soft shuffle of the two men's footsteps as they retreated down the hallway. The princess leaned heavily against the doorframe for support, frozen with shock. Malbrin's guess had been right.

The king had arranged a marriage for her.

*

Margariete yanked the delicate door of her suite harshly, nearly dislodging it from its track as she stormed over the threshold. Both of her servants yelped nervously. Rin hurried to replace the bamboo-framed panel. The princess had strained to keep her composure as she fled the lower floors of the castle, determined to contain her unbearable despair. But now her fury overpowered her self-control.

She expected this kind of behavior from her father, but her brother? He was her twin for Nehro's sake! How could he use her as barter to solidify his own political status? The sharp dagger of his betrayal cut deeply into her core.

The princess raged at her maids as they followed her into the inner apartments of her chambers. Rin and Lya humbly submitted to her every command, removing the princess's cumbersome overcoat and hanging it on a T-shaped stand. Lya fumbled with the complex laces of Margariete's outerdress and received a lashing rebuke. Once the gown was properly stowed in the dressing room's elaborate closet, Rin loosened the ribbons of the princess's corset.

Margariete's strength of will collapsed as the garment's confining grip relaxed, as if it had been restricting the heaving despair of her brother's disloyalty. She doubled over, clutching her body as it shook with sobs of bitter anguish. Her maids attempted to calm her, but Margariete pushed their soothing hands away and ordered them to leave.

Crawling to the dressing table, she pulled herself onto its kneeling cushion. Ripping the veil covering her face and hair, she threw them savagely to the floor. She released the tight bonds of her hair, and the dark locks tumbled down her back, caressing the olive skin of her arms. Margariete glared into the looking-glass at the features of her curse, but her deep sapphire eyes only seemed to scowl back in defiance.

The power of the water goddess assured that the populace of Thyella would imitate the physical traits associated with Her element—ivory-hued skin, white-blond hair, and light shades of silver-grey eyes. Margariete's family was at a loss to explain her dark characteristics. No one in the shard had ever evinced such rich, earth-toned tresses, nor a golden sheen to her skin. Her appearance especially shamed her father, who held conformity of culture in the highest regard. Even her servants were afraid to look upon her long, as if her curse might somehow spread.

Life was a lonely battle for the princess. In a land where convention was rigidly observed, she was an outcast. Only her brothers and swordmaster overcame the silly superstitious nature of her countrymen, and cared for her despite everything.

Or so she had previously believed.

Apparently, her worth to her twin was only that of a marriageable asset. Margariete was politically astute enough to know which member of House Kotrell she would wed. The patron of the Fourth Kingdom, a widower of 58 seasons, was the only eligible male in the royal line. His first wife had produced four heirs, a young son and three daughters near Margariete's own age. Perhaps her father believed that King Hylan wouldn't reject her for the attributes she would pass to more children. Margariete was likely to spend the 18th anniversary of her birth as the wife of a man who was older than her father.

The princess shuddered at the thought of his touch. Her hands gripped the corners of the dressing table, the wood biting into her fingers. In a fit of helpless rage she overturned the vanity. Its looking-glass shattered against the wall, jars of rouge, bottles of perfume, and porcelain ornaments smashed across the bamboo mats. The resounding crash summoned both of Margariete's maids, who rushed into the room in alarm.

"Highness, are you all right?" Rin asked, forgetting to avert her eyes from the princess's exposed features.

Margariete slowly stood, calmly removing her underrobe and replacing it with a washing dress. The act of destruction had abated her fury.

"I'm fine," she said evenly, pointedly ignoring the disarray resulting from her tantrum. "Is my bath ready?"

"As you requested," Rin answered, lowering her eyes.

Margariete turned to her attendants. Lya stood immobile just inside the room, her eyes shifting between Margariete and the broken furniture. Rin reacted swiftly, carefully traversing the field of splintered glass and righting the remains of the dressing table.

"Help her," Margariete commanded as Rin bent to clean up the mess.

Not waiting to see if her orders were obeyed, the princess strode through the dressing room's left door and entered the bathing chamber.

Four obsidian steps led to the raised washing basin. The sweet scent of lavender wafted from the steaming water. A gilded podium stood next to the ten-span square bath, balancing an elliptical bowl. The princess removed the silver laces of her crimson signet glove. As she slid the silk shell from her arm, Margariete felt a calming breeze of liberation drift around her. She couldn't remember a time without the mark of her station. A signet glove was given to every noble child at birth and could only be removed in the washing chamber. It was treason to look upon the naked arm of royalty.

She sank into the basin, disregarding the sound of clinking glass in the adjacent room. The heat relaxed her muscles and seeped into her body, calming her riotous emotions. For several moments, Margariete lost herself in the sensation of water lapping gently against her skin.

Her course of action became clear.

She could never submit herself to marriage with a complete stranger and the princess entertained no allegiance to a father who had only ever treated her with disdain. She felt no love toward the people of this realm. Now, she realized she had not even earned her twin's respect.

The Princess of the Jewel would be gone by morning.

2: MIDNIGHT IN THE QUEEN'S CHAMBERS

Margariete pulled a thin lighting stick away from the coals in the fireplace, setting it against the wick of a candle. Placing the light in its brass housing, she looped a finger inside the lantern's hood ring. She crossed to the center of her bedchamber, searching for two specific thyella mats, each with a tiny blemish on its basted edge. To other eyes, the imperfection would look like a scuff or scrape, but anyone in the royal family would immediately recognize its significance: the almost imperceptible shape of half an open blossom, one on each side of the bamboo flooring.

Hundreds of seasons ago, Margariete's ancestors had built the gargantuan castle complex around a sacred spring that fed seven waterways—the Seven Cascades. Even then, the continent's warring families dueled over territory and resources, often wiping entire clans from the face of the shard. The Castle of the Jewel had taken more than a hundred seasons to complete. To safeguard his family in the event of attack, the original ruler of the First Kingdom had commissioned the construction of secret escapeways from the royal apartments.

Margariete's fingers crept beneath the mat, gently pulling it upward and sliding it along the surface of another. The bare floor revealed a square depression of wood inset with a brass loop. Margariete slipped her hand into the circular lock, grasping the handle and twisting it to the right. A click snapped through the room.

Margariete remained motionless for a few breaths, waiting to see if the noise had attracted the attention of her maids sleeping two rooms over. Assured that their slumber was unbroken, she rolled the pocket door to the left, uncovering a steep, winding stair. A gust of air exhaled from the opening. The candle flickered inside its paper lantern.

Margariete swept down the stairs, gliding down the well-worn steps. Even without the aid of light, she could navigate the drafty tunnel, so often did she engage its use. Most recently, the princess employed the hidden route to avoid her ladies-in-waiting when meeting her swordmaster for her unauthorized lessons.

Now it would provide escape. At the base of the stairs she turned, reaching between the gaps in the last two steps. She extracted a stuffed knapsack, followed by a long sheath and belt. Hanging the lantern on a hook that stretched out from the wall, she lifted the pack and slipped quietly back into her room.

Once there, Margariete retrieved several articles of clothing from the bag. Stripping off her nightclothes, she redressed in a loose green linen blouse, snug brown trousers, and mid-calf leather boots. Then she removed her signet glove, its silver and gold embroidery of intertwined flowers and leaves winking coldly in the lunar light. Almost reverently, she laid it lightly on her sleeping quilt.

The message could not have been more absolute.

Intentional removal of the glove was considered a heinous breach of conduct in every Thyellan society. Margariete smirked satisfactorily as she imagined the incredulous looks on Lya and Rin's faces when they found the symbol of their princess lying neatly on her undisturbed blankets in the morning.

To complete her new ensemble, Margariete covered her arms with common leather gloves. She then buttoned her long sleeves at each wrist and hid the skin of her neck with a ragged wool scarf. The princess examined her appearance in the bedchamber's full-length mirror, carefully ensuring that nothing of her dark skin was visible except her face.

Pleased, the princess reached for the sheath and fastened its belt around her hips. Margariete fondled the sword's pearl-encrusted hilt for reassurance. *Stardawn* was a rare weapon, a blade from the Cursed Land, made before that country's fall into darkness. The sword's presence alone boosted her courage, a secret of metalcraft now lost to the modern world.

Lifting the knapsack, Margariete scanned the assortment of items she had gathered in haste after dinner: a rolled bamboo map, scraps from the kitchen, a purse of coins, and an extra set of clothing. Shouldering the bag, she crept back into the tunnel, pausing to replace the floor mat and hidden panel above her.

Only a circle of muted light from the lantern dusted the corridor. The darkness pressed around her as she walked through the hall, warming in its seductive embrace. In a few steps the route forked; one course led to a hidden stairwell that opened at the base of the Jewel Shrine on the bottom floor of the castle, but the other led to the private chambers of the king.

As the highest ranking woman in the First Kingdom, Margariete had inherited the queen's apartments when her mother passed away. It was fortunate that her brother, soon to be crowned ruler of the city, already occupied the king's quarters. Having no wife, he allowed his twin to keep residence in their mother's former rooms. Their father, ruler of the Third Kingdom, resided in the guest suites when he visited his son's city.

The princess required one more item before stealing her way to the stables, so she turned toward her brother's rooms. Dusty mantels of cobweb blanketed the space between wall and ceiling. After a fraction of an arc she encountered what seemed to be a blank wall. Pressing her fingers against two imperceptible depressions in the stone opened a secret door, revealing another staircase inside.

Ghostly straggles of dust billowed outward as Margariete climbed, dancing in the heat of the lantern. Soon she reached a heavy wooden panel, inset with the same brass loop as Margariete's escape hatch. Twisting the ring to the appropriate setting, she heard a reassuring click as the lock released. She opened the panel as quietly as possible, hoping that none of her brother's servants lurked about.

Margariete lifted herself into a long, rectangular room lined with leather-bound books and fantastic woven tapestries. No fire burned in the hearth. The only light sprang from the princess's lantern or leaked through the shuttered partitions of a gargantuan window in the outer wall. Lilac and rose fragrance wafted through the air, fresh flowers having been placed around the apartment's many decorative tables in preparation for the return of the city's future king. During her brother's week-long absence, their father had been handling the daily affairs of the kingdom. A contingent of the highest ranking knights—members of the Order of Pearl—had accompanied the crown prince on his errand, as well as the Pearl Daimyo, leader of the First Kingdom's army.

The princess padded out of the study and across the hall to her twin's closet. Margariete had never even been in her own wardrobe—her maids had always extracted her clothing and carried them into the dressing room. As soon as she entered the huge clothing storage chamber, the difficulty of her task seemed daunting. Shelves upon shelves of thin boxes piled from floor to ceiling, meticulously organized. Drawers swelled with articles of courtly apparel. Wooden T-stands sported costly robes and sashes. Three beefy iron chests gleamed warily in the center of the antechamber.

Well, I have to start somewhere, she sighed to herself.

Setting the lantern on the nearest trunk, she chose a plain-looking set of boxes and began pouring their contents onto the floor. Making some effort to muffle the sounds of her rummaging, the closet soon sported heaps of tunics, robes, belts and cloaks, some only half freed from their containers. Margariete didn't have time to tidy the strewn garments, for the moon would soon lift its shadow away from the sun, spilling light over the country. She needed to be gone before then.

Kicking some of the scattered boxes in frustration, the princess moved away from the shelves and flipped the lid of the center trunk. A grey woolen cloak lay folded neatly at the top. Margariete smiled softly. She had been looking for this robe particularly. The plain fabric would serve to conceal her, and its fitted hood was specifically designed to cling to the head while riding. The princess possessed nothing so austere herself. Her wardrobe overflowed with only the most embellished attire. Her two training outfits— the one she now wore and the extra set in her pack—had been provided by her swordmaster.

Wrapping the long hooded cape about her shoulders, she fastened the silver clasp and hurried back into her brother's study, carefully securing the hood over her twist of hair. Margariete doused the candle and discarded her lantern on a nearby table. Standing in front of the shuttered window, she braced her courage for the next course of her plan.

Flight through the hidden escapeway wasn't really an option. Designed to provide a quick exit in the rare event that the castle was overrun with enemies, the path descended six floors into the shrine at the center of the palace's ground level. Only three doors led out of the building from there, the first through the main hall, and the others from guard stations. Each route would take her past sentry checkpoints inside the castle. The public verandas surrounding the shrine were enhanced with nightingale alarms—floorboards with creaking springs that sang whenever they were walked upon. During the cycle, these sounds were the delight of the palace courtiers, but at night they provided warning against assassins and spies. Once outside, she would have to scale the castle's inner wall, avoiding the Knights of the Gem, to reach the courtyard stables.

Only one alternative existed.

The Castle of the Jewel perched atop the highest point of a plateau, with the capital city sprawling on lower levels to the north, west, and east. But to the south, the castle peeked precariously over a sheer plummet of slick, glassy obsidian, where seven sparkling waterways plunged over a thousand spans into the lowlands below—the Seven Cascades. The king's study overlooked the countryside through a vast opening that stretched from matted floor to vaulted ceiling, a feature requiring no defense since scaling the massive cliff was an impossible feat.

Rainbow-hued light from the lunar corona splashed into the study as Margariete pivoted the wooden partitions away from the window, revealing the supports of the frame. As glass would dull the view, and paper-paneling obstruct it completely, the king's gallery was left open to the sky, with vertical beams placed every two hands breadth apart along its length. Each beam was three fingers thick on all sides and the space between too narrow for any man's body.

But not a woman's.

Margariete shed her pack and sword, laying them close to the edge. Turning sideways, she slid her leg between the slats, planting a booted foot on the teal roof tiles of the balcony on the level below. Arching laterally, she persuaded her hips through the slender opening as the wind eddied forcefully around her. After a deep breath to flatten her stomach, her torso and shoulders followed. Once free, she braced her body against the building's outside wall and reached back through the beams, retrieving her belongings. The air coiled about her, threatening her balance as she refastened her weapon and pack.

As Margariete peered over the roof's edge, scanning for a possible way down, exhilaration absorbed any bubble of fear that might have previously pulsed through her body. Film from the falls sprinkled the tiles with a slick lacquer. The balcony roof she occupied stretched in a sharp slope before dropping into nothingness. Several other steep roofs jutted from the walls below, disappearing around the corners of the building. At its base, the castle melded with the glassy cliff, visibly separate only by the white coloring of the structure's plaster.

Farther down, three of the Cascades tumbled into a darkness so deep it swallowed the crashing water's song. Only a mournful murmur reached Margariete's ears. The brink of the first set of falls rested more than 20 spans below the castle's foundation, while four other streams burst from cavernous canals that burrowed into the sides of the precipice. The Seven Cascades were said to have been born from the tears of the goddess Nehro, a blessing to the First Kingdom of life and sanctity.

No sentry bothered to patrol this area. No one in his right mind would attempt to enter the castle from this direction. One false step between the rooftops and any would-be intruder faced an unpleasant death on the razor-edged rocks below.

Unless, by chance, he could fly.

Margariete exhaled an excited gasp, elation pulsing through her senses.

"Calm yourself," she whispered through a strained jaw, trying to regain focus.

Closing her eyes, the princess imagined herself riding away from the castle, toward the violet thyella forests that she could see from the castle windows but had never visited. Her heart slowed its pounding, and, after a long moment, she regained control of her breathing.

The Princess of the Jewel did not, as it were, possess the ability of flight, but she did employ other unique talents that would aid her descent. She ignored the steep abyss sinking before her, instead gauging the distance between her position and the graded incline of the next level's roof. Sliding carefully to the base of the triangular canopy, she balanced her body against the wind. Then she calmly stepped off the edge.

The chasm's beckoning darkness reached eagerly to devour her, but Margariete had no intention of complying. As soon as her body began to drop, she bent the air with her will, persuading it to slow her fall. She drifted gently to the slippery surface of the tile below, grasping a golden statue of the sacred kryystil fish for leverage. This roof ran parallel to the west battlements around the corner. At the cliff side of the battlement a small, square turret protected the palace and would provide cover from the guards.

She glanced at the moon to ascertain the arc. The halo of stars that surrounded the black orb was no longer visible, and the lunar corona had begun to brighten on one side. A sliver of sun was just beginning to peek around the moon. An arc or two, perhaps less, and the rays of dawn would break through the nightly eclipse.

Margariete turned left and quickly trotted to the corner of the building, using window sills and shutters for balance. She peered tentatively around the wall.

Two Amber class knights, the lowest threshold in the Knights of the Gem, walked the battlement, surveying the west and south, where a breach of security was most likely to occur. Since the great kingdoms of the shard were currently at peace, and had been so for almost 18 seasons, the castle sentries kept watch with relaxed ease. Margariete slithered around the corner, poised to leap across the gap between the main roof and the guard lookout as soon as an opportunity presented itself. When both guards had their backs turned to her position, she sped down the roof, intending to gain as much momentum as possible. Leaping across the gap, she wrapped her mind around the curves of her body, pulling it forward. As she glided to her target she wove an invisible force against her lower extremities, suspending herself over the stone surface for a fraction of a breath. She lowered herself to the floor quietly.

Margariete sidled against the watchtower wall, considering her next course of action. The stables lay across the courtyard four stories down. If she dropped and ran, one of the knights would spot her. Listening intently to the conversation playing between the two men, she waited for them to move closer.

"Did you hit your head on the trap door on the way up here?" an older, stern voice barked jovially. "You think Lord Terail could win a duel against His Highness, the prince? Have you ever seen the heir apparent fight?"

Margariete's heart faltered at the mention of her swordmaster. Her one regret was that she might never see his crafty smile again.

"I have," a younger, rather offended voice countered, "but Lord Terail is a demon with the blade, and he's His Highness's swordmaster."

"He's been almost everyone's swordmaster for the last four seasons," the older man responded with a snort, "but His Highness surpassed Lord Terail's abilities last trinal. The crown prince practices alone now. I daresay he is the best swordsman to appear since the Fracturing."

Margariete agreed with the older knight. Terail might be the best swordmaster in the realm, especially for a knight who had just reached his 26th season, but if the opportunity had arisen, she would have preferred her twin's instruction. The future king was unmatched in natural talent with any edged weapon. Terail might be known for his tenacity and cleverness in a fight, but against the prince, Lord Terail's efforts were wasted.

"I'm just saying that Lord Terail can handle at least ten Knights of the Gem on his own, Order of Pearl even. Imagine if Amber had to fight him on the battlefield? I bet the daimyo could easily handle 50 of us before we managed to take him down."

"I think you overestimate his abilities," the elder knight stated with a grunt. The pair was coming closer to the princess's hiding place.

Margariete prepared to spring on the two unsuspecting men. Their point was ridiculous to argue anyway. Her twin and Lord Terail were closer than brothers, each trusting the other implicitly. The Cursed Kingdom was more likely to spring back to life before the two would ever do battle with each other.

When the lead knight was close enough, Margariete arched outward from her concealment, spinning into a low crouch and sweeping an extended leg across the warrior's ankles. The older man fell forward as the princess realigned her stance, retracting her attacking leg and lashing out with the heel of the other as she balanced on her palms. Her strike connected with the guard's head. Margariete had executed the spiral thrust so quickly that her victim did not have time to draw breath and shout a warning. He was unconscious before his body crumpled to the stone.

The younger knight managed a strangled squawk before Margariete straightened, leveling her gaze with his and pressing her will into his skull.

"Be silent and kneel," she commanded, invoking the weight of her mind.

The youth's eyes widened, as if surprised by a physical blow. Then he complied, dropping to his knees without a sound. Margariete scrutinized the area to see if anyone else had been alerted, then hastily checked the status of the older soldier lying on the ground. His breathing was even and strong—the princess could leave him in good conscience.

Lifting the chin of the kneeling knight, she pierced his mind with her own.

"You will continue to stand guard and forget you ever saw me. When your partner awakens you will convince him that he slipped and fell," she instructed.

The atmosphere was heavy with her influence. The young warrior was easy to dominate, his strength of will being much weaker than Margariete's. She would have preferred to avoid inflicting violence upon the first knight, but she was only able to exert this type of mind control on one person at a time.

The Amber knight nodded his head once and resumed his duties, treating Margariete as if she didn't exist. Leaping into the courtyard, she once again employed her abilities to float safely to the ground. With a quick glance across the area, she made her way to the stable compound. Once inside, she scanned for guards, but found none.

Margariete dashed to a stall where a beautiful mare shook her mane in welcome. The princess smiled at her steed, patting its flank fondly. Crescent had been a present from her twin on their 16th birth anniversary. Her father had vehemently disapproved, as the horse obviously provided Margariete an excuse to exit the castle confines. The crown prince had given his word that he would accompany his sister on any riding excursion, and bid their father to silence his objections. Bitter satisfaction filled Margariete, knowing that her brother's gift offered her freedom from his treachery.

She saddled her horse and attached a fully equipped saddle bag from the cavalry gear station. Pre-packed for emergencies, a store of travel tackle was always on hand. Then Margariete led Crescent to the door.

Only one obstacle remained—the outer wall's gate. Two guards would be posted there, perhaps more. A woman leaving under the cover of darkness was sure to evoke the sentries' suspicion, especially since she was without escort. Though Margariete could easily lift herself over the fortification with her abilities, her 1200 pound horse was another matter entirely.

This particular segment of her plan had required the most consideration. Margariete had deliberated and discarded several options before the solution presented itself.

A long iron cabinet rested snugly against the entrance wall of the stable, secured with a heavy lock. Inside rested a violet and gold flanged banner adorned with the royal crest: a jasmine blossom superimposed over the silhouette of a handheld fan. The flag was reserved for urgent messages sent directly from the kingdom's ruler. Martial protocol required the castle guard to open the main gate for the bearer of the pennant without delay. When not in use, the standard was locked safely in its cupboard, the only key kept safe in her twin's apartments.

Margariete manipulated the lock springs with her mind, compressing and turning them until the catch released. Pilfering the banner, she mounted her horse and braced the pole in a loop attached to the stirrup. She spurred Crescent forward, racing through the training courtyard as if in great haste. Once in sight of the main gate, Margariete unfurled the pennant, allowing it to stream freely behind her. The princess passed several soldiers who looked on her curiously, but none attempted to waylay her. She steered her mare down the long ramp leading to the lowest defensive level of the keep and approached the iron-shod door of the outer gate. One of the four wall sentries yelled to a companion, who hurried into the gatehouse. The squeal of metal winches pealed through the air as chains lurched around the gate's spools. A thick crossbar lifted away from the double doors, allowing the panels to swing inward, exposing a crevice just wide enough for Margariete to gallop through.

Crescent bounded across the bridge spanning the tributary of water that encircled the castle and rushed through the multileveled terraces of the City of Jewels. Margariete's heart sang as she cleared the city gate and directed Crescent to the deserted highway.

By the time anyone discovered she was gone, the princess would be too far away for her father's men to find her.

She was free.

3: TWO CYCLES OF FREEDOM

A supple breeze teased the dappled trees, cooling Margariete's sweat-dampened temples. She heaved another swing at a dead stalk of thyella bamboo, chopping it into manageable chunks. The trunk refused to submit to the downstrokes of her sword's edge, fragmenting into splinters that flew into her hair and clothing. Margariete glared at her weapon disconsolately. *Stardawn* had always sliced effortlessly through the bamboo of the imitation practice soldiers back at the castle, and she wondered why the task of wood hewing was so difficult. It was almost as if the blade were pouting, sour over undertaking such a mundane task.

The Jeweled Princess cursed at the bamboo stem, berated her sword for good measure, then stretched the cramping muscles of her lower back. A burning throbbed in her limbs. Deciding that she had enough fuel for her fire anyway, Margariete sheathed *Stardawn* and stacked the deadwood within her small camp boundaries. She plopped onto the bedroll she had unfurled earlier, letting the warmth from the crackling firepit ease the soreness from her tired muscles.

Margariete had failed to imagine how difficult the road would be. The need to gather campfire fuel hadn't occurred to her before. Though her sword training had often resulted in a mix of bruises and exhaustion, hacking at stubborn bamboo stalks required a wholly different kind of stamina. Her legs were chafed from long arcs in the saddle, her hips and shoulders ached from sleeping on rocks and twiggy foliage. The princess wondered morosely if she would ever be able to move again.

Her eyes itched for rest. Despite her fatigue, her slumber was constantly interrupted. Having never experienced the forest unaccompanied, she was alarmed by the startling darkness that surrounded the natural world. Small chirping insects filled the night with their music, spinning an illusion of serenity that lulled the princess into anxiety-edged tranquility. Just as sleep laid a comforting hand on her harried nerves, the crunch of dead thyella leaves near her tiny camp jolted her into wakefulness. Beyond the firelight, a gloomy silhouette would dance away, its eyes gleaming.

Worse than seeing those eerie eyes, Margariete's abilities allowed her to sense movement outside the radius of firelight. Motion of any kind sent ripples through the air, like an object wading through water, conveying vibrations that alerted the princess to activity. Without context, Margariete was unable to discern the difference between the swaying stalks of thyella bamboo or the passage of a dangerous animal. The environment was too new, too foreign. Already anxious that the Knights of the Gem were tracking her, the telepathic princess found herself unable to sink into sleep.

What had she expected? Plush mattresses and silk pillows?

After time had passed and sleep still withheld its comfort, Margariete forced herself into a sitting position. Reaching for her pack, she extracted a slatted scroll, its thin reeds tied together with scruffy twine. As she unrolled the bamboo, its glossy surface revealed tiny illustrations of cities, rivers, roads, and forests. By the light of the fire, she noted the location of the castle and ran her finger along the eastward route she had taken—across the highway that followed the border of the lavender thyella forest. Her campsite jutted into the bamboo trunks, about a hundred paces away from the road. Far enough to hide her fire from any of her father's guard patrols, but close enough to avoid losing herself completely in the woods. It seemed from the map's markings that she had travelled almost half of the highway.

Malbrin had once mentioned in a lesson that a lightly-burdened war horse could cover more ground in a cycle than an average horse and rider. Margariete only had a half-cycle head start, but there were five main roads leading away from the City of Jewels. Her father would be forced to split his forces to search for her or risk compromising the security of the city.

It wasn't the knights that worried the princess—they could be avoided in the shelter of the forest. It was the thought of her twin's pursuit that caused her to jump every time horse hooves sounded on the packed soil of the road. He had traveled far to the north to handle a recent rampage of beasts that had crossed over the border from the Cursed Land. Margariete wondered how long it would take a messenger to reach the crown prince's encampment. Three or four cycles? Once he discovered her flight, he would hunt her himself, and with him was Terail, the most skilled tracker in the First Kingdom.

Her first goal was to reach Timberdale, a moderate-sized town situated between the thyella forest on the south and pine woodlands on the north. Her brother, assuming he knew which direction she had fled, would have to trek through the entire Korene Valley to catch her, and there were only a scattering of fords or bridges that crossed the Cohmay River. Taking into account the time needed for a herald to reach him, and the distance her brother would have to cover, Margariete was confident that he couldn't overtake her before she reached Timberdale. From there, she intended to hack through the pine woods that ran along the benches of the Sakuhra Mountain range. After crossing into the wildlands of the Third Kingdom, she would swing northeast around the foothills and make her way through the unclaimed grasslands that bordered the Koungo Waste. Once in the desert, she would enter Hitoshi City, a haven for those who didn't want to be found.

Margariete replaced the map and stretched across her bedroll, frowning. It would be a race between siblings. She knew her brother would never relent.

What was her twin thinking, forcing her to wed a stranger older than their father? She knew her brother's disdain for arranged marriages. The two had often shared their views on the subject, having witnessed the devastating effect that such a union had wrought on Queen Anleia, their mother. Anleia's marriage to the monarch of the Third Kingdom, Margariete's father, had a single purpose—to ally the military might of the First Kingdom, ruled by Margariete's grandfather, with the Tempestguard of the City of Storms. The pact provided the strength for the Jeweled King to crush his most powerful enemy, the Second Kingdom of Thyella, though it cost his daughter her happiness.

Little love was shared between Anleia and her husband, the former a creature of gentle kindness, the latter a man of calculating ambition. Barely a season after the marriage, Queen Anleia gave birth to twins. That very cycle, His

Majesty King Shogan, Anleia's father, was slain in the last great battle between the First and Second Kingdoms. Anleia gained sovereignty over the City of Jewels. When her husband returned from his campaigning abroad, the ruler of the City of Storms was forced to return to his homeland to stem a sudden uprising in his own realm, granting Margariete's mother a reprieve from her husband's attentions.

A ripple of sorrow passed through Margariete as she reminisced on her mother's life. The princess still remembered the first time she realized her mother was dreadfully ill. The image of Anleia's long beautiful hair, swirling slowly as the queen fell to the ground, her body shaking itself into a swoon, was forever imprinted on Margariete's memory. Barely seven, the princess had failed to understand why the healers could do nothing for her mother's ailment. Over the next eight seasons, Margariete had watched the disease slowly consume the queen's life.

At 15, Margariete was left with only her brothers and Terail for company. She grew increasingly closer to her twin, trusting him as mentor and friend. He had pledged to spare her from their mother's fate.

His broken promise rankled sourly in the princess's head. Quickly, Margariete banished the thought of him, vowing not to let tears burn her eyes.

Her fire had almost turned to coals and the night's chill nip was creeping inside her blanket. Gazing at the pile of chopped bamboo across the little campsite, she imagined an unseen hand wrapping itself around a piece of firewood. A single chunk rose gently into the air and glided over to the pit where Margariete ordered it into the fire.

Margariete's mind was the only portion of her body that didn't ache with overuse. Willing the blankets to climb her body, she struggled to find a bit of comfort. Not finding any, she contented herself with thoughts of her freedom and the most important reason she had sacrificed her comfortable quilts back at the castle—a marriage that would never take place.

*

It was still dark when Margariete's eyes snapped open. For a moment, she wasn't sure what had caused her to wake. The embers of her fire popped twice, spewing a puff of ash into the air. The princess watched them, muscles tensed, mind alert. Sentry waves of pressure undulated across the forest like an earthquake of air, yet not a single leaf fluttered. Realizing the sensation was the result of her mind-sense and not the wind, Margariete stood slowly and reached for *Stardawn*.

In the bamboo stalks, Crescent pawed nervously at the ground, pulling at the reins that tethered her. Margariete slid her sword from its sheath, grateful for the aura of calm it provided. Barely any lunar light escaped the shadow of the moon, only a nimbus of stars hemmed its circumference, signifying the deepest part of night.

Margariete brandished her sword, swinging it several times to loosen her stiff muscles. The air was stagnant, as if the entire forest held its breath. No recognizable movement tickled her senses, yet her skin crawled with current. She stood vigilant for a few minutes, poised for action, with the creaking of her horse's leather strappings the only interruption in the silence. Margariete had never felt anything like this before.

A flash of flame erupted so abruptly in her peripheral vision that she lost her balance and hit the ground. The frosty green column of fire burned vividly, preventing Margariete from looking directly at it for more than a few moments. Crescent squealed in panic, yanking madly at her bridle. The mare nearly trampled Margariete, but the princess managed to roll away from Crescent's sharp hooves. By the time Margariete had righted herself, the intensity of the light had disappeared, leaving only small curls of green that wafted around the origin of the anomaly.

The forest returned to normal. Insects chirped, soft sounds of passing wildlife resumed. Margariete estimated her distance from the disturbance: a walk of 250 paces. Donning her weapon belt and tossing her cloak about her shoulders to mask her identity, she trudged toward it.

When she arrived, Margariete saw a wide coil of blackened foliage that opened into a copse of charred bamboo stalks. Cloudy ringlets of sea-green vapor floated through the air, slowly evaporating as she watched. The taste of burnt sap hung heavily in the atmosphere, blending strangely with a sharp scent of something metallic. In the center of a perfectly scorched ring lay the unconscious, naked body of a young woman.

Margariete hadn't known exactly what to expect—a savage monster, some sort of magical disaster—but not something as innocuous as this. Sheathing *Stardawn*, the Princess of the Jewel padded lightly toward the girl, who looked to be barely older than herself. The maid's appearance resembled typical Thyellan ancestry—platinum-blond tresses and a fair completion—though her body seemed more delicate and slender than average. After whisking off a glove, Margariete knelt next to the girl, using her palm to check for breath.

The stranger was alive. Margariete took off her borrowed cloak and wrapped it around the young woman. As the princess turned the comatose damsel onto her back, the girl's hair fell away from her face and ears. Margariete gasped in surprise. The top of the girl's ears stretched into an unusual, yet distinct point.

Whoever this was, she wasn't Thyellan. As Margariete prepared to carry the girl back to camp, the Princess of the First Kingdom wondered just what, in the name of Nehro's Grace, was going on.

4: MIDMORNING ON THE HIGHWAY

The moon lifted its shadow fully from the sun, which eagerly burned away the last traces of the early cycle mist from the ground. Margariete looked at the brightening sky nervously as she buckled the last of her saddlebags to Crescent's harness. She should have been on the road arcs ago. Every moment that passed threatened the success of her flight. The princess's horse rolled her eyes reproachfully as Margariete yanked impatiently on the cinch of the saddle.

"Sorry girl," Margariete said, patting Crescent's mane apologetically.

Margariete rechecked her meager supplies, ensuring everything had been stowed properly. The stranger, still unconscious, lay close to the fire. The dark arcs of the night had passed neither quietly nor swiftly. A deeply disturbed sleep had plagued the pale girl through the night, her eyes shifting feverishly under her eyelids. Her body jerked abruptly every few moments in distress. Margariete had tried to wake the maid several times with a shake of the shoulder and, finally, a douse of water to the face. Nothing seemed to work, and after half an arc, Margariete abandoned the task and spent the remainder of the coming dawn tending the fire.

Troubled, the princess plopped onto the grass. The girl did not seem to share Margariete's need for haste. Just after the first crest of sunlight had touched the sky, the sound of heavy hooves had echoed into the forest. At least five or six riders rushed past her concealed camp. The alacrity of the company made Margariete anxious. What if it had been a troop of knights hunting her?

Margariete brushed a limp lock of hair away from the young woman's forehead. After the night's strange events, Margariete had carried the newcomer out of the blackened foliage with telekinetic power. Once in the campsite, Margariete had dressed the girl in the spare set of clothes from Crescent's pack. Unfortunately, Margariete had not packed an extra pair of shoes.

The princess had considered abandoning the strange girl and riding on to Timberdale, but pity compelled her to stay. Thyellans were prejudiced against the most trivial deviation from the norm. The maid appeared to belong, but subtle differences suggested a foreign nature. In addition to the pointed ears, the maiden's skin, though the same ivory as most of Thyella's inhabitants, had a creamier, more refined texture, lacking flaw or blemish. High cheek bones accented the delicate structure of her almond-shaped eyes.

Forsaking the unconscious girl was not something Margariete could do. The princess felt a kinship with the poor maid, an empathetic connection of differentness. The princess herself stood apart from her people, her coloring scorned for its distinctiveness. If left here, Margariete was certain the stranger would be treated as an outcast, or worse, tormented for her unusual appearance.

But they needed to get moving. Just as the princess decided to toss the stranger over Crescent's saddle, the maid stirred and thrashed.

Wondering what nightmare plagued her companion, Margariete cautiously ventured into the girl's dreams. There was no coherence. Desperate flashes of green fire and chaotic images of blood and broken glass surged into Margariete's head. A sickening terror, laced with overwhelming loss, forced Margariete to break the link.

The princess came to herself in a tremor of heaving breath. To her surprise, the girl's eyes fluttered open. Margariete threw her hood over her head and shrank back, poised to respond if the girl turned hostile.

The maiden seemed more confused than aggressive, however, with a bewildered expression in her unusual shade of green eyes. She looked around, seemingly lost.

"Who are you?" the princess asked, keeping her face hidden deep inside her hood.

The girl turned to Margariete, as if startled to find someone there.

"I—I'm—" she stuttered. She looked down at the grass beneath her, the lavender forest surrounding her and the sky above. "Where am I?"

"This is the thyella forest of the First Kingdom," Margariete said.

"First Kingdom?" The green eyes rose to meet Margariete's gaze, revealing no recognition.

"Yes," Margariete said, wondering that anyone could be so politically oblivious. "Strongest of the three realms. Where are you from?"

"I—" again the girl looked away, pulling nervously at her borrowed clothing, "—don't know."

"What do you mean 'you don't know'?" Margariete probed gently.

"I can't—remember," the girl answered in a quavering voice, her breath quickening with panic. "I don't know how I got here."

Margariete inspected the girl closely. Fear and anxiety surrounded the frail stranger like a halo. Margariete wondered if the maid really couldn't remember or if it was a charade. Discovering the truth would be relatively simple.

The telepath sifted her mental fingers through the girl's mind, filtering through its confused emptiness. Margariete felt a barren void of memory, though imprints of experience remained, ghosts of thought that lay just outside the girl's conscious reach. The princess had never encountered such a feeling. Some people locked their memories away, hidden so deeply inside themselves that neither they nor Margariete could reach them. In those instances, she could almost physically feel the barrier they had erected inside themselves. Others simply denied the existence of their own experience. This was different. Impressions of the girl's life remained, but the memories had dissolved, leaving only bits of residue.

"Do you have a name?" Margariete asked, retaining her telepathic link inside the quivering girl's mind.

Perhaps the princess could help scrape the vestiges of thought into something helpful.

"I—"

A swirl curled within the emptiness. Margariete bore down on the flurry, willing coherence. Wisps of power curled across the link connecting the two girls' minds, breaking the princess's concentration. But somewhere within the confusion, Margariete had reconstructed a name.

"Esilwen," the girl announced, saying the name just as the princess thought it. "I think I'm called Esilwen."

"You're not sure?" Margariete asked, her mind aching from the forced break.

"Not entirely. I can't—" Esilwen paused, tilting her head as she thought. "I'm not certain, but when you asked me, it's the first thing I thought of."

42

Margariete stared at the girl thoughtfully. Perhaps Esilwen was her name, perhaps it was a word from the maid's past. Whichever it happened to be, the name sounded foreign.

"Then Esilwen I will call you," Margariete decided. "I don't suppose you can explain your rather unconventional entrance?"

"My entrance?" Esilwen asked, confusion once again evident in her expression.

"I found you in that clearing," Margariete said, pointing to the circle of charred thyella bamboo stalks. "There was an eruption of green fire last night. I found you in the center, after it died, not a single burn or scratch on you."

"Green fire?" Esilwen repeated.

Margariete considered plunging into Esilwen's mind again, to encourage another memory to surface, but Esilwen spoke before the princess had the chance.

"Fohtian."

Margariete angled her head in surprise. She had heard that name before, in a rather interesting lesson with Malbrin: a lecture that discussed the reigning gods before the Fracturing of the Shards.

"Fohtian, god of fire," Margariete said. "That makes some sense. Most of his myths involve green flame. But that still doesn't explain how you got here."

"I wish I knew," Esilwen apologized, straightening the tunic she wore. "Are these your clothes?"

"Yes," Margariete answered offhandedly, "it was cold last night. I didn't want you freeze."

"I wouldn't have frozen."

Margariete laughed.

"How do you know that?"

"I just do," Esilwen shrugged.

A theory sprang to Margariete's mind. Thyella was the domain of the water goddess. No one worshipped the other gods. Was it possible that Esilwen had somehow passed into Thyella from another shard?

Esilwen was now looking at Margariete with open curiosity, no doubt wondering about the cloak and hood.

"Who are you?" she asked.

"My name is Margariete."

"Do you live near here?"

"I have no home," Margariete said, more acidly than she meant to. Abruptly, she stood and walked to Crescent, her need to get moving renewed. "I'm on my way to the Koungo Waste," she threw back over her shoulder.

"Um, I don't know what that is," Esilwen admitted.

"It's freedom," Margariete answered with a yank on the saddlebags. She heard a rustle of grass and leaves as Esilwen shifted.

"Don't you have a family?"

"I *had* a family."

Margariete turned to look at Esilwen. The blond maid held very still, almost like she was afraid Margariete would bolt in response to any sudden movement.

"Did something happen to them?"

"Yes," Margariete spat tersely. "Greed. Power. Betrayal. They—"

The princess's accusations were interrupted by a sudden surge of flame. The campfire in front of Esilwen burst a vibrant green. All color drained from the girl's face.

"Are you all right?" Margariete asked, hurrying to Esilwen's side. "What happened?"

"I—you were talking about—" Esilwen's body shuddered, her voice quivered and she struggled to breathe. "He—"

Esilwen fell silent, fear draping around her. Her hands covered her eyes.

"I saw *his* face," she whispered.

Margariete had the distinct impression that this was the cause of Esilwen's nightmares.

"What does he look like?" Margariete prompted carefully, unsure of exactly who "he" was.

As the princess patted Esilwen on the shoulder, Esilwen lifted her hand and spread her fingers wide, waving her palm above the fire. The flames blushed and grew warmer. Facial features, distinctly masculine, formed out of the flames. The image lasted a collection of heartbeats, then disappeared in a crackle. Esilwen clamped her hand into a fist and suddenly the fire suffocated.

"Who is this man?" Margariete asked.

Esilwen didn't answer, but her body shook. Margariete changed the subject when it was obvious that her companion couldn't answer.

"You have special abilities. Can you do more than control the fire?"

Esilwen pulled her hands away from her face and swallowed hard.

"You say that like you expect I could do more."

"I do."

"How do you know that?"

Margariete pulled Esilwen to her feet.

"Because I'm different too."

Margariete fixed a stare on her abandoned blanket, commanding the air to bring the cloth to her outstretched hand.

"By Fohtian's Blood," Esilwen gasped, "how did you do that?"

"I've always been able to do it," Margariete answered, "ever since I was a child. And that's only a fraction of what I can do."

Esilwen's brows contracted.

"To be honest, I don't know what other abilities I have."

Margariete took Esilwen's hand, and led her to Crescent.

"Listen," Margariete said as she tied the blanket to the saddle, "you seem to react on instinct. But in my country, using your magic could get you killed. They will torment you—kill you—just for being different. You're lucky that you look like them. It will make it easier to keep you safe. But we'll have to do something to hide those ears."

"Is that why you hide your face?" Esilwen asked, motioning to Margariete's hood. "Because you're different?"

"Yeah, different," Margariete scoffed. The princess pulled off her hood, revealing her dark features.

"But you're beautiful!" Esilwen exclaimed.

"That doesn't matter, Esilwen. The people of the three kingdoms all have fair hair and skin, like yours. When people look at me, they think I'm cursed."

Margariete looked up at the sky, agitated. They had lingered here too long. As she replaced her hood, she looked back at her new companion.

"You and I are similar. Both of us have something to hide. If you would like, you can come with me."

Esilwen's head slanted back toward the charred grove where she had first arrived. Then she glanced over the lonely campsite.

"You have treated me with kindness, Margariete," Esilwen answered. "I will go with you."

5: TIMBERDALE

Esilwen listened to the pleasant harmony plucked by an entertainer wielding a long-stemmed instrument. The hollow twang of the serene chords soothed her discordant nerves, its melody relaxing her tired muscles. Her legs were folded uncomfortably beneath her as she knelt next to a table low to the floor, sipping at the warm, bitter tea. Esilwen admired the intricate designs decorating the palm-sized porcelain cup. Fragile flowers of gold and crimson danced in a frozen swirl around the container's lateral surface. Everything in this realm manifested a purposeful delicacy, whether a small embroidered design on a place setting or the elaborate woodcarvings surrounding the teahouse booths. Nothing seemed too insignificant to embellish.

She sighed wearily as she carefully set the drink back onto the glossy black table. *The Lavender Petal,* named for its decorative violet bamboo carvings of various flora, was obviously tended with loving attention to detail. Though the floorboards creaked with age, the inner recesses were tenderly painted and the wood was sanded to a warm sheen. Partitions of varying sizes, some large enough to accommodate parties of six or seven, littered the two-story building, allowing privacy for patrons as they consumed their meal. Each booth housed a shiny table and supple kneeling cushions on a two-span, raised platform. Esilwen had wondered at this arrangement until their serving woman arrived. The platform allowed her to attend customers without bending her body into an awkward position. Margariete had chosen a small stall across from the second-floor balcony, an area that offered a friendly view of Timberdale's inhabitants as they enjoyed their lunch.

Esilwen liked this town. Pinched on both sides by contrasting forests, it was three times longer than its width. The north wall met the shores of a hardy pine forest as it tumbled down the slopes of the Sakuhra Mountains. Margariete had explained that the blue and green peaks were named for their seasonal flourish of cherry blossom radiance, an event that turned the dour mountain range into blushing shades of pink. The southeast edge of the city was cradled by the thyella forest where they had trekked over the last three cycles. According to her dark-haired friend, Timberdale lay on the main trade route between the First and Third kingdoms and was the primary supplier of raw timber and woodware.

The pair had entered the crossroads town four arcs ago, bypassing finely decorated buildings and shops until they encountered *The Lavender Petal*, eager for a meal consisting of more than musty bread and stale cheese. Margariete devoured her food, requested tea for Esilwen, and rushed out of the establishment to collect supplies, ordering Esilwen to wait for her return. Stiff and exhausted, Esilwen had been too tired to protest. Crescent couldn't carry two passengers for an extended period of time, so the girls had taken turns walking. Though unable to remember anything from her past, Esilwen's body seemed unaccustomed to prolonged physical exertion.

Margariete had promised to return within an arc before she disappeared down the lattice stairs. That length of time and a half had elapsed. Worry gnawed at Esilwen. Still insecure about the customs of Thyellan culture, she wondered if searching for her absent companion would incur more harm than good.

Because of her ignorance of Thyellan protocol, Margariete had spent most of their journey tutoring Esilwen on social expectations. According to Margariete, the focal point of the country's people centered on the perfection of duty. Ritual customs surrounded daily tasks—everything from the correct order of donning one's garments in the morning to blessing one's sleeping arrangements in the evening. Ceremonial courtesy carried special significance. Margariete told her that most people would disregard their own needs rather than risk insulting another, particularly if that someone occupied higher social strata. Social non-compliance was treated with swift and harsh retribution.

Esilwen's gaze was drawn to the musician performing next to the balcony rail. The resonant melody seemed to personify the ideals of the Thyellan people: beauty in perfection, strength in resolve, courtesy in all actions. Only Margariete contradicted these typical standards, harboring obvious disdain toward her way of life. After hearing some of Margariete's childhood experiences, Esilwen could understand why. But the more stories her companion related, the more Esilwen suspected that Margariete was withholding something important. The anecdotes she shared never included proper names of people or places, referring to family simply as "father" or "brother," designating places as "home" or "my city." Esilwen deduced only that Margariete had fled from a high-class family, due to Crescent's bulging money pouch.

Though curious, Esilwen felt that prying would sully the gratitude she felt for Margariete's willing aid. Besides money, direction, and information, Margariete had devised a cunning arrangement of Esilwen's blond locks to securely mask her foreign ears.

Esilwen sighed and took another sip from her teacup. Thinking of her unique ear shape reminded her of how different she was from the people in this realm. She felt empty, a black cavity swallowing the contents of her skull. Margariete had been unsuccessful in her attempts to reconstruct more of Esilwen's memory. Esilwen was unable to recall anything more specific than her own name and a few images of that unknown face. She did, however, recognize general things—pine trees, horses, and grass— but everything about this culture felt odd, though she was at a loss to explain how she knew that.

If she had truly lost her memory, how did she understand the nature of reality? Shouldn't she be like a child, without speech or comprehension of complex thought? When Margariete spoke of "shards," Esilwen recognized what that meant. Somehow, she had crossed through the barriers dividing the universe. But other things, such as how the moon arched across the sky from horizon to horizon, eclipsing the sun in night's cloud as the lunar body reached the apex of its orbit, seemed peculiar. Now that she considered it, it seemed more natural for the sun to move across the sky, rather than gleam from a stationary position.

The voices of travelers filled the air around her. Casting a glance at the crest of the stairs, Esilwen hoped to catch sight of her companion's hooded head. The effort was wasted—Margariete did not appear. According to snippets of conversation Esilwen had overheard, an odd collection of thunderstorms was harassing the southern portion of the Third Kingdom, pushing steadily north. Across the room, an older woman of at least 40 seasons urged a relative to avoid the northeastern border of the pine forest due to bandits. The woman's brother insisted that the rogues were merely rumors spread by insidious merchants attempting to justify the inflated prices of their goods.

One particular topic snagged Esilwen's attention, as it was mentioned at nearly every table—the unusual activity of the Knights of the Gem. Evidently, there were three ranks of soldiers, the lowest class regularly patrolling the highways. Over the last few cycles, knights of the second order, who were rarely seen outside the larger cities, had been spotted in large numbers. The sightings had the customers abuzz with speculation.

The townspeople's interest in the knights' activities led Esilwen to realize that several times during their journey, Margariete had turned away from the road and tugged Crescent into the forest when the sound of hooves and jingle of armored harnesses drew near. The telepath had justified her actions, asserting that because of the girls' lack of escort, it was better if they didn't interact with any other travelers. At the time it had seemed prudent, but now Esilwen doubted Margariete's actions were limited to caution. Why would Margariete be so nervous about meeting a company of the Order of Jade?

"Can I get you anything else, miss? Some more tea, perhaps?"

Esilwen started at the soft sound of the attendant's voice. Looking from her empty cup to the blue-robed hostess, she smiled tentatively.

"Tea would be wonderful, thank you."

The serving girl knelt next to the table, setting a service tray on the floor and carefully straightening her robe beneath her knees. Grasping the handle of the kettle delicately with her right palm, she held the lid steady with her left, skillfully refilling Esilwen's cup. After placing the decanter back on the tray, she deposited the steaming porcelain vessel on the table in front of her customer, careful to offer it with both hands. Esilwen quickly reviewed Margariete's table etiquette lesson before accepting the tea. Raising the cup with her right hand, Esilwen set it snugly into her left. She rotated it three times to the right before lifting it to her lips and sipping it lightly. Then, to indicate her approval, she turned the cup once to the left and bent forward in a shallow bow. The hostess returned the gesture, retrieved the serving tray and moved to the next table. Esilwen released a tense whoosh of breath. She had almost forgotten the bow, which would have been interpreted as an insult to the attendant's service.

The hot tea further relaxed her nerves, and her mind drifted aimlessly on the waves of the musician's next melody. The chords were tinged with an underlying sense of regret, a tang of unfathomable loss.

The face flashed across her memory, an image spewing flames of horrific terror.

The suddenness of her emotion caused Esilwen's palm to spasm, and she dropped the hot teacup before it reached her mouth. Barely saving it from destruction against the table, the momentum of the teacup's fall and Esilwen's quick catch caused the steaming liquid to slosh across the back of her hands. Without thinking, she used a nearby cloth to soak up the spilled beverage. Her task was interrupted by an unexpected crash from behind and a surprised exclamation from the hostess. A deep baritone voice yelled in outrage.

"You clumsy fool!"

Esilwen whipped around to discover the cause of the commotion. A man in expensive silk had risen to his feet from one of the larger booths across the room. The serving maid knelt on the floor, anxiously retrieving smashed crockery. Margariete, fully hooded in her cloak, pushed past them in an obvious hurry, sweeping through the havoc as she approached Esilwen. The blue-robed attendant looked desperately between the angry customer and Margariete.

When Margariete reached Esilwen, the brunette tossed a gold coin on the table. Grabbing Esilwen with a black-gloved hand, Margariete yanked her out of the booth.

"We have to go," she ordered breathlessly, glancing warily at the nearest set of stairs.

Their view was blocked by the raging customer and the hostess. As Margariete pulled her forward, Esilwen deduced that her friend must have collided with the serving maid, causing the teapot to smash on the table and spattering the other patron with boiling tea. The gentleman's costly attire was obviously ruined, and his skin had reddened where the hot drink contacted his skin.

"Hurry," Margariete prodded.

"I don't understand. What's going on?" Esilwen asked as Margariete began weaving through the sea of tables to the second set of stairs.

"I'll explain later, we have to go now."

Halfway to the stairs, Esilwen heard a loud smack. As she looked over her shoulder, she heard the serving maid whimper. The furious gentleman towered over the hostess who clutched her now bruised face with one hand. All other conversation hushed, every eye in the teahouse—except Margariete's—peered at the disturbance. Esilwen pulled against her forward momentum, causing Margariete to lose her grip.

"Look what you've done, wench," the man accused, holding up his arms for everyone to see.

Small blisters had begun to form on his left arm, and a dark splotch stained the lglove he wore on the right. Esilwen remembered that the glove designated something important in First Kingdom society, but couldn't recall exactly what. She was more interested in the man's burns. Earlier, she had been served tea from the same kettle, but when the drink had sloshed onto her skin, Esilwen hadn't suffered any discomfort, much less pain. She looked at the back of her unblemished hand. Was that not normal?

By the time Esilwen looked back at the scene, the hostess had crawled to her knees, quickly prostrating herself before the gentleman in an apologetic bow.

"I'm sorry, My Lord, please forgive me! Another guest bumped into me, and I dropped the tray."

"Do not make excuses for your incompetence!" he screeched. "You will be punished for disgracing me."

The man kicked the girl's downturned face with his leather-clad foot, and she fell backward. Two others at the table laughed as the serving girl sobbed.

Compassion welled inside Esilwen, and she marveled that no one in the teahouse intervened on the poor maid's behalf.

"Esilwen, we have to go," Margariete whispered savagely, pulling again at Esilwen's sleeve.

Incredulous at Margariete's callous apathy toward the situation, Esilwen snatched her hand away.

"We have to do something!" she exclaimed, turning to face her friend. Margariete looked between Esilwen and the man impatiently.

"There isn't time," Margariete argued. "Besides, there's nothing we can do. He has every right to do what he wants. He's a noble."

"What? How do you know?" Esilwen asked.

"See the signet glove on his right hand?" Margariete explained. "If we help her, we could be arrested."

"But you were the one who bumped into her!" Esilwen's eyes narrowed. "It doesn't matter if he's noble or not. What he's doing is wrong. The accident is partly your fault. You have power. You must save her."

Esilwen looked back. The nobleman had drawn a dagger from a sheath at his belt. A murmur rippled through the room, though no one moved. Esilwen thought she might be sick. No status or class could justify this.

"Please, Margariete," Esilwen begged. "Please, stop him."

Margariete stared at the hostess as she was jerked to her feet by the nobleman's henchmen.

"Fine," Margariete compromised ungraciously, "but after this, you do exactly as I say. No questions. Understand?"

Esilwen nodded her head once in agreement. Margariete tossed her knapsack to Esilwen with a growl. Esilwen watched her hooded friend dart toward the aristocrat just as he thrust his weapon downward.

Margariete slid under the strike, thrusting the serving girl and her captors backward. She halted the arc of the nobleman's swing with a crossed counter of her gloved hands. The blade would have undoubtedly pierced the hostess's heart. With one fluid movement, Margariete twisted her palms around the attacker's signet forearm, rotating his arm forward from his body and forcing a lock in his elbow. The instant the knife pointed perpendicular to the floor, she struck his wrist, stripping the weapon from the noble's grasp before either henchman could register that their master had been assaulted. With a vigorous kick, Margariete reduced the man's knee into mush, just as the other two men drew their swords and flung the hostess roughly to the side. Esilwen shouted a warning, but it was lost in the angry howl of the wounded aristocrat.

Luckily, Margariete didn't need it.

Kicking backward viciously, the heel of her boot slammed into the closest man's nose with a sticky squelch, flinging blood everywhere. As he fell, Margariete spun, blocking the second man's sword with the dagger. With her free hand, she hit his arm at the wrist, her palm down and fingers extended, thrusting her opponent's forearm and weapon upward and away from her body. Freed of its parry, she drove the blade forward into the soft muscle of the henchman's unprotected underarm. He screamed and backed away, dropping his sword and clawing at the dagger lodged in his armpit.

Quickly, Margariete hauled the stunned hostess upright and dragged her toward the north staircase. Confused patrons burst into bellows and yells, but no one stopped them.

"Esilwen," Margariete shouted across the balcony, "go!"

Awestruck by Margariete's violent display of martial skill, Esilwen stood in frozen shock. The blonde had expected her companion to reason with the angry nobleman, or use her domination power to force his will, not break his leg!

The nobleman's guards stood between Esilwen and Margariete, one rising from the floor and the other ripping the dagger from his wound. Both quickly rearmed themselves. Esilwen would never reach her friend before the men managed to block her flight.

"Esilwen!" Margariete yelled pointing to the second set of stairs as she descended. "Get moving. Meet me downstairs!"

Overtaken by the speed of the battle and its unforeseen brutality, Esilwen had completely forgotten about the other stairway. Grateful that Margariete had kept a clear head under pressure, Esilwen followed the brunette's instructions and rushed to the first level of the building. Once there, she weaved through milling customers, narrowly avoiding a collision with an older woman delivering a tray of food. Esilwen had entered the teahouse using the other set of stairs, and for a moment she was disoriented. After spotting the tail of Margariete's cloak as it whipped past several dining partitions, Esilwen scampered in that direction, nearly knocking the heavy knapsack she carried into another hostess.

Which, coincidently, had started the entire crisis in the first place.

She met Margariete, serving girl in tow, at *The Lavender Petal's* entrance. Tears streaked the young woman's panicked face. Esilwen grasped the girl's other arm and the trio burst through the door. As soon as they were outside, Margariete pulled them toward an empty side street, charging away from the teahouse. Their pace was impeded by the floundering hostess, who constantly entangled her feet in the long fabric of her blue serving robe. Esilwen offered words of comfort when she could, but her breath wheezed heavily in her lungs.

Flying from one alley to another, Margariete weaved them through the town, not stopping until they reached the north wall. Esilwen's heart pounded, blood roaring in her ears. They hid between two tall buildings close to the gate. Sliding down the cool stones of the town wall, Esilwen dropped the knapsack and lost herself in an exhausted stupor.

"You can never go back to that teahouse, do you understand?" Margariete's words came through a fuzzy barrier in Esilwen's ears.

Esilwen's first impulse was to reply, *Well of course. I'm not an idiot.* Before the comment left her lips, however, the roaring sensation in her head subsided and she realized Margariete was addressing the serving maid.

"That man will have you killed if you do."

"Where will I go?" asked the girl helplessly, glancing between her two rescuers with what looked like despair.

"Leave Timberdale if you can. Head for the Jeweled City. You should be able to find work there," Margariete said, glancing up and down the area to make sure no one had followed them.

The hostess's body shook, and she was quickly overtaken by tears.

"But—my family," she sobbed into her hands, "what about my family?"

Margariete stiffened and remained silent, as if waging some internal battle. Finally, with a frustrated grimace, she stalked toward Esilwen and snatched the pack. Rummaging in a side pouch, she retrieved four gold coins.

"What is your name?" Margariete asked severely.

"Seriya," the maid choked.

"Seriya, your old life is over," Margariete said, using both hands to place the coins in the hostess's palm.

Esilwen remembered that Margariete had once mentioned it was customary to offer a gift with both hands or else the recipient would suffer bad luck.

"This should help you."

"I—I can't accept this," Seriya whispered in awe. "These would feed my family for more than a trinal!"

"Exactly," Margariete responded sternly. "It was my fault you spilled that tea. Consider it my apology."

Margariete shouldered the pack and headed out of the alley, turning her back on the hostess. Esilwen scrambled onto wobbly legs to follow.

"Who are you?" Seriya asked quietly.

Margariete paused, but didn't turn around.

"You should leave as soon as possible."

Without another word, she marched toward the town gate.

6: FINAL ARC OF CYCLE

"Please, Margariete, I have to stop," Esilwen wheezed. Her lungs burned with exertion. It seemed there wasn't enough air in the kingdom to support her. "I can't—run—anymore," she panted between gasps. "I can—barely—breathe!"

Bent over, her palms clutching her knees for support, she tried to ignore the sharp pinch stinging her side. The mad sprint out of Timberdale had only slowed into a quick trot a few miles ago, but the new boots Margariete had purchased for Esilwen back in town did nothing to enhance her physical stamina. She had been exhausted before their expeditious flight. Now her muscles cramped and throbbed, threatening total collapse.

Margariete leaned wearily against a tree, and though she had obviously expended most of her energy as well, the brunette didn't look nearly as spent as Esilwen felt. Margariete stared down the road, surveying the way they had come.

"Still too close," Margariete stated breathlessly. "We need to get farther away."

Esilwen cast her companion a beseeching expression. Margariete's eyes softened, obviously acknowledging her friend's condition.

"Only a bit farther," she promised, "then we can move off the road."

Esilwen inhaled sharply, suddenly assaulted by a fit of coughs. Margariete rummaged in the pack, retrieving a water flask.

"Is that nobleman chasing us? Is that why we can't stop?" Esilwen croaked as Margariete offered the flagon.

The water tasted vaguely sweet. Somewhat refreshed, Esilwen replaced the stopper and returned it.

"Probably," Margariete responded, pushing her weight off the tree and pointedly avoiding Esilwen's eyes. "But it will take some time for him to organize his men. Though if they're all as weak as his personal bodyguards, we'll be fine."

It wasn't exactly a lie, but Esilwen suspected it wasn't the whole truth either. Margariete had been agitated before the confrontation with the noble and his guards. Whatever secret she carried had put them both in danger.

"Where did you learn to fight like that?" Esilwen probed, hoping to prolong their respite for a few more minutes and uncover some answers at the same time.

"An old friend," Margariete responded evasively.

When she turned back to Esilwen, a tremor of regret shone behind the sapphire eyes. Esilwen decided not to press the matter and changed the direction of her inquiry.

"You moved so fast! I thought you were going to kill them," Esilwen said with a shake of her head. "They didn't even have time to block your attacks."

"If I had wanted to kill them, they would be dead," Margariete shrugged offhandedly.

As if to substantiate her statement, Margariete drew her sword in a swift movement, twirled it once and sheathed it expertly. A puzzled expression crossed her brow.

"Why? What did you think I was going to do?"

"Reason with them," Esilwen offered, waving her hand in the air. "Use your mind powers on them. That sort of thing."

Margariete's answering smile flashed condescending. She laughed.

"That would have been the easier thing to do, if the nobleman had been on his own. But his guards made using my mind powers impossible. I can only control one person at a time. Had I attempted to influence him, I would have been an easy target for his men." Margariete nodded her head once in the direction of Timberdale. "Not to mention the large number of witnesses. The point was to remain hidden, ourselves and our powers. We caused enough of a disturbance back there."

Esilwen's breathing was becoming more regular, though it seemed as if her remaining strength leaked into the ground through the soles of her feet. Her legs wobbled dangerously.

"At least we saved Seriya," she mused. "I can't believe that man would kill her over something so trivial."

"I would have let him if you hadn't convinced me to help her."

Margariete's eyes bored into Esilwen with a paradoxical mixture of accusation and praise. One, however, greatly outweighed the other, and Esilwen surmised that Margariete resented her interference. Sighing dejectedly, Esilwen decided that, despite her companion's lessons, she understood less of this culture than she had previously believed.

"Do you really hate your own people that much?" she murmured in a low voice, looking at the ground. "You would allow an innocent girl to die for the sake of a noble's pride?"

When Margariete spoke, her anger cut through the air like a whip, sending a hissing fury inside Esilwen's skull.

"Did it ever occur to you that it would have been better for Seriya if I had? Her life is forever changed, Esilwen. She has defiled her reputation with the law and disgraced her family's honor."

The pressure of Margariete's inflamed temper pressed against Esilwen's head, squeezing heated vibrations into skin and blood. Her vision danced with dizzy red spots.

"The proper thing for her to do would have been to die," Margariete continued, her vehemence slicing through the air like needles. "Her sacrifice would have released her family from further persecution. Seriya's survival will bring only shame to her family."

Esilwen was too emotional to respond. But then the pressure receded out of Esilwen's mind as Margariete regained control of herself. Though Margariete at least offered some vindication for the nobleman's actions, Esilwen knew, to the core of her being, that his measures had been wrong—immoral even. Why would an entire society sanction such unscrupulous behavior from their leaders? How could she befriend someone who supported such cruelty?

But, she countered inside herself, Margariete didn't let the girl die. She risked herself to save Seriya when all the townspeople simply observed the noble's attempted execution. Only a little prodding had urged the telepath to intervene. And then, at the gate, Margariete had displayed compassion, providing the unfortunate hostess with the means to start a new life.

"That's why you gave her the money," Esilwen said, "when we left—"

"Because I knew she could never go home."

"And she refused the gift at first because—?"

"She recognized her dishonor. Seriya didn't want to shame herself further by accepting a gift that condoned her disobedience."

Margariete folded her arms across her chest, as if in challenge.

"Saving her was the right thing to do," Esilwen finished quietly.

"According to who?" Margariete snapped with a lift of her eyebrows.

Esilwen paused. She hadn't anticipated Margariete's argument. Without memory, lacking context, Esilwen was at a loss to substantiate her beliefs. "Because it is" seemed like inadequate justification, but deeper validation was impossible for one who failed to recall the values of her own society.

"Right and wrong in Thyella are determined by traditions handed down from my people over generations," Margariete defended tartly, taking advantage of Esilwen's contemplative musing. "Not by you, not by me, or anyone who thinks themselves above it. That nobleman was probably a councilman of Timberdale. And if that's true, he is the law. It's his duty to oversee the city in the name of the king."

A deep sense of conviction permeated Esilwen. She didn't know its origin; she couldn't provide proof. She simply recognized its truth.

"Each soul has the right to pursue his destiny without the oppression of another. Forcing someone into submission is unacceptable, no matter the circumstance."

Obstinance tugged Margariete's features, but something in the dark blue eyes made Esilwen believe that her friend wasn't angry with her. Some part of Margariete had brooded over that statement before. Conceding verbal defeat, however, was simply not in Margariete's disposition.

"Maybe where you're from that's the case, but not here. Understand this," Margariete declared with finality, "duty and honor are all that matter in Thyella. Fail to adhere to this and you deserve death. In some cases, the dishonor is so great, the only way to restore it is to take our own lives. That is what my people believe."

"Is that what you believe?" Esilwen asked.

The wind blew vacantly through the trees, almost echoing Esilwen's words. Margariete paused, unwilling to answer the question.

"That girl will never be welcomed in her home again," Margariete said at last. "She might even return to *The Lavender Petal* to accept her punishment rather than live in exile. It's possible that the nobleman might spare her if she tells him everything she knows about us. If he likes her, he might force her into his service instead of executing her. If she runs—well, a woman who disgraces her family has only one choice of occupation."

Esilwen guessed what that occupation might be.

"Why didn't we just bring her with us?" Esilwen asked, swallowing a sudden ache in her throat.

"I couldn't have guaranteed her safety. I'm already taking a risk dragging you around." Margariete's voice turned steely and cold with rebuff. "I made an exception because you aren't Thyellan."

"What would you have done if I were?" Esilwen demanded.

Margariete shrugged.

"I would have left you."

Esilwen's look of horror must have affected Margariete because she hurried to explain.

"If you were Thyellan, you would hate me just as much as the rest of them, Esilwen. You would have refused to travel with me. But to be honest, I've kept you around

65

because it's been nice to have someone I felt I could trust again."

The sincerity of Margariete's words caused warmth to spread through Esilwen's body. It gave Esilwen the strength to carve into some unanswered mysteries.

"If you trust me as you say," she began, "why won't you tell me the truth?"

"I've never lied to you," Margariete stated bluntly.

"You've never been completely honest either," Esilwen countered.

"I don't understand what you mean."

Margariete turned decisively away from Timberdale and plodded down the road, leaving Esilwen scrambling to keep pace. Not to be deterred, the blonde willed her aching feet to match Margariete's long strides and continued with the conversation when she caught her friend.

"You intentionally leave out details when you tell me about your past: the name of your brother, for example, or the reason you ran away. And every time you think you hear someone approaching, you drag me off the road into the forest, waiting until they pass us. We've fled Timberdale without explanation, without Crescent, and without the supplies you went to buy. Up until now, I've tried to respect your secrets, but I can't any longer. If we are going to travel together, if you want me to be able to help you, you need to tell me everything."

Margariete didn't stop walking, but her expression hardened into glass. Esilwen put her hand on her companion's arm to augment her entreaty.

"Please, Margariete," she begged, "tell me what's really happening."

Several steps later, with downcast eyes, Margariete confessed. "I ran away because I didn't want to get married."

"Married?"

"It was arranged," Margariete replied. "My supposed fiancé is King Hylan of the Fourth Kingdom, over three times my age and a complete stranger to me."

"By Fohtian's Blood. Why?" Esilwen asked, shock jolting through her bones.

Bitterness bit Margariete's features as she turned.

"Because my brother is to be king. And he obviously desires to rule the entire shard. There are only three great kingdoms left in Thyella. The First and Third were joined through my mother's marriage to King Arahm. The Second Kingdom was destroyed long ago. The only kingdom not allied by treaty is the Fourth."

Tears seeped down Margariete's cheeks, and she continued in a softer, disconsolate tone.

"My brother would sell my happiness to secure his own. I saw what a horrible, loveless life my mother lived while married to my father. I will not suffer as she did."

Esilwen wanted to offer comfort, but felt inadequate to the task. What could she possibly say? This had driven her friend from home, from life. Words lacked substance against such pain. Instead, Esilwen chose to display her support by giving Margariete's arm a tight squeeze. Margariete wiped the tears from her cheeks with gloved fingers, steadying her breathing.

"So, if your brother is to be king, that would make you—" Esilwen prompted.

"A princess, yes. Second in line to the throne of both realms. My twin will take the crown of the First Kingdom in 21 cycles, and then inherit the Third upon my father's death."

Esilwen pondered the revelation of Margariete's heritage. Events were starting to form a sensible sketch. In a culture that worshiped personal honor, a promised daughter who suddenly disappeared would seriously harm a father's reputation. Rather than allow Margariete to seek her freedom, her father and brother must be concerned with their political status. No wonder so many knights were searching for her.

"That's why the Knights of the Gem I heard about in Timberdale are searching the roads," Esilwen reasoned. "They're looking for you."

"Yes," Margariete agreed, her voice strong and resolute, as if apologizing for her previous loss of emotional control, "although I'm surprised how quickly they've rallied. I had hoped to cross the border into the Third Kingdom before enough men were assembled to search for me. That's why we had to leave Timberdale. A pair of knights found Crescent. I think they may have recognized her saddle. It's marked with the royal crest. I didn't even think about that. Now they know which direction I've gone, which means we need to travel with more haste or they'll find me."

"I'm sorry your family has treated you so poorly." Esilwen said. "But how can your own people justify condemning you for your appearance? You're their princess!"

Margariete exhaled a mocking laugh.

"The only reason I didn't die at birth was because I'm a princess. Had I been anything less and my mother not the queen of the strongest kingdom, I would have been killed. It was her power that protected me from my father's hatred, and after her death, my brother. Since my father is only the ruler of the Third Kingdom, he had no right to harm an heir to the First. Even now, my brother holds more power over my life than my father. In these lands, my brother is all supreme."

"I'm so sorry, Margariete."

The pair halted in the center of the road. Moved to empathy, Esilwen suddenly embraced her new friend fiercely.

"Talking about it just makes me angrier," Margariete admitted. "I've blindly trusted my brother all my life. He promised to protect me. I didn't think a time would come when he would injure me so greatly."

Esilwen pulled away from Margariete. The brunette shook miserably, choking on grief.

"You can trust me," Esilwen vowed.

"I know," Margariete sighed with a resigned smile, and straightened. "You wouldn't benefit from disloyalty. If I've learned anything, it's that a person is only as valuable to you as they further your own success. Without me, you are alone in a world you don't understand."

"You believe that no one would help you simply because they care about you?"

"I did once. That's what led me here."

"What about your mother? She cared for you."

"And she's dead."

"What about the friend who trained you? Didn't he—"

"Terail is a loyal, devoted servant of the crown. My brother's closest friend. In the end, he would feel obligated to side with the prince."

Esilwen looked resolutely at Margariete.

"I know your brother's treachery has destroyed your faith in those close to you. But I swear to you, by the Blood of Fohtian, that I will remain true, no matter the cost. You can trust me."

Esilwen saw conflict in Margariete's eyes—the need to believe in someone tempered by the fear of trust. As the sky dipped into evening, Esilwen smiled and trotted down the highway, forcing her tired muscles into obedience.

"I say we run well into the night," she threw over her shoulder cheerfully. "That should give us a sufficient head start. After all, we wouldn't want you to be forced to marry, would we?"

"That would be a tragedy wouldn't it," Margariete returned, jogging to Esilwen's side.

The blonde nodded, ignoring the pain as it stabbed once again into her side, determined to prove that her loyalty would be unshakable.

7: LUNAR TWILIGHT

The future king of the First Kingdom drew tightly on the reins of his formidable black stallion, commanding the magnificent steed to halt. The eastern horizon dimmed with the shrouding eclipse of the moon, plunging the edges of the hilly landscape into dusk. The horse pranced excitedly, sensing the restlessness of its rider. Patting the animal's mane, the prince spoke a soothing phrase to calm its agitation. Moments later, a lanky, well-muscled man in his late 20s pulled his mount to a stop alongside the soon-to-be sovereign. Pointing to the sky, the heir apparent drew his companion's attention to a rapidly growing speck gliding toward their position.

Lord Terail nodded in acknowledgement, lifting his left hand toward the object. A golden ring, set with a glimmering pattern of rubies, adorned his middle finger. Three strokes on the stones caused the ring to shimmer in the dying light, imparting a magical summoning to the bird. The irresistible call urged the hawk to increase its speed, allowing it to arrive safely on Lord Terail's gauntleted arm in less than a 12th of an arc. The kingdom's Pearl Daimyo, highest ranking knight in the Gem class, untied a bamboo tube attached to the fowl's leg. Releasing the hawk, he unlatched the cylinder's catch and extracted a missive from its interior. The prince watched as Terail unrolled the parchment and scanned its contents eagerly.

"You were right," he announced, "she's heading east, just like you predicted. The Amber knights in Timberdale found Crescent near the marketplace. They've taken the horse to the duke's stables."

The prince's gaze surveyed the horizon. Soon smoke trails from Timberdale's hearths would be visible.

"We are half a cycle from Timberdale," he said. "If we rest here through the night arcs and leave before dawn, we can reach the city by midmorning."

"I don't understand that woman," Terail stated in exasperation, drawing the prince's eye. "Why go east? Your father's kingdom is more superstitious than yours. If anyone sees her face, she'll be killed."

"She intends merely to pass through the Third Kingdom," the prince said shortly. "She will turn north around the base of the Sakuhra Mountains. She seeks Hitoshi, in the Koungo Waste."

Incredulity unfolded across Terail's face.

"Hitoshi is dangerous. It's a city of outlaws and slave traders—the only realm not governed by the three kingdoms. What does she think she'll find there?"

The prince exhaled a patient breath. "If I know my sister, it is the only place she feels she can live without fear of discovery. It has been a haven for outcasts before."

"Of a different breed," Terail argued, his lips pulling into a grim line, "murderers, thieves and whores—not those who are branded with a 'curse.' Doesn't she realize what brigands such as those might do to her if she's exposed?"

"She has been locked inside the castle her entire life, Terail," the prince justified gravely, "and has no experience with the outside world. Her view is narrow, seeing things how she wants them to be, not as they are. If she makes it to Hitoshi, even I will not be able to find her. We have to catch her before she reaches the Waste."

"Well then," Terail added with a cunning sparkle in his eyes, "lucky for us, she's now on foot. It should be easier to overtake her."

The prince dismounted and rummaged through the saddlebags. He wondered why his sister was being so difficult. He supposed it was simply in her nature.

"Send a return message to our forces in Timberdale," he ordered. "No one is to pursue her. We will arrive tomorrow with further instructions."

Terail smiled. "As you command, Your Highness."

8: AT THE BRIDGE

Margariete winced as she freed her blistered toes from the leather soles of her boots. She tossed the offending footwear in a heap, surveying the damaged skin. The last four miles had significantly encouraged the throbbing sores across the heels of her feet. With the point of a dagger, the princess carefully sliced each one, relieving the pressure and draining the puss. She wished that she'd had the foresight to pack the healing salve Terail had given her to repair the blisters caused by her sword lessons.

Last night, they had pushed their bodies until it was too dark to see the road. Barely managing the strength to veer far enough from the highway to risk a fire, they found themselves too exhausted to gather fuel. The damp of night had crept inside Margariete's joints and muscles, an unforgiving chill plaguing her slumber. Consequently, she felt weak and uncomfortably stiff as dawn swept into morning. Esilwen, however, seemed unaffected by the cold. Even in sleep the foreigner generated heat from somewhere within herself. Margariete presumed it was another of her companion's abilities.

On first light, they resumed their flight. The most regrettable loss from Timberdale had been Crescent. The grey mare could have not only spared Margariete the sores on her feet, but most of the newly purchased supplies had been stowed in the horse's saddlebags. A pang of regret for the loss of another loyal friend stuck jaggedly in the princess's heart.

Margariete supposed they should be grateful that they had managed to salvage anything. She had just finished buying an appropriate pair of shoes for Esilwen when she had noticed the two Amber knights scrutinizing Crescent's saddle. One had taken the reins, while the other had dashed down the road, presumably to report the discovery to a superior officer. Taking the horse from the remaining knight would have been easy, but Margariete had spotted several other armored men in the market. One, at least, ranked Jade. Fearing exposure, she had raced to *The Lavender Petal* with only the meager scatter of supplies that she had stored in her knapsack.

She cursed herself over the mistake, stabbing with exuberance at a particularly large blister, accidentally drawing blood. Margariete drew a sharp intake of breath. The princess should have realized that Crescent's saddle would bear the markings of the royal crown. By now, a messenger would have been dispatched to her twin.

After running all morning, Margariete finally called a halt at the midcycle arc next to a creek. The highway arched over the gurgling stream with a moderately wide bridge whose shadowed underbelly could provide cover should the need arise. Esilwen had kept pace without complaint, but the princess knew her companion struggled with the effort.

Margariete bathed her sore feet in the cold rush of water, allowing its icy nip to dull the pain. She sighed with relief. Esilwen plunked onto the grassy bank, placing the waterskin she had recently filled upstream between them. After stretching briskly, Esilwen tackled the leather lacing that ran the length of her new shoes. A trickle of pity for the fragile blonde seeped through the princess. New shoes on Esilwen's soft skin had most likely left her feet more swollen and raw than Margariete's. But to the princess's complete astonishment, Esilwen's feet emerged from the rigid leather intact and unblemished.

"Is something wrong?" Esilwen asked in response to what must have been a look of disbelief on Margariete's face.

"There isn't anything wrong," she exclaimed, indicating Esilwen's toes, "that's the problem!"

"How is that a problem?"

"Look at your feet!" Margariete instructed.

Esilwen followed Margariete's directions, running her fingers across skin that was free from irritation. By her puzzled expression, Margariete could tell her friend had failed to comprehend the significance. After a moment, Esilwen giggled.

"Okay," she admitted, "I have no idea what you mean."

"I have sores all over my feet," Margariete grimaced, lifting one foot from the water to display its barrage of boils, "and my shoes are worn in from my practice sessions with Terail. How is possible that you haven't a single blister?"

Esilwen's gaze shifted from Margariete's foot to her own several times before she answered.

"I have no idea," she said with a shrug. "I do remember feeling some pain as I ran. The shoes pinched at my feet, but right after, the pain always just—went away."

Margariete stared. Went away? How did blisters vanish? Esilwen's feet should have been spattered with sores. It didn't make sense, but then, this was a girl who showed up in the middle of a forest fire. As Margariete opened her mouth to argue the point, she caught the sound of a deep, resonant laughter echoing down the road, traveling toward Timberdale. Margariete drew her feet swiftly from the creek, ignoring a sharp stab of pain as they made contact with the air.

"Put your shoes back on," she commanded, deftly wrapping her feet in wide strips of cloth she pulled from the knapsack.

Both girls donned their footwear, quickly gathered their scattered belongings, and dashed under the bridge. Though the overpass was wide enough for a wagon to trundle across, the underside hugged the stream, barely allowing the companions room to sit upright. Margariete huddled with Esilwen under the west end, closest to the sound of laughter so that the unknown travelers would be unlikely to spot them.

More voices joined the mirth, along with the creak of wagon wheels. Margariete felt the vibrations of the group's approach ripple through the air well before she could distinguish words. From the low pitch of the voices, she guessed that the party was primarily male. Their demeanor seemed disorganized and rambunctious, which made her certain it wasn't a group of knights. The Gem code of honor prevented such behavior in public. It was probably merchants. Though not a direct threat, Margariete felt wary about meeting strangers, especially if the company was making its way to Timberdale.

Margariete could only hear pieces of the party's conversation until the lead members of the group tromped onto the wooden boards of the bridge. There they paused.

"Should we stop and water the horses?" a gruff voice inquired.

The traveler's question sent shivers of fear across Margariete's nerves. If anyone approached the creek bank, Esilwen and Margariete were sure to be noticed. The sight of two women huddled under a bridge in the middle of the pine forest would surely arouse interest.

"No, the fork to the Sakuhra Mountains is only three miles away," a stern voice replied, much to Margariete's relief. "We'll water them—and the merchandise—at the spring there."

A scattering of low chuckles responded to the comment, along with several quiet whimpers. Margariete heard a metallic rattle, like chains scraping across wood.

"Do you think we could have this one?" the first voice snickered hopefully. Feet scuffled and a high-pitched yelp squealed fearfully. "She's certainly feisty!"

"Don't touch me!" a young female sobbed.

"I think she likes you, Garu," inserted an oily-toned man.

"Leave her be," the stern voice commanded. "She's worth more unspoiled."

Slave traders. Disgust wormed inside Margariete's belly. A quick glance at Esilwen revealed that the blonde had come to the same conclusion. Human trafficking had dwindled to a choked dribble since the season Margariete's grandfather died. Queen Anleia, Margariete's mother, disapproved of the tradition and quickly abolished its practice inside the First Kingdom's borders. The princess's twin had once told her that a rogue faction of slavers still operated in secret, trading flesh for gold despite the edicts of the crown.

Hooves clopped and laden wheels lumbered across the bridge. More chains grated against the wooden overpass. Sniffles from several prisoners and the distinct wail of a child caused Margariete to shudder. The planks above her shuddered with a sudden thump, and the child's cry transformed into a yowl.

"Get up you worthless rat," Garu demanded harshly.

The little one continued to whimper. Margariete heard another thud, and the child gasped. Esilwen gripped Margariete's arm desperately, pleading with her eyes, but the princess only shook her head fiercely.

"I said get up, boy," Garu roared. Sickening thumps echoed from the top of the bridge as Garu released his frustration on the child.

Esilwen chewed her lip, her chin quivering, when the boy's cries of pain turned into sodden pleas for mercy. Margariete again shook her head. They couldn't save every troubled person they encountered; they had already drawn too much attention in Timberdale. The rebellious look in Esilwen's face prompted Margariete's next action.

Don't move, the princess communicated telepathically. *If you try to help them, you'll get us both killed.*

Esilwen stared at the princess with surprise, never having experienced the brunette's mind voice before. Margariete could hear her companion's thoughts clearly. Would she really die if they helped? Wasn't Margariete strong enough to defeat the slavers?

Not without risk to the prisoners, Margariete answered.

Esilwen regarded her pensively. The boy's beating had ceased. Weak, almost silent weeping sang harmony with the murmur of the creek.

If they've captured these people to sell as slaves, it wouldn't make sense to hurt them just because we intercede, Esilwen argued. *Isn't it more likely that they'll try to only kill us and leave the prisoners alone?*

We don't have time to rescue every peasant that's in danger, the princess argued. *We can't single-handedly save all of Thyella!*

"On your feet," Garu rasped.

More scuffs and grates sounded above. Presumably, Garu had forced the boy up.

I won't sit idle while these people are in danger.

Uncompromising fervor radiated from Esilwen, surging into Margariete's consciousness along with her words.

I can't use my powers in front of these slavers or the prisoners, Esilwen. If they find out what I can do—

Fohtian's Blood, Margariete, then what do you have them for? Do you really think the gods graced you with power so you could hide under a bridge like a coward?

Anger constricted Margariete's eyes, but Esilwen's sincerity remained unwavering, pulsing inside Margariete's head. Before the princess could retaliate, Esilwen continued.

I'm going to help them, Margariete, with or without you.

Margariete glared, but Esilwen seemed undeterred. The groan of wheels on wood echoed into the little gully as the transport lurched forward. Breaking her link to Esilwen's mind, the princess collected the vibrations in the air, assessing the placement of slavers and prisoners above her. Two guards marched at the rear of the party, just beyond a scraggly line of chained captives. The last prisoner was small: the young boy. At least ten slaves were locked inside the wagon, two men flanking each side of the cage. One wagoneer guided the horses, surrounded by three men on foot. A lone rider led the entire party at its head.

Nine guards total, sure to be trained in combat. As Margariete opened her eyes, the picture dissolved inside her head. The fight would be difficult, but it might be possible to defeat them without the aid of her powers. If she killed enough of them quickly, the others might run away.

Margariete looked back at her companion, reinserting her voice into Esilwen's thoughts.

Stay low and wait until I've taken out the rear guards, then help the prisoners escape.

Without waiting for her friend's response, the princess rolled out of her hiding place, using the bank incline to hide her ascent, and crept toward the edge of the bridge.

The wagon had already crossed. An unkempt man in grimy brown leathers tormented one of the female captives. Margariete guessed him to be Garu. Of the nine, he looked the most formidable, with two swords and an array of daggers girding his belt. Most of the other guards carried only one weapon—one carried a bow.

As the last two slavers stepped off the bridge, Margariete edged away from the bank, intending to skulk silently behind them. Unfortunately, the loose gravel of the pavement had other ideas.

An insolent clatter of stone caused the guard on her left to twist around, abruptly reaching for his sword. Just as his fingertips touched the hilt, Margariete's blade slid out of its sheath, cleaving the flesh of his neck in a wild spray of blood. He clutched his throat, a futile effort to stanch the flow, and toppled face down on the hard-packed road. His companion yelped with surprise, momentarily stunned by the suddenness of her attack. Margariete reacted by instinct, rapidly tilting her blade into position. Without hesitation, she thrust the weapon hilt deep into the man's abdomen.

No amount of training had prepared the princess for the crunch of bone that followed the upward slice of her blade as she yanked it from the slaver's spine. Her practice sessions with Terail had not included the acrid odor of iron that accompanied a shower of so much blood. Margariete watched—horrifically transfixed—as the spark of life drained from the man's eyes. Her surroundings melted into a wash of silence, the air too thick to breathe. The lifeless form that had once been a thinking, sentient human fell at her feet.

She had never killed before.

Her sword shuddered with tremors, but she scarcely noticed. The weight of consequence pressed around her, squeezing her body painfully, as if the spirits of the dead men sought revenge from the netherworld. The slavers, prisoners, and forest dissolved into the sight of the dead body sprawled gracelessly before her.

"Margariete!" shouted a familiar voice, frantic with concern. "Margariete look out!"

Esilwen's warning jolted the highway scene back into focus, just in time for Margariete to duck as a curved blade sliced above her. She felt the weapon brush against the fabric of her hood. Twenty spans away, the archer nocked a shaft against his bowstring.

Her next guard opponent smelled of stale beer and urine, rusty-red bracers adorning his arms. She parried his thrust, spinning inward into his body and propelling her lifted elbow against the side of his head. The blow knocked him to the ground, and Margariete hoped he was unconscious. She didn't have time to confirm.

A twanging vibration prickled her senses, like tiny insects running along her skin, alerting her to the bowman's attack. The premonition provided her with a moment to react. Another spin and a parallel sword swipe along the axis of her body brushed the archer's arrow aside like a dried leaf, cleaving the shaft in two. Wide-eyed and dumbstruck, the ranged fighter faltered, allowing Margariete to take advantage of his inaction. Reaching through the air with her mind, the princess attacked the archer's bow, snapping the shaft where the ligament string met the wood at the base. As the tension released, the bowstring snapped across the archer's face, flipping into his left eye. Screaming, he dropped the broken weapon.

Before Margariete could revel in her success, a sharp burst of pain erupted in the back of her head. The attack against the bowman had governed her attention, taking far too long. Dropping to her stomach and rolling over, she barely managed to avoid a blade plunging toward her skull. Instead, the weapon stabbed past her left cheek, pinning her hood against the ground.

Garu's second sword poised to strike. He must have flanked her while she concentrated on the archer. Somewhere to the right, Margariete caught a glimpse of the red-bracered man lurching to his feet. A vicious upward kick knocked Garu backward into his compatriot. As they tried to sort themselves, the princess reached for the hilt of Garu's imbedded weapon. Pulling desperately, she quickly realized it would be impossible to extract from her angle. To her left, a newly alerted slaver rushed around the line of chained captives. At least three more guards still waited at the head of the column.

This wasn't going as well as she had planned.

Alone, her sword skills had proven inadequate. Victory hinged on releasing all the weapons in her arsenal. Hooking a gloved finger around the latch of her cloak, she freed herself from its ensnarement. A quick spring set her on her feet, where she faced slavers and prisoners alike. Her sapphire eyes glittered fiercely from her unmasked dusky face. Garu, Red-Bracers, and the newcomer, a bald, shirtless man jacketed in scars, recoiled in alarm at her appearance. Fear twisted the captives' features, and they shied away from the dark-haired princess. Margariete smirked in both triumph and disdain.

She lifted the palm of her free hand, focusing her mind around the hilt of her first victim's abandoned sword, three strides behind her current opponents. With a twist and contraction of her fingers, the princess willed the weapon to rise and thrust forward. The blade obeyed as if attached to marionette strings, piercing through the bald man's shoulder and erupting tip first from his chest. A gurgle of blood gushed from his mouth as he crumpled to the ground. As if wielded by an invisible foe, the sword yanked itself free of the slaver's body and rushed to battle Red-Bracers just as Margariete sped forward. Garu narrowly blocked *Stardawn's* first strike.

"What cursed magic is this!" Red-Bracers screamed, frantically parrying the assault of the disembodied sword.

Terrified gasps and whispered prayers to Nehro murmured from the slaves' lips. Garu struggled to wrench his attention from his comrade's combat with the dancing blade. Taking advantage of his distraction, Margariete drove her weapon through his ribcage, ripping through the flesh and rending his heart.

Sudden hooves beat the ground. Margariete turned just in time to see the horseman rein in his mount five body lengths away. He calmly leveled a hand crossbow at her breast. Two more slavers guarded his flanks, both pale and tensely gripping their sword hilts.

"Surrender," the horserider ordered.

Margariete responded by planting her free-floating blade into Red-Bracers' stomach, taunting the horseman with a saucy lift of her eyebrows. With a ghastly grimace, the mounted slaver let his bolt fly.

The princess had already gathered the mental strength to thwart the attack. Pushing against the air with only her mind, she commanded the projectile to slow its flight. It halted a dagger's width from her chest, suspended in midair. A collective hiss of awe told Margariete that the sight was not lost on her audience of captives. Preparing a counter-trajectory, she reversed the alignment of the bolt and released it against the marksman. Impelled by the whole of Margariete's will and fury, the shaft tore through the horseman's throat, puncturing cleanly through his body and embedding itself in the bole of a tree a hundred paces away. The spooked horse reared erratically, throwing its dead rider from the saddle.

Margariete fought against a wave of blackness that surged behind her eyes. Drained and dizzy, she refused to show weakness to the two remaining slavers, though her strength was spent. She could neither dominate one nor physically fight the other. Using the throbbing ache in her head to lend vehemence to her glare, she glowered at them, hoping to coerce their surrender.

But before any word of intimidation escaped her tongue, both men fled into the forest, one pausing only to aid the flagging steps of the archer who had lost his eye.

Immediately, Margariete crumpled to her knees. *Stardawn* fell from her listless grasp. She heard Esilwen's approach. Light fingers touched the princess's shoulder.

"Are you injured?" Esilwen asked.

"I'm fine," Margariete lied, shivers of weakness spasming across her body. "Set the prisoners free."

Shuffles and clicks swam through the princess's ears as Esilwen searched for the keys and began releasing the captives. The blonde's words of comfort were lost inside Margariete's rushing head, faint as she was with spinning images of dying slavers. For a moment, she struggled with a churning stomach. She didn't know how long she fought the sickness, but a startled yelp made her look up. A former prisoner loomed over her, his faded green eyes boring into her with hatred. Behind him, Esilwen had just unlocked the women's cage, but a slave wrested away the keys.

Esilwen's scream was the last thing Margariete remembered as something hard connected with her cheek.

9: REKKADELL

A foggy blur glazed Margariete's vision when she opened her eyes. The left side of her torso throbbed with aches and her head was wreathed in torment. Dim eclipselight streamed across the floor. Were those bars, or were they the slats of wood guarding her brother's window? Hadn't she already slipped through them? Did she have to escape the castle again?

Then Seriya fell to the floor, an eruption of green flame devouring everything. Esilwen forced Margariete to attack the slavers, but she had to disarm the castle guards first. Margariete tried to sort through the images, but the scattered events had no sense of time. Had she defeated Garu or the Timberdale noblemen first? Why was the man with red bracers leading Crescent away?

Margariete closed her eyes and shifted to ease the soreness of her side. An involuntary moan croaked from her throat when her face contacted the cold floor. The odor of damp animal feed overwhelmed her nostrils. She tried to sit up, but was surprised to discover her hands unable to move. Scratchy rope bound her wrists. Her feet seemed to be in the same predicament.

"Margariete?" asked a timid voice.

The princess surveyed the gloom. The voice sounded familiar, but Margariete's thoughts spun in wobbly circles. Every thread of memory she tried to fashion dispersed into a vortex of disorder, as if their edges purposely repelled each other. Is this how Esilwen felt when she tried to recall her past?

Where was Esilwen?

Margariete noted three shady blobs that might be walls, one punctured with a barred window. Wooden shafts leered menacingly across the fourth wall, like ghoulish teeth. Wondering if she had the strength to battle her prison's lock, she tried to sit up. Why couldn't her arms move?

Then she remembered. Her arms and legs were bound. The room stretched and twisted in her vision.

"Margariete, are you okay?" the familiar voice inquired.

"Esilwen?" she guessed.

"I'm here."

Margariete blinked slowly. Less than a few strides away, a woman lay propped awkwardly against the wall, restrained with cord. Lunar light teased a shine across her hair. How could Margariete have not noticed her before? The figure's outline was indistinct. Was she Esilwen?

"Where are we?" Margariete asked, the question rolling clumsily out of her mouth.

"I heard the townspeople call it Rekkadell."

"What's wrong with me?" she croaked, trying unsuccessfully to roll over. Her muscles refused to obey her commands. She incongruously recalled the looks of fear plastered across the faces of the slaves she had liberated. Did they leave? What happened to Crescent?

And where was Esilwen?

The woman was speaking, but her voice slipped past Margariete's ears without meaning. Shutting her eyes against the dizzying cyclone of her vision, the princess endeavored to will the madness away. But the darkness only grew deeper, swallowing her in black, velvet night.

*

Margariete's eyes snapped open in response to tense vibrations crackling through the air. A murmuring buzz roared through her head as she tried to sort through the last of a hazy dream. The ache in her skull was reminiscent of the time she'd consumed too much rice wine during her mother's funeral, but her thoughts now conducted themselves with distinct clarity. Most likely she had been drugged and the effects were now wearing off. The back of her head and cheek throbbed acutely, and the slowly brightening sky increased the intensity of the pain.

She looked down. Someone had exchanged her travelling garb for a thin, soiled dress that exposed her arms and most of her legs. Thick ropes wrapped across her midsection, pinning her arms and body to some kind of pole. She jerked irritably at the bindings with no result.

The barking of an angry mob surged around her.

The noise captured her attention and she looked around in surprise. At least a hundred villagers spread around her in a semicircle, spitting both curses and phlegm. She stood on a raised platform, four or five hand spans from the ground. Several men stacked bundles of sticks and piles of thatch at its base. She was tied to a large round shaft that impaled the dais at the center.

Quiet weeping, barely noticeable above the din of the crowd, came from behind her. Margariete tried to turn, but the restraints prevented her from seeing anything more than the long locks of blond hair belonging to another person tied to the other side of the pole.

"Esilwen?" she croaked desperately.

Esilwen's response was lost in a sudden roar of approval from the townspeople. Two burly villagers had pushed a man to the top of the platform. Displaying a signet glove of coarse cloth on his right arm, he faced Margariete with smug import. The man stood slightly taller than the princess, a splash of grey invading the careful trim of his pointed goatee. His pouchy middle was draped in a humble tunic, but appeared to be the finest garment worn by anyone in the village.

The town magistrate, Margariete thought.

He surveyed both women, his watery eyes hard with revulsion. The princess glared back, gathering the mental energy she needed to bend him to her will, but he spun back to the mob too quickly. The previous cycle's combat, combined with whatever drug they had forced on her, made her feel sluggish. She needed eye contact to dominate her target.

With his back to her, the magistrate raised his hands toward the throng, commanding quiet. The mob hushed into whispers.

"Citizens of Rekkadell," he projected with undisguised superiority, "just 18 seasons ago, King Shogan went into the core of the Second Kingdom, only to be swallowed by the darkness that now curses it. It has long been rumored that shadows walked the borders of the Cursed Land."

The magistrate paused while muttered agreement rippled through the villagers.

"We have all heard the reports of monsters attacking our lands to the north, and now, here before us, stand two of them! Behold! The long-eared demon and the dark-haired witch. Both masquerade as humans, making us believe they belong! Who knows what wicked magicks they have used on our homes, on our children!"

Angry shouts of fear exploded from the mass of people. A slimy fruit slapped Margariete in the face. The magistrate shouted to be heard.

"Our own people captured them in the woods, barely surviving with their lives!"

"Only because I saved them," Margariete cried in response to the magistrate's lie. "They would have been sold into slavery if I hadn't stopped the men who imprisoned them!"

The magistrate whipped around, striking her face with the back of his hand, superstitious frenzy spewing from his eyes.

"Silence witch!" he bellowed.

His gaze locked with hers, as if showing his audience he could burn her to ashes with a look. Margariete smirked.

"Let me go," Margariete commanded, keeping her voice so low, only the magistrate could possibly hear.

She pushed her will into his, meeting moderate resistance. The princess sensed his confusion. He fought against her sway, but Margariete simply forced more of herself into his head. An agonizing sprinkle of moments passed, the telepath wondering if her abilities would fail. But, to her relief, the magistrate's body posture slackened, his eyes focusing on her bindings.

"Release her," the magistrate instructed, turning to the nearest villager, probably a farmer.

Near the platform, several members of the crowd looked at each other, puzzled.

"But—Milord?" the farmer sputtered, a mixture of fright and uncertainly draining the color of his already pale face. A raggedy woman, missing most of her teeth, eyed Margariete suspiciously.

"The witch has cast a spell on him," she shouted, her face lacquered with fear.

The farmer glanced between the woman and the magistrate, who ordered Margariete's release a second time.

"Gag her!" the farmer yelled.

Another villager, heavyset with thick, hairy arms, leapt onto the platform. Pulling a handkerchief from his grimy work apron, he stuffed it into Margariete's mouth. She tried to spit out the foul thing, but the man held it firmly in place.

From the corner of her eye, the princess saw the farmer climb onto the podium and shake the magistrate. Margariete's hold on the village leader shattered into splinters.

Anger shook the air around the magistrate as he approached her. Her head snapped to one side as he struck her again. The crowd howled with a cacophony of righteous mania.

"You foul witch!" he screeched. "How dare you use your evil magic on me?"

Margariete fixed him with a stare that promised supernatural retribution. The pompous man trembled, taking a step back despite his bravado. His mind betrayed a stark terror that she might possess him again.

It won't be the last time, she injected into his mind. *You are easily persuaded. If it wasn't for the accident of birth, making you a noble, you wouldn't be considered fit to lead these people.*

Revolted awe cuffed the magistrate's expression. He turned back to the villagers, shouting over their clamor. Soon the people lowered their voices, anxious to hear the proclamation of their leader.

"People of Rekkadell," he announced, "you have seen the polluted magic of this witch! Even now, I can hear her in my mind, threatening me. Insulting me! She will corrupt everything she touches, force you to act against your will— just as she did me! She defies the natural order of the land.

This impurity must be cleansed in the name of the great goddess Nehro!"

A cheer erupted from the mob, uniting them in fanatical fervor. The magistrate's discourse was punctuated with hails to the water goddess and promises of death to the captives.

"We will watch the witch and her demon burn, sending their souls back to the Void! Douse the wood in oil," he commanded, turning back to the farmer.

Thick liquid sloshed against the gathered timber and thatch. The magistrate, farmer, and man in the apron—probably a blacksmith—climbed off the platform as the orders were obeyed.

"I'm so sorry, Margariete," Esilwen sobbed, barely audible over the crowd, "if I hadn't asked you to save those people—"

The pungent stench of the fuel stung Margariete's nose as she surveyed the crowd, fully prepared to agree that all this was indeed Esilwen's fault. If it weren't for the blonde's meddling, they would be safely through the Third Kingdom.

But just then, a particular pair of eyes drew her attention. Instead of fear and hate, the small orbs showed pity and sorrow. Tears ran freely down the small face of a boy, his flesh bruised and torn by the slaver Garu's fists. The child raised his hand toward her, as if begging his people to show his savior mercy.

Margariete gazed into the little boy's consciousness. There she found acceptance, disregard for her appearance, and gratitude for her actions. The child's affection clashed with the behavior of the mob. How could the pretty lady be all the terrible things they called her? She had saved him from those terrible men. Why would his village want to hurt her?

Unable to speak through the gag, Margariete projected a repentant reply into Esilwen's head.

No, she reassured her friend, *you were right. What do I have these powers for? I would have regretted not saving those people for the rest of my life. I ran away from home to avoid the same fate. I die only regretting that I couldn't save us.*

"Light the fire," the magistrate yelled.

The sea of people parted for a man brandishing two lit torches. He approached the platform. Margariete thought wistfully of her family—the twin whose betrayal had led her here, and her littlest sibling, Shikun, only 12 seasons. Had it been less than a fortnight since the last time she saw him? He had been giddy with excitement, joining his elder brother and the Knights of the Gem on an official quest. They had ridden to the border of the Cursed Land only cycles before she had fled the castle. She felt sorry that she hadn't taken the time to properly say goodbye.

Her twin, on the other hand, could rot in the Void for all she cared.

As the man handed the torches to the blacksmith and the farmer, Margariete pictured the face of her mother, wondering if there was another existence after this one. Would Queen Anleia be there in the netherworld, waiting to welcome her daughter?

Panic hit her hard when the blacksmith lower the torch to the fuel. With a last, frantic effort to save both herself and her friend, Margariete telekinetically grasped at the lighted baton, holding it motionless in the air. Fearful expressions spread across the faces in the crowd. The blacksmith tugged madly at the floating implement, but it stubbornly remained stuck to nothing.

She would not meekly submit to these senseless, silly people. With her last bit of strength, Margariete hurled the torch to the ground, snuffing out the flames with her force of mind.

The farmer backed away, cradling the other torch. Margariete tried to reach out to snatch it away, but her power was spent. The princess despaired. She couldn't control the minds of a hundred angry villagers at the same time.

She and Esilwen were going to die.

That realization must have filtered through her expression, because the torch-bearing farmer suddenly gained a measure of courage. He stepped toward the platform, preparing to light the thatch.

As he bent, an arrow zipped through the sky, knocking the torch from his hand. It skidded away from the platform. Margariete looked up, searching for the archer who had managed the flawless execution of the near-impossible shot.

Perched atop a mighty black stallion, Margariete spied a figure that filled her with both relief and dread. His gloved right hand gripped the shaft of a Thyellan longbow, though he made no move to nock another arrow. His presence alone belied the need for a weapon. Thick leather armor spilled across his body, overlaid with a white overcoat that billowed softly in the breeze. Authority and wrath radiated from his twilight eyes as he swept the village with his gaze. The townspeople, recognizing the seal on his silver-trimmed signet glove, fell to their knees in fealty.

"Margariete, who is he?" Esilwen whispered.

Was that awe or fear in her companion's voice? Margariete couldn't tell.

Margariete answered telepathically, resentment in her silent voice.

Heir to the throne of the First Kingdom and sovereign of the City of Jewels. My twin brother, Prince Raeylan of House Viridius.

10: STAY OF EXECUTION

Margariete scowled at her brother's black-and-scarlet armored companion as he mounted the platform, a faint grin on his face. Terail tucked into a graceful bow.

"Your Highness, it seems you're in need of my assistance."

She continued to glower, knowing Terail enjoyed that she couldn't reply while gagged. Though she could communicate telepathically—her swordmaster was one of the few who knew of her secret—silent words seemed less powerful than a spoken retort. She looked away quickly, hoping she could blink away the tears before he saw them. But the only person more observant than Margariete's twin brother was his daimyo general. Terail hooked an index finger under her chin, guiding her eyes back to his. Though he kept the façade of amusement, Margariete saw through the lie meant for the villagers—serious concern hid behind his eyes.

Terail gently removed the gag from her mouth. He ran his finger from her chin to the angry bruise on her cheek, furrowing his brow. Margariete winced. He removed his hand quickly and grasped the hilt of a dagger sheathed at his thigh. Terail winked at her with a smile, and the ropes fell about her like rice stalks to a scythe. Margariete barely detected the upward slice of his blade before he had replaced the weapon.

Her limbs felt lifeless. She tumbled forward.

"Your Highness, are you all right?" Terail asked anxiously, catching her before she slipped off the platform.

"I'm not sure," Margariete answered, ordering her body to obey her brain's command. It stubbornly refused, concluding it would be much easier to rely on Terail's support.

"They gave her something last night," Esilwen interjected, hastening to Margariete's side. Terail glanced at the blonde, lifting his pale eyebrows.

"Who is this?" he asked.

"She's my friend, Esilwen," Margariete answered, turning to thank her companion.

Esilwen's attention, however, seemed fixed on the crown prince, conflicting sensations flickering across her face. Margariete felt the same. She shifted her gaze to her brother. He had rescued and condemned her in the same moment. She experienced a fleeting regret that the townsfolk's attempted execution had been thwarted. Her death would have saved her the greater agony of an impending marriage contract.

But then Esilwen would have died as well, she chided herself, ashamed of such a selfish thought.

Terail lifted Margariete off the execution platform. As they tread through the kneeling villagers toward the horses, the princess noticed several of the Rekkadell citizens moving away from her. Esilwen locked her arm protectively through Margariete's in response. The princess turned gratefully, meeting an encouraging smile. Incredibly, Esilwen seemed unaffected by the experience of being nearly scorched into the next life—physically at least.

Emotional havoc, however, seemed etched into the lines around her eyes.

Raeylan dismounted his stallion and spoke in low tones to the magistrate. Margariete was too far away to overhear the exchange, but the town noble had obviously said something Raeylan didn't like. The prince's face showed stoic displeasure. Margariete had been the recipient of that look before—her twin reserved it for those who violated protocol. The magistrate squirmed as Raeylan issued a reprimand. Just as the trio reached them, the village leader dropped to the ground in a show of obeisance. The prince turned to Margariete, driving disapproval into her heart with his silver-grey stare.

It was not what she had expected. Accusations and lectures on duty she could have resisted, even defied. Despite her resentment toward his treachery, his silent disappointment wreaked havoc inside her. But behind that twilight stare, Margariete sensed the torrent of relief he felt. He had reached her in time.

Outwardly, the prince hid his emotions well. Seasons of practiced etiquette concealed his inner thoughts with polite courtesy—but not from Margariete. Bonds deeper than blood bound the twins together. As Raeylan graciously accepted Esilwen's introduction from Terail, Margariete detected a slimming around her brother's lips, the slight crease of his brow—signs of surprise that were invisible to anyone else. He, like Margariete, had noticed the subtle differences between Esilwen and the rest of the Thyellan race.

After an appropriate greeting to Esilwen, Raeylan mounted his horse, offering a hand to his sister. The princess tossed her dark hair rebelliously, clenching her jaw. A wild desire to run assailed her.

But then she snorted cynically. Even with a head start she had been unable to outrun Raeylan. Margariete accepted her brother's proffered assistance and climbed into the saddle, wrapping her arms around his waist. Terail drew Esilwen onto the other horse. As the two horses charged onto the highway, the princess made a mental vow.

Raeylan could drag her back to the castle, but he couldn't force her to marry. She would join the Seven Cascades in their descent before submitting to the bridal bower.

*

"This is it," Esilwen said, plucking a thin leaf from an emerald-black bush and offering it to Terail. "This is what they made us eat."

Terail accepted the leaf and examined it.

"Kalil leaf," he said, passing the narrow plant to the prince. "Numbs all feeling, usually puts the victim to sleep. After it wears off, the recipient experiences extreme exhaustion and a nasty headache. But," he added slyly at Margariete, "when you need to subdue a dangerous prisoner, it can be a most effective poison."

"Is there a remedy for it?" Margariete asked impatiently.

The throbbing in her head had increased dramatically with the constant rocking motion of Shale, her brother's steed. The party had halted at the site of Margariete's battle with the slavers. Though she was grateful to slide off the horse, Margariete couldn't help darting glances at the bloodied corpses of the men she had killed.

"I'm afraid the only thing you can do is rest," Terail answered.

Raeylan cast her a firm look, and though Margariete sensed something else in his expression, it was too deep for her to recognize. Walking to Shale, he untied a large bundle of cloth from the saddle. The fabric looked familiar to Margariete.

"Open it," Raeylan directed, handing it to his sister.

Margariete swallowed the dryness in her throat. The long, narrow shape of the cloth revealed the identity of the object inside. Raeylan's tight lips indicated that he knew exactly who it belonged to. Unwrapping the cloak she had stolen from his closet, she pulled *Stardawn* from its sheltering embrace.

Relief for the recovery of her precious weapon mingled with unease. This had to mean Raeylan suspected her forbidden sword study. Margariete's next thought was to shield her teacher from dishonor, but claiming that she had self-trained would sound implausible. She had, after all, single-handedly killed five armed men.

"The weapon is yours," Raeylan stated.

Margariete nodded once.

"And these men," he asked, "did you kill them?"

Margariete couldn't bring herself to verbally accept responsibility for her actions. She nodded again, this time with eyes lowered.

"Do you realize," Raeylan continued, "the seriousness of what you have done?"

"She saved those villagers," Esilwen interjected hotly. "If not for her, they'd have been sold into slavery. She was only defending them!"

Margariete felt heavy with guilt. Esilwen had missed the underlying significance of Raeylan's tone. Her brother did not condemn her for helping the slaves. In her place, he would have taken similar measures to ensure the safety of his people.

"That is not the matter of consequence," he said. "The Princess of the Jewel has disregarded the propriety of her station."

Margariete flinched. Raeylan's use of her formal title expressed the intensity of his disapproval.

"What do you mean?" Esilwen argued, flying instantly to Margariete's defense. "Because she learned to fight? Because she can defend herself?"

The prince's steadfast answer stunned the maid speechless.

"Yes."

Margariete had always resented her brother's powerful ability to silence an argument with logic, defeating an opponent with quiet authority. Esilwen looked like she felt the same way.

"I can't hide your transgression," he said, turning his attention back to his sister. "With so many witnesses, our father will hear of the incident, especially since you publically challenged the Duke of Timberdale. Your actions were careless, Margariete."

"The blame is partially mine, Your Highness," Terail inserted.

Raeylan surveyed the bodies that lay scattered on the highway.

"As her teacher, you should have been more cautious, Terail," the prince charged.

Margariete stared at her brother in astonishment. Had Raeylan known about her lessons all along? That suggested he wasn't angry at her disobedience, but worry that she had been exposed. After a pause, the prince addressed his general sternly.

"This indiscretion cannot go unpunished, Lord Terail."

"I understand, Your Highness," Terail said, accepting the rebuke with a graceful bow. "I expected nothing less."

Expected nothing less? Margariete thought, noting the significance of Terail's use of the word in past tense.

She glanced between her brother and her trainer. Terail had known that they would eventually be caught! His intention had been to suffer the penalty alone all along. And she had no doubt that her brother had designed the maneuver to spare her any social repercussions.

"If Margariete hadn't known how to fight, we would have been in a lot of trouble!" Esilwen burst.

"Had she not run away," Raeylan countered, "she would not have had the need." His eyes turned to Margariete, cold with anger. "Do you realize what we left behind to pursue you? Beasts from the Cursed Land have infiltrated our borders. Instead of fulfilling my duty to protect my people, I am chasing after you."

Raeylan's accusation, so offhandedly ignorant of the gouging betrayal she felt, urged the resurgence of her resentment. Outrage trembled at her lips.

"Why should I care what you were doing, or how important it was? You broke your promise to me for your own selfish gain. I'll never forgive you!"

Raeylan stared at his sister in shock. If she had drawn her blade and cut out his heart, less agony would have pained his expression. Since the prince seemed incapable of responding, Terail interceded on his sovereign's behalf.

"Betray you? What could he have possibly done to betray you?"

"He knows what I'm talking about," Margariete spat.

"Well I sure don't," Terail admitted, glancing with unease between the two siblings.

"I heard father talking with one of his advisers," she said, glaring at her twin with hostility. "You signed a marriage treaty with the Fourth Kingdom."

"Ye-es," Terail said, "but why would that make *you* run away?"

The prince's shoulders relaxed and he sighed, understanding thawing the tension in his body.

"Because she thought the marriage had been arranged for her," Raeylan explained.

Terail laughed nervously, scratching the back of his head.

"Well, this is awkward."

Margariete's brows contracted. They knew something she didn't.

"Do you have so little faith in me, sister?" Raeylan asked sadly, suddenly not meeting her eyes.

"I—" she stuttered, unsure of how to respond.

Her brother's behavior confounded her. He seemed so—vulnerable.

"I did sign a treaty," the prince admitted, "but not between you and King Hylan."

"But—father, he—he said I would try and talk you out of it. He's been trying to arrange my marriage for the last two seasons. I thought—when he mentioned the marriage—"

Raeylan looked on his sister fondly, his affection shining from cloudy, grey eyes.

"True, he felt this was the perfect opportunity to use you. But I vowed that I would never allow you to suffer as our mother did, Margariete. I would never break that promise."

"Then—what," she faltered in confusion, "what was father speaking of?"

A flicker of melancholy touched Raeylan's expression.

"I was tired of father using you as political pawn. King Hylan's youngest daughter has come of age. I agreed to marry in your place."

Shame replaced the bitterness that Margariete had felt for the last eight cycles. Not only had she needlessly endangered her life, but she had pulled Raeylan away from important matters, forcing him to choose between his love for her and his duty as future king.

All for nothing.

Raeylan had not sold her happiness; he had bought hers at the cost of his own.

"But Raeylan—"

"The treaty is final, Margariete," Raeylan said quietly, before she could argue. "There will be no more discussion on the matter. I will wed Princess Katrina before the next Sakuhra festival."

"That's only 20 cycles," Margariete said.

"Yes, just after my coronation."

"Raeylan I—I'm so sorry. I feel like such a fool," the princess whispered.

Raeylan wrapped his arms protectively around his twin. As she buried her face into his cloak, she felt the strength of his presence engulf her. Terail politely looked away, but tears freely adorned Esilwen's cheeks.

"All that matters is that you are safe. I was afraid you would come to harm before I could reach you."

"With good reason," Terail added mischievously. "You were gone from the castle for only eight cycles and were nearly burned alive."

"You did leave quite a trail for me to follow," Raeylan admitted.

Margariete pushed her brother away. The cycle had been so emotionally wearisome that she didn't think she could manage a good-natured response.

"So what now?" Margariete asked.

Raeylan looked at Esilwen.

"It seems you have some explaining of your own. But for now, we head back to Timberdale. I'm sure you and your companion want a bath and a change of clothes."

Margariete looked down at her filthy attire. Both she and Esilwen were still clad in shabby execution gowns. Margariete belted *Stardawn* around her waist and slipped Raeylan's borrowed cloak around her shoulders.

"Well done," Terail said, refereeing to her disguise as he assisted her into Shale's saddle. "Too bad it's got a hole in it."

Margariete glared at her swordmaster's smile. She inspected the hood. He was right, a gaping hole rent the fabric. The opening would reveal evidence of her dark hair.

She silently cursed Garu's dead soul.

11: RESPITE REFLECTIONS

Raeylan released the clasps of his armor, meticulously removing each piece of leather and placing it in its proper position on the garment stand before him. As he detached the last greave, he inspected the suit for flaws. The surface was worn, but clean and free of damage. His overcoat, however, was layered with dust. A dark, oily blotch spread across the white fabric where his sister had leaned against him during the journey back to Timberdale. He draped the royal garment over the armor ensemble, mentally noting to have the overcoat tended.

Walking to a small table with a washbasin, the prince removed his finely embossed signet glove. Deep grooves of silver and gold etched the royal symbols of the Viridius line into the leather, runes that were universally recognized throughout the shard. He laved the water gently over his hands, arms, and face, washing the evidence of travel from his body and mind alike. As he pulled the glove back across his skin, he felt the weight of his station press heavily about him.

Shielding Margariete from the consequences of her actions would be difficult. King Arahm would demand retribution. At the very least, he would deny her any more training. He might confine her to the castle permanently. Raeylan knew that would suffocate her.

The prince knelt on a cushion in the middle of the room, placing both hands flat against his thighs in proper meditation posture. Weariness clung to him like hungry leeches, sucking away his endurance. The physical demand of hunting beasts at the borderland and the lack of sleep caused by Margariete's pursuit left his body dry and empty. Concern for his twin's safety had pinched the customary calm from his mind for cycles. When he finally discovered her, beaten and tied to that stake, it had taken the last dregs of his self-control to restrain the tide of wrath that surged within him. The magistrate of Rekkadell had been only a breath from finding his soul relocated to the netherworld.

Regret heaved through him as he delved deeper into a meditative state, drowning him with the disgrace of deserted duty. He should have remained at his post, placing the demands of the kingdom above his own concerns. Never before had the choice between country and sister been forced upon him. Never had he relinquished one in order to preserve the other. He had chosen his sister, succumbed to his need to protect her.

His people would be ashamed.

Raeylan withered, trapped between devotion to his duty and love for his twin. As the fervor of his mental anguish tore through his sense of self, a pair of ice-green eyes glistened in his mind, pouring compassion from the halo of their gaze. Their radiant irises held him mesmerized.

The image was interrupted by a knock that echoed flatly through the room. Raeylan breathed in slowly, breaking free of his thoughts. He raised his eyes to the door.

"Enter."

It slid open and Terail marched through.

"Your Highness," he greeted, bowing respectfully, "I have spoken with the duke as you requested. He was, um, 'persuaded' to relinquish the maid."

Raeylan lifted a hand and indicated the cushion across the table. Terail assumed the same kneeling position as his prince.

"And what was the duke's response to my other orders?" Raeylan asked.

"A few promises bought his silence, but I imagine that will only last until the next time he meets with your father. The Duke of Timberdale is well known for his love of gold. His allegiance follows whichever royal treasury lines his pockets."

Raeylan shook his head. "There is little else we can do."

"If you want my opinion, Your Highness," Terail muttered, folding his arms against his chest, "that pompous excuse for a noble should eat the tip of my blade if he proves unfaithful."

The prince turned the corner of his lips ever so slightly. Lord Terail's vehement loyalty proved a little aggressive in situations of political complexity. Raeylan, however, deeply appreciated the reliability of his general.

"Some in the aristocracy still believe it is my father who controls the First Kingdom," he said, "and I am merely a puppet on the throne."

"That's a far stretch from the truth," the Pearl Daimyo snorted. "Since your mother's death, you have truly been as a king—your father only a steward."

"The rumors provide hope for those who still cling to my grandfather's ideals. They have ruled too long through a system of privilege, basing the value of a soul on birthright and class."

Terail smiled smugly. "Soon your rule will be officially recognized. They would be better served to show complete fealty now."

"Much can occur in a 20 cycles, Terail," Raeylan sighed, feeling the press of his duty once more. "Though I have already assumed the responsibilities, my full right as a ruler will not be solidified until my coronation. Until then, I am only a ghost of a king." The prince shook the gloomy thought from his mind. Other, more important matters needed his attention. "What of the maid?"

"I explained her new occupation," Terail replied. "She knows of Princess Margariete's uncommon appearance and has sworn to carry the secret."

"Good. My sister needs an attendant for the journey. Better that it is someone she knows. We leave tomorrow for the borderland."

Terail's expression rose in question. "Shall I organize a contingent of knights to escort the princess back to the castle?"

"No. Send for Crescent and arrange horses for the other two women. They will accompany us."

Terail failed to mask his shock. "Don't you feel it might be too dangerous for them?"

Raeylan's eyes grew hard. "If my sister returns to the City of Jewels now, she will face King Arahm alone. He will grant no pardon. I must be present to defend her. Besides, I think my sister has more than proven her prowess in battle, wouldn't you agree?"

Terail nodded in understanding. "But what of the stranger?"

"My sister will look after Esilwen," Raeylan answered, his voice softening as he spoke her name.

"Do you think it's true that she comes from the other side of the shardwall?"

"Had I not met her myself, I wouldn't have believed it possible. She's not of our race. That much is certain."

"Well, the pointed ears were a dead giveaway," Terail said with a chuckle.

"It's more than that—" the prince said, but before he was able to elaborate, a knock came from the door. Terail rose and opened it, revealing an Amber knight.

"Excuse me, Your Highness, Daimyo Terail," he apologized with a bow. The knight held his arms outstretched, offering a rolled parchment with both palms. "This just arrived from the border camp."

Terail accepted the message and excused the soldier, waiting until the door slid closed.

"It's from Prince Shikun."

Raeylan waited, silently commanding Terail to relay the letter's message. After scanning the words quickly, Terail summarized.

"He wants to know if you've found the princess and reports that the squad hasn't discovered any signs of the cursed beasts."

"Send a reply, and add news of our approximate return."

"As you command, sire," Terail said with a bow. He paused, drawing a deep breath before continuing. "Your Highness, I wish to apologize for instructing your sister in the way of the sword."

Raeylan's grey eyes smiled. Though a formality, honor demanded his general's request for forgiveness for such an obvious breech.

"You trained her well, Terail. If not for your tutelage, my sister would be dead. I thank you for saving your princess's life." The prince inclined his head in a kingly expression of gratitude.

"And how long have you known about our private lessons?" Terail's lips twisted into a cunning smile.

"Since the beginning," Raeylan answered. "She abandons her maids the same arc every cycle. You disappear at about the same time. The connection was not difficult to deduce."

"I thought I hid it well!" Terail's laughter coiled with mirth. "Then again, I should have known better than to think you wouldn't notice."

"If she had been more discrete, as you were, I might not have. But, I make it a point to always note my sister's whereabouts."

"May I ask why you didn't stop her training as soon as you discovered it?"

"Margariete has always struggled to find happiness. Lessons with you gave her a sense of self-worth. I could not take that from her."

"Now that she's been discovered, shall I put an end to her lessons?"

A flash of sorrow touched Terail's expression. Raeylan knew his friend asked the question only because it was required, not because it was the young general's wish.

"News will reach King Arahm, Terail. Hiding your involvement from him is contingent on the cessation of your coaching. You are the best daimyo the First Kingdom has had in generations. You cannot be replaced."

"It will be hard on her."

"Not if I train her myself."

The pronouncement startled Terail for only a brief moment, then the crafty glint returned to the knight's eyes.

"I'm sure your father will be pleased," he said as he stepped into the hallway and closed the door.

12: AN ARC IN THE WASHING CHAMBER

The warm, poppy-scented water of the bath soothed Esilwen's body. Steam wafted through the cedar-lined bathing house, located in the left wing of the *Timberdale Inn and Tavern*. The pine washtub was short but deep, coated with a glossy resin that made the wood impervious to water. Esilwen's knees rested just under her chin, her hair pinned securely to the top of her head. A cloth protected her blond curls and her pointed ears from view.

Margariete had shown her how to cleanse the dirt from face, body, and hair with a sweet smelling cake of soap before slipping into the water. As she rinsed her skin with a ladle, Esilwen had thought it odd to wash before entering the tub. It seemed more natural to scrub while in the water. Margariete had been surprised when Esilwen mentioned it.

Esilwen glanced at the princess. Margariete's eyes were closed, but the muscles of her face were rigid. The relaxing atmosphere of the bathhouse had not provided release for the princess.

After leaving the road where they had encountered the slavers, Esilwen had little opportunity to console the princess. Upon their arrival at the town's finest inn the next cycle, Terail had hustled the two women into the building, ordered sufficient accommodations, and sent them directly to the washing chamber.

Esilwen sighed, sinking lower into the water. The prince and his general were not the tyrants of oppression she had expected from Margariete's description. Terail's concern for his princess danced clearly in his eyes every time he looked at her. His cheery jibes were obvious attempts to lighten her humor. Esilwen wondered if Terail's interest in the Jeweled Princess was something more than simply the attentions of a mentor.

Margariete's twin, however, scattered Esilwen's thoughts into disorder. The prince hadn't spoken to her directly since the argument at the slaver battle site, but when he looked at her, his stoic grey eyes sent shivers through her body. His regal face carried a constant expression of authority, but real emotion lay hidden behind that mask.

She reminded herself for the thousandth time that he was a prince—one who was betrothed. Esilwen wrenched her thoughts back to Margariete. The Jeweled Princess had barely spoken since discovering her brother's sacrifice. The privacy of the washing chamber offered Esilwen the first chance to help heal her friend's distress, though maid was unsure how to begin.

"Your brother isn't what I expected," she said tentatively.

Margariete opened her eyes, staring into the ceiling.

"I never should have doubted him."

"You couldn't have known, Margariete," Esilwen said, encouraged that Margariete had confided in her so quickly. "Anyone could have made such a mistake."

Margariete closed her eyes and swallowed. "I caused him great pain with my lack of trust. There is no pardon for that. I should have waited for him. I pulled him away from his duty. It will reflect badly on him with the nobles."

"He doesn't blame you, Margariete," Esilwen assured. "He's just happy that you're safe."

Margariete wiped her face with the back of her fingers, suppressing a sniffle. "It's just another of my indiscretions he'll be forced to hide at his own expense. I could live a thousand seasons and never match the sacrifices he has had to make for me."

"Look at me, Margariete," Esilwen commanded.

Slowly the princess rotated her head. Unshed tears shone in her sapphire eyes.

"You are capable of the same devotion, the same selflessness. You've known me only a short time, yet you've risked everything, even your freedom, to help me. If that's not loyalty, what would you call it?" Esilwen didn't wait for the princess to respond. "You ran. It was a mistake. I saw how your brother embraced you. He's already forgiven you."

Margariete's lips wavered into a smile just as the wooden door creaked open. The princess instinctively sank lower into the water in an effort to conceal her skin. Esilwen turned to the door, surprised that she recognized the intruding servant.

"Your Highness," Seriya said, falling to her knees in fealty. "I have graciously accepted the responsibility of your secret. I commit myself to your service."

Esilwen glanced at Margariete, who had pulled back out of the water.

"Who hired you?" the princess asked. The commanding tone surprised Esilwen. It was the first time she had heard stately inflection in Margariete's voice.

"The Pearl Daimyo retrieved me from my former duties at the duke's estate, Your Highness."

Esilwen was unsure what those "former duties" entailed, but was too afraid of the answer to ask. Margariete bit her lip, then shook her head once, as if clearing it of weakness.

"I accept your pledge of service."

Seriya's rose obediently, looking without fear on her new mistress. Moving to Margariete's side, she began untangling the princess's dark hair.

13: Two Cycles From The Camp

The fading light illuminated the gentle affection in Raeylan's eyes as he offered his twin a small bamboo box. Margariete took it as he settled next to her on an ashy rock. A light breeze danced through Margariete's new travel clothing as the gust broke free of the forest confines behind, racing eagerly into the rolling hills of the Korene Valley below. One cycle from Timberdale had brought the company to the lip of the grassy vale. Between scattered clumps of chalky granite, the Cohmay River was just visible on the treeless horizon. Margariete lifted the lid of the box, revealing a carefully folded garment of red silk.

"Little does it match your beauty, my sister," Raeylan said, removing the fabric from its protective shell, "but signet gloves worthy of your station can be crafted only at Castle Viridius."

Sliding the glove across both palms, Raeylan presented the gift for his sister's approval. Two narrow scrolls of gold embroidery twisted around the thumb and forefinger of the scarlet cloth, gliding gracefully to the elbow. A delicate image of the Viridius crest adorned the wrist. The new mark of her station flaunted elegance within simplicity. Margariete accepted it with both hands, blinking back a swell of gratitude. The gift was a manifestation of her

115

brother's absolute forgiveness, a symbolic reinstatement of her position at his side.

She bowed. Raeylan nodded with a pleased smile, then politely turned away from her. Terail and Seriya, who had watched from an appropriate distance, followed the prince's example. Esilwen stood next to Crescent, glancing around in confusion. Margariete smiled fondly, projecting instructions into her friend's mind.

You have to look away, Margariete explained. *It is improper for anyone to see my naked right arm.*

Esilwen seemed dubious, but averted her eyes as directed. Margariete removed the plain black glove she already wore and cloaked her skin with the silk garment. For the first time since her mother's death, the princess felt the dignity of her title, as if her brother's love had somehow renewed her. She would never doubt him again—second chances were rare in Thyella.

"Welcome back, Princess Margariete," Terail announced when she had finished. As he bowed, his eyes met hers with a playful flash. "It's been very dull without you. Not that your brother isn't a wonderful travelling companion, but he's just not as pleasing to the eye. And he never does anything unexpected."

Raeylan rose to his feet and collected the reins of Shale and Crescent. "And to earn my title of predictability," he said, "you and I shall discuss the details of our arrival at the borderland in private. The horses need tending."

"I never get a cycle off," Terail complained.

He winked slyly at Margariete before leading the other three animals to the edge of the camp. The princess laughed, watching Terail join her brother at a small stream 50 paces away.

"Does your brother know?" Esilwen asked, sidling next to Margariete.

Margariete turned to her friend quizzically.

"Know what?"

Esilwen's green eyes sparkled with delight.

"About you and Terail," she said.

Margariete glanced between the two men at the river and Esilwen.

"Of course he knows," the princess replied. "You were there when Terail admitted to teaching me. Raeylan will never let me train with Terail again." She grimaced and sighed. "It's not proper."

Esilwen giggled amicably. "That's not what I meant, Margariete. Does your brother know how you feel about Terail?"

"I don't understand the question," the princess answered somewhat tartly.

"I see the way you look at him," Esilwen said with bright eyes, "and the way he looks back."

Margariete folded her arms defensively. Her heart pounded hotly in her chest.

"He's my swordmaster, nothing more."

Margariete glanced nervously at Seriya, making sure the maid hadn't overheard Esilwen's outrageous speculation. Seriya seemed oblivious to the two friends' conversation, however, entirely engrossed with arranging the sleeping blankets around the fire.

"A very handsome swordmaster," Esilwen declared.

Margariete found it difficult to reply, so she remained silent, turning her gaze back to Terail. His hair fluttered casually in the evening breeze as he rubbed down Esilwen's horse. Noticing her gaze, he granted an easy smile in her direction. She felt warmth spread uncomfortably through her chest.

A dreadful insight left her breathless. How could she have missed her own feelings on the matter? She had always assumed her friendship with Terail was platonic, a natural result of her brother's faith in a trusted ally. But suddenly her anticipation for his lessons seemed more than just the excitement of swordplay.

"You didn't even realize it did you?" Esilwen said. "In all the time that you've known him, you must have read his mind. Are you saying you've never sensed his feelings for you?"

"I only read his mind when I'm training with him," the princess defended, "to determine his next attack. Both Terail and Raeylan guard their thoughts well. Usually, I can only see what's on the immediate surface, and I can't read Raeylan at all."

Esilwen looked surprised.

"You mean people can resist your ability?"

Margariete shrugged.

"Sometimes. Knowing what I can do helps them prevent it, I think."

Esilwen refrained from speaking for a few minutes. Seriya stoked the fire with dead stalks of bamboo.

"Even if you can't see his thoughts," she finally said, "it's clear that Terail cares deeply for you."

Margariete shook her head, dashing the acknowledgment of her feelings for Terail into shards. Her fondness for him was buried deeply inside herself for a reason. She allowed sense to reclaim her thoughts.

"It doesn't matter how we feel, Esilwen. My father will never allow it."

"Why not?" Esilwen asked.

Margariete's voice hardened with her expression.

"Terail is not of noble birth. His knighthood was granted by my brother under special circumstances."

"But he's a general," Esilwen argued. "Doesn't that make him important?"

"The Dasklos family is still a common bloodline. No matter his deeds or title, my father will never see past Terail's heritage."

Margariete looked wistfully into the darkening night. Terail and her twin became dusky figures as the moon eclipsed the sun.

"Can't your brother do something about that? I thought he—"

"Raeylan breaks the rules for me too often," Margariete interrupted with an impatient wave of her signet glove. She needed to squelch this new emotion before it blossomed into something unmanageable. "It's a dangerous political move every time he does it. It's not just my father's opinion that matters. Appearances are everything. A princess married to a commoner reflects poorly on her family, regardless of any king's approval."

"I'm not sure I will ever understand your people's regard for propriety," Esilwen said sadly. "Social rules should not outweigh love."

The blond girl bowed her head in defeat. Margariete wondered if Esilwen's unusual perspective was a product of differences in culture or simply an innate personality trait. The princess left her companion staring into the darkness and moved to the campfire, removing her leather boots as she settled onto a downy coverlet. Soon the crackle of the flames was interrupted by Esilwen's voice.

"May I ask you something?" Esilwen said as she sank onto an adjacent blanket.

"What is it?" Margariete answered, staring tensely into the firepit.

"That glove your brother gave you—you called it a signet glove back at *The Lavender Petal* when you saved Seriya from the Duke of Timberdale."

"Yes?" Margariete turned to Esilwen, grateful for the change in subject.

"Why do you wear them?"

"It's a mark of nobility. The social standing of an individual is displayed by the symbols and elegance of his glove. It's an old tradition stemming from the legendary Glove of Nehro, the water goddess. According to my people, the artifact was entrusted to my ancestors for protection. It was said that during the Fracturing of the Shards the goddess poured her soul into The Glove, and to this cycle it possesses her power. The Glove was right-handed," Margariete displayed her crimson glove in the firelight. "Once worn, it could not be removed without killing the bearer. At least, that's what the stories say. That is why no one is allowed to see our right arms 'ungloved.' Our nobility began making their own gloves to demonstrate their respect for the kings and queens who bore the duty of the goddess's artifact."

"Does your family still have this glove?" Esilwen asked.

Margariete hesitated. Of course it was a natural question, but the fate of Nehro's Glove was one of the Viridius family's most closely guarded secrets.

"Yes," she finally said, repeating the lie that had been bred into her since childhood, "the rightful heir to the throne is always entrusted with its safety. My mother wore it during her rule. My brother wears it now."

"So then the prince has magical powers, like you?"

"If the legend of The Glove is true, then yes," the princess answered hurriedly. "He never uses it, though. According to tradition, the powers of the goddess are only to be expended in great need, though there are those among the nobility who believe the magic is simply a myth to scare the peasants."

Esilwen stared into the fire thoughtfully. An uncomfortable guilt gnawed Margariete's insides. Esilwen trusted her, and here Margariete was, forced to lie about her heritage again. The secret was too delicate to reveal. Only the Viridius family, Lord Terail, and Master Malbrin knew the true reason Raeylan never exhibited Nehro's powers.

The goddess's artifact was missing. The crown prince of the First Kingdom wore only an imitation on his right hand.

King Shogan, Margariete's grandfather, was the last known bearer of the real artifact. His lust for violence had plunged the shard into a bloody conflict that only ended with the obliteration of the Second Kingdom. Just a cycle after the victory, King Arahm found the body of his father-in-law on the border between the two warring kingdoms, stripped of The Glove.

The royal family had successfully hidden the loss of The Glove for 18 seasons—the disgrace would not only ruin the family's honor, but some, especially certain members of the aristocracy, could use the incident as leverage to depose the Viridius line entirely. Commoners would be persuaded that the ruling linage had lost the protection of the goddess. The country could destroy itself in a civil war.

"Are you girls all right?"

Margariete flinched at Terail's unexpected arrival. The knight had moved silent as the darkness. As the firelight revealed the amusement in his eyes, Margariete felt a flush of heat temper her cheeks and she looked away quickly.

"Did something happen in the few moments we were gone?" Terail asked, suspicion evident in his voice.

"No," Margariete lied. Terail pursed his lips skeptically, his usual oblique response when he knew the princess withheld information.

"Keep your secrets then," he conceded fondly. "Your brother wishes to speak with you privately. See the trees by the river? He's waiting for you there."

Margariete rose, looking in the direction Terail indicated. An indistinct collection of river foliage masked her brother from view. Terail tossed a bundle to her from across the fire.

"You better hurry," he said, as she examined *Stardawn*. "If it gets much darker you might get lost, and I'll have to come find you."

An appropriate remark sprang to her lips, but Margariete's voice faltered before it could escape her mouth. She cleared her throat and strapped her weapon around her hips. When she looked back to Terail, he was staring at her oddly.

"What?" she asked.

"Are you sure you're okay?" he asked with some concern. "You're acting strangely."

"I'm fine," she answered, yanking on her boots and stalking toward the trees.

She felt his eyes pressing into her back until she broke through the small ring of trees. Raeylan stood in the center of a cleared area, sword drawn. His white overcoat dangled from a nearby limb. Margariete looked at him in confusion.

"In two cycles we will reach the border camp," he said. "There we will encounter beasts from the Cursed Land. I want to make sure that Terail has trained you well."

"You're going to fight me?"

Margariete felt a nervous squeeze in her spine. Raeylan would of course never cause her serious harm, but he was the best swordsman in all of Thyella. The princess did not want to embarrass herself in front of her twin.

"Not fight you, sister. Train you."

Bewilderment forced Margariete's mouth open.

"And if our father asks," he continued, "I have been overseeing your training from the beginning."

"You want me to lie?"

"It's not a lie."

"How so?"

"I have known about your training since it began. I allowed it to continue." The prince's expression became stern. "Terail's involvement is not to be revealed. Do you understand?"

Margariete nodded. Raeylan was protecting Terail's knighthood. This way the prince would bear the responsibility, and consequences, himself.

"Then draw your sword."

Raeylan arranged his body in a stance Margariete had learned under Terail's tutelage. The princess smiled in challenge. It was the same move that she had been analyzing during Malbrin's last lesson, an attack she knew to be flawed. She had devised an original counter that would slide underneath her opponent's defense, easily disarming him. Maybe this wouldn't be as difficult as she previously thought. Her sword sang through the clearing as she released it from its sheath.

Raeylan's posture shifted instantly, distracting her from the movements of his weapon. Within seconds she was lying on her back, *Stardawn* flung uselessly on the ground beside her. The tip of Raeylan's blade hovered effortlessly at her neck.

"Rule number one sister: when your enemy shows you a weakness, it is usually your own."

14: AT THE BORDER

Shikun lifted a blade, admiring the sunlight bounce off the metal's razor edge. The new weapon gleamed flawless, magnificent in balance. Though the young prince had only seen 12 seasons, weapons-training had been a part of his education since he could remember. Leveling the sword horizontal to his eye, he examined the delicate, almost imperceptible waves of grooves etched along the length its curve. The folding technique of the sword's construction made the steel harder than armor bands, able to slice through skin, sinew, and bone with ease.

But not the scaly hides of the demented beasts from the Cursed Land. Their natural armor turned almost every attack, blunting the blacksmiths' most hardy handiwork. Spears struggled to pry the beasts' rigid scales apart, arrows bounced harmlessly to the animals' feet. Shikun's previous sword had snapped in his last encounter with the demon creatures. Luckily, the company blacksmith had several spares on hand.

The princeling of the Jeweled City grimaced in frustration. If only his knights were equipped with weapons from the City of Blades. The Second Kingdom of Thyella had produced unrivaled swordsmiths before its destruction. Their blades were sharp enough to cleave the swords of their enemies into useless chunks of metal and their arrows pierced rival armor like silk. Few of these extraordinary weapons still existed, and no blacksmith alive could replicate the secrets of their forging.

"This is a fine blade, Delig," Shikun complemented the soot-encrusted artisan, "a true masterpiece."

"Thank you, Your Highness," the blacksmith answered with humble courtesy. "I can also repair your armor if you wish."

Shikun slid his new sword into the empty sheath on his hip. "I wish there was time, but you and your apprentices are already overwhelmed with replacing the men's armaments. Besides, my brother should be arriving sometime this cycle. With the beasts so close, he will want to strike quickly."

"Of course, Your Highness," the blacksmith said, bowing politely before returning to his work in the makeshift forge.

Shikun left the swordmaker's station with the confidence granted by a new weapon, threading his way through the camp toward the command tent. The scouts he'd sent the previous cycle were due to return any moment, hopefully with news of the beasts or of his brother. A guard—Pearl class by the insignia on his bracers—opened the door flap as Shikun approached, lowering his head in respect as the young prince crossed into the tent's dim interior.

Inside, three knights knelt on the floor mats. Captain Hendar, a burly warrior in his mid-50s, stroked his close-clipped beard, a grimace burying vertical lines into his whiskers. Hendar's lieutenant knelt stiffly at his side, candlelight glinting like water across his banded leather armor. Both men were draped with Pearl-imprinted tabards, but unlike the guard standing outside, the hems of their cloaks were trimmed in lavender and gold, indicating command.

Dark red splatters stained the leather gear of the knight sitting opposite them, his hair clogged with mud and grime. It took Shikun several moments to recognize the disheveled knight. Negin, the leader of the scouting party he had dispatched to track the beasts.

"Your Highness," Hendar addressed Shikun with a bow, tightness constricting his usually hearty voice, "Negin has returned with unsettling news."

Shikun nodded rigidly, suddenly infected by the tension of his officers. He crossed to the head of the low table and folded his knees into proper position, hoping he looked as confident as his older brother. A quick nod indicated his readiness to receive the knight's report.

"Our group followed the beasts north, just over the border into the Cursed Land." Negin ran his tongue over cracked lips. "I apologize, Highness, but our previous count of four creatures was inaccurate."

Shikun clenched his fists, suppressing a flinch. Two cycles ago his hunting party had encountered only one creature. Even with three Pearl ranking knights, the highest order in the Knights of the Gem, the beast had escaped with little difficulty, leaving two warriors severely wounded. Though his brother taught him to mask fear with calm, Shikun struggled to restrain the clammy chills of alarm prickling his nerves. Sweat slipped from underneath the blond curls at the nape of his neck, despite the morning crispness.

"How many then?" he heard himself ask, almost outside his own volition.

"Negin discovered the lair of the four we've been chasing," Hendar answered. "Another three ambushed his force from behind. Only Negin escaped. His companions were slain."

The captain's mouth slashed through his beard in a grim line. Lieutenant Tenan's face paled beneath its film of composure. Shikun lowered his eyes in recognition of his men's sacrifice and swallowed a lump of grief. The Knights of the Gem were more than comrades to the adolescent monarch. They were friends. Many, like Hendar, were surrogate fathers, since his own seemed uninterested in his upbringing. Shikun knew every man in the Order of Pearl especially because they were Raeylan's personal military unit.

Negin was a natural woodsman, and the best archer in the scouting party. Kazuki, his second, had been the most talented horseman. Riku's wife had borne him a daughter just weeks before the company left the City of Jewels. Naoto had promised upon his return to train his young son with messenger falcons. The youngest, Taro, had finally gathered the courage to ask for his childhood love's hand in marriage.

The young prince had sent them to their deaths. Men who he had respected as family—men he considered cousins, uncles, and brothers. He felt their loss lean against his courage. Fifteen knights had accompanied Prince Raeylan from Castle Viridius. When he returned, Raeylan would find only 11 remaining, two gravely wounded. Shikun grappled with the failure, squeezing his eyes tightly to control any outward burst of feeling. Inflating his lungs carefully, like his brother had taught him, Shikun released the breath in a steadying mantra. Hendar and Tenan waited respectfully until the princeling regained his composure.

"We will honor their deaths upon my brother's return. Negin, report to the healer's quarter." Shikun managed to keep all but a slight tremor from his voice as he issued orders. As Negin exited the tent, Shikun turned to the captain. "What was the last known location of the demons?"

"Less than half a cycle north."

"Have the men prepare. My brother will want to move against the monsters tomorrow."

Hendar nodded, but exchanged a worried glance with Tenan. "Permission to speak freely, Your Highness?"

Shikun clenched his hands. Captain Hendar made that request only when Shikun's inexperience failed to take all considerations into account. "What is it, captain?"

"With seven beasts at our door, I do not believe a direct attack would be successful."

"You lack faith in our men?" Shikun inquired tersely.

"No, Your Highness," Tenan answered quickly, pulling his crooked eyebrows into a furrow. "The knights in this camp are unmatched in skill, but we will need all our men to handle that many enemies. Prince Raeylan is bringing the Princess of the Jewel with him. We cannot possibly leave her here undefended when we march on the cursed beasts."

Shikun spat an ugly curse word in his head. Of course the company would have to split its force to protect his sister. Why hadn't Raeylan just sent Margariete home? Even with her secret abilities, she was no match for the horrors of the Cursed Land.

"It makes the Knights of the Pearl uncomfortable knowing that the only heirs to the First and Third kingdoms are located at the same, dangerous border camp," Hendar inserted grumpily. "If any of you were to be killed, or all—"

The captain let his words hang incomplete, then finished hurriedly, "You must convince His Highness Prince Raeylan to send her home."

Tension built in the stuffy tent. Shikun's throat felt dry and itchy. As the youngest, he had no authority to question the actions of his brother. But Raeylan thought there were only four creatures and that 15 unharmed knights were available for combat.

"I will be sure to relate your advice to my brother," he conceded. "The appearance of another three beasts changes matters. Your concerns will not be taken lightly, I promise you."

Both Hendar and Tenan nodded their heads, bowing respectfully before exiting the tent. Once the flap closed, the young prince sighed tiredly and prayed the goddess would send his brother back soon.

*

A half-circle of nine knights and their squires greeted the crown prince and his company when they arrived after midcycle. Shikun watched his brother assist a hooded woman dismount, while Lord Terail tossed his reins absently to one of the young attendants. Though Margariete's signet glove was new, Shikun recognized the royal seal embroidered on the crimson silk when Raeylan handed her down. The rest of his sister's attire, however, caused Shikun to stare in perplexed surprise.

A light cotton tunic crisscrossed over her breast, held in place by a stiff leather corset that hugged her midsection. Armored greaves protected her thighs and calves, black riding boots smothered her dark pants at the knees. Leather bracers slid over her gloves, though the right side was shorter than the left, leaving the wrist and hand free to display signet rank. A tight fitting cloak hid the princess's face from view.

Armor of Maidens. When his grandfather's armies marched on the Second Kingdom, only the women were left to defend the villages and cities. Developed in the City of Storms, every woman of age was given armor in the event that enemies overran their homeland, though none of the women were actually trained in combat. After the war, the Armor of Maidens was gathered into the treasuries of each city, safely stored should war plague the kingdom again. Shikun had seen his mother's set hanging proudly in the private armory at Castle Viridius, though hers was much more elaborate than the armor Margariete now wore.

Most surprisingly of all was the weapon secured proudly at his sister's hip. Shikun was unable to mask his shock as Margariete approached, her hooded head scanning the vicinity. Her embrace was sharp, lacking her usual cocoon of heavy fabric.

"How are you, Shikun?" Margariete smiled from deep within the cowl.

"Well, my sister," he answered. "And you?" His gaze unconsciously flicked to her sword.

"Perfectly well," she responded, humor tinting the curve of her lips.

Shikun glanced over to his brother. The eldest prince had already begun a conversation with Captain Hendar, who appeared grave. Terail was helping another woman from the saddle of a brown riding steed. When her feet touched the ground, she threw back her hood, revealing a halo of platinum curls.

As the woman turned in his direction, Shikun felt his breath freeze inside his lungs. The afternoon light reflected her creamy beauty. Her frosty-green eyes absorbed him with an ethereal radiance. Her hair was pulled back into a cascading twist, blond locks tumbling delightfully around her shoulders. With a graceful bow, she thanked the Pearl Daimyo for his assistance, her smile shining with a brilliance brighter than the sun. It was as if Shikun looked upon a lorelei, one of the divine servants of Nehro said to possess more than mortal beauty.

"Her name is Esilwen," Margariete said with a smirk, poking him in the shoulder.

Margariete's sisterly shove seemed to break the spell. Shikun closed his mouth, unaware that it had been hanging open for quite some time. His tongue was dry as the beautiful maiden approached.

"Esilwen," Margariete said, "this is my younger brother, Prince Shikun of House Viridius."

Esilwen smiled sweetly and bowed to the young prince. Shikun's adolescent heart almost stopped when she spoke.

"It's an honor," she said in a voice tinkling like tiny bells.

"The honor is mine, Lady Esilwen," Shikun responded and returned the gesture, his insides churning with prickles. Esilwen giggled timidly. Only then did he note, with a rising flood of horror, that Esilwen's right arm was bare. He flicked a weighted glance at his sister, hoping she could smooth over his breach of propriety.

"It's all right Shikun," Margariete said. "We are addressing her as 'Lady.' She is my companion and guest."

"Princess Margariete," Terail interrupted, stepping forward into their midst, "Prince Raeylan has commanded me to escort you to your tent. Please, follow me."

Margariete, Esilwen, and a maid in blue serving robes followed Terail into the maze of tents, shielding them from Shikun's sight. Esilwen's disappearance seemed to darken the world around him.

"Shikun."

The youngest prince turned toward the sound of his brother's voice. Raeylan stood at the flap of the command tent, poised to enter. Meeting his gaze, Shikun hurried to his brother. The dimness of the tent caused Shikun to blink until the darkness faded away. Raeylan removed some of his outer armor and splashed water over his face and neck. Shikun stood politely at attention until addressed.

"Some of the men are absent, my brother."

Raeylan waited patiently for an answer.

Shikun looked at the ground, a flush of shame burning his throat. "There are more creatures than we previously thought. A scouting party of four men was killed earlier this cycle, Raeylan, on a mission dispatched under my orders."

The enormity of his failure hung painfully inside his chest. Shikun feared to look up, afraid to see disappointment in the person he revered most. A moment of stillness passed, followed by a rustle of clothing.

"Shikun."

The youngest Viridius prince felt the pressure of his brother's palm against his shoulder.

"Little brother, all battles carry risk. Our men meet it with honor. It disgraces their sacrifice if you blame yourself."

Shikun swallowed his regret and looked up at Raeylan. The crown prince's expression was calm, but saturated with underlying feeling, charged like the air before a storm. His words buoyed Shikun's spirit.

The tent flapped open, and Terail strode into the center of the room, bowing to each prince respectfully. "Your sister is settled and has agreed to stay put until she is summoned," he announced.

"Good," Raeylan answered, still holding Shikun in his gaze. "Gather the commanders."

Terail left the tent quickly.

"I have a new mission for you, Shikun."

"Anything, brother."

"I turn the care of our sister over to you. Keep her safe and ensure she does not do anything rash—especially in front of the men. Perhaps you could show her the camp."

Shikun felt his ears burn. Taking care of his sister meant a possible conversation with her new companion.

"Of course," he blurted, cringing at his own eagerness.

"Good," Raeylan returned with a genuine smile.

Terail returned with Hendar and Tenan as Shikun left. The Pearl Daimyo gave the prince a sly wink as they passed in the threshold.

Shikun trotted hastily to the hub of the camp, slowing only as his sister's lodgings came into view. He tamed his hair and readjusted his tabard. The girl in blue serving robes perched lightly on a stool outside the tent, skillfully mending a garment. Her face was pleasantly rounded. As he approached, she stood and bowed politely.

"Your Highness," she greeted, obviously noting the royal crest on his navy signet glove.

"I wish to speak with Princess Margariete. I am to show her and Lady Esilwen through the camp."

"As you command," the girl returned, straightening and entering the ladies' quarters. Shikun waited, straining to decipher the muffled voices within the tent. Moments later his sister emerged, Esilwen at her side. The evening light dyed the blond maid's simple white traveling dress a watery blue, the color of lunar dusk. Next to his dark sister, Esilwen seemed to shine with otherworldly brilliance. Margariete cleared her throat meaningfully, and Shikun, suddenly embarrassed, realized he had been staring again.

"Prince Raeylan has asked me to show you around the camp," Shikun announced formally.

"Has he?" Margariete jabbed. "Or were you sent to keep track of me?"

"Both," Shikun admitted.

"Even so," Esilwen said kindly, "I would enjoy seeing your camp."

Shikun directed them westward, toward a crisp river edging the encampment. Two boys led dappled horses to the water's edge, tethering them to the trees as the young prince and the two ladies approached.

"So Raeylan left you in charge while he went to look for me?" Margariete asked as their feet clacked about the riverbank stones. His sister gazed thoughtfully across the gurgling water.

"Yes. It's the first time I've ever been in command," Shikun said, kicking absently at pebbles. He could almost feel his sister's ability boring into his skull, sifting through his thoughts.

"I'm sure you did well, Shikun," Margariete said. "We are born to lead after all."

Shikun ignored her. Bad enough Raeylan knew his failure. He felt a desperate need to conceal his feelings of inadequacy from his sister's angelic companion.

"This is where we tend the horses," he explained quickly, the words tumbling from his lips in a rushing cascade, "down farther there is a small washing pool. I advise you not to go there in the early morning. Your maid will be given instructions on the proper time for you to use it."

"That would be a sight to behold, wouldn't it?" Margariete laughed from inside the depths of her hood, teeth flashing white.

Shikun felt his cheeks burn as her implication became clear.

"As I said before, your maid will advise you on a proper time for you to use it," Shikun repeated weakly. He turned toward another part of camp and led the ladies forward.

"So are you a knight as well?" Esilwen's musical voice asked from behind.

"I'm not yet of age," Shikun answered. "I'm still in training as a squire."

They reached a wide, voluminous tent. The ringing of hammer on metal chanted rhythmically through the air. One side of the heavy woven canvas yawned open to the night, supported by four tall bamboo posts in intervals. Swords, shields, and armor were stacked neatly along the perimeter of the other three walls. Polished tables and worn work tools huddled in clumped stations. Ceramic basins cradled searing red coals and sparks of flame inside and outside the smithy. Delig and his two apprentices bowed quickly as they spotted the spectators, then ardently resumed their work.

"A squire?" Esilwen asked.

"Of course," Shikun said, turning toward Esilwen in surprise, "before anyone can earn his knightly title, he must first serve as a squire. Raeylan is my master."

Esilwen's brows knit together in confusion, and Shikun realized that she had no idea what he was talking about.

"Basically," Margariete interrupted, eyes rapidly shifting from Shikun to Esilwen, "Shikun makes sure Raeylan's equipment is in order, oversees orders, and prepares Shale for battle. In exchange, Raeylan teaches Shikun how to be a knight."

Shikun suddenly wondered how Margariete had come to know this beautiful stranger. He had never heard of anyone who didn't understand the relationship between knight and squire. Training to join the knighthood was a high honor.

"Can't Raeylan do all of that for himself?" Esilwen asked incredulously.

"When a knight has just returned from battle, he is either exhausted or injured," Shikun explained. "It would be difficult for the knight to do everything on his own, especially if the battle spans more than just a cycle."

Esilwen seemed hypnotized by the spark-spewing hammer strokes of the blacksmith. Finally she asked, "Was Prince Raeylan ever a squire?"

"Yes. You cannot become a knight of realm without first serving two seasons as a squire. I have just begun my term. Afterward, I will be inducted into the Amber class knighthood."

"He will go through Jade quickly though, straight to Pearl," Margariete added, tousling her sibling's hair fondly. "As a prince, he has trained since he was a small child. He could best any Amber class knight now. Judging by his skill, he's probably on the level of Jade already."

"Does every knight here have a squire?" Esilwen asked as Shikun directed them toward another copse of tents. These were smaller, lighter in color and surrounded by multiple fire pits. Knights and their attendants occupied logs and stumps framing each fire, steaming bowls in their hands. Most of the knights sported signet gloves, but many of the squires had naked arms.

"Oh yes, and some even have more than one, based on their rank in the Order," Shikun clarified, turning toward the largest camp hearth. It was vacant. "Terail and the commanders all have two. They have too much business for just one squire to handle. Raeylan has three, including me. As a prince, there are some errands I am not allowed to do—like delivering messages—so the other squires perform those duties."

"That's interesting," Esilwen said.

Curiosity peeled into Shikun's tour of courteous decorum. He couldn't help but ask his next question, though it wasn't exactly polite.

"Where do you come from, Lady Esilwen?"

"Timberdale," Margariete answered before Shikun had finished the question. His sister plopped onto a log. "She spends a lot of time indoors."

Esilwen bit her lip, looking away quickly as she settled next to Margariete.

Shikun wondered why his sister had lied.

"How many men do you have here, Shikun?" Margariete said, her sapphire eyes glinting fiercely, warning him away from conversation involving her friend.

Shikun knew better than to cross her. He would have to ask Raeylan about Esilwen's homeland later.

"We had 15 Pearl class knights to begin with, but three have been killed. There are 21 squires, three healers, the blacksmith and his two apprentices, and a cook," Shikun reported. "Are you hungry?"

"Starving," Margariete said, turning to Esilwen, who nodded in agreement.

Shikun walked to the mess tent and retrieved food. He handed them each a bowl of rice, garnished with fish, then sat across the firepit. During the meal, Esilwen whispered quietly to Margariete. Shikun stared uncomfortably into the flames, wishing he could hear their conversation. His sister's lie bothered him. Did she not trust him? He knew he was incapable of doing anything that would bring Esilwen to harm.

"Why is it that I always seem to enter after something awkward has happened?" Terail proclaimed, stepping out of the evening shade and into the light of the fire with a jovial sigh.

"Esilwen and I are tired, that's all," Margariete said. "It's poor Shikun you should be worried about. Raeylan forced him to watch over me all aftermidcycle."

Terail let his breath out in a low whistle. "I do not envy you, my prince," he said gravely. "This one's a handful. Always running off."

"Very funny," Margariete scorned.

"Which reminds me," Terail said with a crafty grin, "I've been asked by Prince Raeylan to instruct you not to go off into the forest alone. The cursed beasts are nearby."

"I'm not fool enough to wander out there, Terail," Margariete answered fiercely.

Terail hid a snicker behind his hand, keeping his eyes blank. Shikun looked between the two, unable to accurately read Margariete's body language.

"What exactly are these cursed beasts?" Esilwen asked.

"They are monsters from the Cursed Land that sometimes cross the border into our kingdom," Shikun said.

"I've heard this 'Cursed Land' mentioned several times," Esilwen said, "but I don't understand what it is."

Shikun pursed his lips thoughtfully. Everyone knew the story of the Cursed Land. Esilwen was most definitely not from Timberdale. Her green eyes looked at him with gentle innocence.

"Our camp is near the Cursed Land's border," he began, unsure of exactly how much to say. "It was once the Second Kingdom of Thyella, ruled by House Tricahnas. The kingdom's capital was the City of Blades."

"Rightly named," Terail interjected, finally breaking gaze with the princess. "The Second Kingdom was unrivaled in their skill of crafting weaponry."

"Magical swords, so the rumors say," the young prince added.

"They aren't rumors," Terail said firelight burning from his pale eyes. "Your sister carries *Stardawn,* an heirloom of my mother's family. It guards against fear and can slash through any armor. Your brother also carries one. *Moonstone Retribution* is its name, though I'm not aware of its magical properties."

"But I thought everyone here was superstitious of magic," Esilwen blurted, "and that's why the people of Rekkadell attacked us."

"Only of cursed magic," Terail answered with a grin, "and the Second Kingdom's weapons were made before it was cursed."

"How was it cursed?" Esilwen asked.

"There was a war. No one truly knows the specifics, but—" Terail shrugged and tossed a stalk of twig into the fire.

"What Terail means," Margariete inserted, "is that he isn't allowed to speak ill of my grandfather. Only the male heirs of King Shogan's throne can disagree with my grandfather's atrocities."

Shikun's blood pounded loudly in his ears as everyone's gaze turned to him.

"My grandfather was a greedy man. Seasons before Raeylan and Margariete were born, he started a war with the ruling family of the Second Kingdom. Most common people believe the war began because the Tricahnas family suddenly stopped their weapons trade, preparing to invade the rest of Thyella. Another popular story was that the Second Kingdom's elite assassin force, the Feralblades, had already murdered several members of the First Kingdom's nobility. But most of those rumors surfaced after the war had already started."

"So what was the real reason then? Why did the war start?" Esilwen asked.

"Power," Shikun explained. "King Shogan discovered the truth behind the Second Kingdom's weapon smithing. He believed the City of Blades was built around a Well of Nehro."

"Well of Nehro?"

"It's a magical spring of sorts," Terail answered quietly. "It connects the mortal realm to the divine energies of the water goddess. Through the Well, a person has access to some of her power."

"If the Tricahnas family had discovered a way to harness the magic of the Well into their weapons, it could tip the balance of power in Thyella in favor of the Second Kingdom," Shikun continued, "which threatened my grandfather's honor. As protector of The Glove of Nehro, the Viridius family held the most influential position in the shard, and he intended to keep it that way. He demanded access to the Shardwell, but the Tricahnas family refused, denying the Well's existence."

"So he marched on the Second Kingdom," Terail growled.

Shikun thought a scowl stained Terail's features, though it disappeared too quickly for the young prince to be sure.

"Yes," Shikun agreed, "and the conflict cost many lives. Entire cities were burned as the two countries tried to destroy each other. Then, right before the trinal rains, my grandfather's army arrived at the gates to the City of Blades. Not much is known after that. A large magical eruption killed all of his soldiers, wiping out an entire generation of Pearl knights. Our scholars believe that King Shogan tried to use The Glove to destroy the Well, or somehow sought to control it. But something obviously went wrong. A cycle later, my father, King Arahm, found my grandfather's dead body."

"After that," Margariete inserted, "our mother took the throne."

"And she was a generous queen," Terail added honestly, "the entire shard would have been spared suffering if she had received the crown sooner."

"But what happened to all the people in the City of Blades?" Esilwen asked in a terrified whisper.

"Most of the lucky ones died," Shikun replied sadly. "Those who weren't were twisted into monsters by the collision of magic. Beasts like the ones we are trying to destroy out here."

"You mean the monsters you're hunting used to be *people*?" Esilwen gasped.

"It wasn't exactly the Viridius family's greatest moment," Margariete said crossly. "And all for some magical Well that doesn't exist."

Terail rose to his feet.

"Excuse me, Your Highnesses, Lady Esilwen," he said tightly, bowing to each. Moments later he disappeared into the tree line.

"Is he okay?" Esilwen looked at Margariete anxiously.

"Terail lost his entire family during the war," Margariete explained, an unusual note of tenderness wringing her voice. Her eyes followed the path he had taken into the woods. "The Feralblades were ruthless once the war began. They massacred entire villages, slaughtering old men, women, and even children. Terail was barely six seasons when his village was attacked."

Esilwen hiccupped and wiped her eyes with the back of her palms. Shikun drew a silky patch of cloth from his cloak and passed it to her, grateful for the dim firelight that hid the heat streaking his skin as she accepted it with a smile.

"Shikun," Margariete said, drawing his attention. His sister still looked after Terail. "Why don't you escort Esilwen back to the tent? I think she could use some rest."

"It's okay, Margariete," Esilwen sniffled. "I'll be fine."

Margariete faced the blond maiden. The two companions stared at each other wordlessly. Abruptly, Esilwen turned to Shikun, traces of tears marking her cheeks.

"Margariete's right," Esilwen admitted, "I think I need to lie down."

Shikun looked suspiciously at his sister. "Raeylan said I was to watch you."

"Really, Shikun," Margariete said irritably, "I'm not going to go wandering. I would like to finish my food. I think I can find my tent on my own."

Shikun scanned the area uneasily. He had promised his brother, but Esilwen seemed genuinely upset. "You promise you'll come back to the tent as soon as you're finished?"

"Of course."

Shikun glanced once more at Margariete as he delivered Esilwen's empty dishes to the cooking station. When he returned, he offered the beautiful lady his arm, which she accepted happily. Together they wound through the camp, torchlight lining the pathway leading back to the ladies' quarters. Light from inside the tent silhouetted Margariete's lady-in-waiting as she bustled about.

"Thank you for escorting me, Prince Shikun," Esilwen remarked when they reached the threshold. Two knights guarded the entrance for the night watch. Esilwen turned to address the little princeling. "I found it difficult to contain my sorrow. I hope you don't think ill of me. The story was so tragic."

"Of course not," Shikun returned quickly, "I apologize for your tears, Lady Esilwen. My brother told me the story when I was very small. He said it was our duty to mend all the horrible things our grandfather did to the people, as our mother would wish."

"That's good of him," Esilwen said, an enchanting sparkle lighting her eyes.

"My brother is a great leader," Shikun said, mesmerized by the maiden before him. "I hope to be just like him."

"I think you're more like him than you know, Shikun."

A warm tingle spread through the young prince's body as she said his name. His mouth tried to answer, but words refused to leave his lips. Bashfully, he looked at his hands, wondering what he could say to impress such a heavenly creature.

"Thank you," she said again.

Something wet splashed across his cheek. Startled, he lifted his palm to his face, wiping at the moisture. The flickering torchlight flashed red across the dark liquid staining his fingers. When he looked up, Esilwen's gentle smile had disappeared, replaced by eyes wide with terror.

15: Nightfall in The Trees

Margariete set her plate on the log, waiting calmly until Shikun and Esilwen disappeared into the rows of woven canvas. Moments later, she leapt to her feet, grateful Esilwen had agreed to lead Shikun away. She followed the path of her former swordmaster, leaving the warm glow of the fire behind. Muted eclipselight outlined the wildflowers and vines at the camp's edge, hidden by the looming phantoms of thyella tree stalks. Margariete deftly avoided the sentries on duty. They seemed more inclined to watch the forest for unwanted guests than to patrol the encampment for deserters.

Darkness threw its velvet curtain over the princess as she darted into the bamboo trunks, forcing Margariete to pause until her eyes adjusted to the sudden loss of light. She walked forward, nearly blind. Wispy tendrils of plant life brushed against her body as she moved, whimpering wraith-like as she passed. The eerie sounds of midnight creatures echoed through the tree branches, causing her breath to quicken. Margariete's blood surged loudly inside her ears. Terail was nowhere in sight. After a few more forward strides, the princess decided to turn back.

But the forest had closed its black jaws around her. The torches of the camp were swallowed in the dense night behind her. Had she travelled in a straight line, or had she veered to the left?

Urgently, she grasped *Stardawn's* hilt. Her panic dissolved slowly, shriveling like thawing wax. A low murmur, like a breathless voice, pushed the fear into the back of her head. The sharp need for action took its place, compelling her arm to rip the sword free of its sheath. It sang through the night with a thrill that rushed up her arm, like a living thing.

Feeling somewhat calmer now that she was armed, Margariete inhaled deeply and focused on the forest's vibrations, hoping to discern the trail back to camp. Movement slinked from behind. She spun, swinging *Stardawn* to meet the threat.

Her blade clashed against a wickedly-edged dagger.

"What are you doing, princess?" Terail asked.

For a moment, Margariete's ragged breaths were the only sounds between them. His face flashed with amusement in the faint light.

"I was—" she faltered as a wash of foolishness prompted her to lower her weapon.

Terail sheathed his dagger. "You do realize how dangerous it is out here?" His voice betrayed a sliver of gravity.

"Of course I do," she replied crossly, replacing *Stardawn*.

"Yet here you are. You looked anxious. Were you scared?"

Margariete glared at him, noting the past tense of his observation. He must have been watching her. "No," she lied.

Terail's head tilted in interest. "Tell me princess, why are you here?"

"I wanted a walk," she answered lamely.

Terail cocked his eyebrows, unimpressed by the response. "You're not a very good liar."

"Yes," she stated, making herself look him in the eye, "I might have been a little concerned. But I would have found my way back."

"Ah," he said with artificial contemplation, circling around her once, "and here I thought you were running away again."

"I'm not an imbecile, Terail," Margariete retorted, trying to burn away her embarrassment with anger. "My brother explained the situation. I'm not going anywhere."

"Good," he said, taking a step closer to her. He let his mask of levity fall away. "Because to be perfectly honest, Your Highness, I've never suffered more unease than the cycle I received word that you had disappeared from the castle."

Margariete's throat constricted. Her heart hammered spastically in her breast, only this time not from fear.

"That's to be expected when a princess of the realm runs away," she said.

"Is it?" Terail countered softly.

His hand slid inside her hood, drawing it slowly from her face.

"Yes," she answered, fighting a catch in her voice.

He brushed his fingers across her jaw, running his thumb under her ear.

"Margariete, why did you really come out here?"

Terail's hair shone silver in the scattered coronal light. His eyes glittered. Margariete was filled with a sudden need to press against him, to be submerged in the warmth of his body.

"I was worried," she allowed, biting her lip. "I didn't want you to get hurt."

"So you came out here to protect me?"

He smiled skeptically. Cold logic sank into her skull, clanging loudly against the desire boiling through her veins. This was a mistake, a disaster that would only lead to despair. Margariete stepped away from him, out of his reach. His hand fell listlessly to his side.

"Let's go back," she said hastily.

She waited for her swordmaster to compose himself, to replace the façade of numb emotion demanded by their culture—the pretense that two people of differing social status could never love each other. To her surprise, she heard him laugh.

"No."

"What do you mean 'no'?" she said, turning back.

Terail rested casually against the bole of a tree.

"I want the truth," he demanded with an indulgent grin, "and I'm not leading you back to the camp without it."

"Fine," she spat ungraciously. "I can find my own way back."

"Suit yourself."

Margariete tried to stretch her senses into the forest once more, but the air was silent, fuzzy with gloom. Terail wrapped his hand around her wrist, forcing her to face him.

"You didn't come out here to protect me," Terail accused, pulling her nearer.

"You were upset," she admitted warily, committing to nothing more. "I just wanted to make sure you were okay."

"And why would that matter to you?" Terail asked.

"You've been a loyal friend and teacher," Margariete responded, petrified by his proximity.

"Just a friend?"

He bent closer, his breath caressing her lips.

"Like a brother," she gasped.

Terail's right arm twisted around her waist, pulling her body against his. The pounding of her passion smothered reason, awakening a throbbing, hungry ache.

"It can never be, Terail," she said. "Ever."

The knight skimmed his lips across her cheek, whispering into her ear.

"I can dream," he said softly, "and right now, this feels like a dream."

She sighed with pleasure as his mouth teased the skin under her ear, the palm of his left hand gliding up her spine and into her hair.

"I didn't train you, Margariete, because I was just your friend," he confided. "I care for you. When I look at you, I don't see a curse. I see a woman. Someone strong, who fights for her right to exist. I could only ever love such a woman."

His kiss sent rivulets of fire thrumming through her head, infecting her with a pulsating need for more as he pulled away.

"I love you too, Terail," she unwillingly confessed.

A smile broke across his face as he stared into her eyes.

"That wasn't so hard was it?"

"Except that no one can ever know it."

"They won't," he said, forcing her mouth open with his lips.

Margariete lost herself in him, intoxicated by the way his palms moved across her body, swooning in the heady scent of the jasmine blossoms draping the bushes around them. When he finally released her, her head spun dizzily, her blood sweeping through her body like shadows through the forest.

Without warning, the sky erupted in a haze of radiance, spattering the moss with flakes of ice-green light. The air roared with angry vibrations as shouts of alarm skittered from the border camp, followed by unnatural roars. Margariete's heart lurched into her throat as a panicked scream of pain tore into the night.

It was Shikun.

16: HORRORS BEFORE FIRST LIGHT

"Thank you for escorting me back to my tent, Prince Shikun," Esilwen said gratefully, throwing a glance back over her shoulder to see if Margariete was still in view. Sentinels of tents shielded the meal circle from view. "I found it difficult to contain my sorrow," she continued, returning her attention to her young escort. "I hope you don't think ill of me. The story was so tragic."

"Of course not," he said. "I apologize for your tears, Lady Esilwen. My brother told me the story when I was very small. He said it was our duty to mend all the horrible things our grandfather did to the people, as our mother would wish."

"That's good of him," Esilwen answered brightly, thinking of Raeylan's twilight grey eyes.

"My brother is a great leader. I hope to be just like him," Shikun said looking at his hands.

The torchlight flickered in the evening's breeze, tickling the hairs on the back on Esilwen's neck. Forms around her seemed to sharpen in contrast. A metallic tang licked the back of her throat.

"I think you're more like him than you know, Shikun," she assured with a truthful smile, though her eyes scanned the area guardedly. Something felt strange, almost like she was surrounded by a whisper of caution. "Thank you," she repeated distractedly.

A rosy flush spread across Shikun's face, but Esilwen hardly noticed. The ambiance around her suddenly shifted. It crept under her fingernails and seeped into her arms, causing gooseflesh to rise on her skin. Before she could share her unease with the young prince, something black splattered across his boyish face, staining his blond hair. Her eyes widened in fright as four scaly apparitions blotted the rest of camp from her sight.

The thud of flesh and clang of armor resounded from either side of her as the two Pearl knights attending her tent crashed to the ground, each clutching desperately at ragged gashes in their bodies. One gurgled in pain as his life soaked into the grass.

Shikun drew his blade, the scrape of metal stinging Esilwen's ears. He turned to meet the threat, deliberately placing his body between her and the creatures as the demons stepped into the light.

Esilwen could not remember encountering anything so entirely horrific. Despite her memory loss, she could tell that these—things—were unnatural, twisted into being by callous forces of magic. Hulking bodies encased in glinting sable scales stood level with her head, their backs curving in an aberrant arch. They skulked forward on four legs, fiendish claws protruding from their leg joints and talons gouging the ground from their toes. Their bony faces peeled back from a jutting, needle-fanged jaw, mimicking the features of a predatory feline but warped with the attributes of a vicious reptile. Twice as long as they were tall, the cursed beasts brandished their forked tails as they prepared to attack—two from the front, and one on each flank.

Shikun's lone sword would be no match for the monsters before them. Their paws were already tarnished with the guards' blood. The princeling's blade shook. Their best chance of survival was escape, but the creatures had them pinned against Margariete's tent.

One of the downed knights attempted a cry for help, but only a weak babble emerged from his mouth. The beast closest to him plunged its maw forward, engulfing the man's face with its spiney fangs. The knight's gasp of pain was lost in a wet crunch as the predator's powerful mouth crushed his skull. Esilwen's evening meal swelled into her throat. She dared not open her mouth, even to scream, as the creature's blood-sodden face turned back to her.

Tattered shouts gushed from the direction of the command tent, but their meanings were lost in a clacking growl vibrating in the four beasts' throats. Shikun lifted his sword in defense as the gory-jawed creature from the right leapt forward to strike. With an unexplained burst of instinct, Esilwen yanked the princeling back, wrapping herself around him protectively. Just as she braced her body for the rending claws, a wall of flame dashed in front of them, shielding the pair with a vertical barrier of ice-green fire that rose as high as the bamboo stalks. The attacking animal yelped in pain, rolling madly against Margariete's tent.

Other tents flared into a blaze as the burning wall touched them, lighting the night sky with an emerald glow. The two forefront creatures were caught on the opposite side of the barrier, completely blocked from view. Caught unaware by the fourth beast, Esilwen cried out as its sharp jaws clamped on her shoulder, snapping her collarbone. The powerful monster wrenched her away from Shikun, hurling her backward onto the grass. When she hit the ground, she rolled onto her back, trying to push herself upright. Her broken shoulder refused and she could only manage to prop herself up on her uninjured side.

Esilwen saw the First Kingdom's princeling fight valiantly with the wicked beast, but its shiny scales turned his every blow. The flaming wall was flickering away. The second creature—charred and limping—circled in on Shikun's flank. Concentrating on avoiding his first opponent's snapping fangs, Shikun hadn't noticed the other monster's approach. Esilwen heard herself call out a warning, but her voice vanished in the agonized screams of the young prince as the two demons ripped into his body. His bloody sword fell to the ground.

A woman's shriek mingled with Shikun's ghastly cries. Seriya burst out of the burning tent, wielding a small dagger. She charged the closest beast, whose teeth still clung to the prince's torn flesh. Esilwen only blinked, and the first creature, which had been between herself and Shikun, was suddenly standing beside Seriya. Even if it had leapt over its fellow, it couldn't have repositioned itself so quickly. Nevertheless, its head bashed into Seriya's midsection, flinging her back into the smoldering tent. Wood cracked and the burning canvas collapsed on top of her.

Frosty trickles of cold burned through Esilwen's shoulder, an odd sensation that erased the pain of her broken bone. But she didn't have time to ponder it. The firewall had died, and two of the beasts were unaccounted for. Shikun was flat against the ground, one beast gnawing on his chest and the other turning back to him. As Esilwen hobbled to her feet, knights and squires flooded around the fallen princeling, engaging the monsters in combat. Esilwen felt hope as the reinforcements hacked at the beasts with their weapons.

Her body had purged itself of pain, but before she could rush to Shikun's aid, a clacking growl from behind drew her attention. As she turned, she saw the forked tail only a half-moment before it slashed across her face, knocking her again to the ground. Esilwen used her hands to break the fall and scanned for her attackers. The two missing creatures loomed over her.

One sank its teeth into her ankle, yanking her forward and away from the burning tents. The second beast lurched toward her, and then—almost comically—turned its attention to its hindquarters. A young squire bravely slashed at the beast's scaly hide, boldly battling its armored tail. The beast whipped around, and Esilwen lost sight of her would-be rescuer as the thing pounced.

The creature holding her foot began dragging her swiftly away, toward the dark line of trees at the forest's edge. She clawed frantically at the grass, trying to loosen the grip of its vice-like jaws. Esilwen managed a kick against the beast's nose. The pressure on her ankle slackened somewhat. Just as she tried to slip her leg from its mouth, the cruel jaws compressed harder. Her body spasmed with pain as the delicate bones splintered. The creature resumed its path, roughly dragging her to the camp's perimeter. Soon she could no longer see the knights or the boy who had tried to save her.

17: MOMENT OF BATTLE

Raeylan knelt in the center of the command tent, facing the canvas entrance. He focused on a small crystal resting on the surface of the room's only table. Fragments of azure stratum pulsed through the mineral, flickering with the rhythm of the candlelight. The jagged gemstone was more than rare; only one was produced every generation. To the majority of the Thyellan populace, the transportation crystals were merely legend, a popular device used by tavern bards to rescue the heroes of epic ballads at the last moment, ensuring the captive attention of any audience. Few knew the magical stones to be more than myth.

The unique crystals grew in only one place in all of Thyella—the Royal Shrine, a private spring in the center of Viridius Castle. Its sacred waters protected the translucent kryystil fish, a creature blessed by the goddess with the gift to bend the flow of space around itself. Raeylan remembered being fascinated with the diaphanous water breathers when he was small, enraptured by the fish's ability to phase from one part of the spring to another. Many of the fish had seen the passage of hundreds of seasons, as if time itself had overlooked them. Removing a kryystil fish from the spring caused it to shrivel, transforming into a notched crystalline stone. None of the current fish had produced offspring in the crown prince's lifetime. Raeylan knew of only four existing stones: three stored safely in the royal vault, and the one resting on the table before him.

The prince lifted the blue crystal and rolled it across the bare palm of his left hand, allowing its rough texture to bite his skin. The stone had been given to him on the anniversary of his eighth season. He still remembered the gentle smile of his mother, masking the worry that continually haunted her eyes, as she placed it in his hand. She had told him that the crystal would take him home, and should dire peril arise, he need only crush it in his palm. The prince had carried it on his person ever since.

Obviously, the crystal would go to Margariete. Raeylan had only managed to rescue his sister from the fanatical inhabitants of Rekkadell by a breath of fate. Now that the princess had tasted the exhilaration of adventure outside the castle, the prince was sure he would be incapable of denying his twin the freedom offered by future excursions. Raeylan was determined to protect Margariete in every way possible, and the crystal would ensure her a means of escape under any circumstance.

Satisfied with his decision, he slipped the glossy object into a small leather pouch and tied it securely to his belt. As he did so, the flames from the thick wax candles on the table wavered ever so slightly.

Raeylan gripped the hilt of *Moonstone Retribution* with his gloved hand, rising to his feet. The world around him seemed to hesitate as he tapped into the sword's magical senses. A breeze pricked his skin, the air tasting salty against his lips. Though his eyes were closed, he could feel the form of a hulking creature as it squeezed itself through the thin panels of space that shaped reality, its scaly hide outlined by pinpricks of bursting light. Having practiced his sword's sensory capabilities on multiple occasions in the kryystil fish shrine, the prince had become an expert on reading the movements of teleportation.

Just as the beast materialized on Raeylan's left, *Moonstone Retribution* caught it by surprise, gouging a bloody trail through the creature's eye and into its brain. The sharp, needle-toothed jaw of the malformed demon sagged in humorless mockery as its lifeless body flopped to the ground. The prince's enchanted blade slid free of the cursed beast's skull as the monster fell, as though the sword had pierced nothing more resistant than the surface of water.

Raeylan burst toward the exit, leaping across the table in his haste. Lifting the tent flap, he prepared to shout a warning to his contingent of knights.

"Ambush!" Captain Hendar shouted before the prince had a chance to part his lips.

The captain's alarm echoed through the northern quadrant of camp. As Raeylan dashed from his tent, a young squire standing sentry outside stepped away in startled confusion. Seeing the naked blade in his commander's hand, the youth quickly drew his own. Before Raeylan could determine Hendar's situation, the brine lick of teleportation once again drew his attention. When a dark scaly hide blinked into existence behind the squire, the prince pushed the boy aside. The beast lifted an enormous paw, striking the empty space where the youth had once been. Raeylan dived into a roll, avoiding the brunt of the attack, though the cursed beast's lethal claws raked through his armor and tore into his shoulder.

With experienced ease, Raeylan regained his feet in a perfectly balanced defensive stance. A quick scan of the area revealed Hendar combating a second beast at the perimeter of the camp. The older soldier stood between the intruder and Lieutenant Tenan, who righted himself with a drunken lurch. Tenan's hand cradled his left eye, blood escaping between his fingers.

"Lieutenant," Raeylan called loudly as he turned back to his own assailant, "send a trio of knights to Shikun and Margariete. Then assist the captain!"

As the prince completed his orders, the monster he was fighting cracked its forked tail toward Raeylan's face. Tossing *Moonstone Retribution* into his uninjured left hand, he smoothly blocked the attack, then with a deft twist, dismembered a portion of the creature's scaled appendage. A high-pitched scream of pain pealed from the cursed animal's throat as large dollops of brackish blood splattered the grass.

Tenan's response was almost lost as Raeylan dodged the snap of the beast's demon jaws. Curling away from the creature's rancid maw, toward its thickly armored foreleg, the prince drove his blade into the animal's upper shoulder joint, ripping through muscle and sinew to the kneecap. An aberrant shriek stung the prince's ears as his adversary crashed to the ground beneath its own weight.

Raeylan made to sever the beast's precarious bond with life, but he halted mid-strike as a wall of green fire boiled across the camp's southern array of tents. Lurid emerald light drenched the entire encampment as three of the tents ignited.

Raeylan was sure one of them had been his sister's.

The prince's hesitation cost him the winning blow in his skirmish with the cursed beast. As Raeylan belatedly completed his sword stroke, *Moonstone Retribution* met with nothing more than clumps of dirt. Having lost his concentration, the beast managed to teleport undetected behind Raeylan. Its damaged tail grazed his cheek as he sidestepped its forward jab. Too late, the prince realized that the creature had herded him into a compromising position. Heaving its bulk forward with a powerful lurch, the beast knocked Raeylan prone and *Moonstone Retribution* spun cleanly out of reach. Malevolent intelligence flashed across the creature's milk-dulled eyes, and Raeylan knew his enemy recognized him to be weaponless.

With a triumphant snarl, the beast reared onto its hind legs, preparing to pounce with curved claws. Setting his mouth into a grim line, the prince calmly called to his blade. *Moonstone Retribution* obeyed in an instant, materializing in Raeylan's hand like a thousand burning stars. He met the creature's attack with enchanted steel, carving a deadly channel the length of the beast's abdomen, spilling death across the ground.

The prince had barely drawn a breath when Shikun's tortured scream of agony rippled through the night. He turned toward the sound. Torn between the need to rescue his brother and his duty to assist his soldiers, Raeylan watched the green light in the center of camp wilt into darkness.

"Go," shouted Hendar's rough voice, yanking the prince's attention back to the fight. "We can hold our own here!"

Light wounds dripped over the unarmored parts of the gruff captain's body, but his foe remained unscathed. Three squires and Tenan had the beast flanked. There was a high probability that when Raeylan returned, his men would be dead. The prince nodded once to Hendar and rushed toward his little brother's position.

The beast cut him off abruptly, blinking away from Hendar and the knights to block Raeylan's path. Lacking the time to slow his momentum, Raeylan bent his body into a slide, cutting upward into the beast's jaw as it tried to maul him with its fangs. Pushing upward with his calves and thighs, Raeylan stood, driving *Moonstone Retribution* through the creature's jawbone and out its snout, throwing the animal onto its side. Without wasting the effort to finish the monster, the prince charged toward Margariete's tent, knowing that his knights would end the creature's life in his stead.

Raeylan unraveled the beasts' tactical plan as he ran. All three creatures had targeted him specifically. Two had attempted an ambush, and the third had abandoned battle with his men to intercept him. He was unsure that he could have handled all three intruders simultaneously. This wasn't just an ordinary hunting party that had strayed over the border. The creatures had deliberate objectives. It seemed likely that the other four had marked Shikun.

Concern lent speed to his limbs, despite the heavy weight of the steel-studded armor protecting his body. As the tents thinned, he spotted two figures racing from the woods toward the origin of Shikun's cry: Terail and Margariete. The Pearl Daimyo's long daggers glinted in each hand as he sprinted forward, Margariete's hood had slipped from her head and her dark hair streamed behind her.

A whimper of pain from the tree line caused the prince to slow his pace. He recognized the sharp scream that immediately followed—the Lady Esilwen. As he scanned the murky darkness that bordered the camp, Raeylan discerned three shapes: two large and feline, one humanoid and captive. All three would soon be swallowed by the forest.

The two creatures horribly outmatched the pretty blond maiden. Without immediate rescue, she was sure to be lost. The thought squeezed Raeylan's chest painfully. He took a moment to consider Margariete and Terail's progress. Both had disappeared behind the smoldering tents and had, no doubt, reached his youngest sibling. With two monsters assailing Esilwen, that left one for each his sister and his general. Knowing that the pair of fighters would survive until he could return, Raeylan quickly changed course, dashing behind the creatures who were dragging the helpless girl into the night's gloom.

Before Raeylan could reach them, a bright flash of green flared around the muzzle of the beast who had clamped its teeth around Esilwen's ankle. The creature growled, angrily pawing at the flame, but it refused to release its grip. The second beast, running alongside its companion, swatted its grimy claws at Esilwen's abdomen, scouring her belly. As she screamed, the fire shrank away.

Raeylan's first blow caught the attention of the second beast, and it blinked aside before his sword connected. Though *Moonstone Retribution* slashed harmlessly through the air where the monster had previously stood, Raeylan could still sense it as it skulked through space. Thinking to avoid the strike, the cursed beast simply shifted to the opposite side of the prince's swing. Faster than the creature could react, Raeylan reversed the angle of attack, his steel biting hungrily into the intruder's bony face as it appeared. The monster snarled in surprise and backed away.

Esilwen's captor finally released her, phasing its charred body to Raeylan's right. The prince knew his position to be risky, but Esilwen's unmoving body lay almost directly beneath them. He worried that if he retreated from his current position, the creatures would damage her further during the fight.

Twisted talons and pronged tails charged him. *Moonstone Retribution* met each expertly, forcing both enemies to recoil. Raeylan granted the monsters no reprieve. Wielding his weapon in a dazzling array of parries and counters, the beasts were unable to breach his guard.

When the burned creature overextended on a particular strike, the prince curved the path of his blade vertically, cleaving the monster's skull in two. Attempting to take advantage of the opening, the other beast surged forward. Raeylan sidestepped and dipped to his knee, driving *Moonstone Retribution* into its chest, ending the wretched creature's existence.

Though other battles clanged in the distance, the prince was only conscious of Esilwen's struggling breath. Yanking his weapon free, he knelt next to her broken form. Her dress enveloped her in tatters, its white fabric spoiled with crimson. Blood leaked from the corners of her mouth as she struggled to breathe. The prince had seen similar wounds on the battlefield before. The creature's weight had crushed her ribs and punctured her lungs.

Panic coiled its strangling fingers around Raeylan. With tender grace, he lifted her to his chest, cradling her last moments of life. She hung limply in his arms, choking in a fit of coughs and splattering blood across his white overcoat.

"Esilwen," he pleaded softly, "please, don't leave."

Despite her tortured state, Esilwen clutched at Raeylan's wounded shoulder. Pain scraped angrily down his arm and back under the pressure, but he didn't flinch. Esilwen's body convulsed and the prince strengthened his hold on her. Green fire spewed suddenly from the rips in her flesh. Her throat rebelled with agonized cries of pain, tears swarming violently down her cheeks.

At first, Raeylan held her in horror, then his alarm gradually transformed into awe as her injuries melted themselves whole. When the flames finally diminished, her skin shone smooth and unbroken. She sobbed, shaking weakly, and hugged him tightly. He stroked her hair soothingly with his ungloved hand, speaking her name gently to calm her.

Then she suddenly pulled away, dread rising to the surface of her eyes.

"We must save Shikun," she whispered.

18: TIDES OF POWER

Terail's swift steps resonated in Margariete's ears as she maneuvered around the collapsed shell of canvas and wood that used to be her quarters. The tent corpse was bordered by the remains of two sentries. Three injured knights and two squires battled a duo of hideous malformed creatures adjacent the devastation, the men forming a protective wheel around a prone figure who lay curled on the ground.

Hot worry raised bile into the princess's mouth as she recognized the balled figure to be her little brother. Shikun held his mangled torso together with his arms and hands, a deluge of blood seeping into the soil. His eyes bulged in agony, spasms wracked his thighs. The princeling's mouth moved with silent words. Esilwen was nowhere to be seen.

Margariete identified Negin among the defenders. His former wounds bled as much as his fresh ones. The other soldiers seemed to have fared far worse. Rends in their armor exposed deep gouges in limbs and trunks. One of the squires bled copiously from the base of his head. Few of the tired men attempted to attack, instead choosing to conserve most of their energy for defensive parries. The young boys swayed unsteadily, as if will alone kept them standing.

Both grateful and dismayed by their presence—the knights would require her to use her abilities with discreet care—she loosed *Stardawn* from its sheath. She felt the blade absorb whatever fear the sight of the cursed beasts had produced, leaving only the concern for her brother's welfare. Margariete charged the hindquarters of the beast pressing forward against Negin. The magical sword slid between the animal's scales with ease. The beast snapped its jaw in her direction. From the edge of her vision she saw Terail engaging the second creature.

Her opponent's reach fell short and Margariete confidently twisted *Stardawn* into the animal's bone. It howled in frustration, but before she could withdraw her weapon, the creature vanished before her eyes.

The princess blinked in astonishment. Had it been destroyed?

A burn across her thigh belayed that thought as her adversary's claws scored her flesh. Only her armor saved the muscle from being completely severed, but she nearly toppled before managing to shift her weight off the injury. Somehow, the beast had moved behind her. Margariete turned and parried its next swipe, cleaving three of its toes from its paw with a flick of *Stardawn's* edge. The thing withdrew a surly step, as if rethinking its strategy. Sticky warmth dribbled down the back of Margariete's leg, along with razor streaks of pain.

Taking advantage of the creature's momentary lack of confidence, Margariete opened her mind, driving her power like arrow-tipped threads into the beast's head. She met an intelligent rage, a raw need to vent violence. More than anything, she felt a sentient presence, a potent image of what the twisted creature had been before the magic distorted it. Beneath that lay a driving urge to obey the wishes of its master, a single focus: *kill the biped princeling*.

The creature's ruthless drive to murder cuffed Margariete like a physical blow, drawing fear to the surface of her mind like a flesh wound drew blood. At once, a grey cloud of calm crawled into her consciousness, *Stardawn* automatically clearing it of chaos.

Margariete barely dodged the creature's tail as it launched toward her abdomen. Maintaining the connection with her opponent's mind, she focused on reading only its immediate aims—when and where it would attack— determined to outwit it. The princess was ready for the feint of its razor claws, which was meant to force her in range of its snaking jaw. She lunged forward and ducked. The monster's teeth closed a thumbnail's length above her head, spewing foul-smelling saliva into her hair. She deflected a second swing of its tail, her blade nipping shallowly across its protective scales. Wondering briefly what had happened to Negin—his training should have brought him to her side—the princess retreated several strides, positioning herself so that the Pearl knights were guarding her back. The beast paced in an irate arc, possible tactics filtering through its head.

The princess attacked, clipping the beast's chin with her sword as it danced backward. Margariete read the animal's intent to teleport an instant before the creature evaporated into the darkness. She twisted to the left as it rematerialized, plunging *Stardawn* into the meat of its hulking shoulder. Surprised anger seethed from the beast's howl, though Margariete cursed vehemently. She had miscalculated its shift. Her intent had been to stab its throat.

Her rotation brought the other knights back into view. Negin and a fellow soldier stared at her in open-mouthed wonder, more stunned at her appearance than the cursed demons attacking the camp. Her opponent effectively isolated her from the safety of the group. Its massive body stood between her and the two frozen men.

"Fight, you idiots!" came an irritated command, sheathed in Terail's voice.

The general's orders appeared to startle the mesmerized soldiers into action, though both men noticeably averted their eyes from Margariete's features. Unaware of the two knights stalking its rear, the beast stepped forward to battle the princess. She kept its interest, slicing *Stardawn* horizontally to prevent it from dodging to the side. The beast shrieked as Negin—brilliantly discerning that his own blade would fail to open a new wound—wedged his weapon into the injury Margariete had dealt with her first strike. A downstroke tore chunks of muscle from the monster's hindquarters, maiming its leg.

With a clumsy lurch, the beast twisted to face Negin and his comrade, lashing its tail toward the new threat. Negin managed to evade, though he was knocked off balance and stumbled. The creature's tail slashed the other knight squarely in the face, severing the man's jaw from his skull.

Morbid delight pulsed across the conduit connecting the princess with the beast, followed by a brief flash of tactical assessment. Through its thoughts, she saw Terail rip his dagger from the other beast's eye, his arm coated in dark gore. The monster lay lifeless and unmoving. The company's healer and his apprentices dashed into view. Margariete felt the beast's unease as it realized it was outnumbered. The battle was lost, and it intended to flee.

Margariete vowed to make the thing pay for attacking Shikun. Ignoring the protests of her wounded leg, she sank *Stardawn* into the monster's torso as it made to escape, drawing her weapon the length of the demon's side. Hot murk spattered her armor as she ran parallel to the beast's body. She felt the creature's despair as its life ebbed from the damage. Without slowing her pace, the princess rushed to her brother's side, sliding to her knees as she reached him.

"Shikun!" she cried, releasing *Stardawn* to clutch her brother's hand.

The young prince turned bleary eyes to his sister.

"Mar—Margariete," he whispered between great heaves of breath, "am I—am I dying?"

Her hand shook as she squeezed Shikun's fingers. Tears choked her eyes as she glanced at the healers. Unmoving, they stared at her in horror, bandages forgotten. Reflexively, Margariete brushed their minds, one after the other. Their dismay stabbed sharply into her stomach, like a festering sore. Now that the rush of combat bled from her body, she realized why Negin and the other knights had hesitated to aid her melee with the beast. Her hood lay limply across her back, revealing her appearance to everyone during the frenzy of battle.

Perhaps they hadn't known which cursed being to attack.

"What are you doing?" she snapped, her voice cracking with concern for her sibling. "Help him!"

The healers continued their dumbfounded stare, as if her words were beyond comprehension.

"Your princess has given you an order," inserted Terail's angry growl. "Do your duty and save our prince!"

All three men cringed at the Pearl Daimyo's harsh tone, quickly turning their attention to Shikun's glaring injuries. They seemed to fall over themselves in their haste to avoid the princess, tending to the dying boy clumsily. Just as she was about to remonstrate them for their lack of skill, Margariete felt a strong arm wrap around her waist, pulling her away from her little brother's side.

"Let me go!" she demanded of her captor.

"You need to give them room to work, Your Highness," Terail explained calmly. "You're distracting them."

As Terail drew her away, one of the apprentices took the space she had occupied, his hands working furiously. Finally acknowledging the bite of pain caused by the wound in her leg, she allowed Terail to assist her as she sat, though she never took her sapphire eyes from Shikun.

"Terail," she whispered desperately, "is he going to be all right?"

"We need to bind your injury," he replied, avoiding an answer.

Margariete heard the rip of cloth and felt a squeeze against her thigh. When she looked at Terail, his eyes were guarded.

Terail rarely evaded questions. She feared the implications. When she glanced back at Shikun, his eyes were round with dark hollows, the lids closed. The princess hardly felt the sting of the bandage as Terail pulled it taut. A loud clanking from the direction of the command tent caught her attention. She looked toward it hopefully, sure that Raeylan would emerge from the darkness.

Her stomach turned to mush as Captain Hendar materialized in the dim light instead. He surveyed the area quickly, counting the dead knights, noting the healers, and pausing only briefly on the princess.

"Where is Prince Raeylan?" he asked Negin.

Margariete's gaze traveled to Negin when he didn't answer his commander. The knight seemed entranced by the princess, his grim stare unreadable. Opening a link to his mind, she immediately felt his uncertainty. He had been startled when she charged into the battle, her sword glinting unnaturally in the eclipselight. At first he had

169

thought another aberration from the Cursed Land had arrived to claim his life. But for the scarlet signet glove— embroidered with the royal crest and identifying her as the Jeweled Princess—he would have attacked her. Now his mind clamored with confusion. Should he fear or honor her? She had killed a cursed beast single-handedly, something three men and their squires had failed to accomplish. Only the Pearl Daimyo himself had managed the same feat.

"Did you not hear me, Negin?" Hendar barked impatiently. "Where is Prince Raeylan?"

Margariete felt an uncomfortable wrench in her mind as Negin's concentration focused to his superior. She cut the connection and turned back to Terail.

"They fear me," she said, trying to stand.

"Princess Margariete, you really should rest."

"I don't need rest," she snarled. "I need to make sure Shikun is all right."

Pushing Terail away, she hobbled back to her unconscious brother. The daimyo walked beside her, ready to catch her if she fell. Angrily, she yanked one of the apprentices out of the way, resuming her place at her brother's side. She glared at the healer.

"You must save him!"

"I cannot, Your Highness," he replied gently, "the wounds are too deep and he has already lost too much blood."

Cold disbelief petrified her limbs.

"You must save him," she demanded again, as if her authority alone could banish the edicts of mortality.

"It is beyond my power, Your Highness," he answered.

"Don't give me excuses," she yelled, "there has to be something you can do!"

Terail penetrated the flurry of panic that clouded her reason.

"Princess Margariete," he said, resting a palm on her shoulder, "he's lost."

"No!" Margariete shouted, her voice clogged with tears. She struck Terail's hand away. "No, I won't believe it!" She placed her hand softly on her brother's cheek. "Shikun please, you have to fight. You have to come back!"

The princeling's ragged breath tickled her skin, his chest rising more slowly each time he exhaled. She watched, every moment an eternity, as Shikun's life force seeped into the netherworld.

He couldn't die. Not Shikun.

Unable to withhold her grief, she collapsed onto his shoulder, sobs hurtling from her body. As if from a distance, Hendar's voice pervaded her grief.

"By Nehro's Grace, it's good to see you safe, Prince Raeylan," the captain said with relief. "I was concerned."

Margariete turned from Shikun's dying chest. Raeylan stood stiffly, the torchlight turning his white overcoat to blood. Or perhaps it was covered in blood. Margariete couldn't tell. Esilwen, pale but composed, fluttered from his side and touched a healer with light fingers.

"Please, move aside," she instructed.

Startled, the healer obeyed. Esilwen knelt next to Shikun. Raeylan stood solemnly behind her, his face carefully expressionless, though Margariete noticed his ungloved knuckles were white.

Esilwen studied Shikun's injuries, biting her lip in concentration. The wind was silent, and the quiet surrounding the mourning group of knights felt alive. Margariete held her breath, afraid that Shikun's spirit might flee the shard entirely at the merest trickle of sound.

"I need a knife," Esilwen finally said.

Though her voice had been barely audible, the words rang loudly in Margariete's ears, like the cackle of ravens over a carcass. Raeylan offered a lean dagger from his belt, hilt first.

Without explanation, Esilwen pulled the sharp blade along the creamy skin of her forearm, which began to drip tiny cascades of scarlet.

"What are you—" Margariete cried in alarm.

Esilwen only smiled with gentle reassurance and pushed back the bandages holding Shikun's mutilated torso together. Placing her torn arm above the young prince, she deliberately allowed her blood to drip into his wounds.

Nothing happened. Twelve heart beats thrummed in Margariete's ears.

Then Shikun inhaled abruptly, a frayed gasp that seemed to last forever. Esilwen's blood sparked into thin strands of ice-green flame, and he screamed. Raeylan hurried forward, pressing down on his little brother to keep him from flailing.

Esilwen's blood continued to rain emerald fire, though her cheeks turned pale and her breathing came shallow. Just as Margariete decided to end her brother's suffering— by forcefully removing Esilwen if she had too—she saw the gashes in Shikun's torso begin to mend. Bone knit, organs healed. The princeling's shrieks faded to moans as the healing fire dissipated.

His body was whole again. Margariete looked from Shikun to Esilwen. The blond healer sank wearily against Raeylan's shoulder.

"He's going to be okay," she promised.

The princess joyfully sought her twin's gaze, but Raeylan was scanning the crowd around them. His eyes were dark as a wave of suspicious whispers rippled among the men.

19: DAWN RITES

Shikun swayed as another wave of dizziness threatened to overwhelm him. Smoke from the smoldering encampment rose dourly into the sky, great streaks of dreary streams that stained the heavens. The simple act of standing exhausted the princeling. Though Lady Esilwen had mended his body, he was afflicted with a physical weakness that only sleep could cure. For the benefit of his honor, he resolved to remain conscious throughout the mourning rite, though it taxed his will to its limit.

So much had been lost in the span of a single night. Mortality had touched the young prince poignantly. Four knights dead in the forest before Raeylan's return, their bodies lost forever. Now the remains of four more—plus a squire near Shikun's own age—draped the funeral pyres, awaiting passage into the water goddess's netherworld. Only a turn of chance had kept his own soul attached to his body. Had Lady Esilwen not been present, the cycle's funeral may very well have been his.

Raeylan approached the first bier. The prince had washed the blood from his hands and face, though his armor and overcoat still sported the garnish of war. General Terail followed closely behind, a porcelain bowl cupped carefully in his palms. The symbols for time, death,

173

and House Viridius adorned its surface in jeweled relief; blessed water filled its interior. Shikun watched Raeylan dip his fingers into the vessel, offering the soul of the fallen squire to Nehro with a whispered prayer. With the wetted tips of his fingers he touched the lips of the youth— Toshi, Shikun remembered with regret—cleansing the squire's spirit for the journey into the arms of the goddess.

Tears gathered in Shikun's eyes. Few honors were considered above this. To be commended into the River of Time by the heir to the throne was a respect only granted to the most honored members of the nobility. For giving his life in the service of his prince, for sacrificing himself in an attempt to rescue Lady Esilwen, Toshi would be honored by his family above all others.

Raeylan completed the rite by removing Toshi's plain grey signet glove. A bandaged Negin stepped forward and presented the squire's journey urn to the prince. Though Shikun couldn't read the inscription from where he stood, he knew a sacred poem was etched on its base. The spidery script contained instructions Toshi would need for his soul to safely cross the Seven Cascades and reach the eternity of the afterlife. Specially designed, the urn held two compartments. In the first, Raeylan solemnly placed the folded glove, followed by seven golden coins—fare for the ship that would bear Toshi into Nehro's misty realm. The second partition would carry Toshi's ashes back to his family after his body had been sanctified by fire.

As Raeylan and Terail stepped back, Hendar and Tenan advanced, unrolling a long white cloth. The crest of the Pearl Knighthood graced its center. Even the stoic knights surrounding Toshi's pyre shed water from their eyes at this unforseen mark of respect. No squire in the history of Thyella had earned the Pearl Shroud. Gently the sheer fabric was lowered over Toshi's body. Two squires then hurried to bathe the wood with scented oil. Raeylan and his knights moved to the next departed knight, but Negin lingered a moment longer. Placing his gloved hand over Toshi's veiled brow, he whispered a quick prayer of gratitude for the dedication and loyalty of his former apprentice.

The passage rites were repeated for the four remaining soldiers, all of whom were fully ranked Pearl class. Hayden, a skilled weapons expert and scout in his 25th season and Johtin—barely 18 and the youngest man of common birth in history to reach the Pearl rank—had fallen at Margariete's tent. Yehisu, who had just inherited his family holdings after his father's passing and who was responsible for the welfare of two younger siblings, had died in the early arcs of morning from wounds he'd received while patrolling with Shikun three cycles ago. The last bier held Kengo, the brave knight who had defended the princess alongside Negin. His spouse and three children would sorely miss him.

In all, only seven Pearl knights remained, many scarred with damage that would never entirely heal. Tenan's left eye was beyond repair. Margariete still limped and Terail's arm injury had thoroughly soaked its dressing. One of the surviving knights lay unconscious on a makeshift litter. No member of the camp had escaped the skirmish unscathed, not even Raeylan, the most skilled swordsman in the kingdom. Margariete's attendant, Seriya, would have died from internal bleeding if Lady Esilwen had not used her fire magic to heal her.

The thought of the pretty blond stranger would have brought a rosy flush into Shikun's cheeks if he had not felt so faint. At least now he understood his sister's wary evasion of questions regarding Esilwen's origins. Though Shikun recalled little of his experience with Esilwen's healing powers, Margariete had described the event in detail. He did, however, remember the vivid wall of green fire that had pushed back the cursed beasts' first attack. It wasn't hard to deduce that Esilwen had somehow been responsible for that as well.

Who had given Esilwen her power? The lady's benefactor was not Nehro, that much was certain. Thyella's patron goddess held sway over a particular domain: water, time, and space. Never had the water deity graced her people with the gift of magical healing, much less the ability to manipulate elemental flame. Shikun's head felt murky as he tried to recall the names of the other ancient gods and the spheres of their influence, but nothing rose to the surface. He wished he had paid closer attention to Master Malbrin's lessons.

Shikun flinched in surprise as Margariete slipped her hand into his gloved palm. Only a few arcs ago he had awakened to find her hunched at his side, eyes dry with sleeplessness.

The odor of burning wood and bodies stuck to his skin. He ached uncomfortably, so he shifted to relieve the stiffness. Quiet whispers between Terail and Raeylan caught his attention, and he peeked toward them.

"But, Your Highness," Terail was objecting softly, "don't you think it would be wise to remain and allow the men to regain their strength? Most are barely standing."

"We cannot linger, Terail," Raeylan answered, his eyes deep with regret as he stared at the funeral fires. "We are at a disadvantage. Last night's attack was neither random nor unintentional."

Terail snorted. "Are we going to believe the crazed thoughts of a mutated beast? Margariete was injured. It's possible she misread them."

"You would doubt Margariete's word?" Raeylan's voice was eerily calm.

Shikun shivered involuntarily.

"No," Terail responded politely, "but I would question our enemy's sanity. We may be overestimating them."

"There was no mistake," Raeylan asserted. "The beasts were after royal blood. It is better to overestimate the enemy than sacrifice my men. We break camp and make for the Jeweled City the moment the funeral rites are completed."

"Very well," Terail conceded. "Shall I give the order?"

"No," Raeylan said. "I must speak to them myself."

The crown prince took ten steps away from the pyres, then called to the assembly. Captain Hendar, Lieutenant Tenan, the two knights still capable of standing, the healer and his apprentices, Margariete, Shikun, the 18 remaining squires, the cook, the blacksmith, and his two students turned to face Raeylan's summons.

"You have all met the events of the night past with honor," Raeylan began. His eyes found each person in the crowd directly, his gaze lingering especially on Margariete. The princess returned his stare with pride and Shikun thought the crown prince almost smiled. "But," he continued, his expression turning somber, "there are two matters I wish to address. The first concerns the Lady Esilwen."

The future king's men remained obediently still as Raeylan paused. Shikun could tell his brother searched for the right combination of words to complete his thoughts.

"You each witnessed her extraordinary abilities. I do not know from whence they hail, but I thank the goddess for sending her to us. Lady Esilwen has thrown herself upon our mercy, risking everything to save the maid Seriya and my younger brother, Prince Shikun. Had she concealed her healing gift, we would be mourning the loss of two more of our party. I do not believe she is one with our enemies. Her actions have won my deepest respect. I pray you follow my example."

Raeylan's head bowed piously, his eyes searched the ground. Shikun felt a particular ache in his heart. He had never seen his older brother so tired. When the elder prince looked back at the crowd, lines had deepened in his face.

"Come to my side, my sister," he requested.

The Jeweled Princess turned her hooded head apprehensively toward Terail—Shikun noticed her gloved fingers clenched into a fist—but she stepped to her twin's right side. Gently, Raeylan removed the mantle, presenting her, fully unveiled, to the men. Several nervously looked away.

"You now know the truth of my sister's identity. I assure you, she is not cursed. Look upon her!" he commanded majestically. As the men cautiously obeyed, Raeylan's voice intensified, profound in its royal regal. "Why Nehro has blessed Princess Margariete with such beauty and strength, I do not know. But she is more than worthy to stand with us. She has battled alongside you, with great skill and without fear. She has demonstrated the cool mind and faithful bravery that is required of any warrior.

"Four cycles ago, Princess Margariete saved the lives of 15 villagers from the town of Rekkadell. They witnessed not only her strength, but also her dark features. She acted as any of us would, risking herself to save innocent lives from the torment of slavery. Despite her heroism, they tried to execute her, their thanks swallowed by fear." Raeylan paused as a tremor stained his voice. Shikun was forced to choke his own emotions away.

"I ask only this: that you protect her as I protect her, honor her as I honor her."

Stillness blanketed the camp like a shower of sakuhra blossoms. And then, like a great wave rolling from the sea, armored knees bent to the ground in steadfast fealty. Knights, youths, and artisans bowed their heads in acceptance. Margariete's cheeks shone with tears. Raeylan smiled openly, a rare event.

"The rest of our people are not so tolerant," the prince warned. "My brothers, I know I can rely on your discretion."

PART 2

20: MORNING IN THE CITY OF JEWELS

The City of Jewels reflected the sunlight in a spectrum of colors, blazing like the faceted surfaces of a thousand gems. Esilwen had to blink several times as she gaped at the city's majestic perch. Water wound around its perimeter. Shikun identified the tributaries as the Seven Cascades, three of which ran through the city, ferrying water to a small lake near the capital's central market. The wayward branches then disappeared under the towering black rock that thrust Viridius Castle into the sky. According to the young prince, the rivers burst from the southern cliff face, plunging into the lowlands below the castle's edge.

Once the group neared the east gate—a heavy black stone bridge spanning the river, its far end girded by two iron banded doors—Raeylan dispatched a messenger to fetch a more appropriate mode of transit for Margariete and Esilwen. While the company paused, Raeylan had a small tent erected near a grove of trees.

Two maids arrived within the arc, each hauling several wrapped bundles, accompanied by a gilded palanquin. As four husky servants lowered the platform to the ground, the two handmaids hustled the princess and Esilwen into the tent.

Margariete called each by name—Lya and Rin—as they removed the princess's armor with grimaced faces and smothered her in waves of silk. Gold and silver thread embroidered fanciful designs of flowers, trees, and birds. Ribbons spilled from eyelets, jade and ruby buttons tumbled over sleeves. With their skilled fingers, the princess's attendants soon had her showered in three layers of robes and a sheen of veil to hide her face.

Simultaneously, the two women turned to Esilwen, clucking their tongues at the state of her attire. Bloodstained and filthy, her dress was beyond repair, her cloak in desperate need of washing. Rin squawked with concern when she noticed that Esilwen wore no signet glove, but Margariete ordered the maid to resume her duties. Both maids acquiesced with grace, but Esilwen noticed an underlying tension between the princess and her servants. Neither would look directly at Margariete.

Soon Lya had Esilwen stripped, wiping away as much grime as possible with only a small basin and washcloth. Rin enclosed Esilwen's body with heavy robes that were less sophisticated in design than Margariete's. The boning in the padded corset pinched Esilwen's lungs uncomfortably, and the long sleeves threatened to trip her newly slippered feet.

As soon as the women were dressed properly, they were handed into the palanquin. The four servants dropped the sheer curtains around its frame and hefted the wooden poles onto their shoulders. With Raeylan and Shikun leading, the company crossed into the Jeweled City.

Esilwen peeked through gaps in the transparent curtains, trying to ignore the suffocating grip of her new clothes. The city glistened with a glaze of freshly fallen rain, and the aquamarine tiles of the closely packed buildings were painted with wooly moss. Most of the structures were dark pinewood, like those of Timberdale, though the filigree carvings around the doorframes and windows put Timberdale's artisans to shame. Bridges of all styles and sizes leapt over the waterways, some of whitewashed wood, others of various colored stone.

Viridius Castle perched atop a flattened mound, its foundations desperately burrowing into a deadly precipice. Blinding white enamel coated the towering structure, its tiled roof punctuated by golden statutes at every corner. The entire complex was encompassed by its own guard of mossy stone walls. A tumble of wide steps meandered down the sharp incline, connecting the palace grounds with the city. Halfway between the castle's feet and the city proper was a second tier, drenched with ornate manors and halls. Tree-filled greenery dominated the gaps between the large buildings. When asked, Margariete explained that only members of the aristocracy were permitted to live there.

As the crown prince and his knights marched through the city, the sea of people crowding the streets parted. Nobles paused in their business, commoners backed against the lantern-lined shops, and merchants left their fabric-draped thresholds. All dropped their knees to the cobblestone pavement as their sovereign passed. Many looked on the palanquin with astonishment before they properly lowered their eyes. Esilwen wondered how long it had been since Margariete's transport had been seen in public.

"Your city is beautiful," Esilwen whispered to Margariete, marveling at the perpetual vapor that clung to the sky from the southern waterfalls. In the sunlight, the misty water droplets glittered like suspended jewels.

"Only if it's not your cage," Margariete complained.

"It's not so terrible anymore, is it?" Esilwen said. "You aren't getting married after all."

Margariete's head turned to the front of the palanquin, her veiled face gazing steadily into Raeylan's back.

"It isn't my cage I speak of."

Esilwen swallowed, thinking of the prince's impending marriage. Less than a fortnight and he would be bound. The injustice of the arrangement had been foremost in Margariete's conversation for the entire six cycle journey to the city.

Raeylan had steadfastly avoided Esilwen during those six cycles. At first, she supposed the duties of leading the company had consumed his time, but the longer she pondered, the more she decided his evasion had been intentional. Once, late on the fourth evening, she had inadvertently glanced across the camp and noticed his twilight eyes on her. With a carefully guarded expression, he had slowly turned away.

Esilwen shook herself free of romantic notions. What was she thinking? There was no reason to suppose Raeylan's attention hadn't been one of curiosity. She had, after all, evinced powers unknown to any magic ever seen in Thyella. And who was to say the prince didn't already feel affection for his future bride?

At least those she had healed were doing well, Esilwen reminded herself. After saving Shikun, Esilwen had used her gifts to restore Seriya, who had suffered broken bones and ugly burns. The effort required to heal Seriya had caused Esilwen to faint. Later, she learned she had been unconscious for many arcs. During the next few cycles she tended to other injuries with more care for her own strength—especially with Shikun hovering over her anxiously the entire time—including Margariete's leg and Terail's wrist. Raeylan had declined her assistance for his own wound.

A jostle brought her back to her surroundings. The entourage had halted before the panes of two black pine doors, heavy with inset bands of steel. Stairs climbed the mountain behind it, offering ascension to the castle. A wide, chiseled ramp ran next to the staircase, presumably for horses and wagons. Raeylan called to the guards, and the gates parted. After a few fragments of an arc, they met another gate, this one an ornate portcullis of polished silver. Here the stairs settled into a horizontal path and turned away, leading toward the manors of the nobility on the second tier.

The guards opened the portcullis as they recognized the two princes leading the party. Esilwen noted the symbols on the guard's tunic were only a partial image of the jasmine blossom design worn by the Pearl knights she had come to know. When she asked Margariete, the princess answered that it meant the warriors at the gate were a lower order in the Knights of the Gem, only class Amber.

Wide avenues of black stone wound from the rectangular courtyard to the castle's entrance, flanked by a surf of glittering sand. Lichen-kissed rocks floated in the ocean of crushed particles, and small bamboo water features clicked at the borders.

A large detail of knights waited to greet them in the courtyard's center, in descending rank from Jade to Amber. The front line, however, displayed colors that Esilwen didn't recognize. Tabards of deep blue, almost indigo, draped their silvery, full-plate armor. A bladed, ivory whirlpool enclosed by a matching circle adorned their breasts. In front of them stood a grim-faced, richly-dressed man of about 50 seasons.

"Margariete," Esilwen asked, as the palanquin lowered to the ground, "who are those men?"

"The Tempestguard," Margariete said under her veil, "the highest ranking soldiers in the City of Storms—my father's kingdom."

"Then, the man in front is your father?"

A rude noise was Margariete's only affirmation.

King Arahm's eyes looked unforgiving. His greying beard and mustache drew Esilwen's gaze to the angry line that was his lips. Not a single blond thread of hair dared escape the tight thong at the nape of his neck. Emeralds and rubies dripped from the hems of his azure and burgundy attire. An abrasively green signet glove flashed from under his sleeve cuffs. Esilwen couldn't help but wonder if the monarch's sour expression had somehow distorted his face into sharp angles, because she could see nothing of Raeylan in him.

Seriya drew aside the palanquin's curtains, and both Esilwen and Margariete stepped onto the stone terrace. Raeylan and Shikun approached their father, each bowing respectfully. Arahm noticeably refused to return the formality. A tense hush engulfed the court as the crown prince and his father stared at each other, the first stoically blank and the other tight with displeasure.

Unsure as to the correct procedure, Esilwen followed Margariete's actions closely. The princess abruptly strode before King Arahm, dipping into an elegant curtsey. Esilwen mimicked the motion. As the Jeweled Princess properly retreated behind her twin, a cloud of fury infused the glare of the Third Kingdom's king, its full intensity aimed at his daughter.

Raeylan shifted, protectively blocking his sister from Arahm's direct line of sight. The king rewarded his son with a scowl. Arahm jerked a folded slice of parchment from the inside pocket of his signet glove and thrust it into Raeylan's hand. The prince's eyes lingered critically on his father for a moment before he coolly turned his attention to the letter. Though already broken, the halved wax seal reminded Esilwen of the insignia she had seen on Timberdale's flags. When the prince finished reading the correspondence, he handed it back to his father.

"The matter is more appropriately discussed inside my castle's halls," Raeylan said calmly. "I will convene with you after I have seen to the needs of my men. Our errand was most difficult."

Arahm's face bulged purple. "We will discuss it now, Raeylan."

The expressions of the gathered knights darkened with disapproval—especially those who had accompanied their prince to the borderland. Esilwen surmised that the public informality with which Arahm addressed his son had been an insult.

"This is not the proper place for such a delicate issue," Raeylan reprimanded, his eyes flicking across the assembly of men.

"You cannot protect her from this!" Arahm snarled, waving the letter for all to see. "Not only has Margariete dishonored the family by running away, but she attacked the Duke of Timberdale."

"The duke has abused his station and my people," Raeylan replied evenly.

"Do not make light of the matter," Arahm continued to bluster. "Margariete defied her duty. She has learned the art of swordplay in secret. She removed her signet glove. Both are forbidden. By the goddess Nehro, she must be punished!"

"What is done cannot be changed, no matter how you wish it. Punishing her now will only serve to please your own sense of retribution."

"How dare you!" Arahm yelled, spittle flecking his lips. "Her actions have shamed our ancestors! This could very well upset our alliance with the City of Glass!"

"His Majesty King Hylan is a respectable and wise man. Under the circumstances, he will no doubt show clemency."

"Margariete's actions are unforgivable!" the king accused, rudely indicating the princess with a finger.

"If this is the case," Raeylan said, a warning thrum low in his voice, "then there is nothing I can do. An unforgivable offense can have no atonement and therefore renders this argument pointless."

"You allow your love for her to blind you. She is a disgrace!"

Esilwen dared not interrupt, though her insides burned with the desire to defend her friend. Before the prince could rebuke his father, one of the Pearl knights stepped forward.

"If it weren't for the skill and courage of the Princess of the Jewel, I would have perished," Negin defended softly. "By her sword, she has earned both my loyalty and gratitude."

Esilwen was astonished to see that King Arahm's face was capable of spewing more anger. The Tempestguard nervously fingered the hilts of their weapons, aware of their sovereign's agitation.

"She has shown herself to be a capable warrior," Captain Hendar inserted, stepping forward to flank his fellow knight. "I would gladly lay down my life in her service."

"Insolence! She is a woman, nothing more," the king roared. His rage washed back to his eldest son. "Your men are undisciplined! They should be flogged for speaking in such a manner. Their impertinence is the mark of an ineffective commander."

"Our prince is—" Hendar began, but Raeylan motioned him to silence.

The First Kingdom's heir faced his father with dignity.

"Their err in decorum is no greater than your own," he charged.

"I demand governance over my own daughter! She should be executed!"

Arahm's challenge settled around the courtyard like rocks dropping into the sea. The only sound was the muted song of the Cascades behind the castle. A savage pounding reverberated in Esilwen's head. Raeylan's form stiffened, and he took care with each breath, as if battling to restrain himself.

"I must refuse your request," Raeylan answered formally. "Do not forget, Your Majesty, that this is my castle. My city. Princess Margariete may be your daughter, but she is my sister—heiress to the First Kingdom of Thyella in her own right. Her fate is mine to decide, not yours. You have no authority here."

His quiet dignity blistered Arahm with intimidation. The king recoiled. The crown prince strode to his castle's entrance, forcing his father to move aside. As he passed Arahm's shoulder, Raeylan paused.

"You are only here by my leave," he warned. "If you ever impart such public injury to me again, I will rescind that courtesy."

"Is that a threat?" Arahm demanded.

"No. Simply a consequence you bring upon yourself through your gratuitous arrogance."

Raeylan's knights filed out of the courtyard at their prince's heels. Esilwen and Margariete followed after, leaving the flustered king behind to wallow in resentment.

21: Viridius Castle

"Master Malbrin," Raeylan said, "may I present the Lady Esilwen."

Esilwen smiled politely and bowed to the man of many seasons who hunched unsteadily before her. Grizzled hair hung to his chin like brittle strands of straw. His brows were lost in a tangle of wrinkles, though his eyes were bright with intelligence. A crisp, pale-grey robe draped his parchment skin. He seemed a personified extension of the musty library. If the ancient scrolls around the room could take physical form, they would look something like Malbrin.

"The pleasure is mine, My Lady," Malbrin returned. "I hear you have great patience," he said when he had straightened his back as far as his ancient bones would allow.

"I, um—" Esilwen trailed off uncomfortably. She had barely been in Viridius Castle for one cycle. What could the old mentor have heard about her? "I'm afraid I don't know what you mean, sir."

"I was informed by young Prince Shikun during his morning lessons that you are quite close friends with the Jeweled Princess, and even spent a few cycles alone with her in the wilderness."

"Yes," Esilwen confirmed hesitantly.

"And yet you have remained by her side," Malbrin continued with a toothy grin. "Thus, I must presume you possess a manner of patience rivaled only by His Highness Prince Raeylan."

Humor laughed across the old man's face.

Esilwen glanced at Raeylan from beneath her eyelashes, hoping to determine the correct response to Malbrin's wit, but the prince had turned his face to the window, hiding it from Esilwen's view. The teacher's attention turned to his student.

"Something troubles you, My Liege?"

The prince didn't answer. Esilwen fidgeted with her fingers nervously, feeling like an outsider.

"Were the horrors of the Cursed Land as terrible as the reports led us to believe?" Malbrin asked.

"Worse," Raeylan replied evenly, still gazing through the thick-paned glass. "Nine perished at the border camp."

Malbrin's head bobbed regretfully, and he sighed softly.

"However, that is not the dilemma I wished to present to you this cycle, Master Sage," Raeylan stated.

The tutor turned back to Esilwen, a knowing twinkle in his eyes. Of course, the prince had questions about her. He was hoping Malbrin could provide some answers. She felt a little embarrassed, wondering if Malbrin had known Raeylan's purpose from the beginning. Nothing seemed to escape the sharp perception of this wizened old man.

Raeylan finally turned from the window, though he looked only at his mentor. A wistful pang pricked her. It seemed that even in her presence the prince wished to avoid her. Esilwen wondered unhappily if she had accidentally offended him during the past few cycles.

"Lady Esilwen is not of our shard," the prince said.

Her throat tightened. Esilwen trusted Raeylan, but found the revelation of her foreignness unnerving. Oddly, Malbrin's crinkled eyebrows lifted in interest instead of surprise.

"Is Your Highness certain?" Malbrin asked.

"Yes," Raeylan asserted. "Margariete found her in the bamboo forest."

Malbrin opened his mouth to propose a question, but the prince stepped forward and brushed away the golden locks concealing Esilwen's pointed ears. Tingles raced up her arms at the lightness of his touch, but the prince stolidly kept his eyes on the tutor.

"Extraordinary!" Malbrin gaped as he shuffled forward for a closer look. He replaced Raeylan's hand with his own, holding her hair away from her ears. After a few moments, the old mentor turned Esilwen's head back and forth, examining her face more thoroughly.

"Yes, yes. Now I see it! Something different in the structure of the bones, the shape of her eyes."

"Margariete spoke of magic," Raeylan continued, moving to the opposite side of the library.

With quick speech he recounted Esilwen's arrival, her loss of memory, and her healing magic. Esilwen waited quietly, acutely aware of the manner in which the prince discussed her—as if she were not even present. Disappointment ran through her, and she bit her lip to keep it from trembling. With an inner sigh, she wished that Margariete and Shikun hadn't been instructed to wait outside the cluttered library. Their company would have been a comfort.

"I will need to research this matter," Malbrin said when the prince finished. "It may take several cycles. My own tomes lack information that would be considered useful to us. I must visit the archives at Nehro's Grand Temple in the shrine district."

"Of course," Raeylan returned with a nod.

The prince strode from the chamber without another word or glance. Esilwen blinked her eyes sadly.

"Always so focused," Malbrin said with fondness.

She turned away from the doorway where Raeylan had disappeared, bobbing her head at the tutor in agreement.

"Our prince tries so hard to secure our future," he continued, walking to the nearest shelf and shuffling through rolls of painted parchment, "that he often forgets about the present. Sometimes, he doesn't notice what is right in front of him."

"I'm not sure I know what you mean," Esilwen replied absently, her mind distracted by the thought of the prince's impenetrable grey eyes.

"That is unfortunate," Malbrin said with an elderly chuckle. He picked a scroll, examined it, and then discarded it. "A very close friend once shared a sensible lesson with me: guide the fish to water, and he will drown more readily."

Esilwen raised an eyebrow, her lips scrunched with confusion. Her perplexity seemed to amuse the old tutor.

"It means," Malbrin explained, "though I have my suspicions, I cannot tell you why Prince Raeylan left this room without comment. My interference would simply complicate things. And I don't want to be held responsible when those events spiral down with the Seven Cascades."

"I still don't understand," Esilwen said apologetically.

"You will my dear, it's only a matter of time," Malbrin answered kindly, "and by Nehro's Grace, there's not much of that left."

Esilwen looked at him, puzzled. It seemed Malbrin delighted in riddles.

"I am an old man," he explained, abandoning the shelves and coming closer to her. "My life has been full of successes and mistakes. Yours will be no less adventurous."

Malbrin placed his hand against her back and guided her gently to the door.

"Now if you will excuse me, My Lady, I must prepare for my departure."

Before she had quite realized what happened, Esilwen found herself outside the library. Margariete and Shikun had been kneeling patiently on several cushions next to the wall. Both rose as the wooden door slid shut. A hopeful grin touched the young prince's face. The princess's veil made it impossible to read Margariete's expression. Esilwen wished the mask was unnecessary. Her friend's life was difficult enough.

"What happened?" Margariete asked.

Esilwen related all that had transpired with Malbrin, leaving out only her misgivings surrounding Raeylan's distant manner.

"We should have answers soon then," Shikun said enthusiastically. "Malbrin is the most knowledgeable man in the kingdom. If there's truth to discover in any of Thyella's scrolls, he'll find it."

"Let us hope," Esilwen responded, suddenly unsure of her new position.

She had enjoyed spending time with Margariete while they travelled, learning of Thyellan culture. But ever since the night of the beast attack, she felt as if the others involuntarily emphasized her differentness. Malbrin's search for her identity would draw attention to other distinctions. A surge of pity for Margariete crossed her. Esilwen supposed this was how the princess had felt her entire life.

"So what now?" Esilwen asked the royal siblings.

"How about a tour of the castle?" Shikun suggested cheerily.

Esilwen smiled at the youth, and a familiar swell of red tinged his cheeks.

"That would be wonderful, Shikun."

Esilwen walked side by side with Margariete as Shikun led the way. The ladies' slippers scuffed the wooden floor, their lavish robes swept behind them. The interior of the castle was open to the sky. The chambers and rooms lay between the building's outer wall and central garden. Balconies and hallways overlooked the inner courtyard on every floor. When Esilwen asked Margariete how they kept the partitioned rooms warm during the cold portion of the season, since there was no roof in the center to store the heat, the princess looked at her oddly.

"You know," Esilwen elaborated as they walked to the circular stairs, "when it's winter."

Margariete and Shikun shared a confused glance.

"When the plants go into hibernation," Esilwen continued, "and it snows?"

"I have never seen such a thing," Margariete said, taken aback. "It only snows at the top of the Sakuhra Mountains, and few who go there ever return."

"Every season is broken into trinals," Shikun explained. "Spring, summer, and the rains. There is no trinal called 'winter.'"

Esilwen pondered silently as the three wound down the stairs from the fourth to second level. Though she was unable to recall a specific experience, she felt certain that the "seasons" from her home shard had been broken into quarters, and that there was a short time where flowers and trees slept as the air grew cold. The concept of "spring" and "summer" were recognizable, but she had never known a third of the calendar to be consumed by rain. She described to her friends the effect winter had on the weather and landscape.

"How could such a thing be possible?" Shikun asked rhetorically, as he stepped out onto the second floor. Margariete seemed speechless.

The west mezzanine was a simple corridor of polished wood and lavender mats that stretched from the stairwell to the Gem Gallery. Rows of unlit candles hung in cradles of sculpted iron along the walls and rails. When lit they pushed away the night like flickering fireflies. The soft sound of chirping beetles drifted from the garden below.

Beneath them, trees burst in varying bouquets of leaves and blossoms, some drooping in delicate pink petals, others boasting manicured spines of spiky boughs. Tiny streams of water gurgled over stones, following a sandy path that meandered through the lively foliage. Bamboo stalks stood sentry at the borders, and stone figurines and wooden benches peppered the walkways. The glassy reflection of a central pond gleamed up at the open sky. Near the southern tip of the shrine, an ivy-draped partition shielded a portion of the garden from public view.

"This is the Jewel Shrine, part of the sacred Spring of Nehro," Shikun commented as they strolled through the open veranda. "It actually has two parts. Behind that partition is a smaller, secluded spring that is only for the royal family. My father says the water appears here magically, but Master Malbrin has a theory that the pressure of the rocks beneath us forces the water up into the spring."

"Which do you think?" Esilwen asked pleasantly.

"I think," Margariete interjected, and though her face was concealed, Esilwen imagined from her tone that it scowled, "that there are bigger concerns right now than worrying about where the water comes from."

Shikun swallowed his reply as the trio entered the Gem Gallery, where two arms of ivory stairs bridged the second level to the first. Fragmented jewels formed lavish murals on the walls and ceiling of the Grand Hall on the main floor, where a set of three heavy doors led outside to the castle grounds. As the trio descended, richly clothed courtiers and noblemen quickly moved away, murmuring whispers of astonishment as they spotted Margariete's veiled form.

After passing through the rectangular columns that supported the palace's main entry hall, they mounted two steps onto a black pine colonnade. Its metal fastenings sang sweetly as Esilwen sauntered across it and gasped in delight.

"It sounds like bird song!" she exclaimed.

Shikun smiled.

"It's called a nightingale floor," he said as he indicated a left turn with his arm. "Come with me, and I will show you Nehro's temple."

"I thought Master Malbrin said the temple was in the shrine district, somewhere in the city?" Esilwen asked as she turned to follow.

"He meant the Grand Temple," Shikun clarified. "It's the largest sanctuary in the entire shard, but the castle has its own temple."

"What for?" she asked.

"So the royal family and guests can worship privately," he answered as they reached a large archway. "Before any diplomatic meeting takes place, the nobles pray here. Also, if the castle were ever besieged, we would still be able to perform sacred rites asking for the goddess's protection."

Rising in the center of the temple was a graceful glass statue, sculpted in the general form of a woman, though her face lacked any features. Water cascaded down the transparent effigy, creating the illusion that she danced with liquid life. Shikun explained that the goddess statue had been crafted by artisans in the Fourth Kingdom, given to the Viridius family long ago. Unlike the majority of the rooms in the castle, which were layered with woven bamboo mats, the shrine's floors were made of slatted cedar beams. Two fingers could slide through the gaps. Clear water rushed beneath the openings, either to or from the garden, Esilwen couldn't tell.

When Esilwen stepped across the threshold into the temple, she halted, her muscles inexplicably paralyzed. The watery statue of Nehro dissolved into mist, replaced by another image—a golden icon with eyes of scarlet, its flaxen talons cupped around a glimmering crystal goblet. Her mind burned. She knew the goblet was something significant, but she could not dredge its meaning from the depths of her forgotten memory. Visions swirled sickeningly in her head, one after another. Soon they came faster than her mind could process. The chalice shattered into bloody splinters, a sword raced toward her neck, her eyes closed into darkness, and a heavy mantle of water stole her breath. A blur of motion was the last thing she remembered as her body slumped to the floor.

22: NOON ON THE PLAZA

Only on occasion did Thyella grow so hot that the sun tortured anyone unfortunate enough to stand beneath it. Margariete grimaced under her veil. Not even the wind stirred the late-summer cycle. She shifted, trying to dislodge the sticky silk clinging uncomfortably to her back without bringing attention to herself. Sweat dribbled under the edge of her corset. At least her veil shaded her face from the courtyard's glare. The others in the assembly squinted in the sun.

An echo of the citizenry's welcoming applause rose to the palace grounds. Somewhere on the city's cobblestone streets, the procession of House Kotrell, the royal line of the Fourth Kingdom, ambled toward the castle. Tradition dictated that the entrance of the future queen be met with particular ceremony. Raeylan and his family were required to wait until King Hylan and his daughter reached them. The rite had begun a little over an arc ago, when the moon touched its midcycle horizon.

The princess gazed across the front of the gathering, envying the lightweight indigo tunics worn by her brothers. Thyellan kingdoms each possessed customary wedding attire—King Arahm and his gentry were weighted with gratuitously ornamented costumes, overcompensating for their inferior riches and strength. The royalty of the First Kingdom had no need of such boast, their position as the most powerful realm in the shard was common knowledge. Therefore, the princes wore simple garments lacking decoration. Their only accessories were the lordly signet gloves on their right arms. Even the women of the court wore robes simple in embroidery and jewels. Only the actual ceremonies would warrant more extravagant apparel from the Viridius household.

Both the wedding and Raeylan's formal coronation would take place nine cycles hence. Margariete ground her teeth in frustration. Her twin had developed an affinity to shield his inner self from her mind-reading abilities at a young age. Knowing that her magical skills would be useless, the princess had attempted to glean a hint of his state over the past few cycles through insight.

Her effort proved useless. Raeylan had spent the last cycle making preparations for the Fourth Kingdom's arrival, seeing the guest apartments made ready, and arranging the particulars of the welcoming banquet. This morning had been devoured by details of the impending entourage.

To the palace residents, the prince seemed in sufficient spirits to receive his betrothed—he was, after all, naturally reserved in public. But his sister knew him better. Though expert at concealing his emotions, Raeylan did allow a smile to touch his face now and then, even letting laughter ripple across his eyes. The prince's recent retreat into rigid resignation was a clear sign to Margariete that he was unhappy. Several times she had tried to convince him that the marriage need not take place, but Raeylan refused to discuss it.

Margariete wished he wasn't so determined to face everything alone.

Esilwen shared the sentiment, though her friend would never have admitted it. Too shy—or forlorn—to acknowledge her own concern for Raeylan, Margariete thanked the water goddess that Esilwen's mind wasn't guarded. Esilwen's sensitivity for Raeylan flooded the telepath's mind every time his name was mentioned. Slight nuances in the healer's conversations with the prince— which were few as he seemed determined to avoid her— revealed underlying significance. If ever the princess mentioned a topic pertaining to her twin, Esilwen quickly changed the course of discussion. Though the healer tried to quash her fondness of the prince, Esilwen's affection for Raeylan grew every cycle. Margariete felt her head would burst with the melancholy of it.

Soon after realizing Esilwen's interest, Margariete had taken to studying her brother closely, hoping to discover if he felt the same. Unfortunately, every time the princess managed to corner him, he seemed too busy to trifle with her company—particularly when Esilwen was present. It seemed his curiosity about the green-eyed healer had vanished with the cursed beasts. The only exception to his evasion happened the cycle Esilwen had collapsed in Nehro's temple. He had called for the best healer in the city, hovering at the physician's elbows. Esilwen's swoon lasted only a few arcs, but Raeylan excused himself as soon her eyelids began to flutter.

The rhythmic thrum of the guards' drums announced the approaching dignitaries, and the silver gates to the courtyard lifted. Horses decked with golden bells pranced through the gates, bearing heralds with the Fourth Kingdom's pennant: a three sided figure enclosing a crescent sun. The Silver Protectorate marched behind, their saffron-and-black-belted robes flashing brilliantly in the sun. Each stamped the butt of a brassy pole-arm on the ground as he walked, the rods' trident shaped heads draped with loops of chiming silver. Margariete knew the staves were purely ornamental. The island nation of the Fourth Kingdom relied mostly on their naval troops, rarely having need for ground soldiers. These monks were most likely the personal guard of House Kotrell's sovereign, trained in a secret art of hand-to-hand combat that required no weapons but their own limbs.

When the Fourth Kingdom's leader crossed onto the terrace, the Jeweled Princess caught her breath in surprise. She had expected another harsh ruler, his face bent by political intrigue—reminiscent of her father's. But the middle-aged king had an oval face, lines of kindness turning at the edges of his genuine smile. His garb was a deep, crimson-embroidered ocher, hemmed with flanged crystals. Instead of a metal crown, he wore a beautiful circlet of tinted glass, fashioned around tiny eyelets of brass. A silver and glass palanquin followed behind him.

As the parade came to a halt, King Hylan hopped from the saddle with a level of energy that usually eluded a man of 58 seasons. He dropped his reigns into the hands of a robed boy who had been walking beside the horse. The Silver Protectorate surrounded their king in a curved wave, as tradition demanded, when Hylan approached Prince Raeylan. After both men had exchanged customary bows, signet gloves crossed ritually over their breasts as befitting one ruler to another, King Hylan gestured to the palanquin.

"As sovereign of the Fourth Kingdom," he announced to the assembly in a fatherly manner, "and ruler of the mirrored City of Glass, I give to you, Prince Raeylan, heir to the First Kingdom and its City of Jewels, our youngest daughter, Princess Katrina of House Kotrell, to wife. May this union bind our realms in friendship."

After King Hylan's public proclamation, all eyes turned as one to the palanquin's sheer curtains.

A maid emerged from the draped cocoon, wreathed in radiant beauty. Her gown was wrought in the style of her warmer homeland climate. Layers of lemon silk draped her curvy form in a blossomed cloud. Tiny embroidered filaments of crushed glass danced across her filmy sleeves and rosy signet glove. A wide belt of silver held the garment in place at her waist, the yellow cloth petal-flaring outward when it reached her thighs. Flaxen curls slipped gracefully to her waist. Though she wore no crown—it was considered bad luck for any bride-to-be to adorn her hair— her throat and wrists were encircled with thin bands of twisted silver.

Princess Katrina kept her eyes modestly lowered as her handmaiden led her to stand before Margariete's twin. A polite curtsey was her only introduction to her future husband. The Prince's grey eyes remained detached as King Hylan took Katrina's gloved hand and placed it ritually into Raeylan's.

Margariete sank with misgiving. The custom indicated formal recognition of the marriage, a declaration more binding than a signed treaty. Nothing could stop the wedding now.

*

"What is this party?" Esilwen asked as Seriya tied the last ribbon on the healer's voluminous ivory sleeves. "I thought last night was Princess Katrina's honor banquet?"

Margariete straightened her veil. "It's a congratulatory celebration for the bride," she said as she, her three attendants, and Esilwen exited the queen's chambers. "Princess Katrina will meet the noblewomen of the city, who can now attempt to become Katrina's favorites and elevate their social status. They'll bring her presents, and she'll flatter herself."

"Oh," Esilwen said as they walked out of the queen's chambers and crossed the hallway. At the top of the stairwell she paused.

"I'm not sure I can do this, Margariete."

The princess halted her descent, turning toward her friend. Esilwen stood trembling, biting her lip.

"Meet us downstairs," she commanded her handmaids, "we will be there shortly."

Rin and Lya obeyed without question, but Seriya glanced at Esilwen in concern before following her lady's instructions. When they had disappeared, Margariete climbed to Esilwen's side. The princess placed both hands on her friend's shoulders in comfort, but the blonde had dropped her gaze to the floor.

"I, too, must bear Katrina's presence," the princess soothed. "But King Hylan seems a kind and worthy man. His daughter is sure to possess some of his goodness."

Margariete twisted her features under the veil, thankful that Esilwen couldn't see them. The princess knew very well that a parent's demeanor didn't always influence a child. King Arahm was the perfect example—none of the Viridius children shared his perspective. Margariete knew only one thing about Katrina. She was the youngest of three sisters, and, until the prospect of marriage with Prince Raeylan, would have been the lowest ranking member of her family for the remainder of her life. But as the queen of the First Kingdom, Katrina would be the envy of them all. Margariete had felt the mad rush of excitement from Katrina as her pending change in station guzzled all other thought. Margariete worried that her new sister's obsession with station indicated a superficial personality. The Jeweled Princess was unable to determine any more of Katrina's character, however, as Margariete was forbidden to attend public banquets. She had spent last evening trapped in her quarters.

Esilwen offered a frail smile. "Thank you, but you're only saying that to ease my discomfort."

"Partly," Margariete admitted, "but I also need to convince myself. We both love my brother—"

Tears glistened in Esilwen's eyes as she raised them. Margariete continued on, determined to help her friend face the unalterable circumstances that would break the healer's heart.

"—and wish him happiness. Katrina is here. That's the end of it."

Esilwen bobbed her head weakly.

"Come, we are already late," Margariete said gently, leading Esilwen down the stairwell.

The girls walked in quiet contemplation as they descended to the first level, Margariete squeezing Esilwen's arm tightly. As the two crossed the nightingale floor, they met Margariete's three maids and a few other attendants who were standing just outside the Ivory Parlor doors. A titter of genteel laughter echoed from within.

"You must enter behind me and sit on my right," Margariete instructed, low enough for the servants not to hear. "Kneel only after I do."

Esilwen nodded that she understood. Rin and Lya each knelt on either side of the door while Seriya slid it open. Straightening her shoulders, the Jeweled Princess swept into the room.

"Ah, ladies! And here she is," Katrina's musical voice announced, "my new sister, Princess Margariete. We are honored that you could join us, Your Highness."

As decreed by Margariete's station, all the ladies present rose in a flutter of motion, the lowest ranking courtier first,

Katrina last, to pay homage to the Princess of the Jewel. Each lady bowed in turn, waiting to reseat themselves until Margariete chose a cushion to kneel upon.

"I saved you a place by my side," Katrina announced to everyone, motioning to a collection of women Margariete barely recognized. Only rarely did she encounter the gentry in such an intimate setting.

"Thank you," Margariete responded with the appropriate amount of courtesy.

Katrina's perfect smile glistened, though Margariete did notice it falter as the Glass Princess ran her eyes across Esilwen. Obviously, Katrina was not pleased by the blond healer's attendance. With a little too much enthusiasm, Katrina led Margariete to her place.

The Jeweled Princess knelt gracefully, feeling the eyes of the noblewomen boring into her. Few of them had ever seen her up close. Margariete considered just ignoring them all, until a wrinkle of gasps swelled through the assembled courtiers.

As instructed, Esilwen had settled onto her knees next to Margariete. Unfortunately, she had managed to do so before Princess Katrina. Margariete cursed softly—how could she have forgotten to warn her friend of such a breach in protocol? By kneeling first, Esilwen had inadvertently announced her social status in the First Kingdom's hierarchy to be above that of the Glass Princess.

Katrina managed to keep her expression fixed, but Margariete saw through its meaningless veneer. Raeylan's betrothed took her place prettily, her extensive rose ruffles billowing about her as she examined Esilwen from head to foot.

"Well this won't do," Katrina said with a sickeningly sweet smile. "Ladies, I think we have a stowaway."

The courtiers giggled like misguided puppets as they returned to their cushions.

"Your friend is not wearing a signet glove," she whispered to Margariete confidentially, just loud enough for all to hear. "Don't you think she would be better suited outside, waiting with the servants?"

When Margariete glanced at Esilwen's bare arm, her friend slipped it self-consciously out of view. Margariete turned and glared blades at her new sister.

"She is a lady," Margariete defended. "It is an honorary title for the assistance she has rendered to the royal family."

Katrina's face leaked merry amusement. "Oh, so it was an act of charity," she said, bright with innocence, "dressing up a commoner. Ladies, my beloved Prince Raeylan is so generous."

The Jeweled Princess remained silent as she contemplated a retort, loathing the pink-petaled creature that was marrying her brother.

"I used to pretend, too," she said to Esilwen, "when I was younger of course. Obviously, I didn't have to pretend to be a princess. Let's play along ladies. My father, His Majesty King Hylan, taught me to be to be kind to those less fortunate than myself. And when I am queen, I will expect you to follow my example."

Margariete held her breath and counted. She had promised her twin that she would observe decorum and treat his bride with respect, but the more Katrina talked, the more anger throbbed at the dark princess's temples. The Glass Princess pretended not to notice, placing a palm of reassurance on Margariete's leg.

"Don't worry my sister. Though that veil hides a terrible visage, I am sure that the time will come when Nehro blesses you with a man who does not care for beauty."

A low sound of encouragement came from the other ladies and Katrina turned to converse with them. Margariete refrained from returning the insult, reminding herself that she would bury her temper for her brother's sake.

It grew more difficult as the party continued.

Now that the Jeweled Princess had arrived, Katrina could receive her gifts. As the Glass Princess was showered with jewelry, gowns and other personal adornments, Katrina made sure to show the appropriate gratitude for each, though Margariete could tell her new sister was simply equating the expense of each gift into a measure of allegiance. The procedure was sickening to watch. Worse, for every compliment Katrina aimed at her new court ladies, the Glass Princess made sure to jab a sheathed insult at Esilwen. As the last sips of ritual tea were taken, Margariete found her patience spent.

"So tell us about your exodus, Princess Margariete," Katrina began pleasantly. "I hear it was quite the scandal."

The clinking teacups were clearly heard as the women fell silent. Only Margariete's sword training gave her the strength to keep her body from trembling with the force of fury that blazed to life at Katrina's offensive comment. She worded her response carefully, controlling the clench of her jaw.

"I don't believe that is your concern, Princess Katrina," she returned, leveling her sapphire eyes on the Glass Princess.

"Oh come now, Princess Margariete," Katrina said. "We have all heard of your flight from the castle. Tell us how you managed to slip past the guards unseen."

That was the last grain of rice in the cart. Margariete obliquely ignored Katrina and called to Seriya.

"I will be returning to my chambers," she said. "Have Rin and Lya draw my bath."

Disappointed whispers filled the room as the Jeweled Princess stood.

"How very selfish of you, Princess Margariete," Katrina accused. "Though this party was to be in my honor, I have been generous enough to share the attention with you. You dishonor us all by refusing to participate."

Margariete could feel the suppressed mockery circulating the room. She motioned for Esilwen to rise, fully aware of the offense that her early departure meant toward Princess Katrina. She decided the consequence would be worth it, as the alternative of staying would most definitely lead to some form of violence on Katrina's person.

"I guess it's not surprising," Katrina said sadly. "I heard you delight the defying propriety. There were rumors you dabble in skills that do no befit a lady, and that you openly ignore the edicts of your own father. I had given you the benefit of the doubt, knowing the vicious lies commoners often spread about their betters. Alas, I see I have been too magnanimous."

Katrina stood with an air of hurt dignity.

"As your new sister, soon to be Queen, I insist that you stay. However, your 'friend' must leave."

Disgust boiled Margariete's blood, accompanied by an alluring desire to strike the conceited Fourth Kingdom Princess across her heavily rouged cheek. Esilwen's light touch on the dark princess's arm, however, soothed the wild craving. Esilwen bowed graciously, as if nothing during the bridal party had caused offense, and apologized for leaving. Margariete opened her mind to her friend and drew strength from what she found there. Though Esilwen recognized Katrina's cruelty, the blond maid was in no way threatened by the Glass Princess's arrogance. Though still unsure of her place in this foreign kingdom, Esilwen's faith in her friends was absolute. Katrina could never undermine that.

Margariete returned to her kneeling cushion as Esilwen left. "My 'flight,'" she said to Katrina, "is nothing beyond Prince Raeylan's capabilities to handle. It would displease him for us to continue discussing it further."

The pronouncement floated through the air like the dust in Malbrin's library. The ladies looked on Katrina nervously. The Glass Princess quickly initiated a benign line of conversation. Katrina's smile never faltered, but Margariete could see into her sister's mind quite clearly as realization struck the soon-to-be-queen.

Katrina might be Raeylan's wife, but Margariete would always have his loyalty.

23: Measures Of The Future Queen

The royal family's private armory was located on the fifth floor of the castle, accessible only by a set of stairs on the top level, the royal apartments. Here, away from the demands of leadership, the Viridius family could enjoy a measure of privacy. Margariete was still required to enter in appropriate attire—cloth and lace concealing every feature but her eyes—even though the weapons chamber was only ten paces and a short stairwell's distance from her rooms. It hadn't always been so, but recently Katrina had taken to visiting the upper floors unannounced. Raeylan had cautioned his sister to take care that Princess Katrina never discover the true nature of Margariete's face.

Following closely behind Margariete were Esilwen and the only maid the princess genuinely trusted—Seriya. Though Rin and Lya had served Margariete for many seasons, their allegiance was to their kingdom, not to her. They kept their mistress's secret out of duty.

It hadn't taken Princess Katrina long to covet the skilled hands of Margariete's attendants, especially the gifted Seriya. Two cycles ago, without consulting anyone, the Fourth Kingdom's princess had conscripted all three into her own service.

Margariete strained her jaw at the recollection. It was just another shameful act that Katrina employed to assert her authority.

Instead of confronting Katrina directly, as the Glass Princess had probably intended, Margariete went straight to her twin. It took little to convince Raeylan that her handmaidens, who knew everything about the dark-haired, olive-toned member of the Viridius family, should remain at their former post. Though Seriya was ecstatic to come back to her lady, Rin and Lya returned with reluctance. Somewhere in the castle, Princess Katrina pouted, upset that her husband-to-be had supported his sister over his future wife.

The dispute had rewarded Margariete with an entire Katrina-free cycle.

In other matters, however, Margariete was less than successful. Before the incident with the ladies-in-waiting, Katrina had completely rearranged the inner workings of the castle to her liking. Servants rushed about in disarray, unsure of their new duties, with the realm's most important ceremony only three cycles away—the crown prince's coronation and wedding. Margariete was convinced that Katrina's meddling would plunge both events into a confused disaster.

Raeylan, however, seemed unconcerned. Whenever Margariete complained about the interference of his bride, he simply reminded Margariete that Katrina would soon occupy the throne next to him, and it was her duty to oversee the daily routines of the household.

The Jeweled Princess huffed indignantly as Seriya opened the heavy armory door. The scent of well-oiled steel and leather clung obstinately to anyone and everything that crossed the threshold, including the trio of women who stepped lightly into the chamber. Rows of spears and blades lined the wooden walls, bamboo bows and arrow shafts surrounded the door.

Had it really been only seven cycles since her brother's monster bride had invaded the castle? It was obvious that Margariete would never have peace again. If Katrina wasn't busily rearranging everything Anleia and Raeylan had previously established, the Glass Princess was stalking Margariete, purposely instigating episodes of camouflaged humiliation. Margariete even had to forgo the normal pleasure of removing her veil in her own quarters, as Katrina frequently entered without warning. Once Katrina had burst in so suddenly that the Jeweled Princess wondered if she had caught an accidental glimpse of dark hair. Katrina disappeared as suddenly as she arrived, before the telepath had a chance to read the invader's thoughts and confirm the suspicion.

Worse, was the constant attention Katrina required of the castle residents. She demanded a never ending barrage of social gatherings in her own honor, insisting Margariete attend each one: parlor parties, evening socials, and tea ceremonies.

The most infuriating offense, however, had occurred moments after Katrina's hideous bridal party. The future queen had practically swooned with distress when Margariete led the cluster of noblewomen into the hall where the wedding ball would take place. The Opal Ballroom had been Queen Anleia's favorite room—so naturally Katrina hated everything about it. With a copious amount of tears and hand-wringing, all charmingly displayed in view of the female gentry, she convinced them of the ballroom's inferiority. Later that cycle, she dictated a list of alterations for the castle workers to complete. No one seemed to care that the new specifications revolved around glass baubles and garish sculptures the new queen had conveniently brought with her—supposed gifts from her father to help her remember her homeland.

Margariete watched in despair as the elegant figurines of rosewood cranes and lovingly crafted lavender tapestries, some woven by Queen Anleia herself, were stripped from the walls, replaced by dreadful yellow smear and unrecognizable glass statuettes. For some reason, gargantuan mirrors were required to infinitely reflect the images of the ugly sculptures.

Only for love of her brother did Margariete bear the Glass Princess's vanity. Though these traits were commonplace in all of Thyella's aristocracy, the crown prince of the First Kingdom valued generosity and compassion. Margariete suffered for him, because she knew: Raeylan would never love Katrina.

Seriya lifted the heavy overcoat from Margariete's shoulders, and Esilwen removed the princess's veil with a friendly smile. After stripping several more layers of fabric off the princess's body, Seriya replaced the formal attire with the women's armor Raeylan had acquired in Timberdale. Esilwen aided wordlessly, assisting with the latches that ran the length of the leather girdle. Though she turned her lips kindly, little light touched Esilwen's eyes.

Esilwen endured far more punishment from Katrina's petty malice than the Jeweled Princess. The healer's closeness to Margariete automatically earned her Katrina's distaste. But Katrina's dislike exploded into outright jealous fury when Esilwen was granted access to the Royal Shrine in the central garden. Only direct members of the Viridius family were awarded that honor. Katrina herself would not be permitted on its hallowed ground until after her marriage. The Glass Princess made great show of her wounded pride in front of her favorite courtiers, then stormed into Raeylan's council chamber with a great amount of flair. Margariete didn't know how Katrina had broached the issue with Raeylan—most likely with transparent whining and complaint—but she looked thoroughly chastised when she left.

Since then, Katrina had taken pleasure in tormenting the gentle healer. Some of the Glass Princess's harsh insults even raised the brows of her fawning followers. Esilwen soon began taking refuge in the private shrine to avoid Katrina, as it was the one place the future queen could not find her.

Despite the malevolent treatment, Esilwen seemed to find strength deep within herself, tolerating Katrina's rudeness without disrespecting her tormenter in return. It amazed Margariete that anyone could be so serene. Even Raeylan sometimes lost his temper—no matter how quietly—once in a while.

But Esilwen's potential future in the City of Jewels worried Margariete. As of yet, Katrina was only a princess, controlling only partial authority of a promised position. That would soon change. Protecting Esilwen would become impossible. Margariete was at a loss. She had already discarded many scenarios in her mind, everything from relocating with Esilwen to the country, to hiding her in the thyella forest. Unfortunately, in every circumstance, Margariete would want to accompany her friend, but she knew her twin would never allow it.

The princess wished Terail was available to give advice, but he had left the cycle after they had returned from the border camp, seeking candidates to replenish the ranks of the Pearl Order. He wasn't expected to return until the morrow.

Unbidden, the memory of her evening interlude in the forest with the Pearl Daimyo triggered an unnatural flush to climb her cheeks. She hadn't spent much time with him since. Their only contact had been a few stolen smiles aimed in each other's direction, Margariete's hidden beneath her veil. The thought of Terail's touch sent her heart racing.

"Your sword, Your Highness?"

Seriya's voice brought her back into the armory. For eight cycles, *Stardawn* had been locked safely on the fifth floor. The sword seemed to be sulking in its confinement as Margariete grasped its sheath with both hands. She shook her head free of the silly notion.

Her first training session with Raeylan since their return to the city would begin in a few moments. She forced herself to relax as she fastened the weapon. Soon, the sweat of combat would wash away her troubles, or at least consume her attention long enough to forget them for a while. She would need her full concentration to avoid Raeylan's strikes with *Moonstone Retribution*. Margariete felt an equal surge of anticipation and dread at the prospect of practicing with her twin. His ability was far beyond her own.

"This is beautiful," Esilwen said in wonder, drawing Margariete's attention. Amidst the racks of weapons, wooden stands displayed armor from every period of Thyellan history. One set of armor captured Esilwen's gaze. Margariete moved to her friend's side, touching the crafted leather tenderly.

"It belonged to my mother," Margariete said fondly. "I only saw her wear it once. When I was seven, the bandits of Hitoshi attacked the villages along the base of the Sakuhra Mountains. Even though she wasn't able to fight, she accompanied the Pearl knights to put an end to the plundering."

Lavender lavished the tunic, gold thread hemming the collar and sleeves. Queen Anleia's armor draped across a polished wooden display, its soft leather corset dyed with a tint of crimson. Stylish designs were etched into its surface, silver fastenings and belts running horizontal across the waistline. The greaves sported similar characteristics, with the Viridius crest artfully painted on both. A pair of worn boots rested at the base of the stand.

"What was she like?" Esilwen asked softly.

"Like Raeylan, though not as serious," Margariete answered. The princess ran her fingers over the armor's shoulder guard. "But her kindness had no equal."

"She sounds wonderful."

"She was," Margariete said, abruptly dropping her hand.

Turning toward the door, the princess walked into the corridor that led to the practice room. Esilwen and Seriya's footsteps echoed after.

When they entered the training hall, Raeylan and Shikun were standing side by side, performing a weaponless training routine. Like a harmonized dance, the two brothers executed several hand-to-hand blocks and attacks, though Shikun was less graceful than his older sibling. When complete, they respectfully bowed to each other.

"Good, Shikun," Raeylan complimented, rewarding the princeling with a smile. "Though you must increase the force of your overhead strike. Don't forget, the strength comes from your body core."

As the crown prince turned his grey eyes to the trio of ladies, his smile dissolved into an emotionless mask.

"You are late, sister," he reprimanded.

Margariete answered with a plain nod. His gaze flicked across the princess's two companions, then back to his sister.

"I apologize, but I must ask that Lady Esilwen and your attendant leave. It is necessary to minimize distractions."

Astonishment grazed Margariete's expression. She knew that Esilwen had been looking forward to watching the training session all morning. Turning to her friend, Margariete noticed that Esilwen blinked quickly. With a small voice, Esilwen answered.

"As you wish, Your Highness."

Raeylan didn't even glance at her. He simply strode into the center of the practice hall.

Esilwen managed a sad smile and then turned to Shikun.

"Would you mind escorting me to the castle gardens?" she asked kindly. "I would like to see that rare flower you've told me about."

"Of course," Shikun answered, practically leaping with excitement. Esilwen, Seriya, and Shikun disappeared into the hallway.

"Let us begin," Raeylan announced, *Moonstone Retribution* singing from its sheath.

Margariete refused to draw *Stardawn*. Raeylan's conduct had been nearly cruel.

"What's wrong, Raeylan?" she asked.

"Begin," he repeated, dipping into a preparatory stance.

Margariete didn't move, other than to fold her arms tersely across her chest.

"Why are you ignoring Esilwen?" she accused acidly. "You haven't spoken to her since the border camp."

Raeylan lunged forward suddenly. Margariete barely managed to pull her weapon from its sheath in time to block. Though she knew he would never cause her actual damage, the force of his blow left her forearm numb. She spun, pressing an attack of her own. He parried easily.

"Answer me, Raeylan," she growled as their swords clanged together. "Why are you avoiding her?"

Raeylan swiped at her face, but as she dodged she realized it had only been a feint. The flat of his blade left a stinging bruise on her inner leg, just above the knee.

"She is not of our world. Until I know more about her, I will maintain my distance. Does that satisfy your curiosity?"

The princess winced as she stepped out of *Moonstone Retribution's* range. She lowered her weapon.

"You confuse my concern with curiosity," she clarified evenly. "You haven't behaved as yourself lately."

"Everything is fine," Raeylan answered impassively.

"If everything was fine, Raeylan," she spat irritably, "you wouldn't be marrying Katrina."

"Princess Katrina, Margariete," Raeylan corrected her tiredly. "Trust me, sister. I do what is best for the kingdom."

"So you admit you do not love her."

"That is not what I said. You assume too much."

Raeylan sprang to her side in an instant, wrapping his foot about her ankle. A swift tug sent her sprawling to the floor.

"Like now, when you believed our duel was in respite. You allow your heart to guide your every step, Margariete. That makes you reckless."

"I would rather be guided by my heart," Margariete argued.

Raeylan's expression remained unchanged—clearly he was not surprised by the news.

"Not everything has to be about duty," she argued.

"That is where you are mistaken, Margariete."

She rose to her feet, opening her mouth to disagree.

"Our time is short," Raeylan said, interrupting her. "I will not squander it in dispute."

Moonstone Retribution flew in her direction and Margariete abandoned her retort.

*

The moment Margariete reached the outer door of her chambers, she knew something was amiss. None of her maids knelt by the panel to open it. The throb of the purpling bruises on her body fled with a sudden rush of adrenaline. She reached into the rooms with her mind, searching for the cause.

Four people bustled about her apartments, one directing the movements of the others who were hauling objects around the room. Understanding hit her with seething rage. Margariete stormed through the sitting and dressing rooms, slamming the doors open as she went. Entering the bedchamber, she confronted the trespassers.

"What are you doing here?" she demanded through her veil.

The Fourth Kingdom Princess turned to her in innocent surprise, as if Margariete were the intruder, and not the other way around. Seriya, Rin, and Lya paused in the process of stacking wooden storage crates near the closet, the looks on their faces plainly conveying their uncertainty of whether they should continue their duties. From their actions, as well as their minds, Margariete discovered Katrina's orders: remove the Jeweled Princess's belongings to make room for the new queen. Katrina dared to bow politely, a coy smile turning her lips.

"Isn't it obvious, sister?" she replied sweetly.

"These are my private apartments," Margariete snapped. "You have no right to be here without my consent."

"On the contrary, Princess Margariete," Katrina cooed brightly. "These are the queen's apartments. They belong to me."

Fury spewed around Margariete, squeezing her lungs with its barbed tendrils. She took a step forward, spots dancing behind her eyes. Katrina's smug expression faltered. She obviously wondered how far she had pushed the Jeweled Princess. The future queen turned to the maids.

"I didn't say you were done," she scolded. "I want it finished."

"Get out!" Margariete ordered everyone in general.

With apologetic faces to Katrina, Rin and Lya obeyed, scuttling out of the room like whipped kittens. Seriya, however, glared emphatically at the Glass Princess before exiting. Noticing suddenly that she and Margariete were alone, Katrina appeared weak and frail. With the countenance of a wronged victim, she confronted Margariete.

"Now look what you've done," she complained with a fabricated sigh. "How am I supposed to get my things situated if I have no servants?"

"You are not the queen for another three cycles, Princess Katrina," Margariete said, emphasizing the title.

"Did you know that you smell terrible? What have you been doing?" Katrina proclaimed, waving her hand in front of her nose. Surveying Margariete's armored apparel she continued. "Ah, I overheard some servants discussing your—" she swished her hand dramatically as she seemed to search for the term "—sword-training. How unladylike. Your disrespect never seems to cease. First you belittle me at my bridal party, and now you refuse me my rightful position in the castle. The top floor of the castle is reserved for the king and queen alone."

Margariete struggled to suppress her temper. Feeding Katrina's malice would only hurt those she wished to protect—Esilwen and her brother. When the rushing of blood subsided in her ears, she countered Katrina's declaration.

"When you are queen, I will surrender these rooms. But for now, these are my apartments. You have overstepped your position. I demand that you leave."

Katrina feigned a sigh of humility, but was unable to produce another point of opposition.

"Of course," she said, gliding to the door. "But I will soon be your queen. It's time you showed me the proper respect that comes with my rank."

With that, Katrina stomped through the threshold with an offended flourish. Seriya and the other maids returned only when the Glass Princess was completely out of sight.

24: ECLIPSE OF REGRET

"I am pleased by your return, Terail," Raeylan said, looking up at his Pearl Daimyo.

"I'm glad to be free of my horse," the general responded with a tired chuckle. "I haven't slept in a proper bed for almost two fortnights."

Raeylan scanned the list of 30 names Terail had provided—all worthy men who received the daimyo's recommendation for testing. Each possessed strength in different areas, but none were completely ready for the Pearl Order.

"Good work, Terail," Raeylan stated, setting the list onto his large desk for later study. "I assume these men journey to the castle?"

"Half of them are already here, Your Highness."

Raeylan nodded his approval, noting the state of Terail's attire. Still garbed in travel-stained armor, the knight seemed out of place in the crown prince's pristine receiving chamber. The rugged appearance of his friend reminded Raeylan of the freedom of the road. He missed the autonomy it granted, even if the journey took him in the direction of more cursed beasts. The prince would gladly fight an entire army of the hideous creatures rather than spend time with another type of demon that now walked the Viridius Castle halls.

"Then I suggest you take your rest as soon as possible," Raeylan jested, "as Shikun and Margariete will be excited by your return."

"From what I've heard, you could use my help keeping them distracted," Terail offered.

Raeylan sought the view out the slatted window of his library—the same gargantuan portal that Margariete had used to escape the castle. The moon was nearing a full eclipse of the sun. The last strands of light reflected coral off the oily marshlands below the Seven Cascades. A perpetual thunder of water crashed below.

"Shikun accepts his duty without question," Raeylan said affectionately, "but Margariete struggles. Sometimes I envy her passion—though it leads her astray on occasion."

"You sacrifice much for your people, my prince."

Raeylan's mind unwillingly wandered to Esilwen. Banishing her eyes, he wondered—not for the first time in the past six cycles—if Nehro was testing him. To be facing such a wife as Princess Katrina, when Esilwen was right in front of him.

Yes, he agreed silently, his sacrifice was great.

"I do what I must," he answered. "As for my sister, the past few cycles have been difficult for her. She could use a diversion."

"As you command," Terail pledged with a polite nod.

"Thank you, Terail." Raeylan couldn't keep the fatigue from staining his voice. "You are a trustworthy warrior and friend."

"And not necessarily in that order," Terail said faithfully.

The general's black-and-scarlet armor creaked as he bowed and retreated from the chamber. Raeylan continued his pensive stare out the window.

Never before had he questioned his duty. Never before had he resented the sacrifice demanded by his station. He had decided to marry in his sister's place without hesitation, driven by the need to protect her. Raeylan had never been deluded into thinking he might be free to marry for love—his mother's union had taught him that—and he had always taken special care not to become too attached to any maiden of the court.

Esilwen complicated everything.

The temptation to relinquish reason and duty increased every cycle. Margariete was right. When officially king, he could dissolve the marriage treaty with the Fourth Kingdom if he so wished—but that would plunge his realm into war.

Tense with the disappointment of his own weakness, he turned from the window and approached a hidden panel on the chamber wall. A quick alignment of the wooden combination freed the locking mechanism, and the pane rotated open, revealing a secret tunnel. After lighting a small candle, he stepped into the musty corridor.

The secret passageways that connected the king and queen's apartments also led through the core of the castle to the Royal Shrine on the first floor. Raeylan had already determined that he would not reveal the tunnels to Katrina. It would be difficult enough to avoid her when she officially moved into the suite next to his. If she wanted to visit the private spring, she could use the main gate that separated the Royal Shrine from the rest of the garden.

He paused when the passage forked in two directions. The right led to the queen's chambers, the left continued to the stairs that led to the Jewel Shrine. Staring into the darkness of the queen's way, he pondered how he would deal with Katrina's presence in his life. Hopefully, her interest would remain focused on herself and her position, leaving any heirs to be raised without her damaging influence. He was determined to keep her vanity from tainting the future generation of Viridius sovereignty. Dealing with the selfish woman during social gatherings would also challenge his patience. Her incessant barrage of social intrigue was bound to erode his tolerance.

His real concern was for Esilwen's welfare. The blood relation of his twin allowed him to protect Margariete, but the blond maid by her side was not so fortunate. She couldn't remain in the castle—the mere sight of her stole the breath from his body—but neither could he send her away, a foreigner in a narrow-minded country. The only people Esilwen knew were in Viridius Castle, friends who loved and cared for her.

His only option was to appoint Esilwen a place in the aristocracy, awarding her a residence on the nobility tier of the city. Lessons with Malbrin would prevent any more accidental offenses like the one that occurred at Katrina's bridal party. The Glass Princess's objections to Esilwen's presence would be restricted. Margariete's right to keep a noble companion to entertain herself would overrule any of Katrina's protests.

Raeylan turned to the left, beginning the long walk down the stairs. The meek candle in his hand did little to combat the darkness, but he knew the path well. His boots crunched softly as they ground against the loose gravel at the bottom of the stairwell. Raising the candle to the blank wall before him, he searched for the trigger—installed by the first king of the Viridius line—that would open the portal into the shrine. As the stone noiselessly retreated into the ground, Raeylan stepped into the cool night.

Far above, the sky shone with a halo of coronal light, casting the shrine into soft hues of blue. Supple moss carpeted the ground, shrouded by a cloak of mist from the garden's central fountain. Cherry trees wept white blossoms around a small path of crushed granite, their limbs cradled by the comforting satin blooms of rosebushes. A trickling spring fed the kryystil fish pool, girded on both sides by the vines of the silver Starlight Flower—an uncommon plant that grew only by the sea. Its silky petals echoed the eclipselight.

Sitting at the water's edge was the blond maid whose presence caused so much conflict within him.

Her gentle fingers teased the crystal water of the spring, forming ripples that swelled across the pool's melancholy surface. A melody of gentle longing glided from Esilwen's lips, though the words were in a language the prince had never known. The sweetness in her voice captivated him. Raeylan's mind told him to retreat, but his rebellious feet carried him forward. Soon he stood but a single stride behind her.

As the lullaby reached its conclusion, Esilwen's head tipped sadly, spilling the golden locks of her hair forward. Raeylan struggled with himself, incapable of abandoning her, yet knowing he shouldn't stay. While he wrestled with indecision, Esilwen lifted a hand to wipe away the moisture that had collected under her eyes. She turned. When she saw him she stiffened.

"Prince Raeylan," she gasped, "I—"

Esilwen tried to rise too quickly. Noticing that her foot caught the hem of her gown, Raeylan leaned forward, catching her in his arms before her fall took her to the ground. Her body trembled at his touch, though he held her gently, as if a breath of wind might steal her from his grasp. She looked at him with eyes rimmed in grief.

"I didn't know you were here," she admitted, taking a step back and looking away. "If you wish, I will leave immediately."

Raeylan's arms dropped to his side. Her words stung him to the core, though he knew very well they sprang from his callous disregard for her.

"Your song," he asked quietly, "what was it about?"

"A woman who lost her faith," she answered timidly, drawing her hand across her ivory sleeve, "and the angel who took mortal form to save her. It's been circling my mind since I went into Nehro's temple, but I don't remember where I learned it."

Another tear drifted to her cheek, and Raeylan stepped forward, brushing it away with his bare thumb. He cradled her cheek with his palm, savoring the sight of her lovely face. She met his gaze, drawing him closer with her beautiful green eyes.

Duty and propriety were forgotten. The arcs he had wasted with Katrina dispelled into vapor—for him, the only thing that existed was the precious maiden in front of him. He touched her lips softly with his own, the melody of her song bleeding into his soul. Forever his heart would be hers.

But his life would belong to Katrina.

Stony reality forced him away, though his hand refused the command to release Esilwen's cheek. Regret scorched his chest, and for a moment he couldn't breathe for the pain.

A poorly masked crunch of gravel wrenched his attention back to the garden's entrance. Obligation returned to him like a knife in the flesh. His sister stood in the threshold of the secret opening, staring at them with her mouth agape.

For an instant, the only sound in the garden was the rustle of leaves and the gurgle of falling water. Then the prince tore himself away from the only woman he had ever loved, trampling the moss as he marched through the main gate. Raeylan welcomed the mournful wail of the nightingale floor as he made his way out the front doors of the castle.

25: In The Practice Room

Margariete lashed at the wooden practice dummy. The common blade she wielded felt clumsy in her hand, far inferior to the smooth balance of *Stardawn*. Unfortunately, her enchanted sword would have destroyed the training manikin. Every time she attacked, the wooden construct's face turned into Katrina, making Margariete's thrusts and slices that much more vehement. Therefore, the princess had to settle for an ordinary sword from the royal armory that connected to Raeylan's personal training room.

"If I didn't know any better," a familiar voice said from behind, "I would say something's upset you."

Margariete whipped around. Terail leaned against the wall. Her already excited pulse throbbed faster. With more than a little aggravation, the princess wondered why she hadn't sensed the displacement of air vibrations caused by his arrival. Had her anger somehow inhibited her ability?

"How long have you been there?" she demanded, still startled.

"Long enough to notice your temper's been loosed," he responded. Glancing at her weapon he continued. "You've improved."

"You have a talent for false flattery," she returned, turning back to the dummy to hide the flush his compliment produced. "I've only trained with Raeylan twice. Hardly enough time to amplify my skills."

"You underestimate yourself, princess."

"How very considerate, but I expect your compassion has some ulterior motive," Margariete accused.

Terail laughed.

"Why do you think any compliment I give you is a disguise for something underhanded?"

Margariete smiled, glad for his company, but feeling a lingering guilt. Terail's return was not as joyous as she expected. It felt unfair, indulging in his presence when Raeylan and Esilwen were forced apart.

"Have you seen my brother this morning?" she asked, diverting the conversation.

"Yes, we just ended council."

"I tried to speak to him," Margariete grumbled, "but he refused me entry to his office."

"Really?" Terail teased. "Maybe he wasn't prepared for you. It's unusual for you to be up so early. Whatever you wanted to discuss must have been important."

"Don't mock me, Terail," Margariete said, throwing her wrath his direction.

"Why unleash your anger on me?" Terail asked raising his hands in defense. "I'm not the one who tried to evict you from your own quarters."

Margariete's anger deflated, remorse washing over her with cold fingers.

"Forgive me," she apologized.

Terail let out a low whistle.

"This Princess Katrina must really irritate you, if you're willing to apologize so easily."

Margariete's hatred flared.

"She's a fiend from the Void," she spat.

"Ah," he said, pushing away from the wall and approaching her nonchalantly, "not a pleasing choice for your brother?"

"No," Margariete answered, lowering her eyes. "He loves someone else."

"Really?" Terail wondered, slowing his pace as he drew nearer. "How do you know?"

Margariete quietly explained what she had seen in the shrine the night before. When she looked up, Terail looked surprised.

"That is a problem," he said as he reached her.

Margariete hurled her weapon to the floor, clutching her arms about her body dejectedly.

"I want his happiness, Terail. But as long as Esilwen is here, I fear they will both live in agony."

Terail stared at her, pondering for a moment before speaking. "Is there nowhere else she can go?"

Margariete shrugged hopelessly.

"Then what does His Highness plan to do?"

"I don't know," said Margariete, shifting uncomfortably. Terail's closeness both calmed and flustered her. "As I said, he refuses to speak with me."

Terail's eyes narrowed with sudden thought.

"You're not thinking of trying to stop the wedding?" he charged.

"I will if I have to."

"It won't work, Margariete," Terail promised, shaking his head. "Prince Raeylan has signed a treaty. No matter how much he might care for another woman, breaking that treaty would lead to war."

"I don't care," Margariete said defiantly.

Terail's eyebrows rose. "But the families who are forced to grieve their men will."

Margariete sagged in defeat as she stepped forward and laid her head on Terail's chest. His arms wrapped protectively around her.

"Your brother surrendered himself to protect you and his kingdom," Terail murmured softly into her hair.

Margariete looked up at him, a guilty wave gnawing at her insides. How could she have a relationship with Terail, when the people she loved were suffering?

"Prince Raeylan would not want you to yield your own happiness on his behalf, Margariete," he said, reading the remorse in her sapphire eyes.

He bent his mouth to hers, kissing her deeply.

Margariete gave in to his advance, her jumbled emotions kindling her passion. Terail was right, but she couldn't simply brush away the misery of Raeylan's sacrifice, no matter how intoxicating Terail's embrace might be.

26: SCROLLS FROM THE PAST

"Please, kneel," Malbrin instructed, indicating a floor cushion with a wave of his hand.

Esilwen obeyed, wondering why the wrinkled mentor had summoned her to his library. Malbrin settled opposite her, a short table between them. Six scrolls of various sizes caught her eye. They were stacked neatly in a row, each wrapped tightly about a painted rod. No two were exactly alike in composition. One was definitely slatted thyella bamboo, woven together with string, and another looked to be some kind of treated animal hide. One was a torn piece of fabric. The other three were varying types of parchment, though foreign to anything Esilwen had seen Margariete use. All looked worn by age, their edges yellowed and cracked. Next to the scrolls sat a plain wooden box.

"Here," Malbrin said pushing the small receptacle toward her, "a gift from the royal family."

Esilwen accepted hesitantly. Malbrin watched with a shimmer of fatherly eagerness in his eyes as she lifted the lid with trembling fingertips. She exhaled a small gasp. Inside was an elbow-length glove, its silky fabric the same shade as her eyes. Delicate silver buttons ran from the wrist to forearm. Lightly embroidered flowers of lavender gold wrapped across the material's surface. She lifted the gift from its cradle and looked quizzically at the aged tutor.

"A signet glove?" she asked.

"Prince Raeylan has bestowed upon you the official title of 'Lady,'" he answered pleasantly. "You are now a citizen of the First Kingdom."

Malbrin looked away politely.

"Please, put it on."

Esilwen pulled the cool silk onto her arm and fastened the buttons.

"Why would he do such a thing?"

"For your protection, My Lady," Malbrin said, turning back. "I think we are all concerned by Princess Katrina's public displays of animosity. She will now have to be more careful. Remember," he added, "you can never take it off in front of anyone."

Esilwen nodded, the memory of her interlude with Raeylan in the Royal Shrine causing her chest to ache. There was more to this gesture than Malbrin knew. The prince's stolen kiss had taken a portion of her soul with it, robbing her of cheerfulness. The thought of Raeylan's impending marriage was now even harder to bear. The moment had torn away the denial she had used to disguise her own feelings. She was grateful for the signet glove he had given her, but during the sleepless, early half of dawn she had reached a decision. Raeylan valued his kingdom above all else, and Esilwen knew her presence was damaging his resolve.

The only choice was to leave.

"I heard that something very intriguing happened to you when you entered the Temple of Nehro," Malbrin said, trying to regain her attention.

"Yes," she admitted.

"Tell me, have you shared the details of what happened with anyone? Our Jeweled Princess perhaps?"

Esilwen hesitated. If she answered Malbrin truthfully, the clever mentor might pressure her for further information. The healer had kept her strange visions to herself, both to keep her friend from unnecessary worry— Katrina's arrival was frustration enough—and because Esilwen feared what the images meant. Were they memories? Prophecies?

"I just fainted," she fibbed quickly.

"Disease and dishonestly often have the same effect," Malbrin responded, obviously unconvinced. "They make us feel weak, and eat away at the inner self."

Malbrin smiled encouragingly. He had already guessed that there was more to her swoon in Nehro's temple. Perhaps the kindly tutor could make sense of her experience. She pushed her apprehension away and dropped her gaze to her hands, the sight of her new glove giving her strength.

"I saw things," she confessed. "But I didn't understand them."

"Maybe if you explain them to me," he suggested, "we might be able to cure you of confusion."

"They came so quickly. I barely remember them. But they all end the same way." She swallowed, dropping her voice to a fearful whisper. "Four different visions, and in all of them, I die."

She looked up at Malbrin, expecting disbelief, but Malbrin studied her shrewdly.

"They aren't visions, Lady Esilwen," Malbrin answered calmly. "They are fragments of your memories."

"How is that possible? A person can die only once."

Malbrin chuckled with his leathery voice. "Have you ever heard of Shardwell magic, My Lady?"

Esilwen shook her head. Malbrin lifted a scroll, the first in the row, and unrolled the slatted bamboo gently. The wood made clicking pops as he did so.

"This is very old," he explained, "and carries much knowledge about our patron goddess, including descriptions of her Wells of power. Almost a thousand seasons ago, Thyella was part of a much larger land; only one in a collection of worlds. This collection was so large, it was believed no one could reach its end in the span of his lifetime. Here, there were fountains of magic, called 'Wells.' They connected us to the gods."

"I don't understand how this relates to me."

Malbrin chose another scroll, this one of brittle parchment, and offered it to Esilwen. She opened it tentatively, afraid it might crumble in her fingers. The inked outline of a golden bird, its talons clamped around a goblet, decorated the upper margin of the scroll. The scarlet eyes reminded her of the icon she had seen in her vision the cycle that she fainted in Nehro's temple. Tiny crimson letters marched across the parchment's surface.

"Read it aloud," Malbrin prompted.

"One hundred and eighteen years have passed since the Fracturing," Esilwen read, automatically equating the term "years" with the Thyellan measurement of "seasons." "The armies of Skoh corrupt our land, razing anything that is not of their dark goddess, though the Mistress of the Void herself is long destroyed. To protect our people from annihilation, Calmic, our sovereign, has taken upon himself the Blood of Fohtian. The power of the Phoenix Angel burns within him. Neither death nor injury hinders him, and fire itself obeys his will."

Esilwen's hands shook as she read. The story sounded familiar. She continued to read the words on the scroll. Calmic, the last true Paladin of Fohtian, battled the servants of Skoh, purging their foul race from the fire god's realm. With his quest complete, he returned Fohtian's Blood to The Chalice and the holy artifact freed his soul from eternal life.

She set the scroll on the table when she finished. "You knew who I was all along," she said, still looking at the ancient parchment, "didn't you?"

"I had suspicions, nothing more," Malbrin answered. "I knew only that this scroll recounted the legend of Calmic. I cannot read it. Only Nehro's scroll," he pointed to the slatted bamboo document, "is written in the Thyellan tongue. The rest of these are in languages I do not understand."

Esilwen glanced at him with a measure of surprise. "Then how was I able to read it?"

"I believe that you are now the carrier of Fohtian's Blood, just like the knight in the story. If what I have learned from my research is correct, the god's power allows you to comprehend any language. It is a gift given to all artifact bearers."

"Artifacts?"

"Even to learned scholars, the details of the Fracturing are still a mystery, but when the gods warred amongst themselves, they shattered the universe into isolated realms that we call 'shards.' Though the gods disappeared around the same time, each left a relic retaining the remnants of their powers—the deity's 'essence' you might say. I presume you have already heard of the one Prince Raeylan bears? The Glove of Nehro? Her power blesses the Viridius line."

"Then can he understand any language as well?" Esilwen wondered.

"As I said," the tutor repeated.

The blonde turned her face quickly to hide a sudden wave of bewilderment that rose to her face. Malbrin was the second person to tell her that the crown prince wore The Glove. Margariete had been the first. But just last night, Raeylan had asked Esilwen to translate the words to the song she had been singing in the private spring. If the prince indeed bore the water goddess's artifact, he should have known the song's meaning.

Someone was lying.

"The Wells are important to your story," Malbrin was saying, "because after the Fracturing they were left untended."

"I don't understand," Esilwen said anxiously—she had lost the thread of Malbrin's explanation. "Are you implying that I'm a Well of power?"

"No—you are something more. The Wells are merely conduits that bridge the planes of magic with our own. A person may partake of this Well and perform feats of power specific to a god's domain. You, on the other hand, embody what is left of Fohtian himself.

"Once the gods controlled the Wells, but now, only two things can influence them: one is a celestial servant of a god, but most of them are gone—lost or destroyed. The other is the bearer of an artifact."

Esilwen dimly recalled the first image in her vision, the golden bird with its crimson eyes. Something had shattered, but the rest was lost in a blur of fire. She repeated as much to the wrinkled mentor.

"But how do you know I carry Fohtian's artifact?" she posed. "I don't remember—"

"You don't remember because of The Chalice," Malbrin interrupted, "the crystal goblet that holds Fohtian's Blood. By drinking it, you were reborn through holy fire. This is why the fire god is named the Phoenix Angel. The process burns away your memories. From what I've researched, when your quest is complete you are supposed to return the god's power to The Chalice. But you said you saw it destroyed in your visions?"

Esilwen nodded.

"Then I have no more answers for you, My Lady. Nothing in my reading explains what might happen if Fohtian's Chalice was irreparably damaged. There are only warnings that it be kept safe. Others have used Fohtian's powers, like Calmic, without crossing the boundaries between worlds."

Esilwen sighed. More mysteries.

"How do you know so much about Fohtian and his artifact if you can't read his scroll?"

"How I know doesn't matter," he stated offhandedly. "More importantly, we need to discover why you came through the shardgate and why you appeared to Princess Margariete specifically. Perhaps it was random circumstance, but it is too serendipitous to be coincidence. Maybe the artifact sent you to her purposefully, knowing the protection our Jeweled Princess would give you. Another possibility is that a shardgate was near the princess's campsite. No one knows for sure just how the shardwalls separate reality, only that they contain multiple openings. These, however, are impossible to locate or unlock."

"If no one has ever found one, then how do you know they even exist?"

"Because you sit before me, Lady Esilwen," he stated with a wise smile, "and you are most definitely a stranger to our shard."

"Everything seems so complicated to me," Esilwen said, overwhelmed.

For cycles she had wondered about her past, but the more answers she found, the more tangled her existence seemed to become. Malbrin was silent for the passing of an entire quarter arc.

"When I first discovered these truths," he said finally, his gaze buried in the myriad shelves of scrolls and parchment lining the room, "about magic, the gods, and the nature of worlds, I found it difficult to measure the value of my life. Like every other Thyellan, I have lived to serve the crown, misguidedly believing my country to be the center of all things, my culture and beliefs the only correct way of living. My loyalty even helped to destroy an entire kingdom. That is what it means to be Thyellan. Duty first, everything else second."

Malbrin paused, then turned to Esilwen.

"But the vastness of the truth—its depth and history—overshadows anything I have seen or done. My influence on past or future will be inconsequential compared to your own, Lady Esilwen. To be granted Fohtian's power is no small gift. Your destiny may very well determine the fortunes of all the Thyellan people."

"And what if I don't want this responsibility?" she asked.

"Like the rest of us, My Lady," he said, "you may not have a choice."

27: Ceremony In The Swan Hall

As far as Katrina was concerned, the legendary splendor of the City of Jewels was exaggerated. She couldn't deny that it was beautiful, or that the sunlight dancing through the Seven Cascades' vapor was fascinating, but the First Kingdom's capital seemed dreary and flat compared to the exquisite architecture that graced her home. And though the rivers somewhat improved the view from Viridius Castle, Katrina detested the marshlands that spoiled the landscape below the falls. She desperately missed the misty glow of the sea, the midcycle tide capped with white foam as the waves stroked the sandy beaches of her homeland.

She would have to bear it, generously suffering the pangs of homesickness for the benefit of her people. Though she would sacrifice some of her usual comforts—Kotrell Castle was a sprawling complex of open buildings and cozy luxury compared to this stuffy fortress—she consoled herself with uplifting thoughts of the envy her sisters felt, now that Katrina was soon to be queen of the most powerful kingdom in the shard. None of her sisters had managed more than an ordinary noble marriage, the most prestigious to a duke. Prince Raeylan, the most influential royal heir in Thyella, would be hers in a cycle's time. Then she would have everything she had ever dreamed—all before she reached 17 seasons.

Still, her arrival hadn't started out exactly as she had imagined. In her own kingdom, she was the most sought-after maiden of age. She never failed to captivate a young nobleman with her beauty. They showered her with courting gifts, each hoping she would accept his offer of pursuit. Katrina had expected her groom to be just as fascinated.

But Prince Raeylan had barely spoken to her and sent her no engagement tokens.

To make matters worse, Katrina had endured tremendous maltreatment from her soon-to-be sister, that horrible Princess Margariete. The veiled troll had been nothing but rude to Katrina since the Glass Princess's arrival, even though Katrina had tried her hardest to befriend her. But nothing was enough—Margariete was determined to dishonor Katrina in every way.

First, the Jeweled Princess had invited that wretched peasant, Esilwen, to the bridal party. And when the lowly commoner had broken protocol in front of the gentry, purposefully embarrassing Katrina, Margariete had failed to berate Esilwen for the propriety breech. Then, the Jeweled monster had complained when Katrina exercised her right to rearrange the household servants—her new sister self-importantly demanding the best handmaidens for herself. Margariete had even managed to turn Prince Raeylan against Katrina on the matter. And finally, the utmost disrespect: Princess Margariete had refused to vacate the queen's apartments until the last possible moment, hoarding the most impressive chambers in the castle, while Katrina's wardrobe gathered dust and wrinkles from its overlong stay in the abysmally cramped guest quarters.

Really, who could be expected to live in a miserly domicile of two antechambers and a closet that was only half the size of the bedroom? Katrina could barely contain the shame.

But the most horrific part of her first week in her new home had come with the discovery that even when joined with Prince Raeylan, Katrina would not supersede Margariete's political position. Before coming to this realization, the Glass Princess had believed that upon marriage, she would be the most important woman in the First and Fourth Kingdoms. But until she conceived an heir, that awful Margariete would be equal to Katrina's social standing, and could even claim the throne if something unforeseen happened to Prince Raeylan before Katrina bore his child.

That was ridiculous. She was going to be queen for Nehro's sake!

So, Katrina decided she would have to defeat the conceited Margariete on the Glass Princesses terms. Since she would be unable to outrank the Jeweled Princess for the time being—long enough for an heir to be born and survive well into its fifth season or so—Katrina would win the loyalty of the local aristocracy, gaining favor with those whose social status might be of value. This would compensate for the intrigue that followed Margariete's steps. All wanted to know what lay concealed underneath that veil.

The native princess's reluctance to attend social gatherings would work to Katrina's advantage. It had been easy enough to spread the rumor that her rival hid a ghastly disfigurement. As queen, Katrina would make it clear that the only opportunity for social advancement would be within her inner circle of supporters. Just this morning, three of the more prominent ladies of the court, each feeling insulted by a previous exchange with Princess Margariete, had quickly joined Katrina's cause.

This was the first indication that things had finally turned in Katrina's favor. The second, to her delight, came in the form of an unexpected invitation from Prince Raeylan, requesting her company for a midmorning stroll. Luckily, she had been preparing for an outing with her new friends and was already finely dressed for display in an off-the-shoulder lavender gown, a current fashion in her own kingdom. Katrina wondered why the nobility of the First Kingdom still insisted on layered robes and corsets. She mentally noted to add that to her list of household improvement.

When the appointed arc arrived for her interlude with the prince, Katrina rushed from her quarters to meet him. Though Raeylan's demeanor was stiffly formal, he offered his arm politely. Giddy with excitement, she accepted gracefully, allowing her cheeks to blush prettily—which she knew would accent the ivory cream of her neck and shoulders. He escorted her away from the guest chambers, toward the fourth-level balcony that overlooked the central garden. The prince asked after her state of wellbeing and whether she was satisfied with her new home. She answered every question with proper enthusiasm as they walked, forming inquiries of her own.

What she learned quickly quashed her exhilaration.

Not once did he comment on how the sunlight highlighted her golden hair or how her new dress brought out the pale loveliness of her eyes. There were no promises of undying adoration, no vows pledging his devotion to fulfill her every desire. In fact, he didn't offer any flattery at all. His conversation painted him dull—always referring to the state of his kingdom or some other boring aspect of duty.

"I hope the Opal Ballroom has been altered to your satisfaction," Raeylan mentioned, grasping the wooden balcony railing with his signet glove hand. He glanced at her.

"Yes, it is perfect. The improvements remind me of home," she said with a flutter of her eyelashes.

The gesture didn't affect him, however. He turned back to the garden. Katrina pursed her lips petulantly, thoroughly displeased.

"Good. I hoped it would help you feel more comfortable here," he said.

"Oh yes," she returned. "I must say, the magnificence of Castle Viridius has me stunned. I don't imagine I shall ever tire of it. There is always something spectacular to captivate my gaze."

Katrina had led him into the perfect opportunity for a compliment—something like "The only thing that captivates me is your remarkable beauty" or "The castle's splendors pale compared to you," but the prince remained silent. He hadn't even responded with a nod, an annoying quirk that indicated his attentiveness to the conversation. She did notice a sudden tightening of his muscles. Wondering crossly what had distracted him, she followed his gaze.

He wasn't staring into the garden. Across the opening, on the opposite side of the castle, the fabric draped figure of Princess Margariete strolled away from the library. The pensive footsteps of Esilwen followed, Prince Shikun at her side. The young princeling chatted amicably to her and she returned his attentions with a frail smile, but ultimately her head tilted toward the floor. After a few moments, Esilwen lifted her eyes, almost as if she felt someone watching her, and looked across the balcony with eyes streaked in sorrow.

Then Esilwen paused, absently raising her arm to brush stray threads of hair away from her face. Katrina gaped in surprise, utterly flabbergasted. A green signet glove encased the loathsome maiden's arm! Since when was it permissible for a peasant to wear a glove of rank? Esilwen hadn't been wearing it the cycle before, Katrina was sure.

This was completely unacceptable! Katrina turned to her betrothed, preparing an objection, but the words slid back down her throat unuttered.

Katrina didn't like the way Esilwen was looking at Raeylan, but she was especially piqued by the way Raeylan was looking back.

Jealousy scraped the Glass Princess's heart into needles. Knives of envy severed her pleasant expression. How could Prince Raeylan drown Margariete's vile friend with generosity—granting her special privileges reserved only for the royal Viridius line, bending the rules of protocol to give her a title—when he had yet to present a single courtship gift to Katrina herself? By the Void, what made the dreadful girl so important?

Realization cut Katrina so quickly that her fingers grew cold. Of course—he must have taken the filthy peasant as a concubine. Why else would a prince lavish attention on someone of such base birth? Esilwen must have earned her favor through Raeylan's bed.

The Glass Princess was no fool. As soon as her marriage was consummated, she would have Esilwen turned out of the castle for harlotry.

Across the way, the Jeweled Princess took Esilwen by the arm and hastily led her away. Katrina was certain Margariete noticed the animosity breeding on her—Katrina's—face. Raeylan turned back to his bride immediately.

"May I escort you back to you quarters, Princess Katrina?" he inquired politely. His eyes were impassive. "The cleansing ceremony is scheduled to begin two arcs from now."

Like a perfect lady, Katrina masked her displeasure with a courteous bow.

"I would like that very much, Your Highness."

*

Princess Katrina entered the Swan Banquet Hall on the arm of her father, a polished smile gleaming at her lips. Tiny flowers embellished the glass and silver hairpins trimming her flawless upsweep, all delicately blown to resemble seashells. Two hundred nobles stood in neat lines bordering the room, dipping their heads in homage. All admired the Glass Princess as she entered, but that was to be expected. A small fortune had been spent on her cleansing gown. The white frock swelled about her knees and ankles like the tips of ocean waves. Minuscule glass sea creatures clinked musically at her wrist and collar. Real seaflowers in full blossom crossed from her shoulder to her waist, their crimpled aqua petals cascading the rest of the way to the hem.

Her attire's only blemish was the plain, unadorned signet glove she wore. Custom dictated that she show proper humility and gratitude for her goddess during the ceremony, symbolized by a simple mark of station. She reminded herself that she only had to endure the thing for a short time, and found comfort in the thought of the glove she had requisitioned for her marriage ceremony. It had cost more than the cleansing dress.

King Hylan led her to the end of the rectangular chamber where a long table waited. Princess Katrina surveyed the figures kneeling behind it. His Majesty King Arahm—the only sensible member of the Viridius family—

had chosen a place as far away from his wayward daughter as possible. Prince Shikun, who seemed so enamored with Katrina's beauty that he hadn't spoken to her even once, perched next to his sister.

Margariete hadn't managed to dress in anything more splendid than her usual finery. Katrina's smile wavered only briefly as her gaze flashed across Margariete's insubordinate sapphire eyes. Prince Raeylan, magnificent in his kingly white cleansing robe, remained motionless, his grey eyes characteristically expressionless. Katrina was pleased to note that the Jeweled Princess's fraudulent friend was nowhere within sight.

The Pearl knights stood at attention behind the royal family, the Pearl Daimyo in the center, decked in glorious ceremonial armor.

Inwardly, Katrina huffed. Terail Dasklos was just as offensive as Esilwen—another commoner masquerading as a noble. The First Kingdom was grossly negligent in their separation of the social classes. Her prince's attachments to family and friends weakened the proper order of things. As queen, she would have much to correct.

When Katrina reached the table, escorted by her father, the royals of the First Kingdom rose to their feet in respect. All parties exchanged bows. Prince Raeylan circumvented the table and moved to Katrina's side. King Hylan kissed his daughter's cheeks, his eyes wet with pride. Raeylan then took her hand as the Fourth Kingdom's monarch retreated behind the table. The rest of the assembly bowed as one. Katrina nearly fainted with gratification.

The doors to the hall opened again, allowing a group of holy men to stream into the room. The monks of the Grand Temple of Nehro were dressed in bald blue robes for the occasion, their necks roped with jade and opal beads. Their leader carried a silver tray, which he set on the ground as he reached the betrothed couple. The glossy platter held two shallow drinking vessels and a fired clay bottle. As his companions chanted a holy prayer to the water goddess, the monks prayed for Nehro to bless the union.

When the chanting finally came to an end—Katrina thought it abysmally overdone—the cleric poured a clear liquid into the small cups. The first was offered to Prince Raeylan, a show of respect for the greater might of his kingdom. Katrina received the second. After a ritual bow, the royal pair lifted the bowls to their lips, consuming the rice wine in a single swallow. The alcohol burned Katrina's throat as she drank, though she forced herself not to cough. Any disruption in the ceremony was considered bad luck for her marriage. As was proper, Katrina waited to return her cup to the monk until after the prince's was safely back on the tray.

Then the monks swept from the chamber. Servants entered wielding bowls steaming with rice. As each member of the aristocracy received a dish, other servants— the very three Margariete hadn't been willing to share— erected a small table in the center of the room. They dressed the table with two empty ceramic bowls bearing the lavender fan and white jasmine crest of the Viridius dynasty.

Katrina was then led by one of the handmaidens to a raised dais in the right corner of the room, the platform designed to keep her kneeling body level with the eyes of the standing gentry. Raeylan occupied a similar podium on the left. When both the bride and groom were settled, the emissaries of the ceremony—Prince Shikun and Princess Margariete—took their places beside the newly delivered table.

The pledging ritual then began.

Each noble approached the emissary's table. After kneeling, the aristocrat deposited a single grain of rice from his bowl into the empty one in front of the emissary. The women offered their pledge into Margariete's bowl, the men into Shikun's. The procession began with those of lowest social rank, moving upward to the gentry of higher political importance.

Katrina waited impatiently during the three quarter arcs that passed as the nobles presented the symbol of their allegiance. Every so often she would peek shyly at her groom, but Prince Raeylan showed no outward signs of discomfort. Not once did he turn his eyes in her direction. Grumpily, she returned her attention to the monotonous ceremony.

The Glass Princess silently blessed the water goddess when the rite was at last complete, and the two emissaries gracefully lifted the now-filled bowls. Shikun walked toward Raeylan, while Margariete approached Katrina. The Jeweled Princess knelt as tradition required.

"You finally show me proper respect, Princess Margariete," Katrina whispered, low enough so no one could overhear.

The Jeweled Princess rose without reply, though her eyes smoldered with resentment. She clenched the bowl in both of her hands and turned to face her brother, who would partake of his rice first. Katrina couldn't suppress a triumphant smile.

"Tomorrow, I am your queen, and I will see to it that your outrageous behavior comes to an end—including the inappropriate attention you waste on that disgusting commoner of yours."

Shikun passed the rice bowl to the prince with both hands. Margariete tilted her head.

"I don't know what you mean."

"It's quite clear, sister. Your brother belongs to me. I refuse to share him with anyone, especially Esilwen."

"Lady Esilwen," Margariete corrected harshly, loud enough that several courtiers looked at them disapprovingly.

"Still upholding that pretense are we? She wears a glove, but I notice she's not in attendance this cycle. It's mandatory for all *real* nobility, not whores given titles for their exploits in the bedroom."

Katrina was first aware of loud crack as the rice bowl smashed against the tiled floor. Margariete turned so quickly that the Glass Princess barely registered the movement. The next thing Katrina knew, a blurry streak of crimson struck her cheek so hard she was knocked from her perch on the cushioned dais.

Gasps filled the room when Princess Katrina tumbled ungracefully to the floor. Margariete raised her scarlet fist in preparation of a second strike. Fear rushed into Katrina's head, causing her knees to tremble as she looked up at her veiled assailant. But before the Jeweled Princess managed another attack, the Pearl Daimyo yanked her backward. Prince Raeylan arrived an instant later.

"Take Margariete to her room and keep her there," the prince barked. Katrina noticed that Margariete wilted under Raeylan's dark glare. Lord Terail whisked her from the Swan Banquet Hall as tears of loathing teemed down Katrina's face.

28: JUNCTURE OF REVELATION

Margariete twisted her fingers nervously as she waited in her bed chamber. She had paced the room for nearly two arcs, anxiously awaiting the summons of her twin. At first, the princess had frothed with the innumerable insults she longed to heap on Katrina's self-important head. But as the sky through her window turned to dusk and the guards still attended her door, her temper transformed into self-recrimination.

Hostility between herself and Katrina in private was risky, but was at least restricted by rumor. The assembled host of nobility who witnessed Margariete's breech of decorum would expect to see consequences.

The ceremony must have continued after her expulsion. Her cooling fury was quickly replaced with the dread of Raeylan's imminent visit. She wished he had confronted her immediately so she could use her rage as a shield.

She gazed around her chambers, her home since the seasons following her mother's death, knowing this was the last night they would be hers. Tomorrow she would vacate the rooms to make way for Katrina. Somewhere in the unconscious part of her mind, Margariete had hoped that Raeylan would abandon the treaty, yielding to his love for

Esilwen. But with the cleansing ritual complete, the walls protecting that hope tumbled into rubble. The following cycle, the 18th anniversary of their birth, Raeylan would be officially recognized as the First Kingdom's sovereign. He would marry in the evening.

Margariete bit her lip. Katrina's threat had been sincere. Though the Glass Princess was mistaken about the nature of Esilwen and Raeylan's relationship, the new queen had somehow discovered the prince's affection for Margariete's friend. Katrina would never relent until Esilwen was gone.

The Jeweled Princess wasn't surprised when Seriya entered the room. Margariete sensed the maid's approach as clearly as if the walls were made of glass.

"Your Highness," she addressed with a proper bow of respect, "Prince Raeylan has requested your attendance in the office within his living quarters."

Margariete's mind registered the waves of air that suggested the guards had finally left their post. She felt their vibrations as they disappeared down the spiral staircase. Reaching up, she liberated her face from the confining veil and tossed it to her attendant. Margariete's abilities confirmed that Raeylan was the only other presence on the castle's top floor, making the veil unnecessary.

The short trek to the king's rooms was loud with the uneasy beats of her heart. Seriya followed closely behind. When they reached the door, Margariete turned to her servant.

"I must go in alone," she instructed, wresting for control over her voice. "Please look after Lady Esilwen. I believe she is still in Malbrin's study. He provided her with some scrolls to read earlier this cycle."

"I fear for you, Your Highness."

Margariete's eyes fell to the floor. Seriya's thoughts betrayed her devotion plainly.

"I have acted rashly," the princess stated, "and must bear the penalty. My brother will protect me as much as he may."

Seriya, unconvinced, bowed and vanished into the stairwell. With a steadying breath, Margariete faced the elegant doors that sheltered her twin's apartments. She slid them open noisily as she entered so that Raeylan would be alerted to her approach. The two antechambers leading to his library slipped away quickly, like the last moments of a condemned prisoner who faced execution.

When she reached the threshold, her courage failed. Raeylan leaned against his desk, his usually guarded expression roiling with conflict. Anxiety struggled with fury, affection clashed with duty. More than anything, her brother's uncharacteristic turmoil dissolved her nerve. Even against the ferocity of the cursed beasts, she had not been this terrified.

"Have you completely lost all reserve?" Raeylan demanded, unable to filter the anger from his voice.

Margariete attempted to revive her bad humor to aid in her defense as she stepped into the room.

"Katrina provoked me! If you knew the things she said—"

"I know very well the state of Katrina's character," Raeylan interrupted, his words impatient. "As do you. Yet you give in to her pettiness. I thought you above it."

"And what of you?" Margariete countered. "I caught you alone with Esilwen. You kissed her—"

"A mistake. One that will never happen again."

"You can't marry Katrina, Raeylan. Not when you love Esilwen," Margariete protested.

"And what does love matter, sister?" Raeylan asked sadly, turning away from her. "I have given you love, forfeited duty and honor to protect you. Yet you squander my sacrifice."

"Marrying Katrina will only bring you misery," Margariete said. "I cannot see you suffer the way mother did. You have a chance for happiness. Esilwen can give it to you."

"I will not break the treaty."

"Curse the treaty to the Void, it's—"

"Stop, Margariete!" Raeylan yelled, spinning to face her.

Margariete nearly collapsed in surprise. Her twin had never shouted at her in her entire life.

"Our position is precarious," he continued. "I choose to marry Katrina for reasons even more important than a simple peace treaty. I am securing the First Kingdom—and your safety—within it."

"What do you mean?" Margariete asked, suddenly wary.

A peace treaty inside itself was no small commitment. What could be even more significant? Whatever it was, Raeylan hadn't shared it with anyone, and Margariete wasn't sure she wanted to know.

"Our political balance is fragile, sister. The First Kingdom could face the might of a single other nation and prevail, but if two joined against us, our country would perish."

"You're anticipating a war?" Margariete asked in astonishment. Since when had hostilities arisen between their kingdom and another? "But the Fourth Kingdom has always avoided conflict," she argued, "remaining neutral even when the Second Kingdom threatened the entire shard. And father would never side against you. He is not foolish enough to attempt such a thing! What is it you fear?"

"King Arahm is joined to us by marriage, but his treaty was betrayed 18 seasons ago." Raeylan looked at her, his eyes heavy with burden. "We are not his children, Margariete."

Margariete's corset seemed to tighten.

"What?" she whispered with horror.

Raeylan softened into sadness. "Mother called me to her side just before she died. Do you remember?" he asked.

"She wanted to speak to you alone. You wouldn't tell me what she said."

"She divulged her infidelity." Her brother rubbed his temple tiredly.

"And Shikun?"

"He is Arahm's."

Margariete felt the shame of her actions squeeze her insides. Her assault on Katrina had put everything at risk.

"Do you now understand?" Raeylan sighed. "If this is discovered, Arahm will try to supplant us both. We have no claim to the Third Kingdom's throne. Only Shikun is the true heir to both the First and Third Kingdoms. Our brother is still moldable, young. He would bend under Arahm's will."

"Then Arahm would effectively hold all might within the whole of Thyella," Margariete said weakly, imagining the injustice that would be left in Arahm's wake. "It would only be a matter a time before the Fourth Kingdom fell."

"Or surrendered," Raeylan added. He turned to Margariete, his face etched with lines of gravity. "Only you and I know of this. I do not suspect Arahm will ever discover the truth, but if he does, we will need the marriage treaty to support us. Hylan will honor his promises as an ally. Arahm will not be able to move against us."

"But if you believe he will never learn of it, why marry Katrina at all?"

"I am convinced that Arahm already plots our destruction. Whether or not he will act, I am uncertain."

"How do you know he will betray us?" Margariete inquired. The startling revelations of the conversation set her head spinning.

"He has a second son, and he knows he can easily sway the people against you," Raeylan explained somberly. "I believe he expected me to follow his lead when I was young. He did not anticipate that I would remove myself from his control. Arahm's demands have always been corrupt. Knowing he wasn't my father made it easier to defy him. But it has turned him against me. His belief that I am his son is all that stays his hand."

Margariete swallowed, feeling sick. She was torn between compassion toward her twin and resentment that he had concealed such a secret. Did he think her not strong enough to keep the confidence?

"Who is our real father?" she finally asked.

"Mother refused to tell me."

Margariete pondered, gazing moodily at her scarlet signet glove. "So, what of Esilwen? She loves you."

Sorrow made her brother's shoulder's slump. No longer did he seem the indestructible prince who could slay any demon, who stemmed the tide of all political dilemmas. He was a young man, barely 18, tortured by duty and insurmountable sacrifice. Raeylan moved behind his desk, resting both palms on its surface.

"I will regret always that I cannot give Esilwen her happiness."

His voice almost broke. Margariete stepped forward and laid a hand of comfort on his shoulder. It seemed to give him strength.

"But I must protect my kingdom."

29: INTERLUDE IN THE QUEEN'S CHAMBERS

Margariete surveyed the bamboo containers that housed her belongings. They lay scattered about her chambers like a collection of broken teeth. Much of her wardrobe would stay in this closet—the majority of her attire belonged to the office of the queen. Now Katrina would own the elaborate robes and corsets.

The dark princess didn't mind. It meant less fuss over layers of silk. She didn't care for gowns or outward appearance, but a tweak of melancholy accompanied her thoughts of leaving this room forever. Her mother had lived here. Being in the same chambers helped Margariete feel closer to Queen Anleia somehow.

When the cycle's ceremonies ended, Margariete's maids would arrive to remove all her things.

Shikun appeared shortly after the coronation to console her. As part of her penalty for attacking Katrina, Margariete had been banned from both the crowning and marriage rites. She was effectively under house arrest until the rest of her sentence was decided. Her little brother perched on the edge of her bed, absently fidgeting with the embroidery on the coverlet. Though he had arrived more than three arcs ago, he had barely spoken.

Margariete smiled. Shikun often came to her for advice in times of worry. Once she had tried prying his questions from his troubled mind, but he had detected the invasion and fled from the room, avoiding her for cycles. Since then, Margariete had learned to suppress the urge to use her powers on him for answers, waiting for him to reveal the purpose of his visit.

"Thank you for keeping me company, Shikun," she said, prodding conversation.

"I was worried for you, sister," he said, looking at her with concern beyond the span of his seasons. "Though, I will admit that I have other reasons to come here as well."

His youthful eyes grew distant, tainted with memory. "Princess Katrina cornered me everywhere I went this cycle, trying to comfort me. She said my 'fancy' of her was a natural emotion, and I shouldn't allow it to prevent us from developing a friendship. She kept patting me on the head—like I was a child."

Margariete's lips twitched strangely, and she was surprised when laughter tickled her tongue. She felt sympathy for her little brother's plight, but the allegation was completely ridiculous. No wonder Shikun had retreated to her chambers.

"And since I am confined to my quarters until further notice—"

"Katrina would never come here looking for me. It was the only logical place to hide." He added hastily, "But as I said, I was concerned for you."

Margariete waved a hand, indicating she took no offense. She was happy to provide an excuse to hide from that self-indulgent monster.

"Don't worry for me. My punishment is well deserved." She looked out the window, suddenly regretful, and asked, "How was it?"

"I didn't realize there was so much involved in a coronation ceremony," Shikun reported excitedly. "Brother was magnificent!" His lip pursed sourly. "But it would have been easier to pay attention if I hadn't been forced to sit next to Princess Katrina. She whispered in my ear through the entire ceremony."

Margariete sighed. Despite her hatred for the Glass Princess, she would have willingly endured the future queen's presence to witness her twin's official crowning.

"And Esilwen?" she asked, trying to avoid contemplating what she had missed.

"She sat in the back of the room with Lord Terail. I saw her when the ceremony ended. She hasn't been herself the last few cycles," he stated obliquely.

From his eager expression, Margariete supposed he awaited an explanation. After a moment of silence, he probed further.

"I think Master Malbrin may have upset her in some way."

Margariete avoided looking at the princeling. She knew the exact cause of Esilwen's unhappiness. The man she loved would wed another. Her friend's outward appearance of sorrow had become more prominent since the stolen kiss with Raeylan. Shikun had only seen Esilwen during Margariete's training session and after Malbrin's private meeting, so it would be natural for him to assume that the fault lay with the aged mentor.

"Malbrin has been studying Esilwen's past," Margariete said. "It would be hard, don't you think? To be in a strange land, wondering who you were or if you had a life somewhere else?"

Shikun nodded, saying nothing. He stared at his hands as they mangled the fringe on one of Margariete's many cushions.

"I saw Esilwen watching Raeylan at the lunch banquet. She loves him, doesn't she?"

Margariete wrapped her arm around her brother's shoulders. She had suspected Shikun to be infatuated with Esilwen from the beginning. The little princeling had been second to Raeylan all of his young life. Margariete imagined it would be difficult not to harbor envy toward his older sibling.

"I'm sorry, Shikun," she comforted.

"It's all right," he answered with a weak smile. "I just— I don't like seeing her so sad. She doesn't smile anymore. Brother's been different too. Does he love her also?"

Margariete nodded. There was no point denying what Shikun already knew.

"It's not fair to keep them apart like this," he proclaimed. "Sometimes I doubt Nehro's wisdom."

"Shikun," Margariete reprimanded, though his blasphemy echoed that of her own heart.

"I do," he confirmed fearlessly. "If she is so great and just, why would she force Raeylan to live in misery? Why would she allow mother to suffer as she did, married to father?"

Margariete waited until the conclusion of his outburst to reply. "I don't know the answers, Shikun. I have asked myself those very questions many times over. But we can't change things. Doubting Nehro does nothing to heal your anger. That I understand."

Margariete looked to the small bead collector on her vanity, and her mind filled with gloom.

"You should go little brother, the wedding will begin soon."

"I wish you could come," he said glumly.

"Me too."

Margariete squeezed him affectionately. Shikun nodded obediently and slunk out of the room. The princess perched unhappily on the edge of her bed, making no move to light a candle, though the sun was soon eclipsed. Smattered lunarlight filtered through the window.

In the dimness, she brooded. It was fortunate that Shikun was spared the knowledge of their mother's indiscretion. The second Prince of the Jewel carried a soul matched in purity only by Esilwen, embracing an innocence bred by the shield of his siblings.

The secret should be withheld from him at least until Arahm passes, she thought, calling the Third Kingdom's sovereign by name, rather than thinking him as "father." The transition felt natural. Even in ignorance of her true heritage, she had never considered Arahm a paternal figure.

The truth couldn't be hidden forever, though. Once Arahm's soul journeyed into the netherworld, Raeylan's code of honor would compel him to relinquish the throne in the City of Storms to his brother, the rightful heir. Shikun would demand an explanation.

Margariete agreed with her twin. It was best to save Shikun from the suffering of the Viridius secrets as long as possible.

Margariete felt the door slide open in the darkness, the heavy footfalls that followed implying a visitor rather than one of her maids. She tasted the vibrations in the air, noting that her guards had been dismissed. Her pulse quickened: only two men in the castle held that authority, and one was currently occupied with preparations for his wedding.

"Why is it so dark, princess?" came Terail's voice.

His body was draped in shadow despite the candle flickering on the surface of the tray he carried. The odor of steamed rice and meat wafted from the platter.

"I brought you some food," he said.

Margariete lifted herself from the bed and met him at the small table that served as her personal dining hall. Terail seemed at ease, regardless of the fact that his presence in the princess's personal chambers was completely inappropriate. He deposited the tray, lighting the candelabra lantern that rested on the table.

As warm light flushed the chamber, Margariete glanced at her bead timekeeper. The marriage ceremony had already begun.

A shock of tears betrayed her distress. Terail embraced her readily, stroking her hair softly as she wept. Soon sobs stabbed her body. Only Terail's support kept her from crumpling.

"Shikun was right," she muttered bitterly, not bothering to recount her earlier conversation with her brother. "Why would Nehro allow this to happen?"

"There was nothing that could have prevented it, Margariete," Terail said quietly.

"No, there wasn't. Nehro's punishing us once more," she accused.

Terail smiled patiently, an amused gleam in his eye. "You think Nehro did this?"

"Yes," Margariete said, pushing roughly away from him. "My mother failed her duty, and now her children are cursed."

Terail looked at her with genuine perplexity. Margariete burned with resentment over her mother's infidelity. When Raeylan first told her, she had been stunned. Over the course of her lonely arcs in detention, she had found reassurance in the thought that Anleia had discovered a measure of happiness, however fleeting. Now, however, she blamed her mother's betrayal for the goddess's vengeance.

Her deluge of tears eventually ebbed, and she lifted her eyes to trace Terail's face. His silver hair danced with the candlelight as he took a step nearer. She loved him and knew that he returned her affection. She would not waste it, not like her twin.

"Anleia was not faithful to King Arahm while he was away fighting my grandfather's war," she confessed.

Terail face twisted in surprise.

"Raeylan told me last night," Margariete explained. "How could mother be so foolish? This whole disaster with Katrina is her fault. There would be no need for the marriage treaty if she had remained true, and maybe I wouldn't have to wear that cursed veil. All of our—"

Terail closed the remaining distance between them, silencing the princess with the fervent pressure of his lips.

"It doesn't help to argue what might have been," he said when he pulled away. "It does nothing to change things. At this moment, your brother is pledging himself to his wife. Do not make things more difficult for him."

"Then what should I do?" she asked, hopelessly lost in the passion of his eyes.

"Raeylan will take care of himself," he promised. "It's time you stopped fretting over him, and turned your attention to something more important."

"Like what?"

"I love you, Margariete," he declared, pulling her close against his body. He stroked her cheek with a calloused palm. "I'm going to ask your brother for your hand."

"Arahm will never allow it," she answered breathlessly, as a thrill of fire climbed her skin.

Terail slipped his fingers across her throat.

"Since he is not your father," he said with a wicked grin, "he will have no say in the matter, now will he?"

Terail thrust his mouth against hers, kneading her hair with one hand as the other loosened the laces of her corset. Margariete's dismay withered in the fever of desire that raced through her blood.

Terail is right, she thought to herself as he laid her on the bed and slid his fingers into her gown, *and it would be selfish of us to squander Raeylan's sacrifice.*

30: EIGHTEEN SEASONS

Terail offered a fluted glass, dark with stormwine, to Margariete. The Jeweled Princess rose from the crumpled bedclothes, covering her nakedness with the blankets. Accepting with a shy smile, she sipped the beverage.

"My maids will be here soon to move my things," she said, a blush shading her olive skin. "You should leave before they find you here."

"That would be awkward, wouldn't it?" he replied with a crafty grin.

Margariete swayed, her eyes rolling back into her head drunkenly. The Pearl Daimyo reacted quickly, catching the glass with catlike agility before her hand went limp, preventing a single drop from escape. As the kalil oil—hidden by the sharp bite of the wine—took effect, the princess slumped back onto the mattress in a heap.

His lips lifted in a vicious smile as he sat next to her, tracing the lines of her face with a fingertip. Only he—the last in his family trade—still understood the secret subtleties that could alter the toxin, methods that would allow him to control the duration of the drug-induced slumber. The properties of the wine would speed the body's filtration of the poison, and a certain combination of particular herbs would bring Margariete awake almost at the moment of his choosing.

He had expected the seduction to be more difficult, but Raeylan's scandalous secret of Queen Anleia's adultery had injured Margariete, providing a weakness for him to exploit. Vulnerable by her faith in his trust, the dark princess had thrown her chastity at him willingly.

Terail fondled a silky lock of her unique tresses. Though she was most definitely the most beautiful of his conquests, he had to admit—he'd had better.

But more important than any gratification of physical pleasure, she had unwittingly provided him with the weapon that would advance his plans a complete trinal sooner than scheduled.

He stripped a wickedly long dagger from its sheath at his belt. One strike with the hilt left a torn bruise above the princess's left cheek, a memento of his gratitude. As he dressed her, he thought it a pity that he had only been able to have her once. He was positive she could be trained to properly satisfy a man.

Terail considered the thought only briefly, however. He had been arranging his retribution for 18 seasons. Revenge would not wait.

And he tonight would have it.

31: Wedding Night

"I am so relieved Princess Margariete was unable to attend the ceremonies this cycle," Queen Katrina spouted to King Arahm and King Hylan. Her gloved hand tenderly touched her bruised face. "I must admit I have never been so ill treated by anyone! If she had been anything less than my new sister—"

Raeylan forced himself to remain emotionless. Katrina's tirade had persisted for the better half of an arc.

"I must agree," Hylan added, "though my precious daughter has always been forgiving. Even so, I do hope Princess Margariete has been properly reprimanded."

All three royal faces turned to Raeylan expectantly. The newly honored king had not divulged Margariete's punishment to anyone. It wasn't surprising that his family members would want a personal recitation of the princess's final sentence.

"Margariete will be moved to a secure location," Raeylan replied. "Her confinement outside the castle will continue until her attitude improves."

"I should hope so," Katrina agreed merrily. "I hate to think of what she might do next. I expect she will be supplied with a tutor to repair her misconceptions of decorum?"

Raeylan nodded neutrally.

"I am glad to see you finally undertaking suitable action as a king, my son," Arahm interjected. He smiled between Raeylan and King Hylan. "Allow me to congratulate you both. This alliance will benefit the entire shard."

The storm ruler shook gloved hands with his glass counterpart.

"And I must say, my son is very lucky. Your daughter will make the most lovely queen in the First Kingdom's history."

Katrina blushed modestly, a trick used by most noblewomen. Raeylan endured it patiently. He disliked the notion of sending his twin away into the countryside, but it seemed the only solution with merit. Margariete needed protection from Katrina's constant provocation. Esilwen would accompany her and be thereby spared the Jeweled Queen's cruelty. With one action he could guard both the women he loved, though it took them far from him.

Raeylan looked at his wife. She proudly accepted Arahm's adoration, which the older ruler showered on her in an endless stream. Her new, over-exaggerated signet glove danced animatedly—touching her hair, smoothing her gown, or tapping her breastbone—subtly reminding her subjects of her own importance. To the casual observer, she seemed to receive her compliments graciously. But her husband wasn't fooled by the charade. Each well-wisher simply stoked the cavern of her vanity.

The fingers on his right hand twitched. His glove remained the same—the imitation of Nehro's artifact he had worn since his mother's death. It could never be removed or the nobility would know it to be counterfeit. The silver-trimmed leather was so familiar it seemed a part of his skin.

"King Raeylan, I must see you dance with my daughter," Hylan requested. "I leave for my homeland on the morrow. I desire to witness the joy you have brought her with my own eyes before I take my leave."

Katrina turned eagerly to her husband. With rigid courtesy, Raeylan held out his arm, granting his father-in-law's wish. His new wife took it readily as he led her to the center of the ballroom. Their intention to dance spread quickly throughout the gathered nobles. All moved to the edges of the chamber, allowing their king and queen an exclusive performance.

The musicians struck a traditional medley, a dance reserved for a single couple. The choreography was intricate, requiring a measure of attention to complete it properly. Katrina didn't deem that awareness necessary.

"I wanted to assure you that I bear your sister no ill will, husband," Katrina began. "Not that I don't feel she shouldn't be adequately punished—you are right to confine her to the country. She has much to learn."

"Indeed," Raeylan agreed politically, concentrating on a point above Katrina's head. Nothing passed between them until the sequence of steps began again.

"I didn't want to anger you further concerning her impropriety," she stated as the movements brought them together again, "but, I must say, I am quite affronted by some of the comments she makes to me."

Raeylan looked at her, lifting his eyebrows. Either of his siblings would have recognized the inconspicuous gesture of warning—evidence that he sensed a fabrication from truth. His wife, however, misinterpreted it as an invitation to continue.

"She has been somewhat jealous of the attention given to me since my arrival," Katrina sighed long-sufferingly. "It is understandable. After all, she has been the only lady in this house for seasons. But the way she treats me in private has made me very uncomfortable. Some of the noblewomen have even confessed that she is spreading hostile rumors about me."

"Were you speaking of Margariete," Raeylan countered calmly, stripping Katrina of her artificial humility with the intensity of his eyes, "or blaming her for your own indiscretions?"

"I—I don't know what you mean," she said. Her hesitation caused her to misstep the next phrase of the dance.

"Princess Margariete must face the consequence for assaulting you, Katrina, but do not think me blind to your arrogance. You provoked the circumstance that led to her retaliation. Always remember, that before husband, I am your king. You will abandon your attempts to ruin my sister."

The song drifted into a carefree tune, signifying the end of their performance. Raeylan exchanged bows with his queen, noting that she seemed less confident, her smile echoing the uncertainty in her eyes. The crowd offered polite applause as he led Katrina away from the dance arena.

Suddenly, a loud clang reverberated through the Opal Ballroom and the doors opened. Maidservants in the traditional red attire of marriage glided into the chamber in rows, littering the floor with dyed Sakuhra petals from their perfumed baskets. Stopping in the middle of the room, they dropped to their knees, awaiting the approach of their queen.

Katrina turned to Raeylan. She whispered, "If you command it, My King, then it shall be done."

Raeylan doubted the sincerity of repentance that smothered her face. He expected Katrina to disregard her pledge the moment her petty nature felt slighted. But he nodded anyway, a concession to her verbal acquiescence.

As the queen strode to the center of the attendants, the most prominent members of the female gentry lined the carpet of blossoms, careful not to disturb them. The red-robed handmaidens then stood and, walking backward, distributed a new layer of petals, this time white, over those laid before. Katrina, head held high and eyes avoiding everyone in the grandeur of her exit, departed for her bridal chamber preparations. Raeylan only watched her leave because it was demanded by tradition. Lively festivities resumed with fervor in the wake of the queen's retreat.

The next arc would be the shortest in Raeylan's life. Afterward, he would be expected to meet Katrina in his quarters.

"It must be a relief to have all of these formalities completed, Your Majesty," Terail said, appearing on Raeylan's left. The king turned to his general, who drank merrily from a goblet of rice wine.

"How is my sister?" Raeylan inquired.

"As you ordered, she has been fed," Terail reported faithfully. "And despite a few tears at your expense, My King, she is now soundly sleeping."

"Thank you for your assistance."

Some of the tension lifted from Raeylan's body. At least one difficulty had been restrained.

"So you really intend to send her away?" Terail asked.

"I'm afraid I must," Raeylan answered as he scanned the crowd.

He spotted Prince Shikun easily. Walking in his younger brother's direction, Terail following, Raeylan dropped his voice.

"With so many witnesses to her behavior, I had no choice."

"Who will you assign as her guardian?" Terail asked, interest in the post plain in his expression.

"The only man I truly trust with such precious cargo," Raeylan jested with a thin smile. "You."

"I would be honored," Terail said as they reached Shikun's table.

Belatedly noticing Esilwen at the princeling's elbow, Raeylan hesitated to sit. The horde of bedecked aristocracy had hidden her from view across the room. Shikun greeted Raeylan's approach with a wide grin, but Esilwen rested rigidly on her cushion, paralyzed by discomfiture. The youngest Viridian cleared his throat when the tension grew thick.

"Hello, brother," he said.

Raeylan regained his composure, breaking his gaze on the sweet healer. Unable to escape without appearing rude, he settled next to his younger sibling. Terail knelt after.

"Lady Esilwen was telling me the story of a great knight, Lord Calmic," Shikun babbled excitedly. "It's incredibly interesting."

Against his will, Raeylan's eyes drew themselves back to Esilwen. Her platinum curls drifted gently around her shoulders. The delicate gown she wore enhanced her benevolent beauty through its unadorned simplicity. Her gaze fixed firmly on the ghastly yellow table dressing in front of her.

"Really?" Terail asked. "We would love to hear it."

Esilwen kept her eyes downcast. "I fear I would bore Your Majesty and Lordship with the tale."

"Lady Esilwen, you are too modest!" Shikun gushed. "You see Calmic was the—"

A gruff voice of displeasure interrupted the young prince.

"Shikun!" Arahm barked.

Raeylan turned, the animosity in Arahm's voice automatically summoning the new king's protective instinct. The Third Kingdom's sovereign glared darkly at Esilwen, as if his disapproval could grind the fragile maiden into powder.

"I will speak with you immediately," Arahm commanded, then turned abruptly and walked away.

With a disappointed frown, the princeling obediently followed. A heavy quiet conquered his absence.

"I'll go get us some wine," Terail offered to escape the awkward situation.

Raeylan nodded, dismissing his general tentatively. Esilwen's fingers trembled, though they folded timidly in her lap. Her characteristic cheerfulness had been replaced by despondency, but sorrow only magnified her grace. The purity of her soul shone with gentle strength, despite her trampled happiness. Raeylan's heart twisted with regret, knowing himself to be the cause.

"Are you enjoying yourself, Lady Esilwen?" he inquired kindly.

"Very much," she retuned softly, but offered no other reply.

Another apprehensive hush swelled between them. Raeylan waited in the stillness. Finally, Esilwen's courage permitted her to raise her eyes. Her ice-green irises immersed him in their grief.

"I have a request, Your Majesty—," she began.

"Anything," he answered, astonished by his own impulsiveness.

"I—I wish to leave Viridius Castle."

Raeylan's breath left his lungs so quickly he felt dizzy. Though he had intended to send her with Margariete, Esilwen's desire to leave battered against his chest like the clash of arms.

"Where would you go?" he asked quietly.

Her reply was hushed, almost lost in the din of music surrounding them.

"Master Malbrin wishes me to accompany him on a journey. He believes he may know someone who can answer my riddle."

"With only the old sage? You cannot Lady Esilwen— the roads are too dangerous."

"Even so," she shrugged sadly. "I cannot stay."

"Because of me," Raeylan said.

Her eyes fell away again, "My presence causes contention in your family."

Raeylan grasped for an argument that would change her mind. Living in a fortress with Margariete, albeit at the edges of the kingdom, would at least ensure Esilwen's safety. Allowing her to gallivant around the realm with only Malbrin as a guard set Raeylan mad with worry.

"Margariete needs you Esilwen. I'm sending her away to our manor in the Korene Valley—"

He paused as Esilwen shook her head. Though he could not see her tears, they were evident in her voice.

"If Queen Katrina didn't dislike me so, Margariete wouldn't have been tempted to defend me. Though I harbor no animosity toward your new bride, I do not wish to be the cause of such trouble."

Esilwen's charity, in contrast to the selfishness of his wife, tore through Raeylan like shards of tempered steel. The healer's altruistic need to forgive Katrina's malice would drive her away forever. He suppressed the desire to beg her to stay, choosing a logical argument instead.

"If this is about what happened in the shrine, Lady Esilwen, allow me to—"

"Please, don't apologize," she interrupted, revealing her tear-streaked face to him. "I do not regret anything that happened within these castle walls. If not for your family's kindness, I might have—"

Her words fell limply. She twisted the end of her signet glove.

"I do plan to return, when I have found my answers."

A response grew from the center of Raeylan's being. When he spoke it, the pledge discharged from his soul rather than his lips.

"I will miss you."

She looked astonished at his forthright admission. She rose to her feet.

"I'm afraid I've had too much excitement this cycle," she said. "I think I will retire to my room."

Raeylan watched the healer as she fled the ballroom. After she disappeared, he wrenched his heart from his chest and crushed it into a crevice deep within him. He reminded himself that he was married, joined by a treaty that would ensure peace within the shard, though he would never know peace himself. Nothing could threaten the security of his kingdom.

For the remainder of the celebration, he wandered through the room, speaking with the gentry and accepting their congratulations. His body performed mindlessly, keeping his thoughts of Esilwen at bay. When the arc had slipped away, a procession of Nehro's monks entered the ballroom, sprinkling sacred water from the goddess's temple over the scattered flower petals. Raeylan measured his steps as he departed, taking care on the slick floor. The entire room, excepting the two other kings, bowed in supplication. When the chamber doors closed behind him, he walked into the public part of the shrine, pausing to inhale its clean, open air.

Soon Terail and five knights approached the king. When they reached him, each knight drew a silver blade and plunged it into the grass. They knelt.

"These men are prepared to replace the guard on your floor, as tradition dictates," the Pearl Daimyo recited.

Raeylan inclined his head and waited for his general to rise.

"Terail," the king said, "thank you my friend. I owe you much. Please prepare the new Pearl candidates. I will replenish my guard in the morning."

"As you command, My Liege," Terail said with a formal bow, completing the ceremony.

As he retreated back to the festivities, he added, "And congratulations."

The remaining knights rose, trailing behind their king as he began the six floor ascent to the royal apartments. He washed himself of all desire as he mounted the steps toward his queen, allowing duty to fill the cracks of his wounded spirit. Over the last few cycles, he had allowed doubt to creep into his mind. He had never resented the sacrifices that his station required of him.

Until he had fallen in love with Esilwen.

Raeylan reprimanded himself as his route took him closer to the bridal chamber. He had acted rashly with Esilwen and feared that his affection had caused her only misery. His lapse of discipline had allowed Katrina to perceive his feelings for the pretty healer. Everything his wife did to Esilwen in retaliation was his responsibility. He would not permit such weakness to challenge him again.

He could not fully give himself to Katrina. Even Nehro would understand that. But he would perform his obligations as husband and king. His people deserved no less, and no matter how much he loathed his bride, her station was entitled respect.

As Raeylan stepped onto the top floor of the castle, he moved aside, allowing the Pearl knights to exchange places with the guards already posted. Two took positions astride the king's quarters, another pair at the queen's. The four previous sentinels hurried back down the stairwell. Raeylan cast a sidelong look at his sister's door. Tonight his queen would sleep in his bed, but tomorrow she would displace his twin.

He hesitated only briefly when he crossed into his receiving room. Then, firmly rendering every element of his body under his mind's control, he stepped into the hallway that connected his library and bedroom.

Immediately, he noticed that his office door stood agape. The sharp lunar light that sliced through the wooden blades of his window revealed a silvered portal of darkness—the secret passageway to his sister's apartments cracked ajar. He stood motionless, listening with a warrior's ears. Scuffles from behind the bedchamber door drew his attention. As he turned to face it, leaden waves of intensity washed against him, sinking around his body like feathers of dread.

Only once had he experienced this phenomenon; only once had his sister pressed her feelings so heavily into the air, infecting the atmosphere around the castle inhabitants with her grief-enraged madness.

The night their mother had died.

Disregarding that he was without arms, he rushed heedlessly to the paper-lined door and threw it open.

Margariete stood in the center of the bedchamber, beads of crimson trimming her dress in pearls of blood. An ugly bruise swelled at her cheek.

With horrified disbelief Raeylan watched his twin rip *Stardawn* from his wife's lifeless body.

PART 3

32: Ruins In The Koungo Waste

A slim hand parted the transcendent curtain that separated the two realities. No two shardgates were exactly the same. This particular portal glittered like glass in the sunlight, peeling open like a vertical sheet of water. Each journey through the barrier was a unique experience, some sticky with unbearable heat, others colder than the glacial vacuum between planets. The woman stepping through the magical doorway had traversed enough gates to expect the unpredictable—once, darkness had plunged so deeply into her mind that she was unable to escape for days, on another occasion, she had floated aimlessly in a vacuous nothing for more than a year—and so she was only mildly unprepared for the suffocating pressure that seized her chest as she tread from one plane of existence into another. The crossing took only seconds, but those few heartbeats seemed like a lifetime of airless hours, her body compressed by an immaterial wall of space that distorted the normal laws of nature.

It was with some measure of relief that she finally entered the realm of the water goddess. Blinking quickly in the bright light—it had been midnight in the world she just left—she surveyed the wasteland of sickly, clumped grass that stretched in every direction. A crumbled edifice of stone hunched several steps away, the corpse of some small shrine or temple. Pale, blue mountains loomed in the distance, but the woman's sharp eyes snatched the gleaming image of a faraway city at their base.

She lifted her luxurious features into a haughty sneer. Nehro's shard. Somewhere in this tiny sphere of reality the goddess's artifact lay hidden, and—if she was lucky—it would be protected by a lorelei. Nehro's water angels were rare these days. The woman laughed with pleasure, low and throaty in resonance. If one of her ancient enemies was indeed concealed here, she would soon hold its salty heart in her fingers.

A length of crimson hair tumbled from the woman's spidery headdress, and she pushed it back with a flick of her brassy wrist. She stretched languidly, tasting the air with her enhanced senses for any residue of magic. Suddenly, her scarlet gold wings arched into the sky with surprise and her eyes burned with ice-green luminescence. With inhuman speed she reached into a pouch at her gold girded waist, retrieving a smooth, colorless stone. A practiced incantation aligned it properly for gate slip.

"My Lord," she said into the magical communication device, "come quickly! Fohtian's Warden is here."

33: CYCLES IN THE DUNGEON

Though the castle's thick layer of brick repelled the brutal sheets of trinal rain, a penetrating chill infected the dungeon level. It was the coldest part of the season, when all of Thyella drowned in heavenly torrents. The mountains were colder still. Malbrin once explained that the rain transformed into drifting ice at their peaks, though Princess Margariete had never seen the phenomenon herself. The thought stabbed her with remorse. There were many things she had wanted to experience. Eighteen seasons had allowed her only a glimpse of life's fullness.

The princess huddled deeper into the dull blankets of her bedroll, the stiffness in her limbs reminiscent of the nights she had spent in the wild. Her eyes wandered the wooden beams in the ceiling, following the flickering torch's wayward pattern. Loose straw padded the hard floor, affording little insulation against the cold that crept through her blankets. Margariete's cell was just long enough to stretch herself full-length on the floor, with arms extended, and only spanned two widths of her sleeping roll.

For half an arc she shifted futilely, attempting to find a posture that conserved the heat of her body. With a frustrated sigh, she sat up and leaned against the wall, suddenly indifferent to her discomfort. She wrapped her arms around her knees and tapped her head against the stone in thoughtful rhythm.

What had she done?

Katrina's lifeless eyes haunted the back of Margariete's eyelids every time she blinked. Crimson droplets trickled grotesquely through her dreams, waking her with their murderous echo.

For three cycles she had lain awake through the night, her brow throbbing, dizziness making her stomach turn. Fear of her own guilt repelled the solace of slumber. The princess's memory was like a red haze hanging over a burning corpse, sharp with the scent of death. Details were lost in its consuming flame. Margariete easily remembered her intimate meeting with Terail, but nothing clearly afterward. One moment she was safe in his strong arms, the next found her skin tarnished by Katrina's blood.

Had she killed Katrina?

Emptiness blanketed the princess's mind. She couldn't remember visiting the armory to retrieve her sword, or following the secret passage into Raeylan's room. But what other explanation was there? *Stardawn* had ended Katrina's short reign as Jeweled Queen. Had Margariete fallen into such a rage of hatred that she had acted without conscious thought?

The disbelief of her twin's expression when he had discovered her yanking *Stardawn* from his wife's dead body had carved a terrible scar into her soul. As he summoned the guards to apprehend her, his inexpressive mask had cracked into alarm. She faintly remembered shouting to him, pleading for something, but the words she had spoken were lost within her own horror.

Tears had abandoned her arcs ago. Her only visitor had been Negin. Three times a cycle he delivered a simple meal, though he did not speak to or look at her directly. On her first cycle, he had provided a simple grey wrap so she could shed her bloody robe.

She waited, plagued simultaneously with hope and foreboding, for a friendly voice: Esilwen, Raeylan, Terail, or Shikun. Margariete longed for an opportunity to defend herself, however unsure she might be of what had happened in her brother's chambers. She craved news of the outside world, would have given anything to know what transpired in the courtroom above. Was her sentence already decided? Had she instigated war?

She hugged her knees tightly to her chest, holding her body together. It couldn't be true. Margariete readily acknowledged her character deficiencies. The princess hated Katrina, but murder?

No. Margariete refused to believe herself capable of such brutality. There had to be some other explanation.

When the soft click of approaching footsteps reached her ears, she quickly forced the trembling out of her limbs. Too despondent to reach out and sense the identities of the visitors, she waited instead. When she heard the key scratching inside the cell's lock, she finally turned her head. Both Raeylan and Terail stood in the threshold, their faces pulled into stoney, grim lines. Her twin's posture was rigid, his hands tightly curled. His grey eyes pierced through her, agonizing in the silence. She didn't dare speak.

"Why?" he asked, his voice carefully modulated.

It took Margariete several moments to find her voice.

"I couldn't have killed her, Raeylan," she finally answered.

She wished he could see into her mind, wanted to somehow project the broken images of memory into him so that he would understand.

"I want to believe that, Margariete," he said, unable to hide the worry that surrounded his eyes. "But only you and

I know of the passages connecting our apartments, and I caught you with sword in hand."

"I know that circumstance supports my guilt, but it wasn't me, brother! One moment I was in my own room, the next—" she trailed off, unable to describe the carnage of that night.

"Your denial alone cannot erase substantial facts, Margariete," Raeylan argued.

"But I wasn't alone—" she began, but Terail, standing a little behind the king, shook his head in warning. He obviously thought their inappropriate interlude would only cause further harm. She quickly amended her testimony. "Shikun visited me, and Terail brought me food, then I—I fell asleep."

"She was sleeping when I left her, Your Majesty," Terail added, giving her an encouraging nod.

Raeylan seemed unmoved by the statement.

"Even if they did visit you, Margariete, both were seen at the celebration before Queen Katrina retired to the bridal chamber. Your accusers will point out that you were unattended during the time of my wife's death."

So there was to be a trial then. Hope brushed her softly.

"But, Raeylan, there were guards at your door! If I had killed Katrina, they would have seen me leave the sixth floor to retrieve *Stardawn*. My sword is kept in the family armory a level below."

Raeylan dashed her hopes against the shore of reason. "The other kings will claim that any other intruder would have been seen entering my chambers, sister, whereas you were not. They will say it is far more likely that you had *Stardawn* hidden in your room, deposited there after your last training session."

"But you were with me then," she countered. "You could speak in my favor!"

Raeylan's voice became sad. "I left before you did, Margariete. I cannot protect you."

Margariete twisted her face in anger, "You're determined to mark me a murderer!"

"I'm determined to uncover the truth," he contradicted.

"You know me better than anyone, Raeylan," she said. "You know I am not capable of murder!"

"That is a good point, My King," Terail interjected. "Even when the Duke of Timberdale and his bodyguards threatened her life, she did not kill."

"And the slavers?" Raeylan asked, turning to his general. "She has proven herself capable of killing."

The king's gaze returned to his twin. Slowly, he crouched next to her, placing both hands against her cheeks.

"Swear to me," he pleaded, "swear to me on our mother's soul that you did not do this."

"I swear," Margariete answered steadily.

Raeylan's hand brushed away the knotted strands of her dark hair.

"I believe you," he said softly. His eyes darkened as he stood. "However, King Arahm and King Hylan have demanded a public trial."

Dread froze her insides. A public trial meant all the nobility would be present, any of whom could claim the right of accusation or express character disparagement. She would be forced to counter each argument, face every alleged insult from her past. The princess would have few defenders.

"You agreed?" she choked.

"The kings have demanded it, and I could not refuse without causing great insult. It was all I could do to persuade them away from outright war."

"What will happen to me?" she asked in a terrified whisper.

"I don't know," he sighed. "The trial will be held four cycles hence. I will find a way to save you, Margariete."

The princess's heart relocated into her toes. A trial would strain all political cords, regardless of whether she was convicted or acquitted.

There was a simpler solution to averting military conflict.

"And what is it you gamble, Raeylan?" she asked quietly. "My life against war? At all costs you must protect the kingdom and its people."

"I don't like where this is going," Terail stately darkly.

Raeylan's expression hardened.

"I will not let my sister die."

"You may not have a choice. If it is the decision of the people and the payment King Hylan demands for his daughter's murder, I will consent to my own execution."

"No," Raeylan maintained firmly. "I will never allow it."

"Yes, you will," Margariete argued. "Duty before all else—isn't that what you've been trying to teach me? Do not deny me, now that I truly understand. You have always taken it upon yourself to safeguard our kingdom, but it is my turn to sacrifice for our country. If my death saves the lives of our people, I will accept it honorably."

34: Trial On The Terrace

Rain bled across the multicolored pavilions that crowded the castle's upper courtyard, soaking them in drizzled gloom. The wooden soles of footwear clattered against the slick black stone as the nobility and their attendants settled themselves for the trial. Raeylan knelt on a raised platform a few yards from the wall, sheltered by a reed and bamboo canopy, Terail on his left and Captain Hendar on the right.

Each awning bore the family insignia of its patron lord. It seemed every family in the realm was represented, including a handful from the Third Kingdom. More than 500 bodies crammed themselves onto the slate flagstones. The king noticed with carefully controlled concern that most of his political opponents had gathered themselves together in the middle of the assembly, the Duke of Timberdale heading the group. Each of these men had brought more than the allotted number of attendants, arguing outrageously when the extra bodyguards were required to wait for their masters in the outer courtyard.

Raeylan had expected something like this. Even with the surplus soldiers, the duke's faction didn't have strength enough to successfully take the castle, but Raeylan thought they might use their military support to force the trial verdict.

Despite this display of antagonism, Raeylan felt some comfort that he still commanded the loyalty of more than half the gathered noblemen, many of whom stood within the ranks of his army. A half-circle of Pearl knights branched across both ends of the castle walls and the raised platform, leaving only a center opening for the viewers to see the Jeweled Princess when she arrived. Lieutenant Tenan was positioned at the edge of this opening and had orders to close the gap should an emergency arise. Twenty Jade knights supplemented the forward ranks—at a word the king could instruct them to forcibly escort the gentry and their bodyguards out the main gate, leaving the Pearl knights free to protect the castle doors. As a further precaution, teams of Amber guards patrolled the edges of the courtyard; six attended the entry gate.

Raeylan felt confident that his knights could control the crowd should chaos erupt, but Arahm was a complication to the Jeweled King's defensive plan. The Storm King had insisted that a full complement of five ranking Tempestguard accompany him, as stated by both law and tradition. Arahm and his soldiers stood inside the ring of Pearl and Jade, the customary location of Accuser. The role legally belonged to King Hylan, but the Sovereign of Glass had declined the title, requesting that Arahm proceed in his stead. Politically, this was the worst development Raeylan could imagine.

At least King Hylan was a rational leader—even under the weight of his daughter's death—unlike Arahm, who harbored open loathing for Margariete. Unfortunately, Hylan stayed only until the cycle Queen Katrina had been entombed in the royal burial chambers beneath Viridius Castle. Consumed by loss, he had left within the arc, relocating his entourage to an inn near the edge of the city. After appointing Arahm as the Accuser, the Glass King left Raeylan with an unmistakable promise.

If Katrina's murder went unpunished, the Fourth Kingdom would interpret it as an act of war.

In the courtyard, only emptiness separated the five Tempestguard and the circular platform where Margariete would be displayed for the public. If Raeylan exonerated his sister, Arahm would object, and might even attempt to arrest her with his own soldiers. It was for this reason that Terail knelt on Raeylan's left. It gave the Pearl Daimyo less ground to cover if he and Raeylan were forced to intercept the Tempestguard before they could reach Margariete. Satisfied that he accounted for every possible obstacle, the king mulled over the coming trial proceedings.

The evidence strongly implicated Margariete's guilt. As Accuser, Arahm would scour every breach of decorum that the Jeweled Princess had committed. Witnesses to these violations of conduct would be called upon to support the Accuser's allegations. Margariete herself would be forced to recall events that could damage her cause.

Somehow, she would have to prove her innocence, but as Arbiter, Raeylan would be unable to speak on her behalf. That left only Terail, Malbrin, and Shikun to support his twin.

Raeylan looked sideways at the platform on his right. Esilwen was the only woman present. The healer had insisted on attending, however unconventional, pleading that she be included as a character witness for Margariete. Though he had welcomed her enthusiasm, Raeylan was bound by law. A woman—other than the Accused—could not speak during such a public hearing. But since Shikun offered to escort her, the Jeweled King had been able to grant her request to come.

A change had transformed Esilwen over the past few cycles. Shedding the listless mantel of sorrow, the healer now burned with protective fervor, rallying all arguments that could back the princess's defense.

A thin wail of drums signaled the Jeweled Princess's entrance. Her gloved hands were heavy with iron restraints, her simple grey robe and veil drooped under the thick sheets of rain. Negin guided her to the accusation platform, where she would face Arahm. A murmur rolled through the crowd as Negin remained at her right—a clear defiance of protocol. The Accused received no such honor. Inside, Raeylan beamed at his officer's show of devotion, though he firmly kept it from leaking into his expression.

A calmly raised hand indicated the Jeweled King's permission to begin. Malbrin, kneeling next to Shikun, struggled to keep his ink and parchment dry as he scratched the events into record. Arahm's feet slopped through the film of water that glazed the courtyard floor. The Accuser's face bristled at Negin's blatant rebellion. With a distinct lack of regard for the Arbiter, Arahm turned his back to Raeylan and addressed the audience in a voice that rattled like the rain.

"Noblemen of the First Kingdom, I beseech your good judgment as I present the affliction that shames the Viridius Family name and dishonors this country. The Jeweled Princess has forsaken the responsibilities of her station and brought our allied sovereignties to the edge of war with our brothers in the City of Glass. Princess Margariete of House Viridius has attempted to regain her former station of rank by murdering Her Majesty Queen Katrina of the City of Jewels. Unfeeling as to how this attack would affect the rest of the realm, the very night the whole of Thyella celebrated peaceful union, this—"

Arahm paused in a confounded bluster, seeming to struggle for a word that could adequately describe the woman standing before him, though Raeylan knew the speech was rehearsed. The Accuser was attempting to rile the gentry's temper with his performance. When Arahm resumed speaking, he pointed to Margariete and spat the word.

"—this creature assassinated the good queen in her own bridal chamber, using a weapon forbidden to her gender."

One of the Tempestguard stepped forth and unsheathed *Stardawn*. The rain slid down the blade like tears as he held it aloft for the nobles' inspection. Arahm snatched the weapon from the solder's grip, brandishing it in Margariete's direction.

"The Jeweled Princess disrespects the duty of her rank and exploits the generosity of her king. She consorts with commoners," at this charge the Accuser pointed *Stardawn's* tip at Esilwen, "to steal the privileges of station and supersede the rights of the nobility to favor those of lesser birth.

"Just two fortnights past, Princess Margariete fled the castle, leaving its safety in a fit of pride. She stole a horse and the royal banner and endangered the lives of the many good knights who were sent to retrieve her. She journeyed to Timberdale, where, unprovoked, she attacked Duke Unsaga, permanently injuring his leg. The Duke of Timberdale offers proof that he was unwarrantedly assaulted by this woman as he attempted to uphold the law in his dukedom, interfering with the punishment of a peasant's misconduct!"

The duke's faction shook their fists and threw verbal denunciations of Margariete. Even the higher ranking nobility loyal to the Jeweled King scowled in disapproval.

Margariete's actions brought into question their own right to lead their respective provinces. With a captive audience, Arahm continued on his rampage of accusations.

"Princess Margariete consistently disregards our honored way of life. She openly disobeys the statutes laid forth for the protection of women within our society. Against proper conduct, she has even studied the way of the sword!"

Arahm threw *Stardawn* against the base of the accusatory podium, where the blade lay naked at Margariete's feet. The muted clank clamored through the courtyard. Every eye widened in shock, except those who already knew the truth. Raeylan steadily refused to display any form of emotion, hoping his subjects would follow his example.

"This restriction maintains order within society, keeping our wives and daughters free from violence. This breach alone can account for her rebellious and abusive behavior. Many of you witnessed Princess Margariete's vicious attack against Queen Katrina just one cycle prior to the murder.

"Princess Margariete believes herself above our laws! She refuses to accept her place and withholds the truth from all of you! It is time you see her for what she really is!"

Arahm turned, his face rigid with malice, and advanced on Margariete. The bold action caught Negin off guard and he reacted too slowly, belatedly knocking the Storm King's arm aside. One swift yank of Arahm's hand loosed the veil and hood from Margariete's head, exposing her to the assembly.

The collective gasp of the aristocracy covered the courtyard like a dark fog. Margariete's hair tumbled freely down her back, darker for its saturation in the rain. Her bright sapphire eyes refused to acknowledge the crowd, but pierced her Accuser with proud hatred.

"You have overstepped your authority, Accuser!" Raeylan announced, fury boiling into his words.

He would have leapt from his platform and drawn his sword against the Storm King, regardless of his duty to remain neutral as the Arbiter, had not Malbrin interrupted.

"The Accused is not on trial for her appearance," the old tutor reprimanded, his words carrying clearly over the splattering rain, "nor for her lack of propriety, King Arahm."

But Raeylan could tell the damage was already irreparable. Swells of abhorrence crested through the audience, punctuated with loud remarks of "witch" and "demon." Superstition would reign over any arguments that might have buoyed Margariete's defense.

"The shame of the Viridius family is revealed," Arahm stated simply. With a confident smile the Accuser addressed Raeylan's sister. "Princess Margariete, do you deny that you despised Queen Katrina?"

"I do not," Margariete responded steadily, offering no more than she was asked. The crowd groaned angrily at her forthright admission.

"And this is what drove you to murder her?" Arahm pressed.

"I did not murder Queen Katrina," Margariete asserted over the noise of the audience.

Her response caused them to grow quiet. Then Arahm laughed scornfully.

"Your king and brother witnessed the murder of the queen at your hand, as you stabbed her with the very blade at your feet!"

The Accuser turned to Raeylan, who rearranged his expression into a steadfast glare. Arahm had distinctly distorted the facts.

"I only saw her remove the blade," he corrected evenly. "I did not see her deliver the blow."

Arahm seemed taken aback by the interruption, and scrambled to realign his argument. He indicated the sword.

"*Stardawn* is its name, is it not?"

"Yes," Margariete answered cautiously.

"And you received it from the Pearl Daimyo, am I correct?"

"Yes," she repeated.

"Furthermore, you and King Raeylan are the only two persons with knowledge of the secret passages connecting the king and queen's apartments?"

"Yes," Margariete responded, but this time her head tilted toward the ground in defeat.

"The guards on duty that night professed that they did not see you leave your chambers that evening, yet you were somehow discovered in the king's apartments. The evidence speaks for itself."

"Perhaps," Raeylan interjected, "but Princess Margariete maintains that she remembers nothing that night, only that she awoke to find the queen already dead and removed the sword. It is just as likely that she was framed by the real assassin."

"You ask us to believe such a farfetched supposition?" Arahm asked the crowd. "We have only her claim of innocence—and of what worth is the word of a liar?"

"That is a brazen accusation," Raeylan rumbled dangerously, but Arahm seemed indifferent to the warning.

"Only if you believe her character true and unblemished," Arahm responded caustically.

Raeylan glanced at his sister in alarm, but she refused to meet his gaze. Her olive skin curdled like sour milk. The king felt stones grind unhappily in the base of his stomach, knowing that Arahm had information that she had kept hidden.

"Gentlemen of the court, our princess has thoroughly tarnished her honor. Mere arcs before the murder of Queen Katrina, the Jeweled Princess took Lord Terail Dasklos as her lover."

Another round of gasps revolved through the courtyard. Even without the charge of murder, a conviction of fornication would warrant Margariete's execution.

"To sustain this allegation, I call upon Lord Terail to speak."

One look at his twin's trembling form and Raeylan knew the accusation was true. A maddening sense of helplessness overwhelmed him. He had known his sister to be reckless, but this? And who had revealed such a damaging indiscretion to Arahm?

"Terail Dasklos," Arahm said as the Pearl Daimyo stood, "did you share Princess Margariete's bed?"

Unexpectedly, Terail leapt from the Viridius platform and approached the Accuser. For a moment Raeylan worried that his general meant to do Arahm harm. The skirmish might allow Margariete a chance to escape, but would cause damage to the kingdom in the long trinals to come. But Terail halted a few steps from the Storm King, bowed politely, and turned to Margariete, a wicked grin peeling across his mouth.

In that instant, Raeylan knew who had betrayed the Viridius family.

"I did," the Pearl Daimyo stated, "though I must say it was rather disappointing."

Margariete flinched like a whip had struck her face. Anger and shock staggered drunkenly through Raeylan's veins. His heart pounded with stunned fury. Five seasons of trust, of friendship, cast into the Void. And for what? What incentive had Arahm promised Terail for his treachery? If Raeylan had been given the power to strike a man dead with thought alone, Terail would have been nothing more than a bloody smear on the flagstone. As it was, the king leapt to his feet and tore *Moonstone Retribution* free from its sheath.

"Why Terail?" he demanded.

"Because," the general answered with a sneer, "you and your sister defile the First Kingdom's throne."

Silence deeper than death settled around the courtyard with black wings. Raeylan knew he should command the guards to arrest Terail for his insolence, but a seed of fear choked the order back. The look of triumph on the general's face revealed Arahm's next allegation before the Accuser voiced it to the crowd. Raeylan realized that Margariete must have told Terail their mother's secret.

"In the heat of her passion," Arahm said loudly, his only acoustic competition the soft weeping of the rain, "Princess Margariete confessed to her lover the true cause of the curse that afflicts the Viridius family. For 18 seasons their lies have poisoned the Jeweled Kingdom, but no longer. The people demand justice."

Arahm paused. Not a single man dared to breathe. Raeylan felt his hands turn to ice on his weapon hilt. The Accuser spat on the ground before Margariete.

"This woman is not my daughter. Nor is her brother my son. They are the children of my late wife's infidelity. They are a shame to the Viridius honor!"

The revelation confounded the crowd. Margariete's face ripened with wretchedness, her eyes pleading to

Raeylan for forgiveness. But Raeylan's condemnation was reserved for Terail alone. Not only had the general destroyed the First Kingdom's royal family, but Raeylan had no doubt his former ally had both murdered the queen and arranged Margariete's appearance of guilt.

"It is my ruling," Raeylan said calmly, "that Princess Margariete of House Viridius is innocent in the matter of Queen Katrina's murder. This trial is over."

"And why should we listen to a bastard king who deceives his own people?" Arahm spouted. "Or do you still claim to bear the holy Glove of Nehro?"

Raeylan stared down at Arahm, undaunted by the Storm King's wrath. "I have never claimed to wear The Glove," the king stated.

"But is that not an imitation on your right arm, King Raeylan?"

"It is the indication of my rank as sovereign. I never asserted it as anything more."

"A lie of omission is little better than admitted deception," Arahm yelled to the populace.

Faces peered through the courtyard, many heads nodding in agreement.

"King Arahm is right!" the Duke of Timberdale concurred, stepping out from the throng. "The Viridius line is cursed! I will not swear loyalty to false nobility!"

He drew his weapon, his attendants following suit.

"So be it," Raeylan said quietly, and charged forward, *Moonstone Retribution* glinting through the storm.

35: THE FIRST KINGDOM'S LAST ARC

Esilwen was pulled to her feet by Shikun as Raeylan charged. The Tempestguard surrounded Arahm with naked blades, escorting him toward the throng of nobles. Twenty or so men near the duke threw off their cloaks, revealing the silver-and-blue emblems of the Storm King. Captain Hendar belatedly followed his sovereign's lead, but it was evident that Margariete's position would be overrun before he could reach her. The courtyard had transformed within moments from an assemblage of aristocracy into a maul of clashing weapons. Bodyguards loyal to defecting lords attacked the Gem Knights of the First Kingdom, though Esilwen could tell that many of Raeylan's soldiers had changed their allegiance, siding with Arahm and the duke.

"Esilwen, get inside the castle!" Shikun commanded as he dashed into the fray. "Quickly!"

The two curved arms of Pearl and Jade knights attempted to close ranks, preventing enemy access to the royal family. Many of the Tempestguard had already broken through the lines by the time the formation could be realigned. Arahm's army swelled not only with traitors, but reinforcements that pushed their way onto the terrace from the outer courtyard. The Gem Knights found themselves battling adversaries on both sides, defense lines spread thin.

Esilwen watched the princeling as he tried to reach Margariete. He had only crossed half the distance to his sister when she was surrounded by three of the Tempestguard. Negin intercepted two of them, parrying with his sword and dagger. The third launched his blade at the princess, though she rolled into a twist and his weapon slashed harmlessly above her torso. The soldier's unimpeded momentum carried him forward and Margariete spun into a kick that drove him to the ground. His weapon sloshed into the ripple of water stretching over the flagstones.

Somehow, Margariete shed her manacles. Through the thick sheet of falling rain Esilwen couldn't see how her friend had managed to escape them. *Stardawn* leapt obediently from the ground into the princess's outstretched palm. In two strides Margariete had moved to Negin's aid. One of his opponents had been felled, but the other had pinned him to the stone, blade plunging toward his throat. A well-aimed blow struck the Tempestguard dead and as She searched for a new foe, the Gem Knights' defensive perimeter faltered. Skirmishing bodies surged between the Jeweled princess and Esilwen, blocking the view.

The blond healer prepared to retreat into the safety of the castle, but she hesitated. A small pair of flailing arms had caught her attention. Between the ebb and flow of combatants, Esilwen spotted Shikun. Two burly Tempestguard were hauling him toward the duke's column of soldiers. They were taking him to his father. The princeling bent and pulled, but the larger men easily countered his resistance.

She scanned the area frantically, seeking help. Margariete had mended the breach in the defender's line—

all were focused on holding their position against desperate odds. Raeylan and Terail were mired in a ferocious duel, their blades crashing against each other with vicious speed.

The battle pitched toward Esilwen. Shikun was dragged farther into the melee. She wasn't a warrior. What could she do?

The answer came unbidden. She wielded Fohtian's artifact. She would trust its power.

Esilwen rushed forward, scooping up a discarded sword along the way. It felt heavy and awkward in her hand and the wet hilt almost slid from her untrained grip. Weaving through the battlefield, Esilwen avoided the sharp edges of steel and the driving bulks of armor. Once she was forced to halt as Hendar ground his weapon into a Tempestguard, throwing a dispatched carcass to the ground in her path. He looked at her with astonishment as he noticed the blade she carried.

"What are you doing here, Lady Esilwen? Fall back to the castle!" he ordered as he plunged a dagger into the throat of another foe.

"Prince Shikun," she explained, breathless in the rain, "they took him."

She pointed toward the middle of the courtyard, but Hendar's attention was demanded by another skirmish. Esilwen snaked around him, the captain's incoherent words lost as she thrust herself into the enemy ranks. Since she seemed an empty threat with her limp sword nearly dragging against the ground, many of the Tempestguard ignored her. More than once she accidentally tripped over the prone forms of dead or wounded men. She had almost caught up to Shikun's captors when something snatched her wrist and curled it painfully. With a yelp she was roughly spun around. An Amber knight raised his weapon to strike her.

Fohtian's Warden acted without forethought. She simply willed her body to arrange her release. The man screamed in agony as green flames burst through the fingers that gripped her. Superstitious fear powered the downward arc of his uninjured weapon arm. She met the slow attack with a clumsy deflection of her sword. The man's eyes widened with terror.

Icy rims of fire licked the length of her blade, turning his steel molten orange as their swords met. The Amber knight dropped his useless weapon and fled.

Esilwen pressed forward, aware that her sword danced with the fire god's power. None dared confront her bewitched blade, and soon she stood before the Storm King. Shikun struggled at his side.

"Witch!" Arahm roared in disgust and drove his sword forward.

Pain spread like scalding layers throughout her body. Her weapon darkened and clattered shallowly against the slate paving stones. She heard her heart pound once loudly, as Arahm tore his blade from her torso.

Esilwen blinked into the grey-streaming sky, wondering when she had fallen.

"No!" came Shikun's sunken voice, seemingly muted like the gurgle of water.

Scuffling told her that the princeling wrested with the men restraining him. Her heart thrummed again.

"Stop fighting, Shikun," Arahm commanded. "She is nothing! We must get you out of here."

Blood spilled into Esilwen's lungs, pressing forward by a steady rhythm. The liquid's metallic tang coated her throat as she tried to breathe. She coughed, drowning in her own life.

"I will not leave!" Shikun declared hotly. "My loyalty is to the First Kingdom, to Raeylan!"

Esilwen turned her head and the Storm King came into view. Arahm's hand struck his son with a loud crack.

"You will do as you are told," Arahm barked angrily. "The First Kingdom is ours. I will make you king of all Thyella."

"I will never betray my brother!" Shikun shrieked. "I refuse to be king!"

"You cannot refuse to perform what you were born to do! You will honor me with obedience." Arahm turned to his men. "Take him," he ordered.

Shikun shouted at his father as the men pulled him toward the silver gate. Arahm looked down on Esilwen's crumpled body.

The eleventh beat rattled her veins. Esilwen was dismayed as she felt the first prickle of healing fire. What would Arahm do when he saw her wounds close, when she rose whole and undamaged in the center of his troops? She was not strong enough to save Shikun by herself. Raeylan and Margariete were so far away.

"Fohtian, save us!" Esilwen prayed.

Green fire erupted from her chest, agonizing needles tearing through her nerves. The men escorting Shikun halted in amazement.

"What manner of demon—?" Arahm thundered.

Esilwen drew a proper breath, slowly standing. The ground shuddered. Shouts of alarm rose from the courtyard as its shell of stone cracked and splintered. Arahm stumbled. Soldiers tumbled to the ground. A high peal, like the fierce shriek from a bird of prey, rose from the bowels of Thyella. The slate under Esilwen's feet grew white with heat. Rain curled in vapor tendrils as it struck the ground around her.

Arahm staggered back, barely escaping the liquefying circle of fire that suddenly lashed outward from Esilwen's body, surrounding her in a protective shell. Esilwen looked down, her gaze disappearing into the depths of an open portal. Infinite fire undulated across the land beneath her feet, as if she hung suspended above an ocean of writhing green flame. Far within the jade sea, a beam of deepest crimson flashed, gathering in speed and form as it raced upward toward her toes. She braced herself as a creature of scarlet-and-gold burned through her body on its path into the air. The majestic bird stretched its fiery wings, nearly the width of the castle, across the grey sky, turning the rain into mist as it passed. The gate below Esilwen's feet vanished like a breath extinguishing a candle. She landed heavily on the crystalled flagstone.

With a snap of its tawny beak, the gigantic phoenix screeched again, fixing its gleaming green eyes on Esilwen's foes. All stood petrified in the courtyard, transfixed by the massive feathered giant. Its scarlet quills were tipped in gold, ablaze with sparks of emerald.

"Free the little prince," Esilwen ordered.

The servant of fire glanced at her, nodded and obeyed. It dived with outstretched talons at Shikun's captors, rending their bodies and compressing the remains into the ground. Esilwen scrambled to her feet and rushed to Shikun's side. He had fallen before the enormous fire elemental. Grabbing at his hand, Esilwen urged him to stand.

"Hurry, Shikun," she said as he struggled upright.

Arahm clambered to the silver portcullis that led out of the inner courtyard.

"Kill the demon!" Arahm screamed, mad spittle flecking his lips. "Save your Prince! Bring me my son!"

Then the Storm King fled from the terrace.

Reluctantly, the Tempestguard surrounded Esilwen and Shikun, the phoenix hovering menacingly above them. A hot breeze scorched the air around them when the majestic bird spread its wings. As the knights raised their weapons to attack, the phoenix screamed, bursting apart in violent green flame. Its feathers flared outward like hundreds of blazing arrows, piercing the soldiers. Each man struck crumpled into ash. Large grey flakes fluttered through the air like boiled snow.

Esilwen choked on the scent. Though the phoenix had disappeared, the remaining Tempestguard and turncoat Gem knights retreated through the gate. Raeylan's warriors let them go, too exhausted to follow.

"Lady Esilwen, are you all right?"

Raeylan's gloved hand closed around her arm. Concern filled his eyes. She nodded, suddenly aware that her wet hair stuck to her skin uncomfortably and her limbs shivered. A great weakness washed over her, and she leaned against Raeylan for support.

The king surveyed the courtyard. Esilwen followed his gaze. One side of the inner wall had blasted outward, the edges of its broken stone frozen into glassy pricks. Hendar and Tenan patrolled the rubble, meeting out death to any enemy that had straggled behind the rest of the fleeing army.

"Go," Shikun said to his brother, moving to support Esilwen. "I will make sure Esilwen reaches the castle safely."

Raeylan squeezed the princeling's shoulder in gratitude. With *Moonstone Retribution* in hand, he moved to join his officers.

"We should see if Margariete is safe," Shikun suggested, turning back toward the castle.

Esilwen and Shikun eased their way through the drifts of cinder corpses. Rain mingled with the blood and ash, coating the stony terrace with a slippery paste.

Consequently, it took a few moments to reach the Jeweled Princess.

Margariete knelt next to her broken trial podium, cradling something in her lap. *Stardawn* lay discarded behind her. As Esilwen approached, she recognized Negin. His body lay still; his sightless eyes stared into the ash-gloom sky. A bamboo shaft protruded from his chest.

"He's already dead," Margariete croaked when she noticed Esilwen. "No manner of healing could help him now."

The arrow had pierced his heart.

"I could try, Margariete," Esilwen whispered hopefully. "We do not yet know the full extent of my powers."

The princess shook her head. "Healing Shikun and Seriya when they were so close to death almost killed you."

Esilwen's sorrow joined Margariete's. Shikun wrapped his arms around his sister as sobs shook her.

"I was—that bird—it—," Margariete explained haltingly. "I didn't see the archer. Negin jumped in front of me and—and—"

Shikun's hold on his sister tightened. Esilwen looked back through courtyard of graves, her tears mingling with the rain.

36: QUEEN ANLEIA'S TOMB

Raeylan had spent many arcs learning the art of monarchial policy from his mother. Queen Anleia had always been meticulous about the details of directing the kingdom. One of the most intriguing discussions they had ever shared was also one of Raeylan's most nostalgic memories. How would he, when king, stop an opposing army from taking the City of Jewels?

As a youth, Raeylan had simply scoffed at the possibility. No one could defeat the leader of the First Kingdom, because no adversary would dare challenge the bearer of Nehro's power. His mother had smiled sadly at his juvenile exclamation, her expression worth more than any word or phrase. It would be seasons before he fully understood Anleia's answer.

Certainty of belief was deceptive, she had said, and brought even the most powerful sovereigns to ruin.

At the time, he had pondered the statement, but remained resilient in his conviction that the Jeweled Kingdom would never face invasion. Now, standing at the precipice of the fallen wall of his castle's inner courtyard, Raeylan wondered if his mother had ever considered techniques to drive an enemy army from its foothold in the city with only a handful of soldiers at her disposal.

The Third Kingdom had entrenched a force of several hundred soldiers—some from the Storm Realm, but at least half were traitors of his own aristocracy—positioned in key areas across the city. Squads held the gates into the City of Jewels, marched across the bridges, and ejected citizens from their homes. The rest of the opposing army stalked the barred entrance into Viridius Castle's courtyard, laying the foundation of a siege.

Raeylan wished his mother had devised some magical formula for retaking the Jeweled capital with a mere 41 Gem Knights and 50 loyalist nobles. Only Pearl and Jade warriors had remained faithful to their king. Those of Amber class had been easily swayed to the Storm Ruler's side. The castle held plenty of supplies for a meager militia. As long as they kept the enemy from raiding the castle, the defenders would be secure.

Until the rest of Arahm's army arrived.

The 2,000 Storm knights were just visible through the grey horizon, and would most likely overrun the city near the last arc of the cycle. Raeylan suspected that King Hylan had sent for the might of the Glass Kingdom as well. The small force occupying the city hadn't tried a frontal assault because they were waiting for reinforcements.

At least Arahm was allowing the inhabitants of the city to flee unhindered—encouraging it even. For three cycles, a steady stream of people poured into the countryside. Now, only a small trickle of merchants willing to stake their lives against the coin of the invading soldiers was left inside the city proper.

Raeylan peered through the rain that shrouded his city. The Storm King's ambush had been well-conceived. That fact alone convinced the Jeweled King that Arahm was not responsible for the plot's design. Though a political genius, Arahm's tactical strategy was limited to "more soldiers win the war." Raeylan's true opponent was Terail Dasklos. The turncoat daimyo had provided the exclusive information that had caused the nobles to defect, and no one but Raeylan's most trusted general could have smuggled scores of disguised Tempestguard into the trial. Terail had even handpicked the guards stationed between the inner and outer courtyard. It was they who had allowed the extra 80 "bodyguards" to slip inside the silver portcullis once the battle began. Arahm's troops had the advantage. The coup would have easily defeated Raeylan's small group of loyalists if Fohtian's elemental hadn't intervened.

The fiery apparition had eliminated over a hundred of Arahm's men. A host had fled back into the city. Those who stayed to fight were eventually defeated. Twenty-eight prisoners now occupied the dungeon cells underneath the castle, 14 of them traitors. By law, these should be executed, but Raeylan had already exceeded his fill of death for a season. He would spare them if he could. In addition to the enemies killed by the phoenix, nine of Raeylan's personal guard had perished during the battle.

"The last of the bodies have been cleared, Your Majesty," Captain Hendar said, interrupting the king's solemn brooding. "I apologize, My King, but we don't have enough dry wood to give proper funerals to our fallen men."

Raeylan only stared at his city, imagining how Terail would deploy the new soldiers when the Third Kingdom's army arrived.

"After the battle, we will salvage wood for pyres from the inner wall," Raeylan decided. "Have Tenan position our troops as soon as possible."

Hendar was silent for a moment, restraining his argument in respect for his sovereign, but the old commander's pragmatism proved too strong to withhold.

"Your Majesty," he began, "I do not wish to sound defeated, but 90 men against 2,000? Even behind the castle's walls, we haven't hope of victory."

Raeylan turned, fixing his grey eyes on his captain.

"Trust that we have more than hope, my friend," he assured.

The king climbed from the broken wall and left Hendar to his duties.

As he stepped onto the nightingale floor inside the castle, Raeylan couldn't help but remember the triumphant grin that had revealed Terail's true character. Raeylan and his daimyo had shared a bond deeper than blood for five seasons, trusting each other, Raeylan had believed, without reserve. They had saved each other's lives on multiple occasions, risked personal honor to support the other more than once. Terail would not have sold his allegiance for something as paltry as money.

But Raeylan obviously didn't know his general as well as he had thought. During the battle, the former Pearl Daimyo had used powers only the water goddess could grant. Like the cursed beasts at the border, Terail could teleport at will.

Moonstone Retribution's capacity to see the general's ethereal jump was all that had rescued the Jeweled King from Terail's deadly daggers during the battle for the courtyard. Raeylan was the better swordsman, but the ability to teleport gave Terail the means to match the king's skill with the blade. Only Esilwen's intervention caused the general to withdraw.

The only plausible explanation for Terail's behavior was that he had feigned friendship from the beginning. He had moved into the castle the season of Anleia's death, had painstakingly broken through Raeylan's stoic guard, positioning himself as the heir's most trusted confidant.

Terail had befriended the lonely princess, wooed her into loving him. And betrayed them for—what? The chance to destroy the First Kingdom?

What would drive him to such obsession?

In light of Terail's newly discovered powers, the mystery of Katrina's death became clear. After drugging Margariete, Terail must have teleported into the bridal chamber and murdered the Queen with *Stardawn* as the king began his climb to the sixth floor. The ability to bend space had given Terail ample time to collect Margariete, wake her, and arrange the appearance of the princess's guilt.

"Is something wrong, Your Majesty?"

Lost in his musings, Raeylan hadn't noticed his prolonged pause on the colonnade. Esilwen drew his gaze. Her smile brightened the crystalline green of her eyes. She filled him with a dichotomous concoction of melancholy and joy.

"I go to my sister," he said. "Would you grant me the honor of your company?"

The pretty maiden blushed.

"That is, if you can get her to come out of her room," the healer returned. "She won't let anyone in, even me."

They ascended the staircase in silence. Halfway up, perhaps uncomfortable in the stillness, Esilwen spoke.

"Are you worried about the upcoming battle, Your Majesty?"

"There is always a measure of unease that precludes a battle," Raeylan answered, "but no. I have faith that Nehro will grant us victory this cycle."

"Then what troubles you so?" Esilwen asked when they had reached the fourth floor.

Raeylan paused and turned, sorrow welling through him. Though his actions in the next arc would save his family, his kingdom, and the woman he loved, it would also bring forth his doom. He smoothed the golden strands from Esilwen's lovely pointed ears with his ungloved hand, drinking in her otherworldly beauty.

"My mother believed that happiness was beyond a monarch's reach, a gift we could provide for others, but never taste ourselves."

His fingers brushed her lips gently.

"Why are you are telling me this?"

"Because I love you," Raeylan replied softly. "My heart cannot deny you. But though you are a part me, my actions this cycle may divide us forever." He kissed her cheek tenderly. "And for that, I must beg your forgiveness."

Raeylan could see Esilwen's breath quicken with panic, and though she didn't understand, she didn't press him for answers.

"If forgiveness is what you desire of me, Your Majesty," she said, her lilting voice cracking with heartache, "I grant it willingly."

He lingered next to her for the span of several moments and then led her to the sixth floor. Seriya knelt by Margariete's chamber door, distress evident in her expression.

"Your Majesty, thank Nehro!" she exclaimed, almost forgetting to bow in respect. "You must do something! Princess Margariete refuses to eat and has forbidden me to enter. I fear she might do herself harm!"

Raeylan strode forward, sliding the door open. Margariete's voice rang hoarsely from within.

"I distinctly ordered that no one enter, Seriya," she reprimanded.

"The king takes orders from no one, my sister," Raeylan announced as he passed into her sleeping quarters.

Margariete immediately rose from the bed, flinching at the sound of his voice.

"R—Raeylan—"

"Calm yourself," he said. "I am not here to torture you further. I will be arranging a meeting in the Jeweled Shrine. I wish for you to attend." He touched her chin with his thumb affectionately. "It is of the greatest importance, Margariete."

"If it will please you, brother," she said.

Raeylan pulled her to his chest, wrapping his arms tightly around her.

"Do not despair," he pleaded. "I will make Terail answer for his crimes. He will die for the cruelty he has shown you."

Margariete returned her twin's embrace fiercely. "I cannot atone for the secrets I betrayed, brother. How can you still call me sister?"

"You are no more guilty than I. I also mislaid my trust in Terail."

As he released her, Margariete took a retreating step, self-hatred twisting inside her sapphire eyes.

"I was a fool. My idiocy has ruined us."

"On the contrary, we are liberated," Raeylan replied, holding his sister's gaze steadily. "It is because of you that the Viridius line will reestablish its claim to Nehro's Grace."

Margariete's brow furrowed.

"What—"

Raeylan raised his hand to stay her question.

"The Third Kingdom will assault the castle soon. We must meet our commanders."

*

Once in the Jeweled Shrine, Raeylan sent Seriya to gather Shikun, Hendar, and Tenan. He refused all attempts at conversation, save to stop Esilwen when she tried to excuse herself from the gathering. When all were present, he addressed the assembly.

"From this cycle forth, Terail Dasklos is stripped of his lordship, banished from the ranks of the Gem Knights with dishonor, and expelled from the First Kingdom. He enters our realm on pain of death.

"His defection leaves us with a loss of leadership. Through recent events, my sister has discovered the loss treachery brings. She has earned the right to defend the First Kingdom, to win back the honor that was stolen from her. Our soldiers fight not only for the survival our country, but also for our princess.

"Margariete of House Viridius, I hereby name you Pearl Daimyo, general and commander of the Gem Knights."

Shikun and Tenan looked only slightly taken aback. Hendar actually released a sigh of relief, grateful he hadn't been appointed to the position. Margariete trembled, requiring a moment to control herself before the ceremony could continue. She knelt before her king and the knights she would command, taking a small cup of water that Raeylan had filled from the spring. Pride filled the king as his twin sipped the liquid, accepting the appointment. He knew her momentary lapse of self-restraint would only strengthen her determination and would be reflected in the quality of her leadership.

The ritual was completed quickly. Afterward, Raeylan instructed the company to follow as he led them into the bowels of the castle, past the dungeons, and into the royal mausoleum.

Typical burial custom in Thyella required the burning of the body, whose ashes were later stored in a sacred jar.

The nobility compartmentalized their urns, sheltering both ashes and the deceased's signet glove.

However, the people of Thyella did not believe that their leaders crossed the Seven Cascades into the netherworld. Thus, the corporeal shells of kings and queens were encased in tombs of stone, their souls protecting the kingdom even in death. The urns of royalty contained not only their mark of rank, but the departed spirit's most treasured possession—a keepsake to anchor his soul to the mortal realm.

The king lit the thick candle at the mausoleum's threshold, noting his companions' confusion as they gathered in the flickering light. The vault greeted the small party with the stillness only death can breathe. Raeylan knew the winding maze of tombs well, having visited his mother's burial place often in the first trinals following her death. As they walked, he ignited the large oil sconces that lined the stone walls. Brothers, wives, children, and kin were cradled in the wall's recesses, their urns carefully placed on adjacent shelves, but the arched alcoves were reserved for past Viridian sovereigns. Each coffin mirrored the attributes of the ruler it housed—some flagrant in jade and gold, others delicately carved with a relief of the monarch's likeness.

When they reached Anleia's niche, Raeylan felt his heart accelerate with anticipation. Her ivory marble sarcophagus was smooth and cool to the touch, etched with a single symbol: duty. He traced it lovingly with his fingers, oblivious to his audience until Shikun coughed loudly.

"Raeylan," Margariete asked, "what are we doing here?"

He looked at his twin. Then he stepped forward and retrieved his mother's urn. He had sealed it himself, five seasons ago.

"Our mother carried two secrets," Raeylan said, turning the lavender jar in the light. Lonely golden petals decorated its porcelain surface. "The first: her firstborn children were not of her husband's blood." He set the urn on the flat surface of him mother's tomb, over the carved rune. "The second," he continued, "she used to protect her children from the malady that claimed her life."

Shikun and Margariete shared a worried glance. Then, the Jeweled King smashed his mother's urn.

"What have you done?" Margariete shrieked.

Nothing could bring greater insult to the departed. The princess lurched forward angrily, but Raeylan had already sifted through the porcelain fragments and extracted an object. He held it out to her, watching as a tender softness replaced the mortification in her features.

"Before she died, mother warned me this time would come," he said to his twin, "when we would need to call upon her spirit to protect the kingdom. She commanded me to pass this on to you, Margariete."

A silver chain dangled from his hand, supporting a tear-shaped stone. Anleia had worn the olive-black pendant every cycle since Raeylan could remember. She had never told them its significance. Margariete ran her thumbs over the glistening mineral.

"This was mother's favorite," she said softly, her eyes sore with memory.

Raeylan heard a shuffle behind his sister and spared a glance at Esilwen. She was scanning the mausoleum agitatedly, pulling absently at her gown.

"Lady Esilwen?" Shikun asked in concern.

"I'm fine, thank you," she responded. "I just—there's something—a sense of—like a presence—I can't quite explain."

Raeylan again sorted through the remains of the lavender vase and withdrew the leather signet glove that had belonged to his mother. It was identical to his own, designed to mimic the one worn by his grandfather, King Shogan, the last known bearer of the goddess's artifact.

"Let it be known from this cycle forth," Raeylan announced, "that House Viridius will continue to uphold the sacred duty assigned by the goddess, Nehro."

Reaching into his mother's signet glove with his right hand, the king removed a scrap of frayed brown material that had been skillfully hidden within. Stained and unimpressive, he set the shapeless wad of fabric on the edge of the ivory sarcophagus.

It was a glove.

Without warning, the king ripped his signet garment from his arm, baring his skin to everyone assembled. Hendar and Tenan looked away apprehensively, but the others simply stared at him in shock.

"Raeylan!" Shikun gasped.

The Jeweled King inhaled a steadying breath. Then he lifted the crumpled artifact and drew it over his arm.

A liquid wave seemed to pass through him as the object touched his skin. The material expanded, contracted, and rippled as it melded to him, like a pool of bronze seeping over a smooth plane. Then, in an icy flash of white, Nehro's Glove altered its form. Dark, leather-like material sheathed his forearm and palm, stretching to the knuckles but leaving the fingers free. Gold and silver runes writhed across its surface, dancing with magical life. Raeylan knew he had never encountered the language before, but found he could understand its meaning.

And then Nehro's Glove extracted its price.

Agony pierced him to the bone. His blood pulsed with pain. Unable to stem the cry of anguish that roared from his lips, he fell to his knees, gripping the edge of his mother's tomb with white-knuckled fingers. Another scream tore his throat as his soul was ripped open, his life force spewing into the vast corridor of time and space that was Nehro's domain.

Both Margariete and Esilwen rushed forward to his aid.

"Stop!" he ordered with such ferocity that they froze.

After a moment, when the pain eased, he hefted himself to his feet, trembling with weakness. The Glove continued to siphon his strength, though not as quickly. Slowly, Raeylan covered Nehro's artifact with his original glove.

"Its touch brings a slow death," he explained to his staring companions.

A strange sensation caused him to turn to Esilwen, pulled his mind toward her like a bubble of air that rushed to the surface of a pond. And suddenly, he could sense the power of Fohtian inside her.

"Nehro's power will drive King Arahm from our borders," he declared. "The Guardian of Time safeguards the City of Jewels once again."

37: RIVER OF TIME

"Was it not Lord Terail's instructions that we wait to attack the castle until he returns at dawn?" King Hylan posed quizzically. "Your men have just arrived. Surely they need rest?"

The Storm King curled his tongue, stemming the curt retort that bridged his lips. The common-born general may have provided Arahm with the information that deposed Raeylan, but the sovereign of the Third Kingdom took orders from no one. His army had a tactical advantage. To delay now, on the brink of victory, was foolhardy.

"Waiting gives King Raeylan time to organize a stronger defense," Arahm snorted. "Terail Dasklos has nothing more to offer than what he has already given. My soldiers know their duty. This cycle, the First Kingdom falls to our combined might."

The shorter king at Arahm's side shivered with nerves, his forehead beaded with perspiration. Hylan's eyes had sunken into his pale face, his skin tight around his skull. His unmanly grief frustrated Arahm almost to disgust. Such whimpering over the loss of a girl-child. Katrina's only value had been her ability to merge her father's kingdom to another. Arahm had been contemplating taking the girl as a wife himself, until Raeylan proposed to take the match.

Raeylan. Anleia's infidelity had been no surprise. Her affection as a wife had been stringently aloof. Over the seasons, Arahm had attributed Raeylan's lack of ambition as a weakness from his mother, but suddenly the difference in conduct was made clear. A bastard son, disobedient and proudly spurning the advice of his kingly father, protecting his witch of a sister, and harboring a demon healer from the Void. No wonder the First Kingdom was rotting from within. Ridding the world of the ill-begotten twins would be a gift to all Thyella.

Shikun, however, was another affair. The boy's defiance of his king warranted execution. Fathering another heir was a simple matter, but, after Raeylan and Margariete were properly dispatched, only the youngest son of Anleia Viridius could claim the First Kingdom's throne. The Storm King needed the errant youth to bring the Kingdom of Jewels under his rule.

"Do you not believe that King Raeylan is willing to parlay?" Hylan asked.

The Glass King's gazed through the marketplace, following the outer castle wall with his eyes. Doubt riddled Hylan's expression.

Arahm's patience nearly faltered. It was arduous, having to convince Hylan time and again that war was the only means to cleanse the shard. The Fourth Kingdom's sovereign was simply too soft, his resolve flabby and frail.

"Have you forgotten King Raeylan's refusal to convict your daughter's murderer?" Arahm ground through his teeth.

Hylan recoiled as if struck.

"You are right, of course," he sighed, "my Katrina deserves justice. But still, I wonder—"

Arahm fought the urge to knock the blubbering fool from his saddle.

"The bastard king brought evil into our shard. His sorceress healer pollutes our land, his sister is a fiend. I will show no mercy to one who consorts with such demons."

The clouds turned dark as the moon began its nightly eclipse, hiding his men as formless outlines. Six hundred troops lurked in the marketplace, awaiting the command to surge through the castle's main gate. The bulk of his army—over a thousand Third Kingdom knights, swollen with 500 of Raeylan's own soldiers—was poised on the nobility tier, between the castle's plateau and the lower plain of the city, ready to assault the complex's west entrance. Once inside, it would be an easy matter to raise the central gate. Smaller platoons dotted the city in the event any of Raeylan's supporters attempted flight. A tertiary force had been stationed outside the city wall, prepared to march if needed.

Arahm's only concern was the infernal apparition that the demon healer could summon. Hopefully, the abomination could only kill a hundred at a time. He was confident that 2,500 men would dispatch the defenders before the creature could do any real damage. To guarantee his own safety, Arahm would direct the battle from the tiled marketplace, out of the monster's range but with a clear view of the looming castle above.

"Hail, King Arahm," called the Tempestguard Marshal, his heavy armor stained with rain as his mount clacked across the square.

Five sentries on horseback accompanied him, surrounding a lonely walking figure, probably a herald from the Jeweled King. Arahm grinned. He would show no clemency this cycle, regardless of the terms the First Kingdom might propose.

"Marshal Takaei?" Arahm addressed.

Takaei halted and bowed in respect, worry crinkling his face. As he moved aside, the enemy messenger stepped forward with resolve, undaunted by the mounted foes around him. Arahm's eyes bulged in their sockets.

King Raeylan stood before him, unarmed and without escort.

"I have come to discuss the conditions of your surrender, Kings of Thyella," Raeylan announced with grave authority, flicking his gaze between Arahm and Hylan. "If you leave my city now, I will spare the lives of your men."

Arahm's face soured with fury. When he gutted this pompous fake, he would drape the remains from the city gate for the birds to feast upon.

"Your demon healer and witch sister have addled your wits, Raeylan," he scoffed. "I, of course, decline your demands."

Raeylan's eyes flashed. "The City of Jewels will be cleansed of all enemies and traitors. You condemn your soldiers if you refuse to withdraw," he warned, clenching the fist sheathed in his signet glove.

Arahm laughed loudly.

"A pathetic last resort. Tonight the rain will wash your blood into the Seven Cascades, and my son," he lingered on the word, "will claim your throne."

The Jeweled King seemed unmoved. Indignation flared inside Arahm's head. He could end this now. One simple command, and Raeylan's kingdom would collapse.

"Marshal Takaei," Arahm said, unable to temper the snarl of his words, "kill this fraud!"

Both Hylan and Takaei stared at the Storm King. Few things were more dishonorable than murdering an unarmed courier, especially in a time of war. Arahm didn't care. The First Kingdom would be his, etiquette be damned to the

Void. The Tempestguard Marshal continued to hesitate, weapon sheathed. With an angry sneer, Arahm drew his own sword, vowing to flog the mutinous knight, and urged his steed forward.

Raeylan stared at Arahm with sober disapproval. The Storm King screeched a triumphant roar, swinging his blade in a wild arc, intending to decapitate his wife's son in one swipe.

His weapon struck only the falling rain.

"What? Where is he!" Arahm bellowed with rage, frantically sweeping his head from side to side. His pulse ballooned under his skin. The Jeweled King was nowhere in sight. The Storm King's men scanned the marketplace, the pounding rain their only accompaniment.

"There!" Hylan finally announced, pointing. Arahm looked in the indicated direction. Raeylan's form was just visible at the pinnacle of the castle's battlements, his overcoat flapping ardently, despite the lack of wind.

The thrum of pounding rain stopped abruptly, the cavity of its silence frigid with vibration. Icy puffs strangled the horse's breath. Arahm's soldiers shivered as the air around them suddenly burned their throats with frost. White crystal petals drifted from above, melting on the Storm King's skin like electric jolts, coating the ground with ghostly powder.

Fear crashed against him in a cackling frenzy. He had seen this before, tasted the arctic wrath of Nehro's power 18 seasons ago, when Shogan had obliterated the City of Blades. Arahm leapt from his horse, barking an alarm to his ally. Without pausing to see if Hylan followed, Arahm dashed for the closest double-floored building.

And then the sky wept frozen daggers.

Arahm's feet slid on the cobblestone. The sharp crack of the ice blades shattering on stone rang through his ears.

Two fingerlike knives gored his arms before he managed to duck into his targeted structure. With a grunt, he ripped them from his flesh and threw them to the floor. To his relief, he noted that the walls were sturdy rock—he seemed to be in some kind of apothecary. Pain-filled screams wafted through the doorway, but Arahm paid them little heed. He needed to reach higher ground.

Arahm spotted some stairs just as Hylan and several Tempestguard burst into the building, their bodies peppered with shards of ice. One collapsed, probably from loss of blood.

"King Arahm," Hylan asked, desperate with panic, "what is happening?"

A hissing rumble shook the floorboards, spurring Arahm to action. Ignoring Hylan's question, the Storm King rushed the stairs, bounding up them two at a time. The clatter of footsteps followed, but not quickly enough.

A wave of water pinched through the threshold, slamming foam and surf against the opposite wall. Lurching upward, the water snatched three men from the stairs, pulling them under its malicious shell. Both Arahm and Hylan escaped its filching tentacles. After reaching the second-level landing, they peered cautiously through a window.

The Cascades thrashed freely through the streets, smothering soldiers and horses, battering their bodies against the buildings, plucking them from safe havens on walls and rooftops. Arahm watched, sick with incredulity, as the water heaved his army over the city's cliff, dashed to its death on the marshlands below.

His men on the nobility tier were at the mercy of the death knives from the sky. Bodies layered the ground, the few survivors scrambling over corpses to escape the flesh-shredding ice. Swells of water lifted from Namida Lake, scooping the frayed carcasses into the thirsty rivers.

Through it all, the solitary figure of the Jeweled King stood against the shadow of his castle.

*

"I specifically told you to wait for me, King Arahm," Terail Dasklos snapped angrily as he entered the command tent.

The Storm King glared at the former First Kingdom general. When the waters of Nehro receded, Arahm and Hylan had retreated outside the city. The Glove had spared only the soldiers outside the walls. Though their remaining forces still outmatched that of the Jeweled King, Arahm dared not to re-enter the city gate.

"It is not for you to decide what I do with my armies, Dasklos," he snarled, scratching the bandages on his arm. The rain had returned, but his body was numb with cold. "Get out."

The traitor stiffened.

"And now, here you are, King Arahm," Terail said acidly, "basking in the fruits of your arrogance, your men dead in the marshlands."

"And you think your skills alone would have influenced the outcome? Bah," Arahm growled. "Raeylan has found Nehro's artifact. This is a battle we can no longer win. Even if I had every knight in the shard at my disposal, I could not overthrow him."

"The Glove of Nehro?" Dasklos asked, brows lifted in wonder. "I thought you said it was lost."

"It was!" Arahm yelled savagely. "I saw King Shogan's dead body myself. Someone had ripped the blasted thing from his arm. We searched the area for seasons, but found nothing!"

"Must have been disappointing for you, Arahm," Dasklos said, his demeanor suddenly slack, cool like a stalking hunter.

The defector smiled wickedly, a feral lust rippling through his eyes. The shiver that wracked Arahm's bowels belied him from reprimanding the commoner for addressing him so informally. Though the Storm King had known the former general for seasons, he had only encountered him on occasion, and even then, barely spared the man a glance. Now that the king looked closely, there was something familiar in the way Dasklos twisted his face with such cruelty.

"It was obvious you were scheming for dominion over the entire shard," Dasklos continued. "When Shogan turned up missing, I bet you were the first to scour his dead body, looking for The Glove. Imagine if you had found it. You would already be Thyella's emperor. But it seems the goddess has forsaken you."

Arahm's fear dissolved in the boil of his temper.

"King Shogan was a good man. He defeated the threat of a warmongering kingdom and restored order to the shard."

"He murdered an entire nation," Terail hissed, hands drifting to the hilts of his daggers, "as did you. Know this, Arahm Galenos: if I did not need to you to destroy the Viridius family, you would already lay dead at my feet."

"How dare you threaten me!" Arahm seethed. "I am the sovereign of the Third Kingdom." The Storm King narrowed his eyes. "And what was the Second Kingdom to you? You were barely a child when it was destroyed."

"You are mistaken, King Arahm," Dasklos said, the gruesome grin returning to his lips. "When the City of Blades was destroyed, I was just as you see me now."

Arms outstretched, he presented himself for inspection. Arahm felt the prickle of annoyance.

"I don't understand."

"Not surprising," Terail smirked, "you never were skilled with complexity."

"You have insulted and threatened me. I warn you never to do it again! I command you to explain yourself!"

Arahm blinked when he unexpectedly felt the cold steel of a dagger's edge at his throat. Dasklos' voice sizzled in the Storm King's ear.

"I answer to no one, Arahm, least of all you."

"What are you?" Arahm trembled.

Only the glove bearer had the gift of teleportation. How was it possible that this commoner had the same ability?

"I am what King Shogan made me," Dasklos answered, pressing down on the knife. It pinched uncomfortably. "I will destroy the empire he left behind. The Viridius family will meet its destruction at my hand."

Dasklos roughly released Arahm, and the king stumbled backward. A flick of the wrist and the long dagger was back at the general's side.

A bitter chill stroked the monarch's spine as he stared at the traitor general.

It was impossible, defied all reason. Only misshapen curiosity kept him from calling for the guard.

"You can't be," the Storm King breathed, trying to convince himself. "House Tricahnas fell with the City of Blades. There were no survivors."

"Yet its youngest prince stands before you."

The revelation struck the Storm King like a fisted gale, draining the blood from his face. The last prince of the Second Kingdom had been renowned as the most efficient killer to ever rise through their elite order of assassins.

Countless covert executions were attributed to their prowess, including the death of Arahm's own father. At 16, Kahlos Tricahnas had been appointed lead commander of the Feralblades. Under his rule, the predatory organization had massacred its targets with ferocious ease, the deeds never solidly traced back to them. Arahm had met the prince only once, as a youth of comparable age at the time. Kahlos should be over his 40th season, yet he appeared to only be in his 20s.

"I see you've heard of me," the Blade Prince said with glee.

"How?" Arahm gasped.

He ignored the king's question.

"My kingdom—my inheritance—was stolen by Shogan Viridius. My family will be avenged."

Realization flicked through Arahm's mind.

"You used me!" he charged fervently, drawing his sword and glowering at his father's murderer.

A low growl emanated from behind him. Arahm twisted and redirected his weapon toward the new threat, but his blade bounced harmlessly off a black, scaly hide. Two cloudy, slit eyes confronted him. A warped, needled-fanged snout darted forward and snapped Arahm's sword into useless halves.

"I wouldn't advise that, Arahm," Kahlos Trichanas warned, striding to the beast. He rubbed the creature behind the ear and it wagged its forked tail appreciatively. "Any attempt on my life will bring an end to yours. The loss of your army has diminished your usefulness to me. I might kill you simply for amusement. My comrades and I will deal with Raeylan and his household."

"Comrades?" Arahm murmured, fear pulsing through his blood.

"Say hello to my eldest brother," the Blade Prince grinned viciously, patting the beast. "Raeylan of House Viridius is not the only man to be blessed with Nehro's strength."

38: GRACE OF GENERATION

The slatted beams of Raeylan's library window clenched its wooden teeth against the sky, as if trying to hide the massive marshland tomb a thousand spans below. Margariete swallowed, steeling her nerves against the sight of the heaping corpses that floated through the brackish water. The tattered remains of horses and wagons stabbed the soggy ground. Tearing herself away from the grisly scene, she paced the room, rubbing the soreness from her tired limbs.

Her night had been restless, poisoned with dreams of ruin. After expelling the enemy army the previous night, Raeylan had collapsed, a grimace of pain scoring his face even in unconsciousness. For one terrifying moment, the princess had thought her twin dead. Dawn now smudged the sky, but he had not yet awakened. The waiting gnawed through her. A great number of Arahm's force had survived The Glove's assault and could attack at any moment.

She tread wearily, the creaking of her mother's maiden armor a comfort. One turn traced several paths across the room. Dissatisfied, she crossed the hallway and entered her brother's bedchamber.

Raeylan lay unmoving on the bed, swaddled in quilts. Esilwen knelt at his side, dabbing his forehead tenderly with a cloth. She stared at him with so much concern that she didn't seem to notice Margariete's arrival. The princess leaned against the doorframe, stroking the smooth surface of her mother's pendant that she wore as she watched her friend attend the king.

A full cycle had not passed since her succession to Pearl Daimyo. Her soldiers accepted her leadership, but the slanderous wake of the trial tainted her confidence. Despite her twin's pardon, the princess struggled to stanch the guilt that blistered her gut. The Jeweled Kingdom's doom was her fault. If she had exercised more caution, heated arguments would have been the casualties, not the the hapless lives spent at the bottom of the Cascades.

Terail had been more than he seemed. She berated herself for succumbing to his advances. His mind had been closed to her since their first meeting. That should have put her on guard. Instead, she had simply dismissed it as an anomaly—after all, she was also unable to read Raeylan's mind. She had trusted Terail with foolhardy blindness, had given herself to him body and soul. The thought of her actions caused her stomach to recoil.

Even if the conflict with Arahm was resolved, it would be generations before peaceful relations existed between the First and Fourth Kingdoms. The City of Glass would be slow to forgive the Viridius family for the death of their princess. Margariete could offer herself no clemency for her idiotic folly. Her twin had almost convinced her that there was nothing wrong with her desire to fall in love, to be loved. But he was wrong. She didn't deserve it.

Nor would she ever.

"Princess Margariete," Seriya announced quietly from the hallway, "Captain Hendar has requested to see you."

Margariete turned, nodded, and followed. Hendar and Tenan's voices drifted from the King's receiving room. As she stepped into the chamber, she suppressed an involuntary stab of discomfort. She had been forced to mask her appearance all her life. Though she was glad to be liberated from such oppression, she couldn't help but feel exposed without her veil to shield her.

Malbrin perched on a cushion to one side of the room. His kindly smile bolstered her courage.

"Report," Margariete ordered quickly, waving Seriya away.

"We estimate the Third Kingdom still has between 800-900 troops outside the city walls," Hendar answered with a frown as long as his beard. "It's only a third of the original force, but we don't have enough soldiers to keep them out of the city."

"The threat of Nehro's Glove will do that for now," Margariete said, hoping her voice conveyed an assurance she didn't feel. "What else?"

Hendar looked at Tenan, both men pale under the skin. The lieutenant's dark leather eye patch swallowed the light. His voice dropped lead ingots as he answered.

"At least 40 cursed beasts are in the enemy camp."

"What?" Margariete shouted. She swiveled her head between her two commanders. "Are they attacking Arahm's army?"

"No, Your Highness," Hendar growled gruffly. "It seems the creatures are in league with the Storm King."

Why, by all the layers of the Void, would the cursed beasts join Arahm? The twisted creatures had never worked with humans.

"Forty you say?" she asked, then continued without waiting for confirmation. "When do you think they will attack?"

"There's no way to be sure," Hendar replied.

"With their teleporting abilities, we won't even see them coming," Tenan added tautly. "There's no way of stopping them from slipping inside the walls."

Margariete chewed her lip uneasily. Tenan's mind knotted with apprehension. He believed that if Raeylan didn't wake soon, the castle was lost. The princess shared her lieutenant's sentiment. Perhaps Nehro's Glove could hold back the creatures. Otherwise, the defenders would be severely outmatched, especially since there were only two weapons in the compound that could harm the beasts: *Stardawn* and *Moonstone Retribution*.

"Tell the men," she commanded with only a brief pause. "Separate them into groups and rotate the watch. Arahm may have let us see the beasts in an effort to exhaust us through fear. Our knights need to be prepared for what they may face."

Tenan and Hendar bowed and left to fulfill her orders. Margariete almost returned to Raeylan's room, but Malbrin's appearance caught her attention. He seemed troubled with contemplation.

"Master Malbrin, are you all right?" she asked.

Her voice drew his gaze. Immediately, his expression altered into certitude.

"I must speak with you and King Raeylan immediately, Your Highness."

"He's still unconscious," Margariete said.

"Then we must try to wake him." The old tutor's bones creaked as he stood. "Time is not our ally."

Intrigued and a bit annoyed, Margariete followed him to the king's side. Malbrin called to her twin several times, but Raeylan didn't stir.

"He nearly killed himself," Esilwen remonstrated softly, "he needs to regain his strength."

"It is necessary that he wakes," Malbrin declared.

"He just destroyed most of the Third Kingdom army," Margariete argued with arched eyebrows, her words hard with concern.

"That is not enough," Malbrin said. He turned to Esilwen, "Can you heal him?"

The blond cleric pondered.

"I don't think so," she finally answered. "I repair wounds, not weariness. Even when I restored Prince Shikun's body after the first battle with the cursed beasts, he slept for many arcs."

Malbrin faced Margariete.

"What about your abilities, princess?" he asked.

"I—" she began, but faltered, "wait, how do you—"

"I've known since you were born that you might have magical powers," he replied, brushing the matter aside with a wave, "though perhaps not their actual nature. I will explain once you wake your brother."

Margariete considered yanking the explanation from the old mentor's mind, but the urgency in his eyes persuaded her to reconsider. Forcing Raeylan back into consciousness would be tricky. She wasn't even sure she had the capability. She turned to her twin, full measure of concentration projecting through the borders of his inner self. Hopefully, in his sleeping state, his normal mental barriers would be left unguarded. Reaching deeper than the capacity of spoken words, she called to him, urging him to rouse, showing him images of the new enemies threatening their gate. For a few moments nothing happened. Then he moaned, opened his eyes, and pushed himself up with great effort.

"Your Majesty!" Esilwen blurted.

"It worked!" Margariete said, excitedly looking to Malbrin.

For a brief moment, the mentor stared at her, thoughtfully surprised. The princess plucked confusion from his mind. Her power had manifested in a way he had not expected. Before she could make sense of anything more, Raeylan spoke and disrupted her concentration.

"Now cursed beasts," he vented grimly. "I will never be granted rest."

"You have unleashed several of The Glove's greater powers in a short span of time," Malbrin explained. "You're lucky the effort did not kill you on the spot. Despite this, you must use another. To defeat the cursed beasts, you must close the Well of Nehro."

Raeylan looked startled. Margariete held her breath to avoid spilling into hysterical laughter. The old sage had risked her brother's life to tell him this? She felt her gaze transform into a distasteful glare.

"Are you speaking of the Well Shikun mentioned?" Esilwen asked through the tension. "The one from the story of your grandfather?"

"The Well of Nehro was a myth created by my grandfather," Margariete scoffed, "as justification for war with the City of Blades."

"On the contrary, Princess Margariete," Malbrin countered with a shake of the head, "the Well is quite real. Four seasons before you were born, King Shogan discovered the City of Blades' secret. Generations of their monarchs had hidden its existence—a direct conduit into Nehro's realm. It was a threat to your grandfather's position as the most powerful man in the shard. Using its magic, the Second Kingdom ensorcelled weapons with enchantments of time and space, making its army stronger than any other. King Shogan demanded that the Second Kingdom share their armaments with the rest of Thyella, but they refused."

"He feared the City of Blades would conquer the shard," Raeylan surmised.

Margariete looked at him in concern. His face was pale and his breath shallow.

"King Shogan planned to take the Second Kingdom, and the Well, for his own," Malbrin continued. "King Kensuru of House Tricahnas had commanded his Feralblades to assassinate the sovereign of the City of Storms, King Arahm's father. This gave your grandfather the means to invade the Second Kingdom sooner than expected. By offering his daughter's hand in marriage— your mother's—King Shogan initiated a treaty with House Galenos. Merging the armies of both nations created a force even the magic of the Well could not contest. Your grandfather managed to breach the walls of the City of Blades. Unfortunately, he misused the might of Nehro's Glove and cracked the barrier that controlled the flow of the Well's power. The resulting explosion obliterated the city, killing most of the populace. Those who managed to survive were hideously distorted, transformed into vicious creatures."

As Malbrin paused, Margariete suddenly realized that her mouth had hung ajar for the majority of the narration. Had her abilities not confirmed his every word, she would have derided him as a superstitious dupe.

"How do you know this?" Raeylan rasped quietly.

"Your grandmother, mostly," he answered, a funny sadness glinting in his eye. "Queen Kalariel."

"My grandmother disappeared the cycle King Shogan died," Raeylan said.

"It was she who instructed me to spread that rumor," Malbrin confessed. "The lie that she had perished of a broken heart, that she might rejoin her king in the netherworld. But your grandmother was not who she pretended to be."

Margariete heard Malbrin's declaration form in his mind before he uttered it, and it seemed the phrase was spoken twice—once in her head and once in her ears.

"Queen Kalariel was Nehro's most trusted lorelei."

Raeylan frowned in disbelief, but Margariete could feel the truth of the aged mentor's statement. The chamber hung heavy with silence until Esilwen spoke.

"What's a lorelei?" she asked sheepishly.

"A celestial servant of the water goddess," Raeylan answered evenly. "A divine being who could change shape at will. It is believed that most of them perished with the gods."

Malbrin nodded. "Nehro charged Kalariel to guard The Glove. It was she who entrusted the artifact to the Viridius family ages ago. At first your ancestors upheld their responsibilities to the goddess with honor, but eventually the monarchs of the First Kingdom—excluding Queen Anleia—succumbed to their own selfish lust for power, wasting the goddess's strength for their own gain. So Kalariel married your grandfather, hoping her blood would purify the corruption that had infected the Viridius lineage."

Esilwen peered at the sage curiously. "She lived long enough to watch Raeylan and Margariete's forefathers?"

"According to legend," Raeylan inserted, "the servants of Nehro were gifted with immortality. How did she orchestrate a marriage between herself and my grandfather?"

"Kalariel approached him as many different people, to learn his nature, to discover what pleased him. Eventually, she charmed him as a simple farm girl. He thought her so beautiful," Malbrin said, eyes distant with the past. "They married immediately."

"But," Margariete posed, glancing between herself and her twin, "that means—"

"Both of you are descendants of Nehro's celestial servant," Malbrin confirmed. "Shikun as well. Kalariel would be proud to see you, to know her efforts were not wasted. But," and his face drooped sadly as he looked at the king, "it would pain her to know that, just like your mother, necessity has forced you to don The Glove. Had you not used it, King Raeylan, you would have lived forever."

Margariete started, hammered by the implications.

"What?" she gasped as her stomach reeled.

She knew that the water goddess's power was draining her brother's life, stealing him from her prematurely, but now? That he would die, and she live forever afterward? Her hands shook. Raeylan, however, remained as expressionless as ever.

"I have always lived my life for the sake of my kingdom," he stated. "Knowledge of my heritage does nothing to change that."

"Then you will not hesitate to undertake the quest I pose. Closing Nehro's Well may be the only way to save Thyella."

Raeylan's mouth pulled into a resolute line. "You ask me to abandon my soldiers."

"You must travel to the City of Blades, My King," Malbrin pressed, "and seal the rift in the Well. If it is indeed the creator of the cursed beasts, closing the conduit to Nehro's realm might disrupt the source of the creatures' power, perhaps destroying them altogether."

"Do you know that for sure?" Esilwen asked.

"Your mother attempted it under Kalariel's guidance, but Queen Anleia's ability to wield The Glove was not strong enough. The Well remained cracked, and the artifact's influence shortened the queen's life."

"Why didn't Kalariel do it?" Esilwen asked. "If she was a divine being, she must have had the strength."

"The gods' artifacts are useless objects in the hands of their servants. The Glove will not work for a lorelei."

Margariete's temper flared. She refused to believe it. This was all just some horrific story.

"Then how did my mother use it? How could Raeylan use it, if we are the grandchildren of a water angel?"

"Because you are neither divine nor mortal, Princess Margariete, but vessels of both parentage," Malbrin explained. "You have traits of humanity which the artifact recognizes, yet you harbor the gifts of the immortal."

When the princess didn't argue, the mentor returned to his history lesson.

"Since Anleia was unable to close the Well, Kalariel sent her back to reestablish peace in the shard, to take King Shogan's place. Your grandmother stayed behind, to do what she could to stem the rupture in the Well. Though she was unable to save the Second Kingdom, she managed to halt the leak's progression, keeping the twisted magic from spreading throughout the rest of Thyella. We never saw her again."

"Could she still be alive?" Margariete asked, not knowing whether she hoped for it. The princess had never met her grandmother.

"I don't know," Malbrin stated guardedly. "She journeyed to the battle for the Second Kingdom just after her husband cracked the Well. In retribution for the genocide that he had committed, she took back her goddess's artifact. Ripping The Glove from his arm sentenced King Shogan to an agonizing death. But she touched it. Kalariel was already weakened by its influence when she gave it to your mother."

"If my mother was half-lorelei and unable to complete the task, it is likely I will not fare better," Raeylan stated. "How can I desert my men on such a gamble?"

"It is our only chance, Your Majesty. But you must go quickly. You must go before The Glove drains your strength entirely."

"Then it is even more important that I remain," Raeylan countered. "There will be need to summon the ice storm again."

Malbrin sighed impatiently. "You will not be able to use that power again for some time. The artifacts have limitations, as do their bearers." He glanced at Esilwen. "Fohtian's also. Both the fire elemental and ice storm are not called on a whim. Attempting such great feats so soon could prove disastrous. At best, the magic simply will not function. At worst, the effort involved could claim your lives."

Margariete agreed with Malbrin, but Raeylan's resolve refused to waver. Her brother might feel like he was forsaking them all, but it seemed to be the only choice.

"We have no hope of defeating the cursed beasts, Raeylan," she said. "We don't have enough of the right weapons. The only people capable of harming the beasts are in this room. Esilwen isn't a warrior, and you aren't in any condition to fight."

"I will not abandon you," he maintained with frustrating tenacity.

"We only have to survive until you close the Well. You can get there quickly with The Glove. I can lead the knights in your absence. If Kalariel is still alive, she can help us. If not, our men can defeat the creatures if they no longer possess Nehro's power. Their ability to teleport is their best asset."

"What if Master Malbrin is wrong, Margariete?"

"Then the castle is lost anyway," Margariete reasoned, "and it won't matter."

39: THE CURSED LAND

The warmth of Raeylan's palm made Esilwen's skin tingle as he entwined his fingers with hers. She smiled reassuringly at Margariete, who paced uneasily across the squeaky wood of the castle's nightingale floor. Esilwen opened her mouth to bid farewell, but a flurry of salty wind spiraled about her body, coiling the hem of her skirt and lifting the tips of her hair. The castle burst into a thousand stars, slipping noiselessly into the viscous blackness of space. As the breeze subsided, the pinpricked fragments of light evaporated into something else—somewhere else. A dense curtain of rain framed a river on one side of her, and the tall heads of a spiny wood lay on the other.

This was where they had encountered the cursed beasts the first time. Though the rain had cleansed most of the evidence of their previous encampment, Esilwen recognized the placement of the trees and the small stone rings that had been fire pits.

Mentally she coaxed her muscles to loosen, embarrassed by her anxiety. She had expected the experience of teleportation to be more uncomfortable— painful even, like her own healing power.

It was strange to think that the castle was more than six cycles away by foot, that she had been there moments ago.

Esilwen turned to her escort, then followed his gaze to a small, rocky outcropping just barely visible in the distance. The campsite slid away in a briny gust as they shifted again, and within the instant it took her to blink, she found her feet firmly positioned on the far off hilltop.

Esilwen barely registered the transport when the sharp peak evaporated and the stars floated around her again, the dimensional draft stroking her hair and kissing the tips of her ears. She first noticed the clacking of pebbles as they landed on the graveled bank of a small stream, but before she saw anything about their location, Raeylan whisked them away once again, delving into the borders of the Second Kingdom.

Raeylan explained before they left the castle that teleportation required him to clearly form the image of his destination in his mind. A blind shift could lead to innumerable disasters—anything from teleporting too high in the air, to reforming inside the solid interior of a cliff. He had never been inside the Cursed Land and the closest objective he could safely recall was the former border camp. Though this method—finding something visible on the horizon in the direction of the City of Blades and making several small teleportative jaunts—took a significant amount of time, it was the only choice. Esilwen only hoped that Margariete could hold the castle that long.

Near the end of an arc, Esilwen lost count of the exact number of jumps, especially since Raeylan barely left enough time for a breath before teleporting to the next target. When they had reached the base of the Sakuhra Mountain Range, the king hesitated. Esilwen tugged her hand free and took a step away from him.

"You need rest," she said.

"We must get to the City of Blades," Raeylan argued. He tried to walk forward, but swayed unsteadily. "Margariete needs every moment we can give her."

"Your sister would be angry with me if I let you die before we even reached the Well," Esilwen returned gently. "It will be of no use to them if you cannot close it once we get there."

"A twelfth of an arc then," Raeylan conceded, settling on a flat collection of black rock.

Esilwen lifted a single eyebrow, noting how his body shook.

"A quarter," she countered, choosing a seat a little further away from him, in case he decided to surprise her and teleport anyway. "No less."

The rain sloshed against the gritty ground. He replied with a brisk nod, and Esilwen relaxed. For a long moment she didn't look at him, just listened to the pounding rain. The landscape here was wilder than the plains encircling the Jeweled Kingdom. The trees were dark with age, and the undergrowth untamed, as if undisturbed by mortal hands for hundreds of seasons. Her cloak was soaked through, and the gown underneath clung to her body. But despite the rain and temperature drop, she didn't feel cold.

By the time she looked over at Raeylan, he had stopped trembling. He had shed most of his heavy battle armor at the castle, choosing instead a simple breastplate of leather and matching bracers. Over this he had draped a white overcoat with the Viridius crest embroidered on the back in gold and lavender thread. He was armed, but not with *Moonstone Retribution*. That he had left for Shikun.

"How much farther do you think?" she asked.

"We are close," Raeylan answered. "We should reach the City of Blades soon."

His eyes drew her in, and she couldn't help but wonder aloud, "What will happen after we defeat the cursed beasts?"

"We restore the First Kingdom," he said, "and return my people to their homes."

"You don't think there will be any more resistance from King Arahm?"

"He fears The Glove. Only Nehro knows how he managed to convince the cursed beasts to join him, but without them, his cause is lost."

Esilwen's eyes dropped to her fingers. Her bare hand slid along the green fabric of the signet glove he had given her. She could feel his gaze on her.

"How long?" she asked softly, her hopes fastened to the words. "When we close the Well, how long will you have?"

As she raised her head, he met her eyes with taut determination.

"The Glove feeds on me constantly. It may take everything I have left to close the Well. My strength fades even now."

He stood and approached her, touching her face tenderly.

"Esilwen, I won't survive long after it is done."

Until this moment, she had hoped that after the war they might have a chance for a life together, however brief. But now, as she looked at him closely, the rain and the cold exposing all weakness, she could see the gaunt hollowing of his face, the sickly grey sheen of his skin. A tremor of anguish stabbed through her. The distress she felt over his marriage to Katrina had been sorrow for herself, for something she wanted but would never have. But this— that the man she loved would die in the next precious arcs—this was damage to the soul that transcended grief.

She was glad of the rain, for it hid her mourning with its own shroud of tears.

With more strength than she believed he had, the king helped her to stand. She wrapped her arms around his neck and felt the pressure of his embrace as he tenderly returned it.

"Even after I lay in my tomb," he whispered, "I will continue to love you, Esilwen."

He kissed her once, lightly on the lips, and took her hand.

With every use of The Glove's power, Raeylan shivered, a hard grimace lining his face. Just as Esilwen decided he needed another respite, the gigantic carcass of a broken wall loomed before them. A ruinous waste climbed the mountain's base, the rain weeping over the bones of a once great nation.

The devastated City of Blades lay before them.

The cracked remains of three flat steppes, like the swipes of a sickle into different lengths of grain, soared into the clouds. Only a portion of the tumbled buildings were visible before disappearing upward into the storm. A huge iron gate, splintered by some inhuman force, lay shriveled and rusting in the moss. Esilwen followed Raeylan through the rubble, careful to avoid stepping on the corroded shards.

"It's hard to believe that Nehro is responsible for this," Esilwen said as they picked a careful route through the gap. "Malbrin's stories made her sound kind and caring. Like a mother maybe."

"She is the element of water," Raeylan said, lifting Esilwen at the waist over a particularly sharp-looking pile of debris, "a life-giver when the weather is fair, but unforgiving when swollen with anger. Water does not distinguish between good or evil. It simply behaves as nature dictates it must."

"And you believe Nehro to be so callous?" Esilwen asked as her feet connected with the littered residue of a cobblestone square just inside the gate.

It seemed to be some sort of gathering place, the main market perhaps. Here the mountain had been leveled into a wide terrace, once populated with a multitude of buildings. Most lay in ruin, a wall tipping here or there. The surrounding pine forest crept through every opening into the city, the new growth bent and heavy with rain as it smothered the remnants closest to the wall.

Raeylan shook his head as they wandered into the empty streets. "Not callous," he corrected. "Rather, I think she celebrated balance."

"It is those with selfish hearts who cannot resist the desire for power," Esilwen argued. "Through their choices, the innocent suffer. Some would call that the definition of evil. We shape our own fate through our will. It is not an edict of nature."

Raeylan's head tilted in her direction, a smile turning his lips. "You sound like my mother," he said.

Though the first level of the city looked even, it gradually climbed uphill. Esilwen could see the valley behind them quite clearly. The second partition looked steeper, gouging like a knife into the mountainside, though less wide. The buildings here had fared better, not because they had withstood a lesser force of magic, but for the quality of their construction. Now that she noticed, Esilwen wondered about the explosion that had reduced the city to rubble.

"I expected the city to have been blown apart by some magical force," she mused, "but this looks more like—"

"Time," Raeylan interjected.

"Yes," Esilwen answered, "like the city just crumbled of old age."

As soon as they crossed into the second level, Esilwen gripped Raeylan's arm and bit back a startled squeal. Through the cloudy haze, soldiers dueled each other, their pasty forms distorted by eerie trails of mist. Then, as if pushed by a massive wave, they toppled to the ground, away from the pinnacle of the city, toward the outer wall. Squirming on the ground soundlessly, their mouths opened wide in hideous agony. Limbs convulsed and curled as their flesh rotted and sagged; bones shriveled into dust, leaving only hollow shells of rusted armor to mark their passing.

When the scene began anew, Esilwen clamped her eyes against it.

"Temporal ghosts," Raeylan stated evenly, though Esilwen felt his body tense.

"What?" she squeaked, peeking through slitted lids.

"Spirits trapped between the mortal realm and the netherworld, doomed to repeat the circumstances of their death. We call them temporal ghosts."

Raeylan urged her forward. She tried to avoid looking at the ghastly apparitions, but the dying men seemed to be everywhere. The Gem Knight crest adorned at least half of the warriors' tabards. The others wore a symbol she did not recognize.

"These men were killed when the Well ruptured," he stated. "If they are being pushed that direction," he indicated with his hand, "then we will find the source the opposite way."

"King Shogan killed his own men," she said sadly as they walked.

"My grandfather was not the best of kings," Raeylan murmured. "Come."

He watched the ghosts attentively, their actions guiding his path. Through the drifting rain clouds, Esilwen spotted the corpse of a colossal fortress, the tip of the Bladed City. At first, their route brought them closer, but soon they turned distinctly west, moving away from its deteriorated cadaver and winding through a grove of taller ruins and fallen towers. Here the skeletal buildings squeezed the narrow streets, looming over them like an emaciated nightmare. More than once, Esilwen stumbled out of the way as two warriors scuffled around her, reflexively dodging the edges of their blades.

"I don't like this," she said, peering through the haunted dream.

Raeylan pulled her nearer but didn't slow his pace. As they penetrated deeper into the city, the mannerisms of the temporal ghosts changed. At first, Esilwen was unable to determine the difference. Then, as they passed a tarnished portcullis, Esilwen's stomach turned in horror.

They stood in a former temple of the water goddess, its walls and arches decayed and broken. Several women and dozens of children had taken refuge inside, but the goddess had not spared them. Instead of aging rapidly to their deaths, their small limbs twisted and burst. Spiked claws grotesquely replaced their fingers and toes. In some, mouths peeled backward as needle like fangs ripped from their jawbones, tearing their tongues in the process. They screamed in dreadful silence. Stuck in an incomplete transformation, their tiny forms fell and writhed in distress until they stopped moving altogether. When the last child had expired, the torture began again.

Esilwen pulled away from Raeylan and retched.

"The magic killed them before it could turn them into beasts," Raeylan said tightly.

She felt pressure on her arm as he led her past the gruesome sight.

"Don't look at them, Esilwen."

She watched only her feet, numbly allowing Raeylan to guide her. Unsure of how long she stumbled next to him, he surprised her with an abrupt stop. Not daring to look at what had caused him to pause, she instead looked at his face. His brow furrowed with uncertainty. Gathering her courage, she peeked at the object that had collected his attention.

It was nothing more imposing than a door set into a deep stone frame. A red-flanged blade, rotating thrice from a central point was carved above it. Raeylan's eyes darkened as he noticed the symbol. He reached out with his gloved hand and brushed it softly.

"What is it?" Esilwen said, reaching to touch it herself.

Raeylan caught her hand quickly and forced it back.

"The mark of the Feralblades."

Now that she studied the building, she noted that of all the structures in the city, this one was whole and undamaged, untouched by the hand of time. Raeylan picked up a rock and tossed it at the door. The small projectile seemed normal until it reached halfway across the threshold, then it began to slow, struggling through the air as if muddling through thick syrup. Finally it halted, suspended motionless above the ground. It never reached the door.

"Do you think the Well is inside?" Esilwen asked.

Raeylan studied the area, as if he could see invisible threads of magic and was analyzing it for weaknesses.

"An enchantment surrounds the building, but doesn't touch it," he said. "I don't think the barrier was placed by the Second Kingdom. It's too powerful."

"How will we cross?"

Raeylan held up his gloved hand, his face lost in thought. "We'll have to teleport," he finally answered.

He wrapped his arm around Esilwen tightly and she prayed that they rematerialized intact on the other side.

40: THE ROYAL SHRINE

Margariete struck the surface of the water in frustration, frowning angrily as the last kryystil fish vanished when her hand tried to close around it. She had spent the better part of an arc bent before the Royal Shrine's spring, failing to capture the translucent scaled creatures. Shikun, on the other hand, smiled with boyish pride at the neat row of crystals he had extracted on his own. Four jagged stones, each inlaid with colored veins, lay before him. The princess glared at her little brother. How had he snared the teleporting fish so easily?

The princeling recoiled from her fierce expression, trying to appear innocent. This reaction suggested that he was using more than just his own talent to pluck the magical fish from the pool. Unfortunately for him, his mind was not guarded as his older brother's. As the invisible tendrils of her abilities invaded his thoughts, Margariete's eyes widened in surprise.

"Cheater!" she accused.

"I'm not cheating," Shikun said as innocuously as possible.

"Yes you are!" she declared. "*Moonstone Retribution* is showing you where the fish are going to be!"

The sword's capability was a revelation to the princess. Her twin had never mentioned that it could sense the dimensional shift.

"No more cheating than you," Shikun retorted, folding his arms indignantly across his chest. "You use your mind powers all the time to see what I'm thinking—and you never ask first!"

"I can't help that I was born with magic," Margariete said pointing at him.

"You get to use your powers whenever you want! I only get *Moonstone Retribution* until Raeylan returns." Shikun returned her pointing finger. "You're just angry because you can't catch any fish!"

"I'm only upset because you're using the sword to help you," she argued. "That's cheating!"

"Does it really matter?" Malbrin's voice interrupted.

Both Margariete and Shikun turned to him, pointed fingers still brandished at each other. The wrinkled skin of the mentor's mouth pulled into disapproval. He extended his palm, revealing three azure teleportation crystals.

"If you two are finished," he continued, "I suggest we move forward with King Raeylan's orders to evacuate the servants."

Shikun let his head drop in shame, but Margariete refused to allow any discomfiture into her demeanor. A moment of happy banter between siblings before a battle that might claim their lives was more important than all the preparations in the shard.

"Catch the last of the fish, Shikun," she said affectionately.

Shikun's eyes brightened, and his hand plunged back into the spring, seemingly clutching at nothing but water. Before his fingers fully closed, the last kryystil teleported directly into his grasp. The princeling lifted the creature from the water with a triumphant call. As soon as the fish left its haven, its scaly body shriveled and shrank, until it was no longer than the prince's little finger. A rough stone glittered in his palm.

Margariete rose, inclining her head at Malbrin's open hand.

"Those are the last from the royal armory?" she asked.

"Yes, Your Highness," Malbrin said sadly.

Margariete sighed grimly. Twenty-one of their number were servants incapable of battle, nearly all women. Their helplessness would not matter to the cursed beasts—the demons would slaughter any living thing in their path. At most, each stone could safely transport five people. Exceeding that limit could stop the crystal from functioning, wasting it. It would take all of the fish from the pool to send the noncombatants to the safety of the wilderness, a hidden stronghold on the northern boundary of the First Kingdom.

That left the three teleportation stones from the armory and the one Raeylan had given Margariete at the border camp. Her twin had insisted that both she and Shikun carry one, and if the situation were lost, they were to abandon the castle. Margariete had resisted, knowing that in her place he would never condemn his men to death in order to flee himself. Too tired to argue, he had simply made her swear an oath that she would go.

The princess had decided to send the remaining two crystals with the refugees.

"Are the servants ready?" she asked, taking the stones from Malbrin.

"They await us in the Opal Ballroom, Your Highness," Malbrin said.

Margariete nodded, trading Malbrin's crystals for Shikun's. To operate, the stones had to be bound to a specific location. This required an incantation to the water goddess and a mental picture of the intended destination. Margariete had never visited the secret family estate, so Shikun had keyed the crystals after each was formed.

"Enchant these, then come find me," she instructed as she handed them to him.

Her little brother somberly attended to his task. Margariete turned and, motioning to Malbrin, walked from the private shrine.

"I have collected several important texts to send with the refugees, Your Highness," Malbrin said as they followed the crushed pebble pathway that led from the central garden, "including the six artifact scrolls given to me by your grandmother."

"You will take them yourself, Master Malbrin," she answered. "I am charging you with the duty to lead those who leave here."

As she walked, the Jeweled Princess surrendered to the constant barrage of rain from the open ceiling, resigned to the fact that she might never be dry again.

"Your Highness," Malbrin contended with a shake of his head, "I must protest."

"There is no argument, old sage," she said. "This isn't a request. It is a command. You will accompany the servants to Viridius Manor." Her boots sang against the nightingale floor as she stepped onto it. "They will need your calming guidance. Besides, when this is over, we will require your wisdom to help restore the First Kingdom."

"I would prefer to remain, Your Highness," Malbrin said.

"I know," Margariete acknowledged as they passed the threshold of one of the parlors. Movement caught her eye and she paused. "But I have made my decision."

"Wouldn't it be more logical to send someone younger and more capable to lead them?" Malbrin asked. "A knight perhaps?"

Inside the partially closed door of the portrait hall, Tenan held Seriya against his chest as her body heaved with sobs. A strange warmth spread through the princess as she watched. Her life over the past trinal had been both tumultuous and terrifying. Somehow, she had missed the affection her maid had developed with Raeylan's highest ranking lieutenant. Observing the knight's expression as he clung to the handmaiden, Margariete knew he returned Seriya's love.

Negin had already given his life to save Margariete. Many others had perished on the same cycle—brothers, sons, and fathers who would never return to their families. Were there other women, like Seriya, who wept for them? Life had become as fragile as the shards.

Looking at Tenan, seeing the heartbreak in the couple's embrace, caused an upwelling of determination inside the princess, a need to protect the love these two people shared from the ravages of war.

One swipe of her palm slid the door completely open. Its wooden frame banged loudly. Tenan released Seriya immediately, quickly bowing to his commander. He looked at Margariete through his one good eye, patiently awaiting a reprimand. Seriya blushed deeply, knowing her behavior to be inappropriate in public, and brushed her tearful face with her apron. Margariete relaxed against the doorframe.

"You are right, Master Malbrin," the princess said. "The company will need the protection of a trained soldier. Leadership as well. Lieutenant Tenan, select a Jade knight whom you trust unconditionally. You'll be going with the refugees."

Seriya gazed at Tenan hopefully.

"I cannot possibly, Your Highness," he sputtered. "You have need of me here!"

"You will do as I ask," Margariete corrected, her smile transforming into the grim line of a commander. "Your damaged eye makes you vulnerable to the cursed beasts. The women need escort, and you'll be the one to do it."

"Your Highness—"

Margariete didn't have time to argue. A quick thrust into Tenan's mind forced his compliance.

"You've been given your orders, Sir Knight," she concluded, stepping forward and handing him the teleportation crystals. "See that the refugees arrive at our hidden estate safely."

"Yes, Your Highness," he answered automatically.

Seriya threw herself into Margariete, hugging the princess tightly as tears of gratitude illuminated her face.

"Thank you," she whispered, then followed Tenan to the ballroom.

"Get the two extra stones from Shikun before you leave," Margariete said to Malbrin, satisfied that at least something good would survive this terrible battle.

"Please don't forget the orders of your king," he reminded quietly, turning to follow her instructions. "I know your tendency to defy authority, princess, but this is not a moment for the heart to override logic. If the battle goes poorly, I will expect to see you at the sanctuary."

Margariete rolled her eyes. "I know very well what my brother said."

"Do not allow your stubbornness to waste it," Malbrin lectured, as if they were in his library again, and she his student. The image filled the princess for a wistful longing for simpler cycles, when death was not licking their heels.

"May Nehro's Grace follow you," the princess said in farewell.

"And may the Void fail to claim you," he returned
solemnly.

*

The new Pearl Daimyo swiftly concluded that a battle
with the cursed beasts in either courtyard would be suicide.
Her men might last half an arc in that exposed area, but not
much more. Soon after Raeylan's departure she had
ordered every solider inside the castle, sacrificing the
outside grounds for increased chances of survival in the
closed quarters of the fortress. Scattered about the palace
in small groups, each troop of loyalists would hold key
points on every level, circling the main garden to hinder the
enemy's movements. With solid walls at the defenders'
backs, the creatures would be unable to teleport behind the
Gem Knights. Then they would force the monsters toward
the Jeweled Shrine where Margariete, Shikun, and the top-
ranking members of the Pearl Order would attempt to
dispatch the enemy.

Furthermore, she had ordered barricades of upturned
furniture throughout the hallways and larger chambers. The
heavier doors of wood and stone were sealed. Margariete
remembered clearly the powerful and agile attacks of the
beasts. They relied heavily on their quick movements and
flanking tactics. By limiting these two components, she
hoped to give her soldiers a better chance of survival.

Unfortunately, there was nothing the princess could do
about the open shrine ceiling. She cursed her forefathers
vehemently while overseeing the battle preparations,
furious at their careless frivolity. Generations of First
Kingdom citizenry had admired the inner garden for its
liberated beauty, but this cycle it would prove to be the
most crippling weakness of the castle. Instead of forcing
the cursed beasts to teleport blindly inside, where they
might be destroyed by reforming inside a barrier or wall,

363

they could perch on the tiled roof and select an advantageous destination. Margariete's only consolation was that when the creatures came from the roof, the defenders might have some sort of advance warning.

The princess waited tensely within her troop of Pearl knights, their backs toward each other in a six-point star. The rain pounded relentlessly, making the mossy ground slick.

Margariete's first line of defense would be in the open plain of the garden, one group of warriors assigned to *Stardawn* and the other to Shikun and *Moonstone Retribution*. She hated positioning her little brother so far away, across the garden's pond, but necessity dictated it. Captain Hendar would protect the princeling in her absence. With the two magic swords, the Viridius siblings would injure as many cursed beasts as possible. That way the men could bypass the creatures' armored hides and finish them, as Negin did at the border camp. If the plan failed, Margariete could pull her troops back into the walled portion of the castle. The princess hoped it was enough to keep them alive until Raeylan sealed the Well.

The attack came like shadows, slipping across the tiled roof as a waft of dark cloud. Margariete noticed them first. Quickly, she sent a telepathic warning to her little brother and called an alarm to her men. Allowing her sensitivity to the air to perceive the first enemy before her eyes did, she swung *Stardawn* in a horizontal arc, laying bare the neck muscles of her target. The monster crumpled in a bloody gush. Three more appeared in its place. The princess struck at two, grazing one along the muscled thigh, the other losing half its jaw to *Stardawn's* thirsty edge. In a blink they both vanished, retreating from her in favor of easier prey.

Shouts echoed from the balconies and inner chambers as knights all around the castle engaged in melee. As

Margariete completed an upward thrust into the gut of a third opponent, its sister creature unwittingly teleported into one of the many barricades. The nightingale floor became a torrent of blood as the beast tore itself free, fleshy entrails sagging against the wood. It rolled and flopped, a piercing gurgle howling from its maw as it died.

Suddenly, something hit Margariete from behind and propelled her forward, slamming her into one of the makeshift fortifications. Her armor absorbed most of the shock, but her ears rang. A heavy weight lay upon her. She pushed it away, belatedly recognizing it to be the body of one of her attending knights. Two cursed beasts separated her from her four remaining men. Ensnaring the closest animal's gaze with her own, she bore into its mind with her will.

"Kill your companions," she demanded, driving the command with her power.

A collection of gaping fangs lunged at her shoulder on the left. Preoccupied with dominating one, *Stardawn* rose too slowly to entirely fend off the attack of the other. Though the princess's sword stabbed her enemy through the back of its mouth, the monster's jaw clamped tight on her arm as it died, tearing through her bracer and scraping the flesh underneath. Ignoring the pain, she raised her weapon to meet yet another foe.

The creature she had enchanted crashed into its fellow before Margariete could strike. The two monsters tumbled away, slapping each other with clawed feet. The general lost track of the creatures as both rolled into the pond with frothing snarls. Momentarily free of opponents, she scanned the garden for Shikun. His entourage of knights still held a tight formation, Captain Hendar protectively combating on the princeling's right. With relief, she noted that her brother seemed free of serious injury.

"That trick always impresses me," came a wicked hiss in her ear.

With a panicked start she felt the cold tang of steel under her throat and the hard pressure of a blade held ready in the small of her back. "I've always wondered what it would be like to force someone into absolute obedience. Not as—" he paused, and Margariete could feel him smile, "—satisfying as seduction perhaps, but worth exploring."

Terail pressed his lips against her ear and—without the slightest displacement of his two blades—trailed his tongue the length of her neck. Margariete swallowed the taste of sickness coating her mouth. Terail made her watch as three more beasts blinked around her comrades. One thrust of a forked tail impaled a man and tossed his limp body away like refuse. The other three knights pulled into a defensive ring as the monsters charged.

Another solider thudded lifeless to the ground. It cost her precious moments to wrest back control. Margariete almost lost tactical judgment in a swell of fury. As soon as she could think, she focused her mental power around Terail's dagger. His solid grip on the weapon made it difficult to sweep it from his hand, so she cast her invisible fetters around his arm instead. A quick flick of her mind threw his limb wide, away from her throat. The same moment she spun, knocking his second stiletto aside before it could pierce her torso, though the physical parry broke her telekinetic hold on his arm.

Caution coaxed her to retreat several steps, though rationally the action was worthless—he could teleport to any position he wished. Terail knew the moment she thought it, and a vicious twist warped his handsome lips. A sudden epiphany cracked through her head like thunder.

"You were commanding the beasts all along weren't you?"

Terail cackled with brutal pleasure.

"Why yes," he said, "and if Esilwen hadn't interfered, my attack on the border camp would have left young Prince Shikun dead. She has proven herself quite the inconvenience."

Margariete tried not to blink, but eventually she could no longer resist. Terail vanished with the drop of her eyelids. Assuming he would attack from the rear, she rotated. The miscalculation cost her a rib as he rematerialized at her flank instead and delivered a harsh kick that snapped her bone and drove her into the mossy ground. She heard him crouch beside her. White sparks blasted her vision as Terail cuffed her temple with the hilt of his dagger. His other hand dug painfully into her scalp and he hefted her head by clumps of hair, forcing her to face him. The sky dripped into her eyes.

"Where is your twin?" he demanded.

Margariete spat into Terail's face. With an angry growl he backhanded her cheek so hard her teeth chattered. The iron taste of blood rolled inside her lips. He pressed her broken rib with the weight of his knee.

"Where is he?" Terail repeated as Margariete screamed in pain.

"Why betray us?" Margariete yelled ferociously.

She jabbed in his mind, but couldn't penetrate the barrier that protected it.

"Revenge mostly," he admitted casually.

She swung *Stardawn* clumsily at his head but he met the strike easily with his dagger. Shifting, he slid his blade to her sword's hilt. With nimble speed he dropped his weapon and wrapped his fingers around her hand. Margariete howled in pain as he twisted her wrist into an unnatural angle. *Stardawn* slipped from her grasp. Releasing both her head and hand, he retrieved the enchanted sword.

"My mother's blade always did prefer women," he said.

"Your mother?" Margariete echoed, straining to focus through the throbbing of her head.

"She was a great queen," he continued, "before she was murdered by the greed of your grandfather."

Terail renewed the pressure of his knee, robbing Margariete of breath. She couldn't put her thoughts in order. How could Terail's mother be a queen? The question bit into her mind, bitter as the pain in her body. Hadn't the Second Kingdom's assassins been responsible for the death of his family? He locked his hand under her chin, arching her neck stiffly and digging the top of her skull into the ground.

"Your House destroyed my birthright, cheated me of my throne. Once I was Kahlos Tricahnas—but no longer. The Tricahnas line is extinct. All that remains is Feralblade."

He leaned forward, halting his lips a breath from hers. His hand squeezed her throat.

"Beg me for your life, princess," he sneered, constricting his fingers. "I might allow you to live, at least until I tire of you."

Margariete choked, unable to answer, blackness rimming the edges of her sight.

Never! she projected from her mind in the absence of voice.

He grinned maliciously and tightened his grip.

41: THE SANCTUARY

Esilwen was vividly aware that her feet dangled over the open air. Raeylan pulled her close as they crashed to the ground, absorbing most of the impact himself. A spike of pain drove through her ankle and she lay gasping for air, the king's strong arms still wrapped around her. His breath came in labored gulps. She pushed herself off his chest, wobbling upright as her healing magic repaired her injured foot. Raeylan struggled to stand.

"Raeylan—" she began, placing a hand of comfort on his shoulder.

"I'm fine," he interrupted.

Esilwen steadied him and offered what strength she had, anxious over the amount of assistance he required to climb to his feet. When he was properly vertical, she let her hands remain wrapped around his arm as they inspected their surroundings.

The oval chamber was soft with darkness, light glimmering about a narrow pedestal in the center of the room. The building's supports seemed old but not aged. The large stone blocks of the walls glistened with delicate silver runes, just like the symbols that had first appeared on The Glove. Alcoves flanged the room's edge, each enfolding an ivory statue. Dust dared not clutter the stone floor.

Ancient power resided here. The hair on Esilwen's arms tingled with the cosmic resonance that permeated the chamber. Raeylan led her forward, as if drawn by the central light. A rippling cube, small enough to fit comfortably in her cupped hands, rested on the pedestal's smooth surface. Inside its planar faces, limitless colors shifted and ruptured, rolling over one another in an infinite plane, bent at the center. She could have lost herself in its immeasurable space, forever staring into its incalculable interior, but for an unsightly abrasion on one of the prism's faces. Through this fissure, tiny flecks of stars spurted into the room, sizzling into effervescent froth when it struck the air.

"Is that it?" Esilwen asked.

"If it is the Well of Nehro you seek," spilled a clear, rushing voice, "then yes, you have arrived in its sanctuary."

Startled, Esilwen cast her eyes about the room, searching for the speaker. Raeylan's gaze clung firmly to a statue outside the alcoves, of different construction than the rest. As Esilwen watched, the sculpture shifted, its face turning pale and lovely, delicate like a water blossom but hard and crisp like a finely cut gem. Her eyes remained the color of the stone, deep and fathomless grey. White pearly curls floated around her shoulders and down her back, held in place by a silver clasp.

"Welcome, Raeylan of House Viridius," she greeted, her words like the filmy song of a mountain spring. Her eyes moved to Esilwen curiously, "Which of the gods' artifacts do you bear, elf?"

Though she had never before heard the word, Esilwen felt comforted by it, understood that "elf" encompassed the nature of her being. The woman's beauty shone from the ethereal, a manifestation of the immortal. An undeniable font of trust embraced Esilwen as she looked at the shapeshifter.

"Fohtian's Blood," Esilwen answered. "How did you know I carried an artifact?"

"The rupture in the Well would have corrupted you if you were anything less. My time wall keeps the magic confined, preventing it from spreading to the rest of the shard. But within the barrier, I cannot alter its influence."

"You are my grandmother," Raeylan said, "the lorelei, Kalariel."

The water spirit smiled at him fondly.

"Yes, I am she," Kalariel confirmed. "Things must be dire in the Jeweled Kingdom for Malbrin to reveal my existence to you."

"Yes," Esilwen replied. "The Third Kingdom and cursed beasts have declared war. They could be attacking the castle at this very moment!"

"And Malbrin properly deduced that closing the Well of Space would put an end to the threat?" Kalariel asked calmly.

Esilwen nodded.

"How are you still alive?" Raeylan interjected. The sallowness had lifted from his skin and Esilwen noted that he seemed stronger. "You touched The Glove."

"Nehro's Well sustains me, as it will you, though The Glove has disrupted the one inside us," Kalariel explained, gracefully resting a hand over her heart.

"I don't understand."

"You are a descendant of the lorelei, Raeylan—Nehro's celestial servants. We each carry her power inside us, a Soulwell that connects us to the goddess's domain. When our Well comes into contact with The Glove, too much of

Nehro's magic surges into us. Our Soulwell implodes under the strain."

"So The Glove is only taking my life because I am a lorelei?" Raeylan asked.

Sorrow drifted across Kalariel's eyes.

"Yes. The Glove is only dangerous to those connected to Nehro's power. A common mortal can bear The Glove until time claims him. Shogan used it for nearly 30 seasons."

Esilwen felt her chest contract painfully. Raeylan's fate could have been avoided if they had known, but now it was too late.

"Generations ago," Kalariel continued, "corruption stained the hearts of the Viridius line. By combining my blood with Shogan, I made any future child of Viridius descent vulnerable to The Glove's influence. No selfish king who desired only power would trade his existence to wield Nehro's artifact. Thus I have fulfilled my obligation to protect my goddess's power."

"At the expense of your own kin!" Esilwen accused. "Raeylan is going to die because of what you have done!"

"You are right," Kalariel said. "The Glove will drown Raeylan's Soulwell, just as it did my daughter's. We are lorelei," Kalariel said turning to Raeylan. "Our lives are driven by our duty to Nehro. The cost is great. But our reward will span the length of time."

Esilwen felt Raeylan's hand slip into hers with a comforting squeeze.

"It isn't fair," Esilwen wept sadly.

The back of Raeylan's bare hand brushed her cheek dry.

"I know," he replied softly. He paused to comfort her for a moment before turning back to Kalariel, "Why have you hidden yourself here all this time? Can you not repair the Well and remove its curse?"

Kalariel motioned to the cube leaking stars into the room, "The Well is ever-changing, like the bed of a river, or the flow of time. As it fluctuates, the tear in its barrier grows wider. When Shogan first damaged the Well, Nehro's magic surged out like a tidal wave. It killed the citizens of this city before I was able to reclaim The Glove from him. By the time I returned with Anleia, the magic had already destroyed the countryside. My daughter was not strong enough to seal the Well with The Glove, so I remained, using the last of my own strength to contain the Well's devastation.

"My Soulwell has long expired. To leave the sanctuary would mean my end. Only Nehro's teleportation can breach the time barrier that I have placed around this place. I have been waiting for a new glove bearer to return and finish what my daughter could not."

Raeylan's jaw tightened.

"My mother was half-lorelei. If she was unable to close the Well, what hope have I of accomplishing the task?"

Kalariel's eyes blazed smoky twilight.

"Because of your father."

"You knew him?" Raeylan asked warily.

"Yes," she answered. "I met him once, before he left the shard."

"Who was he?"

"I cannot tell you," Kalariel said looking displeased. "His secrets are his own. But it is his influence that marks your sister."

Raeylan looked surprised.

"That is why Margariete looks so different from our people? Why she can read thoughts?"

"Yes," Kalariel said impatiently. "When in your mother's womb, Margariete drew your father's power to her, as you did Anleia's."

Raeylan looked pensive before asking, "But why can't she see into my mind then?"

"You use your Soulwell to prevent it. Nehro's domain is space and time, as well as water. Thoughts and memories are recorded in time space, or it would be more accurate to say that they are in the space that is time. By halting that flow, you are able to keep Margariete from accessing the thoughts in your mind. Anleia's youngest son never learned how to use this ability, for, unlike you, he had no secrets to hide."

"You know a lot about Raeylan and his family," Esilwen said skeptically. "If you haven't left this room for so long, how do know so much?"

"My daughter often journeyed to speak with me while she was alive," Kalariel said with a sad smile. "Her travels hastened her death. When her visits suddenly stopped, I knew The Glove had claimed her."

"How do the cursed beasts have the power to teleport," Raeylan asked, turning the conversation back to the dire situation at hand, "when they do not have The Glove?"

"Men warped by the Well's magic share that gift—those creatures you name 'cursed beasts.' Their leader wasted seasons attempting to enter the sanctuary, believing that access would give him more power. But I would not allow further harm to the Well. He abandoned that quest almost five seasons ago."

Raeylan's jaw tightened. When he asked his next question, Esilwen had the distinct feeling that he already suspected the answer.

"Who was this leader?"

"Kahlos Tricahnas," Kalariel returned. "He was in this chamber 18 seasons ago, the same cycle Shogan disrupted the Well. Because of his proximity, the magic gave the master of the Feralblades minor powers instead of warping him into a monster. He can bend the walls between space, and his body does not age. He is the only mortal the magic left in human form."

"Terail," Raeylan growled under his breath.

"Kahlos and his followers are linked to the Well's power. When it dies, so shall they."

"And you?" he asked.

"Only the Well keeps me alive," Kalariel said stepping in front of the pedestal. "But I would gladly see it closed. My alternate fate is to remain here, never again to see my goddess's realm. We must hurry; time grows short. There is more at stake than just the survival of your kingdom."

Esilwen felt her heart quicken with fear. What could be worse than the threat at Viridius Castle?

"What do you mean?" Raeylan asked quickly, obviously worried.

"When a shardgate is opened, the lorelei and glove-bearer can sense it. I have felt it open three times."

"Three?" Esilwen repeated.

Kalariel nodded, "Few ways exist to open the shardgates that separate the worlds. Nehro's artifact has this power, as does the Soulwell of a water angel. Since The Glove has not left Theylla, and I have not felt the presence of a new lorelei in our world, some other force has opened the gate."

"What else has the means to open it?" Raeylan asked.

"The raw power of Fohtian's Blood brought you," Kalariel said to Esilwen. "I felt its unusual disruption when you arrived—as did Raeylan, though he might not have realized what it meant at the time. Only when The Chalice of the Phoenix Angel is broken, will its power of resurrection cast you through the shardgates."

"Yes, that's what happened," Esilwen replied truthfully. "When I entered one of Nehro's temples, I saw visions from my past. The Chalice shatters in one of them."

Esilwen stopped, looking at Raeylan. She hadn't told anyone but Malbrin what she had seen the cycle she fainted in Nehro's temple.

"What else did you see?" the water spirit prompted.

"My own death—several of my own deaths, actually."

Raeylan jerked, completely taken off guard. His gaze melted with concern. Kalariel's eyes shifted to a point in the darkness, the irises swinging back and forth rapidly, as if filtering through many seasons of life. When she finished, she looked at Esilwen thoughtfully.

"And you remember nothing else?"

"If it weren't for Margariete, I don't think I would even know my own name."

"The Temple of Nehro in Viridius Castle is blessed by a holy sanctification. Its link to Nehro's power is not potent, but it was strong enough to return some of your memory," Kalariel said. "The rest of what you have lost can be restored by The Glove."

A hope tugged at Esilwen. She could finally fill the empty hole inside her. Yet doubt pricked her. She turned to Raeylan.

"What if it changes me? What if I don't like who I was before?"

"You will not lose what you have learned here," Kalariel promised.

Raeylan squeezed Esilwen's hand reassuringly.

"What of the other two gate openings?" he asked.

"There is only one other way to cross a shardgate: by using a lorelei's heart. It is difficult to defeat a water spirit.

We are powerful, the second in strength of the gods' celestials. I fear something dangerous has followed Fohtian's Warden into this shard, someone with great power and little mercy."

Kalariel reached out to Raeylan, cupping her palm on his cheek.

"You have already lost much of your strength, my grandson. To ensure the successful restoration of your companion's lost memory, you will need to draw energy from the Well as you seal it. I fear that if you wait until after, you will be too weak to accomplish it. I am confident in the strength of my daughter's children and grateful to have seen them overcome Shogan's cruelty."

She released Raeylan's cheek and stepped back, opening a path to the Well.

42: Birth Of The Mind

Feralblade's exhilaration mounted savagely, as it always did before a kill. Death had ever been his mistress—his private slave of the Void. Revenge caressed him like the body of a lover, passionate and sultry, as he stole the breath from the Viridius princess. He could have murdered her swiftly, sliced her open like an animal. But that would have robbed him of her feeble struggling, the pleasing ecstasy of her suffering.

His nails clawed her throat as he compressed her airway. He could feel the curve of her bone. Margariete tried to throw him off, twisting her hips and legs, but Feralblade gripped her solidly with his knees, his weight holding her down. Though he leaned forward to sustain the attack, the assassin maintained care that her reach not meet his face. He held *Stardawn* with his free hand, hilt forward and blade parallel to his elbow. As her breath faded and her eyes started to roll, the princess scraped her fingers desperately against the leather bracer protecting his arm.

He smiled fiendishly. This cycle he would at last damn the souls of his enemies.

"Goodbye, princess. I will send your little brother to meet you shortly."

She stopped resisting. He experienced a moment of disappointment, a fleeting regret that she had succumbed so swiftly. Perhaps he should have savored her torment with more leisure.

He would not make the same mistake with Shikun.

A sudden pain lanced through his wrist, causing a startled grunt through his teeth. Margariete's fingers had extended into sharp talons, pierced his armor and gouged into his forearm. The princess stared at him through incandescent orbs of sapphire, as if her pupils had melted entirely. Uncontrolled fury scoured his head, its stiff bristles like wire, corroding the edges of his mind barrier.

And then she slammed her forehead against his skull.

The force of her strike tossed him the length of three men, but the psychic damage of the blow far exceeded the physical. A honed spike of telepathic energy had snapped the mental defenses granted by Nehro's power, leaving his mind completely vulnerable. He scrambled up, drawing a dagger with one hand and prepping *Stardawn* in the other.

The princess slowly rose to her feet. Wisps of shade absorbed the light around her, like a liquid eclipse rising from the ground. Fear snatched Feralblade's throat as she advanced a step forward. An invisible force yanked *Stardawn* from his grasp and drew the blade to her outstretched hand. His long dagger flew into emptiness.

Night swallowed the shrine in inky nothingness. The screech of beasts and cries of men were smothered into oblivion. Only Margariete remained.

Her power radiated behind her in a windswept cyclone, crackling with electric pulses. As he watched, the gale billowed into the lightless sky, a massive head rearing from its center. Furious cerulean eyes scowled from its serpentine head. The projection's massive wings blew across the horizon and vanished into the gloom. Anger charged the air. Feralbalde could taste the steely energy bite his tongue.

He couldn't run. He commanded his body to teleport, but nothing happened. He was trapped in Margariete's world of darkness.

"Kneel!" Margariete rasped from all around him, her voice grating with inhuman power.

Feralblade complied, despite his violent attempt at resistance. His knees buckled.

Margariete's mouth curled into a snarl. When she clenched her fist, his right arm flew forward in a wash of pain. Then the bone snapped of its own accord.

A gurgle of agony burned his throat, but no sound came. His body was still under her control. He felt sickening pops dash through his fingers and toes as the telepath twisted the joints until they cracked. Needles of misery gouged him like hot irons into his skull. Skin peeled backward from his face and hands. His eyes burst into an anguished mangle of jelly.

And then the darkness was swept away, like fog in a windstorm. Feralblade dropped to his hands as her hold on him evaporated. To his surprise, he found his eyes were intact, his bones whole. For a moment he didn't understand. Then he realized—the attack had been in his mind.

But the pain was as real as any physical injury. Its lingering touch robbed him of strength. As he looked around, he spotted his discarded dagger in the moss. He snatched it quickly.

Margariete looked distracted, blinking at her sword as if in amazement. He didn't know what had diverted her attention, but he didn't care. He had to strike now before the princess was able to infiltrate his mind again. He knew he couldn't withstand another psychic assault.

He teleported behind her, but she sidestepped and his blade was turned by her armor. *Stardawn* met his next swing. In his weakened state, the force of it threw him back onto the ground. His weapon bounced away. Margariete stared down at him in disgust, her eyes sparking with controlled vehemence. Lifting her sword, she prepared a killing strike.

43: MEMORIES FROM TIME

The memories came, not as if she suddenly recalled the events, but as if someone had collected them from the ocean of time and poured them into her head from a flask. In a matter of moments she experienced her lives, from death to awakening. The effect of feeling existence backward made her head whirl dizzily.

Magic's burning fire took over her body as her life dissolved in thick darkness. A strong hand held her head under water until she could bear it no longer, and her lungs inhaled the briny liquid. The man was the village leader of Dayton, a small hamlet along the coast of a shaggy sea. Accused of witchcraft, the town council had sentenced her to death by drowning, a ceremony that would cleanse her soul of "demon grime."

The phoenix flame scorched her old and wasted form, a thousand years following her arrival in Carthis. Her many acolytes surrounded her lavish bed, tears begging her spirit to remain. The people of this shard worshipped the old gods, and her life had been steeped in knowledge and spiritual guidance. A prophecy foretold her coming; her unifying influence had brought balance to countries of elves, humans, and dwarves. In her centuries of leadership, war was unknown to the shard.

She fell to ashes as a horrific crimson-winged woman severed Esilwen's head from her body with a hooked sword. The fire servant pursued the elf on behalf of another.

Lastly, the memory of her first life, her true self, filled the cavity of her mind. She drank from The Chalice, the ice-green liquid inside called for her protection. Kirion had watched first with disbelief, then with a simmering rage as the fire god's power devoured her body. But before she succumbed to the flame, she slammed the crystal goblet against the god's golden statue, shattering the artifact into pieces.

Esilwen clutched her head, aching with the weight of cosmological responsibility. She had found him, Kirion, Lord of Light, asleep behind a multihued barrier hidden in her home shard of Alanis. Bewitched by his raven locks and finely featured face, she had released him from his prison. Naively believing their meeting was fated by the gods, she cared for him, enchanted by his charm and majestic dark eyes. Just as she grew to love him, he left for a time, but promised swift return. Faithfully, she waited, a simple priestess in Fohtian's Grand Temple.

Upon his homecoming, Kirion possessed a mightier presence, a force of power that the elders of Alanis had never seen. A new article jeweled his ear, a black pearl made of shadow darker than night. The elders were afraid, but Esilwen spoke on his behalf, chastising the people for their lack of compassion. But instead of embracing her with love, Kirion demanded the Phoenix Angel's Chalice.

For generations the Paladins of Fohtian protected the fire god's blood, careful to use it only in great need. When they refused Kirion's request, he rained the Void's destruction upon the temple, slaying those within. Only the sacred chamber housing The Chalice escaped his wrath untouched, and Esilwen alone remained.

She knew that The Chalice was an anchor, the harbor for the Warden's self during the time he used the god's power. If The Chalice was broken, the Warden's memories would scatter to the shards, forever lost.

The deaths of her mentors lay like a stone in her chest. The elders had warned her not to unchain Kirion, but she had not listened, infatuated with the romance of her own story. So Esilwen sacrificed her identity, destroying The Chalice to keep the fire god's power forever from Kirion's reach.

The healer swayed, using the etched columns of the sanctuary to slide to the floor. Raeylan stood in front of the Well, his glove arm stretched toward it. Kalariel stared at her with sympathetic eyes as the Well flickered into darkness. By the residual glow of the silver runelight, Esilwen saw Raeylan topple.

"He still has time," Kalariel said with words that gurgled like water, "short though it may be. Do not fear your path, child. Fohtian and Nehro will guide you."

As she spoke, Kalariel slowly evaporated into mist. Her body vanished, but her heart remained suspended momentarily above the floor, beating a measured tempo. Gradually it dimmed to grey, hardening into a lump of crystal flecks, some of which drifted to the floor. In a sudden whoosh the heart broke apart and collapsed to the stone, a glittering pile of salt the only evidence of the lorelei's passing.

Esilwen turned to Raeylan's crumpled form, placing her hand gently on his cheek. His breath was shallow and his skin damp with sweat. She brushed a straggle of blond away from his face so it wouldn't be in his eyes when he woke.

She loved him, trusted him, and she knew that he returned those feelings just as deeply.

She had loved the Lord of Light when she was just a girl, when she was young and easily beguiled. Her affection for him had long ago transformed into fear, his face burned into her subconscious as a thing to flee. He pursued her not out of tenderness, but for the hope that he might still be able to extract Fohtian's power from her.

So why did she feel an urgent, lingering pull toward Kirion's dark eyes?

Because she still believed she could save him. She yearned not for him, but what he should have been, or once was: The Lord of Light, honorable and just.

Like Raeylan.

Still lost in conundrum, she took a small pouch from Raeylan's belt and gathered Kalariel's remains. Replacing the leather receptacle, she tried to wake him.

If it was indeed Kirion who had entered Thyella after her, they had to hurry.

44: SOVEREIGN OF THE SHARDS

The entanglements of mortals were at least amusing, if bothersome. Their short lives hindered designs beyond the scope of their own shard, their small minds unable to comprehend the cosmic significance of a greater cause. Putting aside their petty disagreements, the inhabitants of the Thyellan shard could join his movement, each contributing to the endeavor of peace.

A peace established under his rule.

Throughout his travels, Lord Kirion had discovered that the shards were broken into a variety of sizes, everything from the dimensions of a continent to multiple planetary systems. This land was a moderate size compared to some he had seen, but its construction was most unique. Like the majority of small shards, it did not possess its own sun. The miniscule worlds were usually dead realms of starless night, frozen and desolate, but Thyella was like a continental greenhouse. The shardwall that stretched across its sky was transparent, staring straight through to the adjacent shard. From here, a stationery sun brought light and warmth to Thyella, and were it not for the path of the moon, this realm would never know night. Every 16 hours the satellite trekked from one horizon to the other, eclipsing the borrowed sun at the apex of its lunar journey.

He had arrived less than an hour ago, finally completing a six day expedition from the shardgate in the northwestern quadrant of the territory. From his perch on the tiled roof of a whitewashed castle, he watched the battle that transpired in the fortress's central garden.

It was a tiring sequence he encountered in most habited shards. Wars for paltry expansion, trivial matters of revenge, or irrelevant consequences of intolerant cultures plagued the worlds controlled by mortals. The universe was sick with it. He had hoped the resting place of Nehro's artifact would be less violent, but he supposed he should have known better. This was simply more evidence that the shards needed direction, a shared religion to guide them.

His religion.

And when his godhood was finally restored through all six artifacts, he would return the universe to its unbroken state.

He had counted three separate battles here, two occurring before his arrival. Four days ago he had felt a Well open into Fohtian's domain, the plane of fire. Most likely that was the cause of the melted wall in the castle's courtyard. Then a distinct influx of Nehro's power had been summoned near the same place. Both artifacts he sought had been here at the same time, but now, as he watched the melee raging below him, he sensed neither.

Nehro's most powerful Well of Space was in this shard, somewhere to the north. He could see the tendrils of power that linked the twisted beasts fighting below to the water goddess's domain. Each thread was fastened to the soul of a monster who had once been a person. Kirion sensed a lingering ghost of the mortals' forms, screaming and writhing within their mutilation.

Only one Well-touched individual clung to his human shape. The power within him was corrupt, the result of

387

some botched spell perhaps. Kirion watched this one closely, intrigued by the man's ability. His teleportation skill had given him a distinct advantage over his opponent, a dark-haired woman.

Kirion's winged general interrupted his vigil. "I have opened the castle gates, My Lord," she reported, dropping out of the sky gracefully. "The wolves have entered without detection."

He did not turn, but continued to gaze into the castle garden. "Do you see something that seems out of place, Thanati?"

The red-haired woman flicked her luminescent green eyes across the battlefield, then ruffled her feathers in surprise.

"After all this time," she said as the olive-skinned woman was thrown to the ground, "I assumed they were all dead. And to find a female! I thought Aeron created only male servants."

Thanati turned her eyes to Kirion with sudden concern. "She may have seen through your illusion, My Lord."

The Lord of Light ran his thumb thoughtfully over his bottom lip. He touched the surface of the dark pearl earring he wore—the first artifact he had found—Skoh's Jewel. With it he had a direct connection to the Void's distortive power. The dark-haired woman's mind-sight would allow her to pierce The Earring's glamour.

"She's too involved in her battle with the teleporter," he finally said, watching the woman try to free her throat from her enemy's grasp. "She could be useful, if she could be persuaded to join us."

"Be wary, My Lord," Thanati argued with a scowl staining her brassy features. "Aeron's kind have furious tempers."

Kirion's smile lit his dark eyes. The woman was exotically beautiful and potentially powerful, a dangerous threat to his lady general.

"You fear I would choose her strength over yours?" he asked with some amusement.

Thanati pouted. "She won't have the chance," she said, pointing to the fight below. "She is weak. The assassin will win their duel. He would make a finer addition to the Faithful Legion, I think."

To a normal observer, Thanati appeared correct. The servant of Aeron seemed to have suffocated. But Kirion could see the dark-haired woman's Soulwell as clearly as her body. It was expanding, drawing a massive surge of magic from her god's plane.

"Don't be so sure, Thanati," the Lord of Light returned with a charming grin.

The force of the woman's rage burst through the garden, washing over everything. All combatants, human and beast, recoiled with fear. She trapped the assassin in his mind, wreaking invisible havoc. After a few moments, her attention focused on her sword and her power dissipated. The lapse freed her opponent and he teleported behind her, but she managed to parry his strike and throw him to the ground.

As she lifted her sword for the killing blow, the threads of enchantment connecting the assassin and his monsters to Nehro's Well snapped in concert. All through the garden beasts howled and shuddered into steamy vapor.

Nehro's Well had been sealed. The assassin shrieked and convulsed, causing the dark-haired woman to pause her weapon's thrust.

The Lord of Light felt a surge of triumph. Nehro's artifact had just been used to close the Well in the north. He was confident it would return.

The assassin, the woman, and one other—a young boy across the garden who also had a weak water Well—intrigued Kirion enough to intervene. He looked at his general, whose eyes flared with excitement.

"Take the castle."

45: INSTANT OF MORTALITY

Margariete's head pounded furiously, the back of her eyelids veined in red. The last thing she remembered was a howl that drove splinters of pain through her skull. In an instant, her magical sense of air vibration had gone deaf. All thought had blended into one massive storm of piercing pain.

She didn't know how long she had been unconscious, but at last the effect of the wail—whatever it had been—was lifting. Fragmented sensations, like the jerky motions of horseback riding, flowed into her mind. Four distinct voices slid in and out of focus. As she became more aware, the realization that she could hear more than one thought stream startled her. Even with full concentration she should only be able to focus on one at a time. She winced as she tried to unscramble them, the effort bringing a fresh pinch into her head. The princess raised a psychic block, but in her confused state it was frail and incomplete, like a sheer curtain that struggled to filter the sun's glow.

Her unsuccessful attempt convinced her to open her eyes. Margariete's vision was blotched and blurry, and it took a few moments for the colored blobs to form identifiable objects. Her arms were bound above her, numb and useless, by a brightly glowing chain. She dangled two spans off the ground in the Royal Shrine.

A sound to the left drew her attention. After looking, she immediately closed her eyes, fighting a gag that rolled up her throat. Out in the main garden two enormous wolves, easily the size of Crescent, tore gory chunks of flesh from Captain Hendar's mangled corpse. The bodies of her men were piled carelessly behind the animals. Judging by the height of the mound, it was all of the knights who had stayed to defend the castle. Tears leaked from her eyes. She couldn't even recall when they had been slain, or how.

A familiar whimper below forced her eyes open again. Shikun wriggled at her feet in a pathetic ball, weeping and cradling his stomach.

"The task is complete, Thanati," a smooth voice announced from near the spring. "The Well of Skoh is opening. Take him to the shardgate."

Margariete turned toward the sound, hatred burning her tears away. A raven-dark head bent over Terail's unconscious body, but the princess could tell that the Feralblade assassin still breathed. Glittering silver scaled armor, embossed with the emblem of a sword encased in a crescent moon, covered the raven-haired stranger. Margariete felt power radiating from him like the light of a star. She sucked her breath through her teeth.

He was definitely not Thyellan.

"I would rather stay by your side, My Lord," his companion asserted.

This must be some nightmare, the princess decided. Her men slaughtered without explanation, gigantic wolves tearing at their corpses, her little brother tortured. Now a woman with two scarlet-gold wings swooping from the center of her back. Margariete wondered if she had gone mad.

"When Esilwen returns, you will no longer be safe," the man ordered, almost sharply. "Do as I command. I have other matters to attend."

When he turned his dark eyes onto Margariete, terror trickled down her spine. How could just his gaze teem with that much power? Who were these people?

The winged woman threw Terail's unconscious form over her shoulder, waltzed past the wolves, and leapt into the sky. When Margariete looked back at the private shrine, the man stood in front of her, poking Shikun's trembling body with the toe of his boot.

"This young lorelei claims relation to you," he said, raising his eyes coolly to hers, "though I find it unlikely to be true."

"Who are you?" Margariete croaked. Her tongue filled her mouth, heavy and swollen.

"Forgive my rudeness," he replied with a charming turn of the mouth. "I am Lord Kirion, master of the Faithful Legion. And you are?"

"What are you doing here?" the princess demanded, angry at the cold indifference he displayed toward Shikun's misery. "What do you want from us?"

"Is it not polite here to return formalities?" he retorted fluidly.

Margariete's expression narrowed in a glower, and she refused to answer. Kirion, however, seemed undeterred.

"Fortunately, your younger brother is not so indecorous," Kirion said, poking Shikun's balled form again.

Shikun recoiled fiercely, ejecting something akin to a hiss. The princeling buried his face into the moss.

"He seemed reluctant to provide information, and it took a bit of convincing to compel him to answer all of my questions—especially those concerning your family, Princess Margariete."

Margariete struggled against her restraints, aching to smudge that sleek smile on Kirion's face with her fist, but the magical shackles refused to loosen. Desperate to determine the condition of her brother, she dropped her psychic barrier and sought his mind with her own.

Shikun, she called silently, *brother, are you all right?*

He wallowed in an all-consuming deluge of anguish and disgrace. All that the princess could gather was that his torture had been brief, intense, and completely incapacitating. The use of her powers caused sharp cracks of pain against her skull, but she ignored the discomfort and suffused herself with power. She looked at Kirion.

"Release me," she commanded, throwing herself into the intruder's mind.

The demand recoiled back on her so hard that it snapped her head backward.

"I think not," Kirion said with a satin chuckle. "Although Shikun has told me much about you princess, he was, however, unable to answer every question. Like why a servant of Aeron is present on a shard clearly influenced by Nehro?"

"Your guess is as good as mine," she snarled.

Her thoughts were elsewhere, busily concocting and discarding means of escape. Her need to save Shikun pressed through her skin like something trying to burst from her body. Though her attempt at domination hadn't worked, perhaps there was something in Kirion's head that would offer a chance for flight. Gathering her focus she reached into his mind.

Her labor returned nothing but a vast plane of unending white, an indecipherable blankness of consciousness.

"Guesses are still speculations," Kirion said. "If you don't know, then tell me of your parents. Perhaps I can solve the mystery."

Margariete presented only a glare. She would give this man nothing. As Kirion tilted his head impatiently, the princess noticed a black jewel in his ear, a dark pearl that stole the light around it.

"I would prefer to have a civil conversation, Margariete," he said with diplomatic ease, "but I suspect The Glove of Nehro will return at any moment, along with an elf I am very eager to collect. Though I cannot affect you with illusion as I can your younger brother," his fingers brushed against the earring, "I am confident I can find other methods to persuade you."

He pointed at Shikun. The youth yelped fearfully at something unseen, and then he bolted upright, like a child experiencing a night terror. Shikun surveyed the shrine in bewilderment, his expression changing from concern as he noticed Margariete hanging from her chains to abhorrence when he saw Kirion. The little princeling rose shakily to his feet, feebly drawing *Moonstone Retribution*. He stood protectively in front of his sister, his body trembling violently.

No Shikun, Margariete screamed, *he'll kill you!*

I have to try, Shikun responded resolutely.

Margariete's throat tightened. From the back of his head he looked so much like Raeylan.

"I will let Shikun live if you join me, Margariete," Kirion offered, amused by Shikun's display of chivalry. "Your kind is rare in the shards. None have been seen since the Fracturing. Your cooperation would be well worth his life."

"My sister would never join you!" Shikun shouted valiantly before Margariete could formulate an answer. "You are a murdering scum!"

Both of Kirion's eyebrows rose and his smile vanished into dangerous indignation.

"Murderer?" Kirion repeated. "You clearly do not understand the scope of my crusade, Prince Shikun. Bringing harmony to the shards is a difficult endeavor. Death is sometimes necessary. These men," Kirion indicated the bier of carcasses, formerly the Pearl knights, "were consumed by trivial matters. Their loyalty to this King Raeylan blinded them to the truth. I simply freed them from their false devotion."

"What truth?" Shikun asked hesitantly, falling into Kirion's verbal trap.

"That I am, now and ever, the one true God of the Universe."

Some of Shikun's bravery returned. His shoulders tensed.

"You're insane! My brother is a great man. When he returns here, he will make you pay for what you have done!"

"I can see your brother's lies have contaminated you, Shikun," Kirion shook his head sadly. "You, also, would have made a helpful addition to my army."

He lifted his hand, touching each finger lightly with his thumb. Their tips lit with dappled tongues of light.

"Be at peace, young lorelei. You will be of use to me, even in death."

As Shikun swung his blade, Kirion deflected *Moonstone Retribution* with a silver bracer. Margariete yelled hoarsely at Shikun to flee, but her warning drowned in her brother's shriek. With his free hand, Kirion touched Shikun's breastplate. The effervescent energy at the man's fingers burned through the youth's chest—armor, flesh, and bone—until Kirion's fist was firmly lodged past the princeling's ribs.

Margariete pulled and twisted against her bindings violently, begging the raven-haired man to stop, to spare her little brother, tears storming her cheeks.

The attacker paid the princess no heed. He rotated his fist and yanked. Shikun collapsed backward. Shikun mouthed her name once, blood foaming at his lips. A gaping hole in his breast spilled his blood over the mossy ground.

Sister, I'm sorry . . .

His small body twitched and his eyes rolled. Then he lay deathly still.

"Shikun!" she wailed.

"A pity," Kirion said, staring carelessly at the bloody lump clutched in his right hand—Shikun's heart. It beat weakly several times, then turned a crusty grey and crumbled into sickly clumps. Kirion inspected it closely, then tossed it to the ground, brushing the residue from his hands like refuse.

"A waste. Useless. Soiled by his mortality."

"I will KILL you!" Margariete screeched vehemently.

Rage and grief boiled behind her skull, dragging her power into blasts of electricity. She gave in to her fury, surrendering control of her magic the same way she had before, when battling Terail. She welcomed its raw hatred, its passionate brutality. With it she would destroy Kirion and avenge her brother.

The stranger seemed unimpressed. He flicked his head toward the main garden once and the largest wolf loped forward. It lifted its jaw to the ceiling and released a mind-

397

scrambling howl. Stars of pain exploded inside Margariete's head. Her power fizzled and died. When her body fell limp, the wolf cry stopped. The princess's sobs were a mixture of defeat and pain.

"You'll have to forgive the Pack Sire," Kirion apologized as he lifted *Moonstone Retribution* and extracted the blue teleport crystal from Shikun's belt pouch. "Threats against the bearer of their lady's artifact are not taken lightly by the Wolves of Skoh."

"You killed him," Margariete said incongruously, grief wracking her body mercilessly.

"I'm afraid that you killed him, Margariete," Kirion countered as he examined the stone. "I offered you his life in exchange for your service. You refused."

"You didn't allow me to answer," she screeched.

"Shikun said you would never join me. You did not contradict him. I assumed you agreed with his pronouncement."

He held up the blue crystal.

"This is a curious stone. What is it?"

"Rot in the Void, you bastard!" she spat. "When Raeylan returns, he will avenge us."

The wolves' chests rumbled. Kirion looked at her intently, his thumb running thoughtfully along his lower lip.

"According to Shikun, your King Raeylan is a lorelei. Unlike you, he does not possess the ability to counter The Earring's illusions. I regret that I cannot trade his life for your allegiance as I offered with your younger brother. I require The Glove in his possession. Forgive me, Princess Margariete, but I must sacrifice both of your brothers this day."

46: ARC OF ILLUSION

The diffused light reflected platinum off Raeylan's hair as Esilwen leaned against one of the pillars. She stroked his face, his head resting comfortably in her lap. Time seemed endless here. He could have been unconscious for only minutes, or perhaps he had slept for days—Esilwen could not determine the difference in this muted stone chamber.

As she waited for the king to wake, Esilwen pondered how she had managed to remember her true name during this lifetime. She had never been able to access it before. When the phoenix fire took her, memories were not buried or hidden. Her life experiences simply scattered into the emptiness of existence. Lost forever.

Margariete must have been the difference in this shard, Esilwen thought to herself, *something she did saved that particular memory before it was completely erased.*

Soon Raeylan's eyes flickered and opened. He gasped for breath like a diver breaking through the surface of the water. His gaze found Esilwen, and he raised a weak hand to her cheek.

"You succeeded," she whispered.

He brushed away a tear that had leaked from the corner of her eye. "And your memories?" he asked.

"There are so many," Esilwen said timidly, "I'm not sure how I would know if any were missing."

"Are you still my Esilwen?" he asked softly.

Concern descended upon his eyes. Esilwen placed her hand over his, holding his palm steadily against her face.

"Yes," she answered, "I will always be your Esilwen."

For the first time since Margariete's trial, a genuine smile illuminated Raeylan's face.

"How long was I asleep?"

"I'm not sure, maybe half an hour—arc," she corrected as Raeylan struggled into an upright position. He looked at her strangely.

"Sorry," she apologized quickly, "my original home called them hours."

She inhaled deeply, slumping with exhaustion.

"Are you all right?" he asked.

"My memory is so full, it's difficult to distinguish what experience belongs to which life," she replied. "I'll be okay. I just need to sort them out, that's all."

"How many lives?"

"Five, including this one."

He pulled her closer, kissing her lips lightly. As they separated, she saw that his smile had been replaced with fatigue.

"We should get back to the castle," Esilwen said. "I think Kirion may have followed me through the gate."

Raeylan's eyes darkened protectively.

"Who is this Kirion?"

"A blight I accidentally released into the shards," Esilwen admitted. "He's after Fohtian's artifact—which is now me. We must hurry back to Viridius Castle."

They stood as one, embracing each other. Raeylan squeezed her tightly to his chest as the world burst into stars. When it reformed, they were inside the Royal Shrine.

Blood stained everything. Carcasses of cursed beasts were heaped like piles of garbage around the private and public garden. Across the shrine's center was a line of fallen Gem Knights, their arms folded across their breastplates with honor as they awaited their final funeral rites. Margariete perched on the edge of the spring, stabbing *Stardawn* into the moss impatiently. Shikun sat on the ground beside her. A red-stained bandage bound his arm. He leaned tiredly against the princess's leg. The instant the king and his healer appeared, Margariete jumped to her feet, causing Shikun to fall backward awkwardly.

"Raeylan! Esilwen!" she shouted joyfully and raced forward to meet them.

Esilwen pulled away from Raeylan and took a step behind him, inexplicably wary. Uneasiness prickled her. Rain pounded through the open ceiling beyond the Royal Shrine, its voice ominous and foreboding. Sickness crawled into her. She should have felt comfort that those she loved had escaped battle unscathed.

Instead, apprehension skulked across her skin.

What is wrong with me? she wondered fretfully, her heart pounding loudly in her ears.

Margariete almost toppled Raeylan when she reached him, her arms assaulting him with a forceful hug. He returned the embrace, somewhat surprised at her intensity.

"Hello, sister," he said with relief. "It pleases me to see you and Shikun safe."

Esilwen breathed heavily, fear pulsing with her blood.

Something was wrong . . .

"I'm glad to see you, Lady Esilwen," Shikun said.

She started, unaware that he had moved beside her. The princeling moved forward as if to hug her, but she recoiled sharply, almost tripping in her attempt to move away. His smile looked ghastly, like an animal showing its

401

teeth. She turned to Raeylan, wondering how to explain the fear she was experiencing.

He was pulling away from Margariete, confusion plain on his face.

"What did you say?" he asked her in concern.

Esilwen! Margariete's voice slammed into the healer's head. *Esilwen it's a trap. Whatever you see, it isn't real. That isn't me, it's an intruder!*

The Margariete in Raeylan's arms hadn't taken her eyes from him. She seemed oblivious to the warning that had just stabbed through Esilwen's mind. With a smile she slid her hand down her twin's arm and slipped her fingers under the edge of The Glove.

"Raeylan, get away from her!" Esilwen screamed, but her alarm was spoken too late.

Margariete yanked on Nehro's artifact, pulling it halfway off. Raeylan grimaced in pain and dropped to his knees, the revealed flesh turning a grisly ash-grey. He clutched at his sister with his free hand, fumbling to detach her fingers from the garment.

Esilwen lunged forward to help but something jerked her backward by the shoulder. Shikun had opened his mouth inhumanly wide, clamping fangs into her flesh. He threw her to the ground, staring at her with carnal bloodlust in his eyes. Inky, black saliva dribbled down his chin. A numbing poison spread through her body and within seconds she couldn't move.

"You're dying, foolish lorelei," Margariete said to Raeylan, her voice uncharacteristically cold. "Fighting will only make your death more painful."

Raeylan's face contorted with concentration, but his efforts proved futile. Using her foot as leverage against his chest, Margariete shoved Raeylan to the ground, wrenching Nehro's Glove completely from his arm.

Raeylan's scream of agony burned a savage hole through Esilwen. She watched, distraught with grief, as he trembled on the moss, his right arm seared black with frost. When he fell silent, a shriek of denial shredded her core.

Margariete stared greedily at her prize, turning the scrap of brown rag in her hand over and over in ecstasy. At the same moment, fire scorched Esilwen's blood as Fohtian's magic coursed through her limbs, countering the poison.

And then the world twisted into a sickly wash of sooty color.

Shikun's body warped into a horse-sized wolf, its weight pinning her to the ground. Its rotten breath was hot against her cheek. The exotic beauty of the Jeweled Princess transformed into the figure of a raven-haired man, surrounded by an aura of light. He tugged a silver bracer off his arm and drew on Nehro's artifact in its place. Pearly runes danced across the magical cloth as it morphed to his skin, changing into a glittering gauntlet of tawny metal.

Behind him, Margariete hung suspended from the ground by a glowing chain of light, tears drizzling down her olive skin. A gag hid her mouth, and blood leaked from one nostril. Shikun's corpse lay discarded at her feet, his chest a gory red cavity.

Kirion stared directly at Esilwen.

"My dearest Esilwen," he said with a charming smile, "I've been searching for you everywhere."

47: The End Of House Viridius

Margariete clamped her teeth against the gag clogging her mouth as she once again struggled with her restraints. She needed to free herself. Raeylan and Esilwen could return at any moment. Kirion had spoken of some kind of illusion and though she had no clear idea of what that meant, she was worried that her twin would be fooled by the intruder's lies.

She had already searched for a lock to pick with her telekinesis, but it seemed the manacles had none. The glowing metal was nothing that she had ever seen before, seemingly smelted around her wrists and warm on her skin. Like Kirion's mind, her abilities were unable to connect with the lustrous material. Exhaustion forced her to surrender the pointless effort. She was trapped.

Her eyes avoided Shikun's body. His lifeless stare and gawking mouth debilitated her with blistering grief. Kirion sat on the ledge that jutted from the spring's pool, absently scratching the Pack Sire's furry ear while inspecting the collection of his captives' possessions. The objects lay in a neat line next to the water: two teleportation crystals between the sheathed *Stardawn* and the naked blade of *Moonstone Retribution*.

Just then, her twin and Esilwen appeared in the shrine. Margariete watched in horror—unable to speak through the cloth in her mouth—as Raeylan embraced Kirion and addressed him as 'sister.' Esilwen seemed agitated and uncertain, peering around with worry as the Pack Sire loped to her side. The princess was unable to see whatever illusion had beguiled her brother and Esilwen.

She had to warn them. Bypassing the gag, she reached out to her twin with an unspoken voice. In response, Raeylan pushed Kirion slightly away, but seemed more puzzled than wary. Desperately, she touched Esilwen's consciousness. At the mention of the intruder, the blonde's eyes flashed with fear, but her reaction was too slow. Kirion already clutched The Glove and had forced Raeylan to his knees.

Painfully aware that Kirion was impervious to her talents, Margariete focused her mind on Nehro's artifact, holding it in place, knowing that its removal would take the life of her twin. Her head screamed in protest with the exertion, but she could not bear to lose a second brother. Blood trickled from her nostril.

The bland metallic tang of the blood was enough to extinguish her concentration, and she lost hold of her mental grip. Kirion tore The Glove from Raeylan's arm. Her brother's anguished cry sliced a devastating wound in her soul, next to the raw fissure that had been her love for Shikun.

Both Viridius brothers lay dead on the mossy bed of the private family shrine.

Margariete succumbed to the despair of ruin. Her family was gone. Only Esilwen remained. The Pack Sire held her friend to the ground with its weight. A nasty bite on her shoulder had just begun to heal. The princess linked her mind to her friend's, saw the illusion shrink away through Esilwen's eyes and experienced the same fear the healer felt.

"My dearest Esilwen," Kirion said, "I've been searching for you everywhere."

Margariete sensed the poison dissipating in Esilwen's blood. As soon as she could move again, Esilwen wrapped both hands around the Pack Sire's leg. Ice-green flames consumed the animal before it had a chance to howl in pain. The princess had never seen Esilwen use her magic with such confidence, or such precision. A pile of ashes drifted around the healer as she stood. Margariete wanted to yell in triumph, but Kirion's cool expression sent icy trembles through the mind-linked brunette.

He laughed.

"Ever resistant, Esilwen," he said.

To Margariete's surprise, hard enmity swelled through her friend.

"You must know that this time," Kirion continued, "you cannot escape me."

Esilwen's thoughts flashed through several rebirths. The elf had lived through more than 2,000 seasons, meeting death more than once, fleeing the image of a man she could not quite remember.

"After all this time, you have nothing to say?" Kirion asked. Then his voice softened, "Of course, you don't remember. Your memories were taken with The Chalice."

"I remember, Kirion," she answered steadily. "How could you? You killed them!"

"It was essential that I gain Nehro's Glove," Kirion stated, walking toward her.

"But Shikun?" Esilwen demanded. "He was just a boy! What possible advantage could you have gained by his death, except to prove yourself a murderer?"

Kirion stopped his advance, astonished. "You fail to see the greater purpose, Esilwen."

"All I see is your lust for power," she said. "You are the face of evil."

"No, Esilwen," Kirion said, genuinely surprised by her allegation. "I cannot restore the shards without first regaining what the other gods took from me."

"These were good people," she declared.

"They were enthralled by their own selfishness, Esilwen. Only I can establish order to the universe. Light will bless all the races once again. These men were unable to recognize the greater good."

"You butcher all who oppose you in your quest for virtue. How can that be the 'greater good'?"

A brooding wrath stared through Kirion's dark eyes.

"You are a fool. I could have kept you by my side until the last moment, perhaps even found a way to save your life when I stripped Fohtian's power from you. But I can see these mortals have corrupted what you once were."

"That 'corruption' is my salvation, Kirion. Through them I was capable of love once more. Only this time, I was not misguided by lies."

Kirion narrowed his eyes and his voice fell dangerously quiet.

"You fancied this man," he stated ominously, pointing at Raeylan's body.

"I loved him, yes," she answered, her confession choking on heartache.

"Have you lost so much of yourself, Esilwen?" he said savagely, looming toward her. "To give yourself to an inferior being—have you forgotten your love for me so readily?"

"I do care for you, Kirion," she answered, "but your obsession has made me your enemy."

Margariete nearly panicked. Kirion had already stolen Shikun and Raeylan from her. Now he was after Esilwen's power. Would he destroy her to get it? There was only one way to make sure that didn't happen.

To escape, Esilwen had to die.

Her friend knew it; Margariete had already sensed the thought dash through Esilwen's mind. Death would send her magically through the shardgate. But a reluctance tugged at the healer. She would forget Thyella, leaving Margariete defenseless and at the mercy of Kirion. Esilwen couldn't bear to lose Margariete, not when so much had been already spoiled.

Esilwen, Margariete thought-sent, *can you hear me?*

Yes, Esilwen replied.

We cannot allow him to have the artifact, Margariete stated plainly.

The princess looked at the spring. The weapons were unattended, but *Stardawn* was still in its sheath. Loosing it would take extra concentration, precious time that might allow Kirion to interfere. Margariete worried, now that he was in possession of The Glove, Kirion could simply grab Esilwen and teleport out of the way. She had to act before he moved closer to her friend.

I can't abandon you, Margariete.

You must, the princess insisted. *He has robbed us of Raeylan and Shikun. I will not let him have you as well.*

What about you? Esilwen asked sadly, but Margariete could feel her friend wavering.

Kirion was speaking again, but neither girl paid him heed.

I am inconsequential. In my brother's place, I must protect you.

Esilwen's ice-green eyes left Kirion and fastened on *Moonstone Retribution.* Under Margariete's control, the blade lifted into the air. Kirion could not see it; it was out of his peripheral range.

You must strike me directly in the heart or I will simply heal, Esilwen instructed. *I will miss you, Margariete. You are my most treasured friend.*

As you are mine, Margariete returned. *May Nehro's Grace protect you.*

Combating the crippling pain caused by the use of her powers, Margariete speared the sword forward. Kirion roared with incredulous rage when he saw the blade, but he could not react in time to counter its flight.

Moonstone Retribution impaled Esilwen through the side, breaking ribs and tearing lungs, its path cleaving directly through her heart.

As she burst into a column of green flame, Esilwen's last thoughts were of Raeylan.

48: THE NETHERWORLD

"Wake up, Raeylan," said a familiar female voice.

His eyes blinked open. Limitless color flushed the liquid space that rippled around him. He floated through it, suspended in an infinite plane of starry hue. The substance flowed around his body petulantly, annoyed by his intrusion. He had seen this place before, winking in the depths of the Well-cube before he had closed it.

A woman with soft grey eyes drifted in front of him, the curve of her tender features instantly recognizable.

"Mother?" Raeylan asked, astonished. Then he pulled his lips in a tight line. "Am I dead, then?"

"No," his mother answered, her long hair swaying with the motion of the radiant tide, "you are here because I summoned you, King Raeylan. I bear only the form of your mother."

"Then who are you, if not Anleia?" he inquired as she lifted her fingers to brush her hair from her face. Her movements were distinctly his mother's.

"You already know who I am," she replied.

Raeylan paused in thought, his mind crisp and clear. The answer flowed into him like a stream of spring water. Who else could mimic his mother so exactly?

"Nehro?" he breathed in awe.

Anleia nodded.

"Why do you look just like my mother?"

"Once, long ago, I had the power to take any shape I wished. But I sacrificed some of myself to create my race of celestials, the lorelei. Now I may only take the forms of those who have passed beyond the mortal realm and into my domain."

The astral gems of the plane did not part around her, as they did Raeylan, but swirled through her. The glittering particles attached to her skin until she was a mass of stellar light. Her body changed, growing taller and broad-shouldered as the radiance faded. Negin swayed in the lustrous sea before the king.

"You gave away a portion your power?" Raeylan wondered.

"Each of the gods did," Negin explained. "There can be no creation without sacrifice. There were those, like Skoh, who were hesitant to give their servants more than simple advantages over common mortals. Because of this, her wolves are plagued by death. My lorelei, Aeron's servants, and Fohtain's erinyes are the strongest of angel-kind. Our strength was traded for theirs. It is one of the reasons the Lord of Light managed to overcome us."

"I don't understand," Raeylan said. "Who is this Lord of Light?"

"Kirion," Nehro as Negin replied, "he who has taken possession of my artifact."

"But you are here, can't you stop him?"

"He is a demigod, neither mortal nor immortal. A human in possession of a god's soul—made stronger through the powers of Skoh's Earring and my Glove. I am but a ghost of what I once was."

"Then what can be done?" Raeylan posed. "If he took The Glove from me, I must be near death."

The glimmering sparks mingled with Nehro once again. Negin's body grew smaller, his limbs lanky with youth. A tight knot curled through Raeylan as he gazed on the form of his little brother.

"Only one son of Viridius will be claimed by Kirion this cycle," she promised with Shikun's voice.

"Shikun—he is—" Raeylan hesitated, unable to finish the question.

"He stood proudly between your sister and Kirion. His death was honorable."

Raeylan's head drooped with grief.

"You will have time to mourn," the goddess continued, "but for now, duty calls you. I have slowed the flow of time, but I cannot hold it forever."

Shikun's face vanished into a mass of wrinkles. Spots of age mired his skin, and his hair turned ashy grey with wisdom. Nehro hunched forward, her crumpled brow heavy around her eyes.

"This is my true form, young king," she said.

Though bent with age, her body drifted elegantly through the prism of starlight, her movements agile with loveliness.

'*Nehro's Grace,'* Raeylan thought, *has always been an actual depiction of the goddess.*

"I am the eldest of the divinities. A part of my soul was trapped within my artifact when the Seven Worlds were shattered, dormant until you used the Well to restore the memories of Fohtian's Warden."

"Has Fohtian awakened also?" Raeylan asked hopefully.

Nehro shook her head from side to side sadly.

"Alas, all that remains of the Phoenix Angel is his power. By shielding us from the clash of magicks, his soul was utterly destroyed. He cannot be revived."

"Why have you brought me to this place?"

"This is my plane, the origin of my power. It was the only place I could manifest myself to you. When I felt Kirion's vile touch on my artifact, I chose to abandon it. Though some of my power will remain within The Glove, my spirit now dwells within you."

Raeylan felt the weight of the universe settle on him.

"Why choose me?"

"Because you remind me of Fohtian," Nehro said with a smile that revealed her cracked and yellowing teeth. "I have seen into your heart. You are honorable. It will be your duty to stop the Lord of Light before he once again disrupts the balance and wreaks havoc on the cosmos."

The looming task of contesting a fallen god filled Raeylan with doubt.

"How?"

"First," Nehro said, "I will close your Soulwell so that Kirion cannot use my Glove against you. Then I will merge my soul with yours, and make you his rival—a demigod in your own right. Through this union, you will have the same powers as my artifact, but you will gain something more, the last of my great powers: influence over time's flow. You cannot stop it, but like a river or stream, you can stem its course."

"And you want me to use that to kill him when I am revived?" Raeylan speculated.

"In time, yes, but not the moment you wake," Nehro instructed. "It will take much strength to close your Well and blend my being into yours. Your body will be weak when you regain consciousness. You must use the new power I have given you to escape, else my gifts to you will be in vain. Both you and your sister must survive."

"What of Esilwen?" Raeylan asked anxiously.

Nehro's eyes revealed the cheerless truth before she spoke. "Fohtian's Warden will pass through the gate before you generate the time distortion. Margariete believes you dead, and she has chosen to kill Esilwen rather than allow Kirion to gain Fohtian's power."

Nehro's body glowed white hot with intensity. Sharp spines of blue slid through Raeylan. The goddess's voice echoed around him.

"You must keep the artifacts from the Lord of Light's reach. Follow Esilwen through the shards. Guard her from Kirion."

This time, when his eyes opened, he could feel the ache of his tired body, though the constant drain of The Glove was gone. A biting pain stabbed through his signet arm, rhythmic with his heartbeat. His fingers were curled into his palm, streaked white with frostbite. Ten steps away Esilwen faced Kirion with peaceful resignation.

Moonstone Retribution pierced her chest diagonally, buried nearly to its hilt between her arm and torso. Her eyes met his and they seemed to smile. The pretty healer's lips formed two words.

Find me.

And then she was consumed by a bright lattice of icy-green flame, sword and all. Not even ash remained where she had vanished. Kirion's shocked expression altered into rage as he turned on Margariete, his anger ringing smoothly through the shrine.

"What have you done!" he roared, advancing on her helpless figure.

Margariete laughed, a sound Raeylan knew to be more hysteria than mirth. The king felt Nehro's power surge within him, but it was turbulent and stormy; untamable.

"How did you do that?" Kirion demanded of the restrained princess, his animosity ebbing into simmering self-control. "Aeron's servants weren't gifted with telekinesis. That is a power the Mystic kept for himself."

Margariete laughed soft sobs, "After what you have stolen from me, you still ask questions. The Void has taken your sanity if you believe I will answer."

"Your death will not be pleasant," Kirion promised crossly.

"I welcome it," Margariete cried in defiance.

Raeylan let go, allowing the magic to drown him. He bid the world to slow its pace. The waterfall spring in the center of the shrine lingered motionless in the air. Time's wave pressed heavily against him, and he struggled to sustain the spell. His body felt bulky and useless, sluggish to obey his commands.

Raeylan lurched unsteadily to his feet, collecting *Stardawn* and the two teleportation crystals from the lip of the pool. An eternity passed as he limped toward his sister, every step encumbered by the thick hand of time.

He experienced a fleeting desire to thrust his sister's blade into Kirion's motionless body, but Raeylan abandoned the thought quickly. Nehro had warned him to use his power only to escape. The king had little understanding of Kirion's mortal state. Would a weapon kill a demigod? Raeylan knew the attempt would require all his remaining energy, and time would resume its normal flow. It was too risky. If the blow didn't fell Kirion instantly, both Raeylan and his twin would die, and there would be no one to protect Esilwen from the Lord of Light.

Just as he slid his arm around Margariete's waist, time slipped Raeylan's leash, and the world surged to life around him. Kirion's face twisted into blank shock. The last thing the raven-haired demigod knew, Nehro's Guardian lay dead by the spring.

"Your weakness, Kirion," Raeylan said, "is your arrogance."

Before Kirion could react, Raeylan crushed the azure crystal in his palm and the shrine erupted into an infinite cloud of glittering stars, dancing within a salty breeze. With a sigh of relief, Raeylan crashed into the rain-soaked garden surrounding the mountain stronghold of Viridius Manor.

49: Reality Scar Extinction

Kirion lifted his hand and the chain of magic that had imprisoned the princess snaked toward him, absorbed by the impenetrable armor of light that constantly coated his skin. As he did so, he turned his right arm back and forth, admiring the golden gauntlet that was Nehro's Glove.

It was always the same when he donned a new artifact. With only minimal concentration, he could peel away the layers of the visible world, separating them into the magical planes of the gods' domains. He could see his own realm, a bright swirl of multi-hued light, the dark shade of the Void, and now, the luminescent Plane of Water. When he retrieved the remaining relics, he would be able to see all six planes and their complex influence on the mortal sphere.

Few beings of the universe knew that the element planes all occupied the same space, stacked on top of each other to create the mortal world. These extra dimensions could only be accessed through special conduits—called Wells by most mortals—that bridged one to another.

There were only three ways to access magic. The lowest level of energy was available to creatures of the material universe through Shardwells. Power drawn through these conduits could be molded into desired effects. Spells, potions, or enchantments were usually generated in this manner. When the Seven Worlds were broken, many new Wells ripped through the fabric of space, creating chaos throughout their surrounding shard. Others were inadvertently closed, leaving the mortals in its vicinity unable to access the gods' power at all.

The expression "Shardwell" was misleading to many mortals. Limited by their concrete understanding of physical laws, they mindlessly expected a "well" to be a round puncture of the local soil. Throughout his travels Kirion had encountered Wells of many sizes and intensities, both stationary and mobile. Some had tangible shape, like a stone or jewel, but others were abstract forms of space or energy.

Another method to harness the gods' power was through a Soulwell—a direct channel that connected a being's soul to a non-material plane. The gods' divine servants were gifted with this phenomenon—the elemental angels—and beings who managed to receive a Soulwell became more than mortal. A person could only harbor one Well at a time. Cosmic gravity would tear a creature's existence apart if two Wells tried to occupy the same soul. Raeylan and Shikun had been attached to Wells of water, but Margariete had been connected to Aeron's plane.

The last and most powerful form of magic was the gods themselves. A manifestation of universal nature, the deities generated their own power, greater than even that of their home domain. They were like stars of magic, radiating their energy into the emptiness of reality—though now only the artifacts remained.

Kirion paced in front of the pond, distracted in thought. Raeylan should be dead—removing The Glove had disconnected him from Nehro's power too quickly. The recoil shock had killed him. There had been no mistake. The Lord of Light had felt the man's Soulwell close. Yet somehow the king had rescued his sister and teleported to safety. It was impossible to return from the halls of death.

Unless—

The newly appointed Pack Sire interrupted Kirion's reflection, padding to his side and lowering its eyes differentially.

My Lord, it sent, *my kin and I will hunt your enemies. They cannot have gotten far.*

Kirion waved his hand dismissively. "I came for Nehro's Glove and Fohtian's Blood. Having retrieved only one, I still must collect the other. We leave immediately."

They dishonored you, the beast argued with a growl in its belly.

Skoh's angels rarely comprehended the larger goal. Kirion supposed he shouldn't have been surprised.

"So they did," he said without malice. His eyes surveyed the corpse of the castle's youngest prince. "I am afraid their insolence has determined the fate of their shard. It will be sacrificed to the Void. Does that satisfy you?"

The wolf grinned approvingly.

It will be a great gift for My Lady.

Kirion flicked his index finger against The Earring. A high ringing chime, like the vibration of a crystal vase, sang through the shard for a thousand leagues. The piercing note tore the sheer silk that shielded the mortal realm from the midnight cavern of the Void. Its sinister mesh expanded hungrily, withering all it touched. Moss, trees, and stone disintegrated, falling into kernels of dark sand that faded into the inky emptiness. Shikun's body crumbled into dreary granules and was lost in the midst of darkness.

The Lord of Light stepped back, the wolves gathering around him. This shard was small. The Earring's spell would devour it entirely within two days. Without The Glove to open the shardgate, Thyella's inhabitants were trapped inside their dying world—including the two who had defied him.

One command to The Glove would take him and his servants to the shardgate, and the second would order it to open. Thanati had already left with the unconscious assassin. Esilwen might have escaped for now, but with Nehro's artifact in his possession, he could find the elfmaid more quickly than ever before. With The Glove's powers, Kirion no longer needed to hunt lorelei, and could lift the ration on gate salt. He could spread his resources freely throughout the shards, expand his armies wider than the confines of the cosmos.

Fohtian's Warden would not stay hidden for long.

EPILOGUE

A king is trained to serve his people, to protect them from harm through toil and sacrifice. A good sovereign meets enemies with honor and averts tragedy through foresight and wisdom.

I spent all I had for my homeland—my strength, my brother, even my own life—yet the end came, despite my efforts. Never in my darkest imaginings had I envisioned a power that could obliterate an entire world from reality so quickly.

Four hundred seasons now separate me from Thyella's last cycles, yet I relive the despair of my people's destruction nightly, its sorrow as sharp now as the dawn we fled through the shardgate. In those dreams Shikun's trusting smile haunts me. The depth of my failure shackles my soul.

Only a handful of Thyellans escaped the black sands of the Void: myself, my twin, my old tutor, Tenan and Seriya, and the 22 servants and knights who had sought refuge at Viridius Manor. By the time Master Malbrin realized the nature of the corrosive magic that swept over our shard, we had only arcs to flee. There was no time to save anyone else. We teleported to the edge of the Koungo Waste and crossed the shardgate threshold with little more than moments to spare.

We journeyed through two lifeless worlds before stumbling into a shard that would support the remnants of our kingdom—a realm of deep jungle with rivers bright with life. Here we encountered a tribal culture that—though wary of our light eyes and fair hair—embraced us with compassion and pity. We called our settlement New Thyella, though the indigenous people named us Hestru—the Outsiders.

Margariete and I stayed only a few cycles.

Before we left, Malbrin gave us the ancient scrolls that Kalariel left in his care, clues to the remaining artifacts and insight into the deadly powers that Kirion may have already discovered. Though I am able to understand any language I encounter through the magic of the water goddess, many of the documents reference places and objects that are meaningless without context. Impossibly, Aeron's scroll is indecipherable. Its puzzle has troubled my waking thoughts.

Kirion expected us to perish, perhaps thinking we could not pass through the shardwall. He soon learned otherwise. My twin and I thwart his endeavors to subjugate the universe with his narrow, misguided dogma. Yet still his support grows: zealots flock to his side, frightened societies submit to his will, opponents succumb to his army.

Time is measured differently throughout the shards, but through Nehro's power I can feel its pulse, like the flow of blood through the universe. The farther we travel from its center, the faster it flows. Perhaps only a decade or two has passed in the shell that was once the place of my birth, but I have watched four centuries of my life pass by. And still we have found no trace of my beloved Esilwen.

Only the gods know who will find her first.

About the Authors

A. Gerry developed an interest in fantasy at a young age. Her fondness for writing comes from many sources, but the most prominent is her devotion to video games. Some of her favorites include *Mass Effect*, *The Elder Scrolls* series, and anything that lets her shoot zombies. She received a Bachelor's Degree from Southern Utah University and teaches at a local charter school.

C. Hall has been addicted to the many realms of fantasy and science fiction all her life. A graduate of Southern Utah University, she now teaches at a local charter school. When she isn't busy designing activities for her Mythology class or going on field trips with the *Star Wars* Club, she is spending time with her sister. C. Hall's favorite authors include J.R.R. Tolkien, J.K. Rowling, and Tracy Hickman.

Also Available from Scribes of Shardwell

PHOENIX ANGEL

SHARDWELL SERIES
BOOK 1

A. GERRY
C. HALL

Made in the USA
Charleston, SC
28 October 2013